# THREE
## · SIX ·
### SEVEN

# THREE
# ·SIX·
# SEVEN

*MEMOIRS OF A*
*VERY IMPORTANT MAN*

*A Novel by*
PETER VANSITTART

PETER OWEN · LONDON AND BOSTON

ISBN  0 7206 0602 0

PETER OWEN PUBLISHERS
73 Kenway Road London SW5 0RE and
99 Main Street Salem New Hampshire 03079

First published 1983
© Peter Vansittart 1983

Printed in Great Britain by
Daedalus Press Somers Road Wisbech Cambs.

*To Lee and Ruth Montague*

Unlawful things, whose deepness doth entice.

Marlowe


The Romans thought it improper that anyone should be left free to follow his tastes and appetites, whether in marriage, the bearing of children, the regulations of his daily life, or the entertainment of his friends, without a large measure of supervision and control. They held that a man's character was more clearly shown in his private life than in his public and political career, and they thus selected officials, one from amongst the so-called patricians and the other a plebeian, whose duty it was to watch, regulate, and punish any tendency to indulge in licentious or voluptuous habits and to depart from the traditional and established modes. These officers were known as Censors, with power to degrade a Roman knight or to expel a senator who had pursued a life of vice and irregularity. They also fulfilled and maintained a general census of property, and register of citizens by their social and political classifications, and exercised a number of other important powers.

Plutarch


The State is the name by which we call the great human conspiracy against hunger and cold, against loneliness and ignorance; the State is the foster-mother and warden of the arts, of love and comradeship, of all that redeems from despair that strange adventure which we call human life.

T. M. Kettle

Now flares across Ellismere
A Roman shadow
The trees take wing and fly
Groaning with disaster

Across treetops, meadows.
Ghosts of a weary land,
Witches of Ellismere,
Here was the despair of Romans.

Plant the oak firm
Against the flying storm.
Winds and waters may rise
Across the districts of your marvelling eyes.

Porter Forrester

# I

Plausible cheats in senate and brothel, camp and bath, or exiled to sunlit, empty islands, viciously condemn the present. 'Nothing has ever been worse.' Their voices strain like bands when wine ferments in the cask. 'Never in all history . . . ,' they shout, eager to win some trivial debate. My story is different.

Though I am exceptional at compiling reports, investing, withdrawing, foreclosing, selling, no Muse has kissed my pen. Yet I have much to tell (and I am, for these contemptible times, exceptionally well-read).

Sallust maintained that Athens' glamour is due less to her achievements than to her historians. Britain has neither. Save for these pages, she may be forgotten, a mere fate-story for children, a rumour in a deserted temple. If she survives further crisis, she will owe more to gods, if they exist, than to her peoples, who exist only to their own detriment. I could have saved them.

I shall tell you more evil than good. A belief prevails that good necessitates evil, lack of conflict inducing inertia. Absurd. In the moderate degrees of life in which you dwell, conflict, pain, challenges, emerge daily, demanding lively choice.

Foolish choice ruined me, judgement not of events, but simply of *that man*. He was calamitous, but has slammed himself into the history books – if books continue to be written, which is doubtful. Reading may soon be as outdated as a chariot. But no poet will rhyme my virtues, which were many; no lonely woman whisper my name while she pleasures herself; my statues never enthralled Milan, Treves, the Sacred Palace, Rome and London.

I am no barbarian, craving to exist only in a horde. I saw horror, which may return. I cannot interest those concerned only with the loins of fading deities, or the twenty-seven charted positions of coitus, especially the eleven legally prohibited. (Several seem geometrically impossible; only with a thin slave did I attempt more than six, and we almost broke each other. Vesta was too timid, Sylviana too super-cilious. Sexual business is splendid in the right place, but a busy man is careful to keep it there.)

I was wealthy, thus, despite current pernicious teachings, a bene-factor. The more we possess, the more strenuously we protect society. Levellers are either bleating incompetents, or terrorists roaring for goods they are too lazy or stupid to earn.


Spring, 367. Marriage rites, songs, flowers, laughter, bells. I myself was not laughing but felt neither jealousy nor self-torment, only curiosity, mildly prurient. Superficially, they paired well, Metellus and Sylviana.

'So tall. So straight. They glisten like saplings. I remind myself how generous life can be.'

'The joy in their faces. And elsewhere, of course.'

'Hush.'

Metellus claimed descent from a rival of Pompey, though through dubious traditions, as he himself admitted, winking over his cups. He also had British ancestors, seldom mentioned, from the midland Coritans, who kept enemies' heads embalmed in cedar oil, a feature unacceptable in Metellus' house, though Sylviana maintained that his father, grossly overweight, must have eaten them.

I myself had never met a genuine Roman settler in Britain. Most of my associates were Gallic or Spanish, though some had long married into what they called the ancient British aristocracy, a ludi-crous concept. Villa magnates, though not always their wives, re-mained loyal, if scarcely fervid, to the Roman gods. Sylviana, daughter of a pushing new man from Jerusalem, was formally Christian, though when I asked what this entailed, she answered only with her shoulders or a tiny, mischievous pout.

The rival priests had now had their say, barely comprehensible. A white bull had been sacrificed, despite the expense, and doves released, to fly into Venus' lap. We were in the gardens of Metellus' uncle, the lawyer, in the centre of Silchester, where, perhaps unnecessarily, he grew garlic, against vampires. The guests, chattering under fresh leaves, were mostly local functionaries of few graces, few vices. Since the troubles, genuine magnates had retired to country villas.

Birds swooped noisily or fled over ramparts to the wide, sparkling Thames below. Slaves refilled goblets, musicians plucked and sang. A

10

bawdy thought was provoked by the decurion Cottanus and his wife, herself too florid from overmuch henna, as though caught in some embarrassing situation. Christians, they copulated, perhaps could only do so, after public worship of chaste or neutered Jeheshua, with his mysterious and perhaps imaginary childhood. (Presumably, they spent the ritual in expectation of pleasures ahead, thus rousing themselves to sufficiency. Cottanus, too heavily haunched, probably did need divine help.)

Sylviana was accepting gifts and praises with her usual air of regarding others as barely endurable intrusions into a day perfected by herself alone. Cottanus saluted me deferentially. 'There's not much to say.' However little there was, he said it at some length, describing a grandson choking to death on a fishbone.

I was more aware of malicious glances eager to prise out my reactions to Sylviana's marriage. These I could ward off, indifferently. If you expect sympathy, you will not get it. I had travelled further and more profitably than these provincials. Nor were my emotions yet precise. Everyone was glad that I had lost a battle which perhaps, very deeply, I had determined not to win.

My ability to shed friends and lovers reassured me that I was driving forward. Indeed, I saw myself as a racer, alert for openings imperceptible to others, rounding perilous corners, thrusting through where rivals hesitated, disclaiming the vulgar crown but grabbing the prize-money.

My affair with Sylviana had never affected Metellus' amiability. We had been fellow students at Autun. Britain had no university, an institution I considered politically undesirable. Students had become rowdier; instruction shallow, colleges degenerating through too much organization, too little work. I myself was successful by being academically inferior to a Metellus; yet my library was the largest in Silchester, and my allusions unrivalled in range. But from my father and brothers I had more assiduously learnt to assess a smile, silence, embrace, the unguarded gesture. Markets must be watched, not merely seen. The most taciturn can be the most informative. While Metellus languished in fine phrases and declining revenues, I was inscribing contracts, leases, deals, outwardly simple yet which, deftly worded, can hook forever the stupid and reckless.

Literature, so cherished by Metellus and Sylviana, does little real harm, unlike dancing and music that shake people like dice. Song can ravage a city, particularly when the words are inaudible. Music, nevertheless, bored me : I was amazed that anyone could tolerate it, save when walking about in tedious discussion. Books are different. No one castrated himself after a bout of Propertius, like those Phrygian lunatics at the pipes and cymbals in Syrian temples. Women actually benefit from reading : exciting themselves with imaginary heroes, they may desist from bothering men. Love poetry, now being loudly recited, I appreciated only when possessing more margin than text. Others' love, others' dreams, are usually less exceptional than their tellers imagine. Show me an eloquent lover, and I show you a bore.

Drinking moderately, I contrived to remain aloof. In my work I was forced to see many, but was not gregarious. Young men, and most girls, fatigued me with their ignorance and conceit; the old, as Horace put it, were walking hospitals. I demanded intelligent discussion of manifest and exciting facts – currency, vintages, textiles, concessions, monopolies – not the vapid philosophic exchanges and sexual suggestiveness that too often pass as conversation. Forced to endure prolonged and obtuse debate about art, I had lately delivered an effective reminder that the Emperor Diocletian, only a peasant, had wisely declared that of all arts, government was hardest. No one thanked me, but I stopped the nonsense. The young called themselves original, but as I often told them, bad art is almost always original art. I myself respected achievement, not wishful thinking.

The Empire, of course, had long since ceased to produce real art. To embellish Constantine's new arch, artists had to rifle the ageing carvings on Trajan's !

That afternoon had outlines fine as a perfectly drawn invoice. Young sunlight, a fresh round sun that, as Metellus observed rather complacently, lay not on, but in, a sky blue and softened. Until now, it had been so hard that the sun was only a squalid rash, but now all was warm, careless, glad. Tiled roofs, red and green gardens of cherries, mulberries, figs, reminded me of carpets, to be rolled up at dusk.

From behind the heads I contemplated Metellus as he greeted guests, fondled Sylviana, his pale clever face under light, thin hair, neat, greenish eyes, leaves around his head, foppish gown and bracelets sparkling. He was always elegant, adventurous in insignificant ways. He had charm, little more. . . . I was never, like him, dazzled by imaginary suns, despite this passing pleasure in light on blossom and ochred tiles. Disdaining practical matters, relying on family groundrents and gambling, he enjoyed hunting boar, swimming a flood for a wager, risking a farm at the cockpit. He disregarded my admonitions that hunting wasted time and transformed men to liars. After a successful hunt, I would have avoided the Divine Hadrian himself.

Metellus preferred only to borrow from me, standing all smiles and compliments while my clerks studied his haphazard repayments and doubled the interest.

Now he had won Sylviana, or appeared to have, but I was immune from lasting hurt. My councils were sought throughout Britain and Gaul. Metellus was rootless as a severed tree. Even Villa magnates could now deal only in silver : I myself, insufficiently refined to be ashamed of success, outbid them with gold, and was freer than all of them.

A rhetor was declaiming an epithalamium by Gaius Valerius Catullus, his trained, unctuous tones hovering above the bubbling merriment :

> 'Gleaming as Venus gleamed before Paris,
> A rare girl creates rare fortune.'

Sylviana was rare, but, whatever else she created, it would not be rare fortune, for Metellus or anyone else.

Feeling their eyes follow me, I wandered between drinkers, studying her from all angles. In yellow-and-white wedding gown and silver ribbons, her usual petulance, real or assumed, forgone, she was now a stranger. Earlier, she had greeted me formally, accepted my congratulations, eyes and skin crocus-bright, then become quietly, enigmatically amused.

'Pull off your coverings,' the rhetor intoned. 'See a new bride.'

At this, aptly enough, each bearing flowers, the twins Flavia and Flavian sidled towards her, smiles rhyming, open without being candid. Their swaying manner never concealed their delight in the opium poppy, imported from Antioch. Promising me the splendours of Olympus, they once invited me to inhale, but I saw only a lump of beef grotesquely magnified and covered with insects. They had laughed as if at a clown.

Still scarcely twenty, they were cruel, like children dissecting a live cat to see how it worked.

They were giggling behind their blossoms at the jurist, Publius Camillus, dubbed by them 'the Frontier' through once remarking, 'If trouble comes, from whatever quarter, I am the Emperor's man. You know where you'll find me. With the troops on the frontier.'

13

Flavian's smile had been ingratiating and insulting. 'Soldiers make marvellous nurses, they should show you rightful consideration.' Flavia adding that she hoped that a few troops actually were on the frontier.

I avoided them, accepted a plate of quails. The best viands were now only in the rural villas, where I was seldom invited, probably due to over-deference, though I confess it irked me.

A dance was beginning to a pipe, all spirals and slow side-steps, touchings and somewhat affected graces, while Metellus and Sylviana, blossom-crowned, watched from a hillock. Bare limbs shone above the grass, through leaves the roofs and walls glowed steadily on several levels. The tiresome rhetor was like an expensive parrot.

> 'Caught in your arms, like a grape pole
> Meshed in the twisting vine.
> Lo! Light dwindles . . .'

Elderly folk sat gossiping about fashions in Bath, a temple scandal at Cirencester, and, as the pipe rose and the dance quickened, sipped further, cutting their wine with honey I had provided (at a very fair price). Children in simple tunics and bright sandals darted between us.

'Pull off your coverings. . .'

When I had last seen Sylviana alone, she had done just that, lying slender and pale; gasping, writhing, netted.

Metellus was laughing, his teeth flashed, several applauded. Unexpectedly I felt a delicious sensation, not of lust, or malignity, but of sheer, unalloyed expectation. Amongst the smiles, songs, spring colours, I could still issue terms to whomsoever I wished.

Barely perceptibly, for the sky remained cloudless, the afternoon faltered. Birds fled with complaining cries. The wine had coarsened, perhaps altered by dishonest slaves. So-called magnates had left, glad to escape the town where their grandfathers had once prospered. Their departure emphasized that too many freedmen were present, former slaves, too pushing, too loud. Several army officers were arriving, swaggering and rough, at odds with the fragile robes and delicate fillets of guests more respectable.

Amongst them was Valentinus, loutish in skin and speech, a bulky, red-faced Pannonian, bald, slightly bandy, with a heavy misshapen nose. Harsh-eyed, scrubbily bearded, he too was a freedman, and sensitive about it.

Pannonia, on the Danube, a savage region, one of the last to withstand Rome, produced the brutal troops that had formerly enabled Lucius Septimus Severus to seize the Empire.

Metellus had described Valentinus' stagnant, difficult voice as that of a horse talking. He was jovial, but I discerned some inner discontent, and indeed he grumbled at his slow promotion, attributing it to jealousies and corruption from above. In profile, his face, with that nose, smashed, he said, while fighting Goths in the Alps, but more probably due to a drunken fall nearer home, was flattish, suggesting tenacity and cruelty. It was an unpleasant reminder that our Praetorian Prefect, and the Exalted Despots of East and West, were alike Pannonians.

Drinking with peculiar, swirling gulps, Valentinus was joined by a lean, black-haired, brown-eyed man, neither young nor old but with abstruse attributes of each, in a well-cut but outlandish red robe with intricately laced yellow cuffs. This personage began recounting, with much play of eye and hand, an Attic mosaic, a musical performance at Ravenna, a dancing ape, and a Roman millionaire condescending to shelter from a storm, suffocating while asleep in a Tuscan outhouse by breathing in too many feathers.

All called him the 'Armenian' though his real name and origins remained undisclosed. He would return without warning from unexplained absences, speaking with casual fluency of Treves, Strasbourg, New Carthage, and unabashed when I trapped him in inconsistency or obvious falsehood. I suspected he went no further than London or Colchester, and was probably a Gallic bankrupt, going wherever his cock led him. Women liked his swarthy, fine-boned features, his flaunting eyes, and doubtless more, calling him a moon-man, thus artistic and unstable. Posing as a Lucretian, he had won repute for intelligence by beginning some trite remark, 'In the phenomenal sense. . . .' (In Southern Gaul he would have been more readily exposed.) He had some knowledge of Greek, though less than he claimed, and I sometimes employed him for documents that needed no secrecy. That he should be invited to Sylviana's marriage was a sign of a poor epoch.

At Valentinus' first sign of impatience, the Armenian detached himself and approached me. Bowing with elaborate, suspect courtesy, then over-familiar, he spoke of some oriental ruler.

'A disciplinarian, you know. A regular Trajan. He condemned himself to be executed for accidentally allowing his troops to pillage some crops. You won't be surprised to learn that he promised to consider the possibility of a reprieve.'

He chuckled, for both of us. I had heard it often before and, quickly dismissing him, I listened with misleading inattention to the voices around me. Gossip, like gesture, betrays.

'They say she was chased to Buxton, then made sure she was taken.'

'The rivers there are strewn with pearls. Our lady would appreciate that.'

'That old husband of hers . . . still, the uninvited guests up north will be glad to taste her.'

The chuckles were an offensive reminder that officers now mixed too freely with their men. Myself, they had the ill-bred stupidity to ignore. Caesar, of course, ignored Artemidorus, and paid for it.

Though our grain tax overpaid their salaries, we professional classes were despised by the military, who believed that their killing of so many emperors, whom they themselves had enthroned, redeemed their repeated inability to withstand the barbarians. Though boasting themselves Roman, few of these porkers could have traced Rome on the map.

'Do you know, we are no longer given that excellent fish sauce! Spanish fish sauce!'

'Certainly, it meant the best of my own youth. That, and a certain discovery between my legs, which is best when shared. Like a joke.'

Metellus and Sylviana were invisible, slaves becoming listless and disagreeable. I moved into the atrium. Wine fumes, flushed, bedizened bodies, dirty feet. The women's dresses, slit at the sides, hinted at bare flanks, or were knotted carelessly enough to raise eyebrows and perhaps more, but by now I had had sufficient. Laughter, jests, contradicted the even world wherein I had my being, trying to make me ashamed of enjoying balanced accounts, the fixed, solid, immutable, more than I did indecent chatter and drunken suppers. I disliked waste of time and income.

I wanted to bid Sylviana goodbye. The whispers, winks, unspoken questions, now irritated. These oafs might need me more than they realized. Even to stand alone in simple sunlight could imperil the Augustus himself. This, however, they had yet to learn.

A girl was smiling up at me. Yellow tunic, white petals between her

16

breasts. I knew her, was civil, allowing her to kiss my cheek. She liked to be called the aristocratic Cornelia, though her family were native Silurians with whom I traded in oysters and pearls. 'Drusus! How brave of you to come!'

The concern in her dark, soft, indolent eyes showed total misjudgement of my long duel with Sylviana. She herself was always drowsing over tales of lovers who died violently on unnecessary occasions. More important, her legs, visible through gauze, though less delicate than Sylviana's, were more available, but, fatigued, I left her, discounting her mercenary sigh of disappointment.

Lamps flared. Faces were hard, alert, fretful.

'He bought himself a girl. She was thirteen. Then settled to drink himself off the earth. In his position, wine's provided free.'

'They do say he's to be accused. The Augustus, through that scoundrel Hyacinthus, claims he's been defrauded.'

'As to that, if I ask you. . . .'

'Please don't.'

'The question is, how much longer? I'm prepared to send a demand to Treves itself.'

'My dear, my very dear friend, am I listening to sedition?'

The laughter was brittle. Informers would be present. Then, from a shadow, Metellus touched my hand.

I did not know how much he knew of my relations with Sylviana. She was adept at speaking frankly only about what later proved to be trivial. His smile was as usual slightly tired, his voice gentle, sauntering. 'My Drusus!' The others left us, and he spoke of the pleasures, not of the marriage bed, but of his garden. The hibiscus, planted after some quarrel : the oak, from which a bore had been considerate enough to fall : the wall fashioned from a deserted shrine, thus encumbered with irritable ghosts. 'My garden is like my library, where each roll has its own past. One I got as a prize, though, yes, I cheated. Others, stolen, borrowed. The two I wrote myself. This one too learned, that one insufficiently obscene.'

He chattered on, while we both probably thought of wayward Sylviana, to whom almost all books were insufficiently obscene. I thought dully of how the three of us would now pass the night. Metellus suddenly quoted Catullus :

'How rank this ease of Lotus land,
I feel death in its dreaming shell.

17

The dreaming towers of Babylon,
How swift they fell!'

He giggled, touching my hand again, though as if not realizing he did so. 'Did you see old Domitia? Menopause tight as a bowstring! Floods of tears, hoots of laughter. I expect Rufus is sharpening his dagger.'

# II

---

It was common knowledge that Britain depended wholly on Rome. Like most common knowledge, this was false.

Memory is as unreliable as an eunuch's promise. Politicians rely on forgiveness from the short memories of a mouse-witted populace, politics itself, as I am sensible enough to know, being little more than the abject flattery of those we despise, its objectives menial, its prizes often fatal. Emperors themselves must accept office or perish. Often they did both.

My own superiority over rivals was based not only on natural acumen but on my verbal felicities. History is being ousted by mere rhetoric and divination. I myself would forbid it being taught, save to the rich, who necessarily wish to preserve society, unless they are touched with the irresponsible morbidity that touched Catiline and my own renegade acquaintances, Flavian and Flavia. Recognition of this denotes the wise man. Roman history, I continue, now promotes only defeatism amongst those few still prepared to listen, or with ability to read. Years ago, Tacitus considered that the most certain way to disaster was to possess an excellent career, and historians will doubtless cite me as an example, along with Pompey, Caesar, Cicero. History lessons should, perhaps, end not with myself but with Marcus Aurelius, in my judgement (and what could be more convincing?) the last authentic Emperor. They should also be very strictly censored. Only contemptible types like the Armenian relish such a tale, whether true or false is unimportant, as that of Emperor Claudius, hustled out of the world by his disgusting wife and a foul eunuch poisoning his mushrooms and tickling his throat with an envenomed feather. Disgraceful, subversive, and, furthermore, noted by vigilant barbarians. The Armenian himself told me with typical, vulgar relish of Julius Caesar's undignified tumble when, during a roaring, spectacular Triumph, his chariot collapsed beneath him while passing, of all places, the Temple of Fortune! Flapping like a heron, the Armenian

19

laughed so heartily that I fancied he would crack his teeth, and indeed I deigned to hope so. People's manners seldom fail to outrage me, and my own fastidiousness has not always ensured me the respect to which I am entitled.

My readers' memories being so imperfect, or dishonest, I must unavoidably outline the decades before the year 367 – to use the preposterous chronology, doubtless temporary, adopted after Theodosius' ferocious promulgation of the Jeheshua cult.

Posterity may not confirm Theodosius' beliefs, and I wonder what Fate will make of them. Descent from a Jewish phallus-deity seems scarcely the best of divine references, and Jeheshua, small, perhaps deformed, certainly sardonic and ill-tempered, with a childhood noted for scandalous behaviour (though the bishops are suppressing reports of this), was a curious rival to the gleaming Olympians, whom many, of course, still respect, in various degrees of apathy or prudence. A few years before 367, the Augustus Flavius Claudius Julian had unsuccessfully attempted to restore the cult of Helios-Mithras-Apollo, the Unconquered Sun.

My own beliefs, scarcely unimportant, will reveal themselves, as posterity will require, to its own very great advantage. I used to consider Jeheshua only a wily, itinerant quack, teaching some form of cannibalism, literally leaving no footprints despite his long and rather tiresome walks. I was amused to discover that, during an undignified brawl at Nicea, 325, Jeheshua was elected a god, by a majority vote. Such is human absurdity. (He may, of course, actually be a god, but not because of Nicea, in itself a horrid and dishonest place.)

Surviving Diocletian's persecution (amply justified), then fostered by Constantine, urban British Christianity was increasing, though rivalled by Isis and Mithras, a formidable pair, particularly in London, cosmopolitan as Alexandria, Antioch, Ephesus, and built to order by us Romans. The ignorant and timid were wearing little crosses, against plague, fire, death. The more sensible explained this talisman as a symbol of vital energies perfectly balanced, a useful stance from which to outwit Fate, or indeed to exploit it. I suspected, however, that crafty Jeheshua was nevertheless inferior to Eneas, Alexander, Pythagoras. Impulsive, intolerant, he seemed not only a joker and buffoon, but a ranter, hating useful if dull social codes, and prophesying Rome crushed by social turmoil under a cloud of fire supervised by some Great One, presumably himself. Obsessed with his own status, he was, like Mithras, over-absorbed with flame. (Have you noted that would-be despots generally share this unproductive interest?)

In my time, Christianity was being riven almost to shreds, by the bawling Orthodox in Rome, and the Arians, often barbarian, who yet included the late Emperor Julian's cousin, Constantius II. Their disputes, always unseemly, often bloody, concerned the apparently ludicrous question of whether Jeheshua was son to his own father, or merely like him. I later discerned, however, beneath this verbiage, a more interesting debate about whether Jeheshua was a god, or only resembling a god. Most barbarians accept the latter, most bishops do not, though it will probably survive the longer. My slaves, with expressions that displeased me, would murmur that he taught that the cunning would inherit the earth. On the whole, they have done so. More capable of abstract thought than most, I tended to regard gods neither as patrons nor clients, but as significant shapes : Jeheshua, very angular, Jupiter a roughly-hewn square, Mithras a circle. They had reality, representing levers by which, in ourselves, we adjust to circumstances. They are symptoms, not of progress, but process. Rather well expressed, I think.

My friend, old Avitus, with more leisure for such matters, possessed a tract concerning Christians.

'Secretly they adore the Great Goddess, Isis-Astarte, whom their leaders try to suppress. At Alexandria, they prohibited all their own sacred books save four. The others, nevertheless, survive underground, to trouble the mind, often in dreams. Statues of Isis, and Ceres, with a man-child, are often displayed openly.'

I began to recognize Jeheshua as, at best, a puny or travestied Hercules, escaping early dangers, refusing a crown, briefly revolting against his father when facing death, at which an earthquake occurred, then ascending in a cloud. Like Socrates, he won early repute for repartee, rejected boorish Hebrew regulations against good living, teased questioners with annoying counter-questions. Also like Socrates, he could have escaped prison, but was too arrogant to do so. As a god he was uninterested in sacrifices – themselves, in our time, a drain on vital resources – but demanded absolute loyalty, accepting no world but his own, a bleak one; though, to do him justice, he commended practical work, cursed the lazy, demanded full payment of debts.

21

As patron of the Empire, he seems incongruous, if not quite as negligible as I had formerly assumed. Corpses sometimes gleam, and his posthumous magic may have entangled his belated patron, Constantine the Great. To defeat magicians, I too have usually professed allegiance to them, thus neutralizing their craving for self-display. In Britain, the Romans foolishly assaulted a Christian oaf, Alban, a wizard, who quickly divided a river to escape them. Later, after execution as a public nuisance, he rather smugly walked off, carrying his own head, at Verulam. They should have pensioned him off and forgotten him.

Christian priests are appointed by manual transmission of *mana,* magic tissue, supposedly originating from Jeheshua himself, whose own hands are likely to have been dirty. His *numen,* spirit, magnetized his followers who, very sensibly relying on more than visions, founded many monastic schools. Silchester monks worshipped Hercules under the name of Christopher, for supporting the world through a flood. I believe they taught a divine trinity of sky, earth, water, whose contact emitted a purifying fire. It was said, probably untruthfully, that initiates had to murder a child and drink the blood, scarcely a tempting proposition. No recommendation either, was that the sect relied greatly on the women and eunuchs of the Sacred Palace. Undeniably it offered easy access of power to the soft-spoken and hypocritical, the opposites of myself.

Gods doubtless went their way, but I was more concerned with human intrigues and ambitions. Like any thoughtful man I could accept that, aeons ago, a god had been mysteriously dismembered, his flesh creating earth and stars, which retained something of his spirit, like capital, with latent powers so valuable in the right hands. Jupiter was everywhere, rather than anywhere in particular. Later, thanks to unusual resources of afterthought, I came closer to Lucretius' belief in atoms, as against my friend Metellus' imprecise notions – he always had notions, rather than ideas – about religion being cords of music binding us to the heart of the earth.

Though sceptical of much of the unseen, I suspected that Democritus too, reducing the universe to those busy, invisible atoms, made good sense, though it might be politically and socially anarchic by restricting choice and responsibility. The tale of him blinding himself to improve his concentration did not attract me : as a contribution to human betterment it was negligible. I have never needed such extravagances. Hard-wrung profits benefited my eyes, and much else.

Some two centuries ago, a few of you may know, the Divine Claudius conquered Britain. His temple at Colchester, if it survives, is solid and commanding, though I disliked the priests' manners. (Crassly, they once mistook me for a grocer, more apposite to the Divine Claudius himself.) Rome tamed the tribes, built cities, fostered communications, mines, farms, mills, vineyards. Abroad, in Germania, in Asia, rulers might flourish or perish wretchedly, and, in the Empire, with the old citizen army long vanished, rootless professional soldiers collected dangerous power. Britain, however, long sat secure in her waters. Hibernia was a swamp festering with madmen : the walls of Hadrian and Antoninus blocked the dreadful Caledonians. Caledonians are inhuman, Hibernians even worse, not human at all. Nevertheless, after 188, ending the line of extraordinary Keepers of Imperial Peace – Nerva, Trajan, Hadrian, Antoninus, Marcus Aurelius – the West faltered. Gods, Tacitus insisted, are interested not in our safety but our punishment. A second Marcus, the loutish successor of Emperor Commodus, perennially distressed by prospects of hard work, would prance about in lion's skin, brandish a club less heavy than it appeared, exchange blows with common gladiators. Cruel and lustful, he invited his own doom, murder by the Praetorian Guards, by then mostly Germans, who at once enthroned Pertinax, former legate in Britain. He gave promise of real authority, so they killed him too and – I would like to believe it sounds incredible – promptly auctioned the Empire to the highest bidder. Rule by the rich, I have said, is logical, is excellent, but I jib at this. Fortunately, the winner, Didius, was allowed but a few days of power before the Praetorians cheerfully dismembered him. Finally the invincible African general, Septimus Severus, methodical, chilly, swift, nerved himself against these brutes, these indolent troopers, and restored the Diadem. Under him, British Villa society won back riches perhaps too blatantly apparent in 367.

Civilized people should learn from me. I always advised discretion, the concealment of hard authority beneath sedate, pleasant smiles, occasional rebates less significant than they appeared, a gratuitous hand-clasp. How seldom I was ever wrong !

Externally, Spain, Gaul, Italy, had long been affected by changes occurring thousands of miles east. Travellers reported gods denying rain, grass dying, disturbances in China, packs of hideous yellow riders turning west. Alarmed Goths and Germans retreated, first imploring, then demanding, lands from the Empire. Marcus Aurelius sometimes fought, sometimes appeased. No ruler should be ruled by dogma. Marcus was admittedly a philosopher, a specimen of which I am generally contemptuous, but he could use a sword well enough, if only in strict necessity. Philosophy, of course, ruins life by making second-raters doubt their own actions, motives, identity, even their own existence. I am no philosopher and proud of it; where philosophers took refuge in analysis of words, trying to pound ordinary life into the inflexible, I took words for granted and assumed command of numbers, continually transforming One into at least Four. I believe Jeheshua, very sensibly, commended those who, with only one coin, lend it at extraordinary interest. Such teachings deserve to conquer the world and seem to be doing so.

Later, the desperate Goths destroyed the great and profitable temple of Diana at Ephesus, stormed Athens, ravaged Italy, captured Emperor Valerian, before being soothed on ignoble terms which included the surrender of Dacia. Though Diocletian attracted many Goths into his legions, the rest continued to threaten Rome and Constantinople, joined by Roman deserters, bankrupts, tax-dodgers and fugitive slaves.

Germans were always violent, both envying and despising superior men in villa and counting-house, and beginning to doubt Roman determination. They had reason. In the scandalous orgiastic dance of power, menials and racial inferiors seized the imperial throne. An Arab, Scythian, Syrian . . . Africans, Thracians, Dalmatians. The despots Aurelian, Probus, Diocletian himself, were peasants. Alexander Severus, cultured and useful, was succeeded by his murderer, a gigantic, illiterate military tribune and wrestler, himself to perish savagely. The State existed only for soldiers and officials in a true desert of spirit (my own phrase, perfect in its precision and doubtless to be appropriated by lesser commentators). Germans flooded Gaul, 276. Before a fatal mutiny, Probus recovered it, then hired the defeated against further aggressive tribes.

In fifteen degenerate years, some thirty emperors 'ruled' from where best they could. As the Armenian put it, ' "Beloved and Divine", they got their heads stamped on a coin, then found them bouncing around on the floor !' (Occasionally, the fellow's coarseness had substance, even sapience.)

Sanity was restored by the fresh blood of the lower-class Dalmatian emperors. Diocletian, victorious in the field, rehabilitated the administration, not from Rome but from his ever-moving camp. When Constantine the Great established the Sacred Palace in Constantinople, the Empire was formally divided into East and West.


You will not be surprised that Britain suffered considerable turmoil. For years, through weakness or misplaced guile, the State had allowed, and occasionally invited, even commanded, Vandals, Jutes, Saxons, Alans, Parisi, Burgundians, Franks, Frisians . . . to colonize waste lands or, a gambler's throw, to defend frontiers. Probus particularly encouraged this, after crushing the British pretender, Bonosus, a drunkard with washerwoman's morals, and establishing Germanic plantations against further native revolts. Emperor Valentinian, of whom I shall have more to tell, settled some beaten Alemans on the eastern swamplands, while deporting British criminals to man the Rhine. Sometimes, barbarian immigrants arrived illegally, the authorities pretending not to notice.

I accept that culture thrives on racial cross-currents, which, in a metaphor notable and exact, adds yeast to stolid traditions. Immigration also, if only temporarily, provides cheap and docile labour as slavery declines. Too much immigration, however, creates resentment and imbalance. As pioneers, newcomers have too much vigour, and sometimes too inventive enterprise, to amuse the natives. Alternatively, they may be mere parasites.

The State, I must tell you, was by now very different from what it had been four centuries earlier, when Pompey the Great stormed three hundred cities and conquered thirteen countries, and Julius Caesar methodically took eight hundred towns. Such heroes also founded cities by the score, forcing the world to blink its aching eyes.

In Britain, internal disorders were at first only seasonal, though under the absurd and despicable Commodus, 184, enigmatic but ferocious Picts rushed the Antonine Wall in mid-Caledonia, which was then permanently abandoned. Perhaps a mistake, though imperial strength was declining.

Subsequently, dangers increased. Clodius Albinus, Governor of Britain, resenting the murder of his old commander, Pertinax, proclaimed himself Emperor and crossed to Rome, denuding Hadrian's Wall, only to be slain by Septimus Severus. Inevitably, hordes of stinking Picts ravaged the northern province – not in itself wholly regrettable, for northerners are unruly and stupid – until repulsed by that unshakeable Emperor Septimus; but, undeniably, the Genius of the Empire had faltered.

I had better say at once that Picts, the Painted Men, are probably unique amongst barbarians, on most of whom walls impose some forbidding mystery, through silence, through sheer and inescapable weight, though, once overwhelmed, they permanently lose *mana*.

Pretentious sophisticates like Metellus and Sylviana joked about Hadrian's Wall, as they did the *agentes*, secret police, but such wit reminded me only of the commonplace elation at seeing a house on fire before ascertaining that it is not one's own. Predictably, Flavia and Flavian, that mincing brace of cretins, carrying their tiny reed hand-bags as they might brimming goblets, drawled that Pictish cruelty derived from the humourless expression on the Wall's monotonous face, but their voices were too tired and faint to detain an intelligent person. Only their petulant affront when anyone could bring himself to agree with their so-called witticisms sometimes made me smile, albeit rather grimly.

After the aggravating Albinus, the Wall never regained absolute mastery, and even the most wilfully purblind could see a spreading blight. The Armenian's nonsense was not always rubbish. 'It's well-known that Italian ladies have been sterile for generations. Lucky for the men, mind you! Lead, let me tell you, poisoning the conduits.' (He need not have 'told me' so importantly. I believe I am to be credited with having first used the word 'pollution' in a formal memorandum.) He added, less convincingly, 'When I was last in Rome I slept with that sticky enticing creature who sees fit to call herself Lady of the House of Life, Shelter of the Dead and Alive. More simply, the goddess Isis, Star of Sailors. Something in that. She's had more sailors between her legs than old Antony put between decks at Actium.'

Uneasiness about the Empire required a stubborn belief in Britain, on which the usurper Albinus had relied. He failed, yet my own belief – which I still largely hold, despite what follows – was not dissimilar. Life was simple, the future could be manipulated, Fate put out to work, for anyone shrewd and, above all, resolute. Britain, rich with possibilities, with more assets than probably anywhere else in the West, had tested her muscles with Albinus and was ceasing to feel shame at being provincial. (I wonder if this has ever been said before – that a nation or empire is only truly viable when 'provincial' is a word of praise.)

Meanwhile, I distrusted defence through walls, which reminded me of athletes who infuriate their backers by an inexplicable fear of winning. Most young men should exist not to lurk behind defences, but to go out and attack, on behalf of their betters.

Under Diocletian, Channel pirates were raiding Britain, an ominous symptom. The Emperor, hard, crafty as befitted one born of slaves, entrusted the British fleet at Boulogne to a Menapian barbarian, Marcus Mausaeus Carausius. Too successful, Carausius subsequently rebelled, overthrowing Diocletian's adopted co-ruler, the peasant Maximian, and, styling himself Augustus, for some years ruled an independent Britain, harshly but competently – and harshness is certainly necessary for workshy, grumbling, over-musical, irresponsive Britons – establishing naval bases, maintaining the fleet, restoring coinage after long debasement. In 367, we were still using those coins, from which his coarse, bearded face gleamed like an extortioner. Very sensibly, he used coins to advertise himself, his intimacy with gods, the Unconquered Sun, with Diocletian.

Old Diocletian waited. Finally, Carausius was murdered by a disloyal though audacious intimate, Allectus (I regret to say, a financial expert). Still, he has never been forgotten : as late as 356, a pretender won some success by calling himself Carausius II, even issuing coins, though poor ones.

After due consideration, I, I myself, might have supported Carausius. Western security was inexorably becoming more hazardous than Eastern, while Britain, whatever the doubtful quality of its ruling personnel, was admirably sited for trade and limited conquests.

Her limitations, however, demanded wholesale remedies, which partly explains what follows. She lacked a national capital, national religion, national spirit, remaining tribal at heart despite the imperial framework. Roman gods, even for ancient magnate families, were like old friends now on half-pay, eliciting little more than conventional good manners; Jeheshua was no fighting man, or pretended not to be and for some years pretended too successfully – now he has been rather extravagantly reversed, witness that bloodshed at his priests' conferences; British gods were dirty blockheads, cut-price Apollos. The province, furthermore, was divided into four cantons, but with certain departments, notably of taxation, stationed outside them, in London. Administration was clogged by officials, who, like

27

their fellows throughout the world, loved to delay, obstruct, evade responsibility. Far too much was referred to the Praetorian Prefect in Gaul, whose jurisdiction included Spain. He would then, far too often, pass it on to the Imperial Offices, where it would probably lie forgotten, particularly if concerning useful reforms and legitimate complaint. Here was the later Empire in a sentence. No civilization can survive stagnant officialdom, and very little culture as I know it. Mark well.

Despite my respect for Rome, City and Idea, I could not have contrived a convincing prospectus for her then. Lofty Rome had sunk to an idle, virtually useless township saddled with too big a name. Her gods had slunk away, in dudgeon or boredom. The louder Emperor Julian praised the Unconquered Sun, the more it seemed to cool. (This remark, my own, I once repeated to Metellus, who forbore to acknowledge it but probably stole for one of his otherwise trivial verses.)

Carausius failed, but had once again shown, if prematurely, the possibility of a successful, autonomous Britain. Allectus, however, frantic for his own hide, again left the Wall undefended, and, abandoning it to Pictish assault, collected all available troops, including Frankish mercenaries, against Roman invasion. Diocletian, admirable at delegating – the secret of authority – dispatched Constantius the Pale, who routed Allectus near Silchester, and was welcomed everywhere, understandably enough. He refortified the Wall. The legions were disciplined under a new appointee, the Duke of Britain, while, from Boulogne, the Count of the Shore directed the fleet.

Constantius' son, Constantine, was born in Britain, where his father, now Emperor, himself died. Constantine had won some respite against the Picts, and was yelled onto the Throne by British troops at York. With these and Germans at his back – which I would never relish – he overcame several continental rivals and reigned supreme until his death. This too assisted British self-confidence, Celts being apt to take inordinate credit for what others have directed.

Constantine continued Diocletian's reforms. Valuable as a remedy which could yet only be temporary, they were less so in disorderly, individualistic Britain. I list them with loathing. Compulsory and total subservience to the State – a gang of eunuchs, place-men, time-servers, freedmen and scared Despot – itself fatigued and short-sighted, replaced loyalty to the Idea interpreted by free yet responsible masters of business. By 367, and I cannot repeat this too often

28

(and can scarcely be reproached even if I do), government meant no more than corrupt officialdom extracting endless subsidies from the real workers, men like myself, who had no rights of appeal. Property entailed obligations excessive and too often intolerable. We had to underwrite huge tax deficiencies, sit unpaid on councils, watch our nominal rulers pocket our dwindling profits. The State's chief, perhaps only, supporters were treated like delinquents : no future in that! I knew of respectable householders selling themselves into slavery to escape forced loans, obligatory public building, extravagant surcharges. Bankers and lawyers would dress in robes soiled and torn, to deceive tax-collectors. Meanwhile, emperors hid from their own generals, barbarian hirelings.

My story, a sermon of major importance, will astonish only those of you not worth addressing. I have, as I am sure you have noted, very decided opinions on government, morals, culture, race, which the combined resources of history are unlikely to refute and which should ensure that my name survives those of most emperors, politicians, and all poets save Vergil and, perhaps, Horace. (Homer, from a misleading view of the world, told foolish and improbable stories about creatures of undesirable behaviour.)

Anyway, as I have said, British Celts took upstart pride in Constantine who, apparently after a dangerous illness, accepted subtle Jeheshua though, an ageing gambler hedging his bets, never actually abjuring Helios, the Unconquered Sun. His heir, Constans, faced new barbarian onslaughts on Britain, 342. Weak and depraved, he preferred concessions to battles, even crediting savages with respect for treaties. Usually, those rodents marked with the signs not of chiefs but of shifty gods, clauses they could not read, and which would have annoyed them if they had been able. They had their own clauses. One tribe, no matter which, volunteered to surrender the moon in a cask. It has not yet done so.

Unbelievably, Constans sanctioned Pictish and Scottish settlements immediately south of the Wall and pardoned illegal German immigrants, flattering their leaders with grandiose titles. This was inserting dry rot into an old mansion, though such policy had been initiated by Caesar Augustus himself, admittedly from a position of strength. I acknowledge that German troops loyally served Caesar Julian, against their brothers.

(Titles, of course, can be inexpensive and effective. Genius knows when best to award them, not invariably doing so. I, with traditional sententious phrases, would ceremonially free my superannuated slaves, thereby saving on household expenses.)

Germans continued to enter Britain. Except on the northern frontiers they were forbidden arms, but often seemed faithful in their plodding way, seldom mating or mixing with their Celtic neighbours. Mindlessly brutal when provoked, enjoying vile beers, gluttony, rowdy songs about squalid gods and kings, quarrels about what they misleadingly termed laws, they shunned Roman highways and towns, gibbered about ghosts, farmed small, dishevelled cattlefolds, worshipped trees, weapons and shadows, fretted at the restraints of peace and blubbered horribly at defeat in war. They enjoyed bellowing words they were unable to write. Some were periodically conscripted for the legions, though scattered to distant places to avoid conspiracy. They fought well, but from brute love of violence, and with equal zest would assault their Roman benefactors. Barbarians, if I may propose a notion perhaps too profound to be readily understood, hate the civilization they so envy.

To no surprise, and to general applause, Constans was murdered, 350, and replaced by his brother Constantius II, a glum Arian Christian, whose beliefs provoked the bishops to impotent curses. Britain soon succumbed to yet another usurper, Gallic or British, Magnus Magnentius. He was briefly master, not only of Britain, but of Spain, Gaul, Italy. Again, and significantly, this episode was sustained mainly by German and British troops, further inflating what has been called, with some exaggeration, the British national mind. His adventure too, weakened British defences.

Constantius, Equal to the Apostles, cautiously cruel, assassin of all his male relations save Julian, put paid to Magnentius, but in Britain the civilized and popular Governor Martinus – it is possible, though uncommon, to be both; I was one but not the other, and do not regret it – attempted to soften Constantius' arbitrary reprisals, but killed himself after failing to control Paul the Chain, a notably evil and, I suspect, barely sane imperial delegate. I believe his shoulder clicked, and the Armenian alleged that he was too proud to read his own letters, scarcely helpful to State secrets! Certainly his harshness provoked further anti-Roman feelings. When Julian, devotee of the army gods, Helios and Mithras, commanded Gaul and Britain, he had to send troops to the Wall, against tribes stimulated by too many concessions. I knew, and despised, the general, Lupercinus, more or less barbarian, thus crude, conceited, bibulous, and, on an important

30

occasion, disrespectful to myself. I reproved him, roundly, though with natural dignity, and inwardly dispatched him a curse which, as it happened, was fatal, a tribute to powers I had not actually claimed.

Constantius II, sour, meagre, but able enough – an impertinent clerk once compared him to myself, presumably intending a compliment – is now overshadowed by the glamorous Julian, author of the anti-Jeheshua tract, *The Mother of the Gods*, and, more importantly, a superb field commander against vile Franks and Alemans. As I have already said, he restored the worship of the Olympian gods, to much popular derision in Antioch and Alexandria, where a malicious joke is applauded more than a victory or commercial profits. Augustus of East and West, Julian perished, perhaps by murder, campaigning quite unnecessarily in Persia. (Why do despots, hitherto successful, need to waste their energies and resources in spectacular but doomed expeditions east?)

Jovian inherited the Diadem. Jovian died. The new Augustus, still in power, 367, was Flavius Valentinian, an officer of Julian's. He appointed his brother Valens to rule the East, as he had continually to defend Gaul from the Alemans. From Paris, he tended to overcome them for a season or two, and, whenever resting, governed from Treves. I doubt whether he or Valens ever visited Rome, and indeed had scant reason to do so.

Most of these rulers at best attempted merely to keep society from falling apart. They lacked curiosity. Poets, Metellus and his like, have too much curiosity, which Plato, quite rightly, condemned. (I sometimes see myself deeply admired by Plato, though not by his degenerate, warm-bath followers.) A Valentinian, a Constantius, has too little. The balance is reached by a prosperous business man, who must pioneer, risk, develop, from premises of reality. He will reach further, and be remembered longer.

Valentinian had an excellent general, Jovinus, victor over Alemans, though in 367 contending with Saxons, 'Short Swords', forbidding appellation, whose threatened recovery from earlier defeats boded ill for Britain. On the Danube, watched fearfully by Emperor Valens, the Goths swarmed and plotted in their new-won lands, though still fearing Huns. And, while barbarian populations swelled, the 'benevolent unconcern' of Roman parents and doctors encouraged infanticide. This, of course, can often be very useful, and mere numbers be socially disadvantageous. In 367, however, I was somewhat undecided about what was best, save in relation to my

31

neighbours' children, all of whom were nasty.

Like the far greater Diocletian and Constantine, the two imperial brothers strove desperately to defend State and Diadem, by decrees seldom possible to enforce. It is important to consider whether legislation can effect genuine change. Has it ever done so? I leave it to you to answer, no doubt under circumstances that themselves direly need changing.

The Emperors forbade breeding with slaves and barbarians, a pleasure often less nauseating than might be imagined. To counter social and political apathy they attempted to re-impose maximum prices and incomes, and make all professions hereditary, like slavery. Public spirit was thus further impoverished, voluntary effort not only ridiculed but penalized. Denying the competitive instincts, vital and more useful than the sexual, the State promoted only frustration and anger. The gifted son of some labouring dolt must remain among pigs : a musician's deaf and dumb son be confined to the harp : the cowardly scion – splendid word – of a great fighter, bear a sword.

Britain avoided as much of this nonsense as she could, and the natives, already disrespectful, were thus set a bad example in civic virtues. In 367 I doubted whether she could ever fully recover under the Roman rule which for so long had fostered my own class. Confiscation, fines, executions, might quell individual subversives, but, continuously, money bought less and less, for reasons perplexing to the untutored mind. (I could scarcely explain it without committing treason.) The splendour of Augustus, Pontifex Maximus, Light of the World, had slumped to the sharp talons of the Fiscal Procurator, demanding ever more for authority, which provided so little. (Nothing, I felt, was more disgraceful to Jeheshua than his intimacy, genuine or crafty toadying, with tax-gatherers. A true comedian – has anyone else observed this? – he was unconcerned with the most serious, the fate of Rome, foretelling evil, like some gloating usurer awaiting repayment. He even transformed water to wine, to dodge the liquor tax. His disciple Paul, a Levantine tent-maker, a writer of poor Greek, I am told was a murderer. A bishop told me that through his knowledge, not of murder but of that very Greek, he properly established Christianity, surely from poor qualifications.)

Energetic, capable, percipient as I have presumably shown, I was aggrieved at being born in times that engendered such mysticism. By now I have outlined all that you need ever know about the Roman Empire.

# III

---

Who am I ?

I am Drusus Antonius Muras, aged thirty in 367. My father, of Sicilian descent, traded in Sens. He married into the Morini, who once proved treacherous to Julius Caesar. My childhood lacked history. My father tolerated no family disputes, which helped make me more purposeful than many contemporaries, who seemed to fight themselves more than they did life's challenge.

As the youngest son, I could expect little from Sens, and early settled in Britain to expand the family business. This, together with contracts to farm imperial monopolies and my flair for selecting information, enabled me to live well enough. Foresight was more essential than courage.

I exported Mendip tin, Silurian gold, Ordovican copper, Wroxeter coal and ironstone : dealt in Chester salt, flax, timber, mules, textiles : imported Aquitaine and Bordeaux wines, Egyptian pepper, Scanian furs, Rhenish glass, Jewish silk. I supplied oats for the cavalry, owned many barns. We had ships, slaves, beasts, but at this time I could seldom risk assembling the long caravans of former days, preferring to dispatch small groups of packhorses down minor roads. Dealings with the north had languished, threatened not only by Picts but the violent Brigantes. These, protected by wide rivers, had led Celtic resistance to the Conquest, accomplished, without them knowing it, for their own good.

My agents were often Jews, with whom I was correct but wary. Beyond their allegiance to a bleak, partisan god, somehow the father of Jeheshua, I know little about them. Their honesty I trusted absolutely, without absolute trust in their generosity. They were invariably courteous, with linguistic versatility, but their sacred books advocated racial exterminations, intolerable to Rome.

My work forced me to live not in a sumptuous rural villa but in Silchester, the old Atrebatan capital, refounded by Trajan, near the

33

Thames, and near Readingas, half a day's ride from London, and paying dues to the cantonal centre, Cirencester. Small and neat, the town had some two thousand citizens and slaves, though, before its defensive walls were erected, it had been larger. London itself had built its walls only seventeen years back. Towns had everywhere shrunk, the rich retreating to villas to escape less the alien unrest than the inexorable Treasury. The Villa magnates were unpopular for dodging taxes and responsibilities through influence, bribery, sheer effrontery, and by selling produce not in public forums but in small, rather covert, rural fairs.

Much of Verulam was adandoned to squatters, elks, foxes. Wroxeter forum, celebrated in Gaul itself, had been gutted, and never repaired. Administration crumbled under levies for defence, postal and medical services, nowhere very apparent, though in Britain, as in Italy, loud demands for these were linked with reluctance to pay for them. And to fulfil one's compulsory civic responsibilities drained one's purse.

Silchester had four old temples, which still housed a few ageing nymphs. A temple to Jeheshua had been completed. Arenas had replaced theatres, though in their homes Metellus and his friends enjoyed satirical or tragic play-readings and dainty recitals.

I had extensive local interests : banking, tanning, iron, glass, with a share in the Farnham potteries. I had restored the elaborate water-mill.

Despite inflation and military uncertainty, Britain still prospered more than Spain, Gaul, Italy, importing less than she exported. Most of the slaves abroad wore British wool. Villa estates, impregnable against price rises, were producing food and goods on a scale unprecedented.

Silchester commanded some crucial roads : to London, matrix of island communications : to Gwynchester, still sacred to the British underworld god : to southern ports, to the Plain and its ghosts, to Bath and the Severn.

London was more an imperial outpost than a British city. It was larger than Lyons, Treves, even Ravenna, with its port (the richest in the West) and its huge basilica, moneylenders ogling on the wide steps like whores. The Fiscal Procurator and his degenerates were directly responsible to the Emperor, with much antagonism simmering between him and the Governor, Praetorian Prefect, local curias, and military command. Nominally inferior to the Governor, the Procurator was thought to spy on him for the Augustus, a procedure which might demonstrate the art of government but was undeniably bad government.

Despite urban temples, the peasantry, dark Silurians, stocky Atrebats, clung to their ancient deities, Bel and Lugus, gods of light, Nodens and Gwyn, capable of little more than scarring a tree by lightning, or drowning a sheep.

The British, long-haired and lazy, while inhabiting our towns, attending lawcourts and curias, seldom became Roman. Their hearts were confused : neither wholly barbarian nor wholly civilized, they accepted the Conquest through hopelessness or greed.

I travelled frequently in Britain and Gaul, visiting my agents and collecting information with which to counter the revenue hounds who spied on my contracts, tried to dictate market policies, and urged me to increase my energies, only to tax me further. Years ago, fury against these creatures had lost Emperor Galerius all Italy.

The future of imperial Britain seemed doubtful, despite enormous trade profits in any quiet year. (Our Leicester concerns, in 363, had earned me four hundred per cent.) However, I could see what stay-at-homes could not. Roads crowded with military deserters, runaway slaves risking the noose, ruined peasants, remittance men, bankrupts, often collected into violent bands – the bacauds – frequently joined by tenants fleeing the taxes their Lords so blatantly ignored.

Everywhere, huge temple investments were endangered. Savings were being buried in woods and fields, barter was returning, while the Treasury insisted on coin, coin, coin. I thought of old Charon, who, for a penny, ferries the dead into oblivion. But on what could he spend it ? An underworld was rising around us too, where our wealth could be used only on shadows.

In a small town everyone knew everyone else. I often saw my old fellow-student, Metellus, and professional associates who formally invited me to dine, but I had no friends of intelligence equal to my own, and suffered the hostility directed towards the powerful and virtuous. Gibes abounded about me sweating gold, vomiting silver, sneezing copper, excreting receipts, combing and finding not lice but jewels. An ox-witted magistrate had compared me to Septimuleius. (Whoever presented the Roman Senate with the head of the radical, Tiberius Gracchus, was promised its weight in gold. Septimuleius succeeded, having first filled it with lead. I would not have risked that.)

35

My detractors had the laughs : I had the profits. I was never entranced by what Metellus called the gradualness of graceful argument. Nonsense breeds rubbish.

'Drusus, I write my verses not because I know the answers but because I do not. Seeking is itself the crown. So the lines come.'

He conducted financial affairs on the same principle, and forgot that his own questions were so foolish. 'Is not sunlight the hard skein of soft gold?' The answer was obvious. Yet the self-esteem of such fellows was insurmountable : they hated real work and resented advice. Metellus' verse, I told him, showed neither observation nor common sense, but he only smiled. More foolish still, he was becoming, for whatever reasons, friendly with Valentinus, the grumbling, foul-mouthed staff-officer.

I did not totally disdain friendships. Some five years previously I met Sylviana. She was then about sixteen. Hitherto, I had slept only with trash : slave girls and brothel boys. Sylviana opened scope I had never suspected. Slender, enigmatic eyes in pellucid skin, short dark fringe. Well enough, but she also had a mind by no means averse to learning. I knew most of what was to be known, from the selling of barley or the manufacture of paper to the inadequacies of Tacitus, and her education was due entirely to me. Admittedly, I myself learnt from her, though her lessons were less precise.

Her spontaneity was accompanied by much that was reserved, deceptive without inevitably being dishonest. Immediately after an intimate embrace, she would stare at me as if I were a badly executed mosaic.

'Most beautiful Sylviana, you don't like me much, do you?'

'You have no charm. Something else seeps through.'

'What does?'

'Yes.'

I certainly learnt exhilarations, brilliant but short, interspersed with broken pacts, exciting truces, sudden feints and false starts. She gave me an expensive Egyptian tortoise shell, after I had mentioned my dislike of this material. I thanked her elaborately, praised the colouring, over-praised its market-value, then stamped it to pieces. She was delighted.

Throughout, we were in some game without defined rules. 'I can sometimes forget you're really a mastiff.' Her small curved smile flitted over her brooding face, then instantly vanished. 'My old Ajax!' I was then only twenty-five.

She would read me poetry, though I so seldom knew whether the authors were serious. Metellus, that minor poet (I suspect very minor), had spoken solemnly about 'the face of a tree, quiet but not indolent'. It was easy to feel superior.

Poets are covetous, polemical and selfish : none wishes others to publish, or even write. Occasionally they irritated me by claiming to delineate more than I could understand. Metellus, Sylviana said, with tiresome appearance of approval, believed that books should suggest worlds beyond their immediate subject. She cited a stupid line he had sent her. 'All, save your smile, is a state of becoming.' I advised her never to be dependent on his account books. 'The difference between you,' she retorted, 'is the difference between a spring shrub and a garden pot.' She forgot that, unless one is a dog, a pot is more useful.

I would listen to her reading, concealing frequent impatience. Verses numbed me, unless, like the Georgics, they gave specific, if sometimes misleading information, or, like the Aeneid, followed, unambiguous as a banker's file, a purposeful human trail. To rebuke the extravagances of Metellus' set, I maintained that literature should confine itself to the language of lawyers and business men, to avoid sacrificing truth for passion and vanity. The death of King Oedipus, the Trojan War, were squalid incidents senselessly enlarged by scribblers, thereby dementing a Nero and an Alexander.

'My poor ugly old man !' Sylviana sighed. Physically, I accepted that I was imperfect. Short in arm and leg, stoutish, I more relied, not on wit, but my wits, which she loved to match.

'Drusus, Drusus. When you tell me that you love me, I realize that I am less lovely than I suspected.'

I liked people to come when needed, vanish after use, like clerks, porters, whores. Sylviana would arrive unexpectedly, inopportunely, yet always leaving too soon. Something in me amused, even stimulated her, other than my millionaire status.

So much of life derives from accident, which apparently, though perhaps only superficially, contradicts fate. The tilt of a head, a slightly uneven walk, an amused eye can refute the irrefutable. Like a risky investment, Sylviana now obsessed me. She was more than a gifted body : bodies alone are but the preliminaries of an exciting contract, and all contracts eventually expire. As if to flout me, she shrugged at ambition. If she had any, it was either absurdly rarefied or intolerably trivial. She professed admiration for Mark Antony tossing away power, though I could tell her that he and his paramour have been misunderstood by the ignorant and shallow. Actium, though a defeat, originated in a shrewd strategy of break-out and recovery, of which poets know nothing.

Undressed, Sylviana never seemed wholly naked. Reticent even when most talkative, in sexual climax she betrayed only a quiet sigh, instantly replaced by a yawn or frown. Like an opal, she flashed unexpectedly, showed colour within darkness itself. When I rebuked her levity, real or feigned, on serious occasions – at her wedding she complained aloud that Juno had played a bloody trick on her – she threatened to sleep with Brunnus, representative of the Cirencester Censor, a cunning plebeian police chief.

'I always wanted to explore the underworld before death. No girl has yet done so.' Her slanted smile was taunting. 'Perhaps that would blind him. Or transform him to a stag. As it is, Brunnus is a stoat. That would help you and your tremendous secrets.'

'He might, of course, see more fiercely, and turn into a satyr.'

'Ah, Drusus, he is a satyr; it's you who see too much. And you feel too little. You're a boxer, but I like to be stroked. Sometimes by a kind hand, sometimes by a friendly tongue. If only you understood.'

'How you would hate it if I did.'

'Yes. How much you know! Or think you do!' She lowered her head, as if to conceal a pert grin. 'Metellus says words are hot or cold. The finest are both at once, exquisitely cooked.'

'Metellus! He has lingered too long in his own childhood. He lives for sensation alone. Does he ever refuse an invitation, a challenge, a ludicrous speculation? Should you not teach him to say no?'

She had quickly accomplished the reverse. Their unexpected marriage left me with an arcane joke or puzzle to unravel. I had never considered them as likely lovers, indeed I had reckoned Metellus too fastidious to risk the strenuous copulations that Sylviana allowed and, in her way, demanded, and the shock forced me to revalue glances, exclamations, silences, laughs. I was unable to imagine her solemnly pledging herself as wife, matron, mother. Nor would her children! She might still find that I had more to offer than flippant, debt-burdened Metellus.

Whatever lay ahead, she would retain the potency of treasure, fallen overboard, almost submerged in sand, but not yet irretrievable. Meanwhile, I accepted this reverse with dignified silence. When we next met her smile was unchanged, ready to skirmish.

'I am delighted by your good news. Metellus is the one man I would have chosen for you. Who else could keep you entertained? For six months at least.'

'That is longer than anyone else has done. And, of course, there is much one knows before one observes it.'

She had this aggravating habit of uttering some such remark with a frowning gravity, doubtless to detract from its obscurity. Seeing my annoyance, she compounded it by adding, 'The god precedes the statue. And surely the statue limits him by being too visible!'

To avoid my reply, she kissed my cheek, then stared at me as if I had made it. With a little-girl attempt to please, she smiled, but spoilt it by saying, 'Does not hazard, fortune, sometimes interfere?' Nodding to herself, as if she had explained the universe.

I left her, consoling myself by reflecting that life with her might at least stop Metellus' empty chatter. It had not yet done so. Indeed, he told me that she was the first line of a poem which would never be written. That, at least, was pleasant to hear, though the same could be said of information vivid but useless, like the story of Sophocles, dying on his hundredth birthday, from a tortoise dropped on his head by an eagle.

I suspected that she accepted Metellus only from the perversity that, so inappropriately, made her join the Christians. With me, she would argue, quarrel, recite, but seldom allow silence. With Metellus, foppish, trivial, his smiles mere ripples of negation, she probably found nothing to say, and welcomed this, as relief, perhaps, from my own mature good sense. Both, I felt, were actually fascinated by me, the rules by which I lived, my wealth, my knowledge of wider worlds.

Metellus, of course, had charm, a quality I did not underrate. *That man* possessed it, perhaps Nero, certainly Caesar. I, for all my powers, did not. It remained beyond purchase, a supple key, minor miracle, a random asset, toy with a sting in it. With charm, even the ugly can buy anything but do not have to.


Supreme elsewhere, I had been baffled by Sylviana, a novel, somewhat honing sensation. I was no celibate, and not given to despair, even about money. Constantly occupied, I sometimes wanted no wife, only nine sisters, divorced and very rich. Almost every woman I instantly desired to see naked, but usually only once. I had insistent curiosity about bodies as I had about all goods, but was too energetic to linger after purchase. In my position, of course, promiscuity had dangers, and I avoided the local brothels, occasionally renting in Gaul a clean, expensive whore whom I could beat with impunity and without embarrassment. Only very seldom did I order a slave into my bed. I imitated Cato in buying slaves both young and ugly, thus cheaper, selling them when old and burdensome, and, after dark, ugliness of course can cheaply attract.

I had one child by a slave. I had them both removed to Gwynchester, where, as so often, Fortune favoured me, both perishing in the peasant troubles. The girl had trim shape and boring tongue that clacked too familiarly about fresh eggs and new clothes. Children I disliked, as I did flies, which buzzed, instead of merely flying. Since then I had remained the same : industrious, capable, public-spirited. When others said they were continually developing they generally meant they were changing for the worse, like the Empire.

(I had better explain my attitude to Fortune. Some, I admit, do have it, like charm, like *aura*, somehow attracting to themselves profitable occasions without striving for them. They seemed to be protected by gods. I claimed no particular Fortune. I won my advantages by labour, skill and foresight, and largely disbelieved in luck, chance, divine caprice.)

Meanwhile, with Sylviana in abeyance, I had to content myself with an orphan, inexpensive, reliable, unsuitably named Vesta, who lived in the poorer district near the Baths with her brother Junius. He too I occasionally bedded : their resemblances and deviations had a curious tang. He was slightly girlish, she a little boyish, and I once suggested that the three of us should indulge together, but her response was hurt and awkward. She submitted to certain demands, rejected by Sylviana as absurd, on my assurance, not quite truthful, that these were but unimportant residue of youthful experiments. I seldom wanted to use her violently : there is no satisfaction in robbing the blind.

Brother and sister shared pallor, slightly tilted nose, small sharp chin, eyes blue and incurious which I wanted to rouse, rough bronze Belgic hair. ('Belgae', of course, means 'the boasters', but neither she nor Junius were that, despite the brother's small, superior smiles.) Away from bed, Vesta was negligible. Junius, more firmly outlined, was proficient at the ball-game played in the cloisters of the old temple of Mars, also a scholar, contributing such unusual, though inessential news that crows were incapable of rape, and that the Trojan Horse was a symbol of racial superiority. Like much that

40

enlivens conversation – the interpretations of dreams, coincidences and the birth of gods – his discoveries were seldom capable of proof.

Vesta was often worried. 'Is it true, sir, that we have abandoned the gods? Or have the gods abandoned us?'

I could have told her that, as a child, I would try to wake early, to see gods hoisting the sky. Instead, more sensibly, I promulgated the religious alternatives available to men, and to a number of women.

Neither she nor Junius displayed much outward gratitude for my attentions. Vesta seemed fond of me, Junius was polite but reserved. For all his learning, he depended on me for employment, and perhaps resented it.

In a small town of straight pavements, my relations with Vesta were no secret, though I naturally forbade her accosting me in public. Sylviana, who, seemingly without effort, discovered everything she wished to, once, drawling, affected, distinct, congratulated me, at Cottanus' table, on 'the Vestal Virgin'.

Vesta never mentioned her husband, murdered in 360. Junius once said his greed for goat cheese had astral significance, I forget what.

# IV

---

Winter had been quiet. Not one of my ships had encountered pirates; Scanians from far north overseas had obligingly captured several of my rivals'. From Treves, the Augustus was withstanding the Alemans. Yet barbarian stillness was untrustworthy as a eunuch's smile or loans to the Court in an age of confiscations. Metellus described that spring as having the pure perfection of an impure gift from the Cyprian. I was more coherent.

I judge a town by its chimneys, pavings, orderliness. On these bright days, Silchester looked passable. Under south walls, vineyards were shooting. The colonnades of Constantine's piazza gleamed. Walking with my usual troupe of clients, parasites, petitioners, I nodded to gods still gazing from friezes, though divinity had faded, like a bland, sunlit cloud. In Forum arcades, matching sun, leaf, sky, gaily clad people sauntered as usual, tossing greetings, gossip, complaints about prices. Streets sloped down to the West Gate and the usual pack of itinerant jobsters. By the rostra, where orators would skin the public, children skipped, squatted over tops and knuckle-bones, and sang meaningless songs.

'I am a fish,
I lie in a dish.'

Smells of fried meats mingled with those of blossom and grass blown from hill and river. Shadow made soft pools behind arches, birds flitted above stalls, alighted on steps, fluttered around the naked, marbled Genius on its mossy pediment before the Basilica. That many streets were patched with clay, many porticoes were still left unrepaired since Allectus' defeat, irritated me less than usual.

Formerly, the rich had freely restored and decorated, from vanity or responsibility; now all was left to the Curia. I myself could have provided stone, cement, new monuments, but, despite fresh herds of

42

jobless, masons were lacking, and municipal slaves and convicts were discontented from food shortages. After the wet summer, much of the scanty harvest had been requisitioned for the army. Nearby quarries were State property, involving the delaying tactics known as civic negotiations, and an outrageous bribe officially designated 'Road Tax'.

Behind the Forum, the Baths were stained by reddish fungus. I wanted the tender to clean them, but the inevitable gifts and licences might be too costly.

Army officers strode harshly through market women, expecting something for nothing as they had for generations; magnates paced slowly to opulent doors or passed in closed litters; children scattered between booths, stealing and cajoling; mountebanks offered cure-alls. From the hubbub, from behind pillar and fountain, I heard scandals and giggles, and shaven Christians arguing under a headless statue. All walls had guttersnipe scrawlings, sexual curses, foul drawings, badly spelt invocations to Isis recommending improvements to life. A former magistrate had presented a special wall for these degenerate exercises but it was left unused, and they were transferred to the columns of his own mansion.

Back in my offices, the slaves and freedmen jumped up respectfully. Their chief, Aurelius, followed me within. Himself a slave, he too owned slaves, on his farm near Readingas.

'In the monks' school, sir. Everyone's speaking of it. All the tables simultaneously collapsed. There's talk of a god taking revenge.'

I said nothing, having long known that dwellings, like pools and woods, could emit influences, particularly upon adolescents, inducing ghosts, unknown voices, disturbances. We both listened to the excitement which my arrival had interrupted.

'Do you know, imagine it, I saw a cloak adrift in the air. With these very eyes. But nothing inside it.'

'Indeed and indeed, we once had much worse. Sounds, under the floor. Running steps, a child's cry. And the dogs wouldn't stop whimpering. They daren't go outside, and, mark me, mark me, why, they were drenched, icy with sweat. Terror!'

I sometimes regretted that we were no longer permitted to slice off slaves' tongues. For the monks I had no sympathy. Schools had helped corrupt the old virtues that respected property, honoured signatures, utilized science, despised the makeshift. Teachers were now mostly panders, distributing inflated nonsense about rhetoric, dreams,

43

the after-life, while coins dwindled, armies mutinied, watched by tribes praying to forest and swamp to reclaim their own.

I myself never ceased to teach Aurelius that not prayer but resolute intelligence can save society. The grandee Hadrian, the peasant Diocletian, knew it. Honour them. They did not consider themselves artists or zealots, but artisans with a job to do. And they went out and did it, offering equity to integrity and ambition. They showed that authority need not be identified with torture and capital losses. They were not ashamed of retribution, only of purposeless retribution. Honour them threefold.

Later, I paused over my documents, satisfied with the mild spring afternoon. Flowers suggested funerals, music a chance to sleep, but I was no dull churl. Green spray of leaves, gold suns, the cleanliness of waves, could sometimes stir me almost as much as a girl, let alone wine or Spanish fish sauce.

My contempt for the superstitions so generally rife was soon being amply justified.

Vergil describes Rumour as swift, winged, ruinous, each feather secreting an unwinking eye, matched by a tongue screeching the terror of cities. He does not lack prescience. Throughout April, rumours sped through the canton, mostly nonsensical. The usual celebrated astrologer, after abstruse calculations, announced that he had persuaded the sun to rise; an image of the Christian demi-god Peter bowed, then sniggered; a painting of Minerva, at Gloucester, had gone so far as to give birth. At Canterbury, a mob attacking shrines to Mars and Hercules had been overcome by blindness and ear-ache, and a brawny slave strangled her baby to propitiate 'Whoever's coming'. Birds were flying with irregular wing-beat : ill-omened, though market reports, a more convincing guide, were satis-factory. In one day, forty-nine cows died in a field, but I would have preferred to hear the secrets of the Imperial Consistory at Treves. In our own Forum, a prancing madman intoned :

'A white spear, iron-shafted,
And from the shaft drips blood.'

A few scourheads will always revere such gibberish. A lawyer, usually sober enough, professed to have seen in a cloud, a Roman temple upside down and a huge eagle in flames, then confessed that this had been a dream. Dreams, I understand, deriving from faded memories

44

and anxieties, had some intimations of the future, and I made sense of this, but not of the report of a serpent born of a duck, from which priests deduced a convulsion in Hibernia. Why gods should be unable or unwilling to employ plain language was beyond my scarcely inconsiderable understanding. Jeheshua also trusted obscurity, communicating through contradictory sayings, remembered in distrustful translations of bad originals. The raucous debates of Christian philosophers best suited the circus.

Disorder in the Empire was conceivably reflected in black skies and blood-red sunsets, though I doubted it. Destiny emerges less from heaven than from lack of character. Celestial magnetism, touching blood and water, doubtless effects minor changes, atoms themselves are not invariably predictable – rocks explode without warning – but few know much of these matters, though many pretend to, and I was too busy, too successful, to care.

Usually, these portents are quickly forgotten. That spring, however, they were prolonged. Women in my own street unexpectedly began weeping hysterically, dancing, then, in a daze, stripping themselves. Business associates from Colchester, itself long restored after its burning by Boudiga, savage British queen or Victorious Mother Goddess, told me that the stone head of Claudius the Conqueror had dissolved. More seriously, a Silchester Gate was suddenly immovable; the Curia ordered its replacement, during which a slave transfixed himself with his own spade.

Such incidents are commonplace, though later eras trace from them the abnormalities of Caligula, the fate of Coriolanus. Tacitus mentions a woman bearing a snake, another killed in her husband's arms by a thunderbolt, but refrains from linking these with plague or civil war.

I settled further into work. A consignment of glass had arrived, I had to decide when to release it. Yet I was not wholly attending. Like unforeseen digits invading a carefully prepared tender, bizarre thoughts invaded my discussions with accountants, bailiffs, brokers. At night, perusing Seneca's essays on right conduct (not only moral instructions but soporifics), I found, lying between me and the script, a most stupid story told me long ago by a family tutor.

A Greek priest had three daughters. Out walking, the eldest saw a precipice and began howling. Her mother and sisters rushed to know why.

'When I marry, my child will fall over this cliff and get killed. O

45

my darling, my lost one, why should I live any more, I'll never see you again !'

The priest discovers the four weeping and wailing, loses his temper, loads his mules, departs, vowing never to return unless he finds anyone sillier than they. Of course, he soon does, and wins a fortune as well.

Annoyed, I walked over to visit my friend Avitus. The streets were quieter, with people talking together in voices strangely hushed, though saluting me deferentially. As always, I was alert for any site on offer. The Armenian once told me that I was known as the gentleman who picked up street-corners, adding unnecessarily that this was at least better than waiting on street-corners to be picked up.

Avitus, a retired merchant, was childless, and I had hopes of becoming his heir. His cloth imports from Arras had been excellent and I acquired many of his interests and ships. I respected him, but would not have invested greatly in his larger projects. Austere, even frugal, he was too steadfast in Catonic virtues, inappropriate to a time of troubles. He preferred giving to taking, in a society that only took. Younger coteries ridiculed his civic responsibility, but he remained, unperturbed, on his bench in the Curia. He always judged an idea not by its wording but by its result. Three men, he would say, may speak in identical terms, but two will be lying and only one speaking the truth. He cherished his ancestral busts, which included Hercules, Scipio and the Divine Vespasian.

A Metellus chuckled at Pliny's *'the unmeasured majesty of the Roman peace'*, a Sylviana playfully blinked it away, but an Avitus knew its worth. In such peace, toil is rewarded, goods fetch proper prices, trade is unrestricted, controls are few, and only barbarians cringe for doles.

I doubt now whether the old man had particular affection for me, but our professional links had been considerable, and of course he enjoyed my gifts of broad discussion and apt quotation. We agreed that philosophers, Greeklings, by despising commerce lacked true imagination. Trade, like politics, combines the finesse of an artist with the insights of a physician. I myself thrived on the curiosity so markedly absent in British towns, where people were like wheels rolled in directions they had not themselves chosen.

Marulla, his wife, showed that elderly women, losing sexuality, can gain that mysterious quality that must underlie ancient religion. There is evidence that ghosts appear more frequently to them.

46

Furthermore, she was from the very best of Villa society, with a pedigree that Jupiter himself scarcely bettered, descending not only from Belgic kings but Etruscan nobles. I always felt somewhat over-weight under her inspection. She adhered to the patriarchal Roman gods, less from piety than from approved custom and sense. Jupiter and Mars had magnified Rome, and, if Rome was to be restored, they must be induced to return.

Avitus' house contained a largeness distinct from its actual size, for, like most Silchester dwellings, it was small. The plain rooms seemed warm and ample, though the floor-heating was damaged, and, save for a rare vase, bowl, image, the fittings were scanty. Dining, you reclined on old couches in the antique way, and were served with just sufficient meat by female slaves who, to the jeers of the Flavias and Flavians, kept on every stitch of clothing and were unimaginable otherwise. It all contrasted with my own home, where I collected books, medallions, pottery : commissioned mosaics, installed lustred tables and smartly-designed hangings. That Sylviana only granted them an offhand, somewhat disparaging smile, I had to as-cribe to an envy understandable but pitiable.

Avitus called for wine, Bordeaux red, not much of it, but served in fine delicate goblets, a gift from myself. The three of us were alone.

Bent, staid, with a fringe of white beard, savouring the wine more often than he drank it, Avitus smiled at Marulla's quiet, waxen face, small, intent eyes, then turned to me.

'Drusus, young man, I will tell you what you already know. With your secret emissaries you would shame Delphi itself. Something's happening to the sea. Perhaps that provokes the preposterous stories they keep inflicting on us. Villages are getting undermined, harbours washing away, meadows filling with salt. There is no doubt of it. Water levels are rising. They have noticed it in the north, they are worried in Kent. The flat lands in upper Gaul are inundated year after year. It is brewing unrest.'

Certainly I knew this, in far more detail than he did, and had already been scrutinizing the possibilities of erecting groynes and ramparts, though once again my chief opponent would not be the sea but imperial officialdom.

Avitus continued, Marulla listening as if at any instant she could intervene with a suggestion surprising but useful.

'If that is not enough, the trees are decaying. You know how Germans love their forests. Their temper is not going to improve.

Some shore people claim to know from tree markings that a gigantic flood once submerged half the world. The fate of Crete still makes me shudder. Well, their priests are telling them that it will happen again. They are looking for higher lands, lands not their own.'

'Honoured Avitus, you remember Seneca advises us to imagine not only the normal but the merely possible.'

'It may be, it may be. Meanwhile, I am not proposing greatly to trust man or god. Neptune helped to build Troy, and he very zestfully assisted in destroying it. You speak of Seneca, doubtless with some accuracy, but what does our friend Vergil say?'

I had the satisfaction of telling him, for which Marulla seemed insufficiently grateful. *'Neptune himself at the task, shattering the walls and foundations cracked by his tremendous trident, and tearing away the entire city from its site.'*

Avitus carefully refilled my goblet, like a schoolmaster rewarding a clever pupil, a comparison relevant to his next observation.

His face, usually so mild, was unexpectedly angry. 'There is what may be more serious. Do you know that even in respectable villas, some tutors are refusing to punish, or even correct, simple errors in grammar, citation, phrasing, spelling and so on! They maintain, and are allowed to do so, that they prefer to conform to whatever jargon the populace is actually speaking! Well . . . there it is! I have had my day. I will not be here to see your generation grappling with the fruits of that. But I do sometimes hear a sound, like that of a stag dragged down. It contains all the pain in the world.'

His smile was tired, and I fancied Marulla heard more than the stag. She had gone still, staring at shadows midway between him and myself, not dreaming but shrewd.

Avitus unexpectedly hesitated. 'Drusus, we are men of experience. You have access to all factions in Britain and Gaul, no man more.' He might have included Spain, but I kept silence knowing that he was very serious.

'I am getting worried. We know the barbarian weakness. Unalterable from the Danube to Hibernia.'

'Feud, passion, superstition.'

'Just so, just so. Now the Bishop has heard it, the priests are buzzing like bees. Something is stirring which no one cares to name. Some leader, perhaps, has showed himself. A barbarian Augustus. Sadly, those two words have ceased to be contradictory. Well, you have resources denied the rest of us. Your fellows cover the land. In ten days the Curia meets. We shall all depend on your views, perhaps on your instructions.'

The Curia would thereby behave more sensibly than usual. Of course, alarms were so frequent that, without further evidence, I could be dismissive. Scots slave-raiders, red Caledonian highland giants eating their own heads. Painted Men invoking insane matriarchal spirits, Frankish pirates . . .

He saw my expression, and leaned forward. 'I can offer you very little. A runaway slave found dead on the road stabbed in a curious way that I do not care to describe. A message in a jar, in that incomprehensible Hibernian screed, signed with a picture which seems like a bear, crowned. A Burgundian, saved from drowning, and mumbling about a "He". Old fools' talk of a great light coming from the sky.'

Only the last really concerned me. Jeheshua's 'Great One' perched on a fiery cloud? Sun motions, said by Junius to last ten years, and causing winds which lodge burning particles in our skins and induce dementia? There was an old tale of humanity reborn on a high mountain, after that world flood, from turds or stones, but never quite shedding the criminal traits that had provoked the disaster.

I mentioned, rather reluctantly, the Armenian's loose talk of the effects of lead. Germans might be deranged by the lead in their hill streams making them as truculent, even virulent, as Christians wrangling about the date of Easter.

Avitus, who had owned lead mines, sighed, and, promising to meet him at the Curia, I departed.

My own house, stone and timber, with fine glass, the lower storey crowded with bales, vats, carts, stood in a neat garden of a few trees and mossy stone herms. No flowers, they poisoned the night air.

The low rooms were tinted with stylized, rather monotonous Celtic designs – leaves becoming birds, bulls' tails changing to lilies, spirals of leaf and twig. As no ancestor had lived there, the place lacked *numen*, the busts in the atrium exuded no *mana*, and referred me to pasts at best speculative, though a reminder that even I was vulnerable to inherited blood-fevers that can actually influence the unborn. I had no relics to treasure for their magnetic properties; the house gods were stock; no friendly spirits gathered at hearth and corner, visible to dogs and children. Metellus kept some remnant of his grandfather in a jar, claiming that nails and hair still lived. For what purpose? He smiled as if at a witticism slightly indecent. A

49

neighbour still deprived himself of his best room, keeping it bolted, to protect his father's ghost.

I had no such inclinations, though that night I needed company. Not ghosts, not Sylviana herself with her slow, luxuriant, questioning voice, not Vesta, who dutifully responded to my moods without initiating any of her own. I was restless, desiring what I could not name. A talk with Junius would have sufficed, but he was at Colchester, on my behalf.

Wine, cheese, rye bread were brought. Aurelius silently presented a roll of news and prices. Nothing unexpected save for an insignificant riot in Arles.

Usually this was a pleasant hour, but Avitus had not dispersed my unease. The priest's foolish women, the low tones in the streets from those standing so oddly still, letting shadows gather about them. A surreptitious murmur. 'Have you all heard? An amber bowl . . . flying over London.'

'What was in it?'

'That's uncertain.'

It had seemed the usual absurd exchanges of vulgar folk, but now brought a foreboding, as if before malaria. Rising seas, a glare from the north, everywhere a lack of the useful; frayed, aggrieved people with too little to do.

Rome! Mother of nations, filling the world with unprecedented shapes, sounds, colours. But now! So many wounds left untreated, bills unpaid, contracts dishonoured. Life blocked by rotting heroes and lost epics. Cowardly senates and disloyal generals. Listless mobs trudging through endless public holidays, clamouring for wine, bread, shows, that they had not earned. Libraries abandoned, or filled not with readers but talkers, sleepers, or, worse, dreamers. Deadly officials preying on emperors who no longer dared to visit their own city.

The Armenian was typical, grumbling about his host's wine and his fee for a job badly done.

Dusk was filling the room. Once, very foolishly, I had envisaged darkness being ripped open like silk, by candle-flame.

I hastily called for lights, then unrolled an amusing portion of Herodotus.

'Gelo brought to Syracuse the rich who had caused the war and thus expected execution, and he enrolled them as citizens; the plebeians, who were absolutely guiltless and thereby expected immunity, he also deported to Syracuse, and there sold them as slaves. This was

50

because he considered that living alongside them was disgusting.'

I smiled less than usual, and later dreamed of ominous seas and criminals left staked on shores at low tide. I awoke, convinced that temples, lawcourts, banks, were wineskins, abruptly punctured, and dwindling to vague heaps.

Pliny's prescription for such dreams, dried dragon's eyes stirred with honey, was academic. The stupid jingle clicked about in my head, together with the witless Greek women and the amber bowl.

> 'I am a fish,
> I lie in a dish.'

# V

Men were running, streets were in turmoil with bewildered mobs continually parting for curial processions, lictors, detachments of cavalry. For once I was glad of Valentinus' bullying centurions.

Messengers constantly scurried to me with missives. The new situation was like a girl's sex, virtually invisible but packed with inescapable implication.

Germans were invading Belgic Gaul, coinciding, perhaps accidentally, with peasant and bacaudic unrest. Worse. By unlucky timing, Picts were assaulting the Wall. The Vicarius, the Governor, with his picked guards, was himself absent in Gaul consulting with the Praetorian Prefect, and likely to be marooned there.

Metellus lounged in, asking my opinion, as he might over new boarhounds. I maintained my usual bearing, confident, sapient, with words deliberately chosen.

'We are the charioteers. Horses, reins, are in our own hands. We need not crash. We need not even race.'

I disliked his laugh. 'You're always right, of course. As you know better than us, you've never once been mistaken. All the same, Drusus, there are creatures who may wish to race us. Very nasty, wouldn't you say?'

I had little time for him and was soon with Aurelius, like a king in some tragedy, receiving from trusted stations throughout the midlands news which, guaranteed or hearsay, was invariably worse than the habitual accounts of bacauds raiding a village, squatters invading a villa abandoned in the earlier troubles through being too large to defend. Bacauds instigated no large revolt, they awaited barbarian incursion or military mutiny, then became jackals.

Aurelius was alarmed, but, while never underestimating these outbreaks, I was not seriously perturbed. To manage, take charge, subdue, was what I enjoyed. I would be needed.

Very carefully, I studied each letter, while the horses clattered through the uneasy din. I swiftly appreciated the situation.

In the western mountains, some farms were being burnt by a handful of Scots, 'Vagrants', perhaps distantly related to Picts, from Hibernia and south-eastern Caledonia. I knew nothing about them of any credit whatsoever. Their raving gods had the morals of a weasel. Fortunately, they were ignorant of siege-engines – rams, onagers and the like. Allegedly, they had originated from Spain. Raiding Hibernia, the earliest band saw a glass tower on an offshore islet. Landing to attack it, they were swept away by a huge wave, some tribal god for once fulfilling his function. A few survivors reached the mainland, their progeny being these lustful, greedy Scots.

If they concerted with Picts, they would need stalwart tackling, though I doubted whether our generals had learnt from 360, when the Picts had been scattered not by a volunteer British army, which the Court probably feared the more, but by Lupercinus' hired Batavians, Burgundians and Heruls, whose habit of killing the aged and widows was predictably condemned by Avitus.

The Armenian visited me, with rag-bag information from badly-defined sources.

'You know of course, Drusus, dear friend and patron, how to behave in the stinking depths of a Scots village !'

I refused to acknowledge so unlikely a mishap, but he only grinned. 'The elders will offer you any wife you can brace yourself to accept. They think any stranger may be a god. Gods themselves can be sacrificed, I never dug out who to. Don't Christian awfuls do something about sacrificing a god to himself? I'd call it rather the long way round ! Anyway, I don't care to punish myself by even dreaming about Scots in their pest-holes. Their cunts are like armpits.'

I had little time to listen further, allowed him a pittance to discover what he could, then resumed work.

Many miles lay between the Thames valley and prospective danger, and both in Gaul and east Britain the tough, intelligent Belgics, though resented by fellow Celts, were traditionally pro-Roman. Much, perhaps, could be left to them. Meanwhile, I had private considerations.

I was in dispute with the sub-procurator, Hyacinthus, absurd name for a venal tax-collector. I once saw him naked, at the Baths, like a yellow, swollen cabbage, his gross belly as if gorged with illicit money-bags and informers' evidence. Like Nero, who shoved respectable senators into the public arena, this Levantine freedman enjoyed tantalizing those more notable than himself, alternately flattering, threatening, reassuring, subtly taunting as if with trident and net. Such as he had precipitated bloody peasant rebellions in Gaul against Diocletian. They could appear a rival government.

On behalf of Flavius Valentinian, Invincible and Beloved Despot, he was claiming dues from me, on alleged shipments of cloth, wine, fir-planks, and from what he termed underpayment of the wheat tax.

Plainly, were barbarians to make any serious, though sporadic, inroads, Hyacinthus, everywhere loathed, would melt into whines, pleadings, silence.

Incidentally, that Jeheshua befriended these repellent tax-officials was credible only as a part of his nagging, insolent humour, unless he thought that he would so transform people that taxes would become unnecessary. From what I knew of them, however, his teachings divided society into debtors and creditors. Pay or be damned. He was the only god I knew who set himself up as a teacher, alongside Plato and his sort. He preached charity, but only for his votaries. The Armenian had a tale of our Bishop's senior deacon, an amiable fellow who married a priestess of Juno to prevent his own indiscriminate hand-outs.

This Bishop, on imperial rescript, had begun demanding tithes. These too I was resisting, though cautiously. I barely knew him but, unlike lay officials, the priests of the favoured religion had considerable popularity, particularly amongst those in ordinary times worthless, but strident and sometimes dangerous during unrest. Despite their nefarious tax-exemptions, monks were excellent farmers and foremost in teaching hygiene and grammar. Some of them were former landowners, who had renounced their estates to escape the stifling taxes.

We shortly knew that, in apparent collusion with Scots, Caledonian highlanders had crushed a Roman colony near the old Antonine defences, while, further south, Painted Men were still swarming towards the Wall.

At this, even some magnates deigned to request, even implore, my advice. I reassured them, but not too much, while inwardly imagining Hyacinthus' dismay, and the tithe-rodents beseeching a miracle.

With no hankerings for suicide, I always refused even elementary barter with Picts and Scots. Treaties, pledged words, were impossible with them. Brute genetics submerged them in mere insensate uproar, inferior, Junius assured me, to animals'. Avitus put it well :

'A Pict promises to meet you in ten days. He swears on the heads of his ancestors. He does not, of course, appear, and has probably cut off the heads. Years later, his folk are still having murderous disputes about the dozen meanings of *promise*, alternative renderings of *ten*, and, ah, the complex reality not of *day* but *days*. Just so. Their memory retains everything, but without discrimination or gradation, being, alas, undisciplined by books or training. Selectivity is unknown. Their minds immediately transform one thing to something else. They exclaim *dog*, but see a black child. They nod when we say *fair trade*, but imagine a bear-hunt and behave like one. I hesitate to call them depraved, they have survived unchanged from primitive chaos, and should, I fear me, be exterminated like epidemics. It is worrying to hear these Asiatic notions of treating all breeds as civilized and cultured citizens, when the facts are so obstinately otherwise.'

Avitus could be a bore of purest quality, but I seldom demurred at his findings.

For German tribalists I had more respect. They loved war for its own sake, clamoured to attack the Empire, but in defeat besought gifts, titles, unlike so many sullen, mercurial Celts. They never forgot the dreadful yellow Riders at their back.

Of the distant Scanians I knew little save that a few reputedly still possessed tails, but Franks were skilled jewellers, Saxons excellent shipbuilders. . . . Most Germans could be lulled and manipulated. Their huge defeats by Julian ensured they worshipped him. The award of a cheap bracelet forced them to weep. They had words for *ransom, bribe, submission, pledge*, without always using them. Sadly, they now manned our frontiers. Their love was dangerous. They slaughtered Emperor Probus, then lamented for a week, cursing themselves. Nevertheless, they had a future, perhaps too much of one. The Picts surely had none.

Picts had been briefly under Roman rule, but long ago, and law, towns, even coins they utterly rejected. They used primitive flints as much as bronze, and whatever iron they captured, and had some ability in carving, also spinning, despite addiction to nakedness inexplicable in the frozen Caledonian mists and fleeting, spectral suns. They retained archaic chariots, and subsisted on cattle of poor quality.

Small, swift, reputedly they tattooed themselves with bizarre geometric and animal patterns, and held ceremonies with demonic cats liable to rip humans apart. Their numbers were increasing, while those of civilized Britain degenerated. Infanticide had been too long countenanced, and I knew of increasing miscarriages, stillbirths, abortions.

Memories were reviving of Hadrian's 9th Legion, allegedly marching north and never reappearing, mysteriously vanishing amongst Picts or Brigantes, the lost Standards now a permanent disgrace. There are other versions, none very creditable, like so much that passes for history.

Pictish learning derived from trees, stones, clouds and song. I had heard that their chiefs were forbidden to wear knots, adored a magic queen, and, though possessing a few stone towns, used them only for rites. They feared intruders, who would break an invisible circle, to be restored only by shamans. There was a story that that they had but one eye, centred in the forehead, through which they saw stars no longer visible to us. They were excellent smiths.

That dark queen with her animal muskiness would have scant allure, for, at a kiss from the truly human, she turned gaunt and stark white.

The Armenian, of course, claimed familiarity with a Pictish village. He confirmed the magic circle, adding that he too could mend it, though at the cost of rheumatic agonies.

'Picts only reached to my shoulders. They glided about, like smoke. And, oh, the screams of cat lust in the night! A child inherits his grandfather's name and spirit. The name is stamped on him at birth, tying him to the tribe. Their personal habits, ugh! I can tell you things that would make your hair fall out, as I see it's already doing without help from them. Try badger's grease. Anyway, the bride, at her wedding, if you can call it that, I myself didn't, is poked by every guest in turn. I contrived to avoid it. How often utter nakedness causes utter disunity! Had I availed myself of her, more than my hair would have dropped off.'

I mentioned Caesar's description of British Celts, their wives shared by some dozen men, especially between brothers, and between fathers and sons.

'Yes, yes.' The Armenian was always uneasy at talk of others' experiences and his lean, swarthy features hardened. 'I know about that. Now, what makes Picts unmanageable is not only that they like to throw poison about – get scratched by them and you twist up and probably die – but that they believe that a lost arm or leg actually increases the strength of the loins, so that they're always grubbing about for a battle. Were I Duke Fullofaudes, I'd keep the legions in barracks and try to get hold of the poison.'

He looked away, as if thinking of something else. 'They feel part not only of their vile ancestors, but of the lands they squat on. Lose lands, lose being. From what I saw of them, and I saw too much, the loss to general culture would be inconsiderable. A terrible lot. Either they have no imagination or they have nothing else. Like whores.'

That he had ever seen a Pict was unlikely, though with his scorched ragged hair and shifty eyes he might have blood unpleasantly alien.

He held my arm. 'I know you're interested in my Julia,' knowing that I was not. Julia was an Atrebatan with whom he lived. He would not have dared bring her to my house. 'I've turned her loose. She's worse than a Scythian, almost worse than a Boetian. One wants from a woman respect as well as easy morals. Between her legs she's crushed velvet, but elsewhere a slut.'

I got ready for the Curia. However exaggerated the reports, Picts over the Wall could be serious, though Lupercinus had swiftly routed them for Emperor Julian. I had to appear composed, even masterful, yet inwardly I felt ambivalent. A temporary crisis would retard settlements with Hyacinthus. But there was more.

While ordering, recommending, warning, I had been resuming very secret calculations about Britain itself. Assets, liabilities, the actual and the potential.

Carausius had revealed the incipient strength of an independent, richly endowed Britain, and demonstrated her unique sea power. I alone could list its metals, pastures, woods, vines, livestock, fisheries. The nine big seaports, twenty wall fortresses, eleven eastern naval towers , the dozens of pre-Conquest hill forts, mostly disused but seldom ruined, and some of the best roads in the Empire, built upon solid tracks of unascertainable age.

All citizens had complained of taxes for military defence. They might now see whether or not their money was being wasted. Interference, compulsory purchases, forced loans, still penalized initiative and blighted trade. All was being taxed at prohibitive expense, to coddle wretched irresponsibles.

I had no instinctive loyalty to Flavius Valentinian Augustus and the dire system by which government existed by permission of armies, in which the men might control the general. Power handled by a scared despot was more frightening than Vagrants or Painted Men, who snarl and bay, then, gorged, creep back to their lairs. I wished to revive a Senate of thoughtful propertied men, the armies merely subservient policemen. This had once been, and I remembered Carausius, raising taxes indeed, but spending them in Britain instead of sending them to remote continental officials. I thought, my pulse quickening, of that Carausian coin enscribed with Vergil's *Come O Awaited One.*

If, in emergency, armed London protectors failed Britain . . . prospects were illimitable. Yet, yet, though indecision was rare to me, I was not yet absolutely assured, having never forgotten Tacitus' biting observation about the British tribes : 'Our most effective weapon against them is their refusal to make common council for the common good.' Then the Armenian's foolish talk of Picts and Scots uncovered an image I kept severely locked in the deepest pits of the mind. The murderous figure looming out of darkness to stab or strangle, not for money but for blood, immune to all reason, to be overcome by strength alone. Better the State, with its follies, its controls, its greed, than mindless barbarian ferocity. Yet – I hesitated, wavered, then reproached myself for such timidity – barbarian raids were as brief as plague, the officialdom endured, continually replenished and augmented by itself : without effort, without meaning, without plan.


Slaves brought ledgers, clerks wrote, Aurelius handed me documents. I betrayed none of my thoughts. Informers surely infested even my own household, and who could withstand the knife, the cords, the slow fire? Nevertheless, I still felt cheerful. Barbarian pressure, more than the debased currency and rising prices, might remind the Augustus that in Britain the bloody reprisals of Paul the Chain on Magnentians and the suicide of kindly Martinus remained unforgiven.

It occurred to me that some of my monies demanded by Hyacinthus and the Bishop might be dispatched to Fullofaudes, Duke of Britain, and Nectaridus, Count of the Shore, on whom so much of my still barely-formulated plans would depend. To induce stupendous rethinking, to challenge the complacent, over-ripe and debt-ridden, was some justification of barbarism, though our resources might be considerably plundered. Let but the officer class earn its keep, however, then we could confront Treves not as a subordinate province but a privileged ally.

I could manipulate some stupid Valentinus easily enough. The real difficulty would be with the Britons : sly, capricious, lazy, drugged on music, they hated discipline. Yet, for brief but crucial periods, they could be inspired by theatrical leadership, be controlled by adroit tactics. We were not facing the infernal Huns and demented Scanians. Many Britons were capable horse-breeders, trainers, riders. Fullofaudes was reputed a useful cavalry general.

I began to enjoy counting opportunities. Could but the Picts and Scots be speedily repulsed, newly-found confidence could stimulate British patriotism. Cunebilinus the Briton had reigned impressively : Caractacus had resisted the Divine Claudius. A British army had threatened the sinister Commodus and toppled his hated minister Perennis. For too long, however, the State had prohibited civilian arms-bearing and military training.

Under the doubtfully sane Emperor Caracalla, all freemen had been granted Roman citizenship. In my future Britain, rights would have to be earned. Even masons' friendly societies or barbers' supping-clubs contain ranks, promotions, liabilities and exclusions.

During the next three days, with no activity from the Curial head-in-airs, still waiting for next week's meeting, I endured Avitus' frets, Vesta's timid sighs, Metellus' witticisms. The Armenian said he had packed Julia off to join her natural associates, the Picts, though I saw her as usual, on hire, by the Constantine Gate. Elsewhere, Valentinus' boasts loudened daily. When Fullofaudes called him, he would make pyramids of barbarian heads, all was prepared, he was Mars' brother-in-law.

I was sceptical, not one of those anxious to leave all to the fighting men. Let one detail suffice. Formerly, to induce toughness and resilience, practice weapons had been double the weight of those used on campaigns. Today, there was feeble drill, no manoeuvres, and when I insisted – to the officers' annoyance – on handling the weapons, I found them of a lightness that would have outraged Trajan and Hadrian. Furthermore, soldiers on the march no longer carried spades. Either these were borne by slaves, or not borne at all. The vulnerability of night camps would be appalling. Picts moved fast by night, Scots were at ease only in filthy darkness.

I then heard a significant admission from Valentinus himself : that barely a quarter of any cohort was able to swim.

From my father at Sens, privy information arrived, secreted in a package of sample flour. The Augustus was indeed in trouble. A murderous peasant outbreak, Frankish harryings near the coasts, and Alemans, recovering from the triumphs of Emperor Julian, in arms along Rhine and Danube. Treves would have small chance, at present, of interfering in Britain.

From north and west, piecemeal reports arrived daily. Vagrants, in greater force than I had realized, were thronging the valleys. Picts, still in containable numbers, had undoubtedly breached the Wall. With diplomatic encouragement, I sent gifts to Fullofaudes.

A decade ago, an imperial commander would have landed from Gaul in unhurried pomp, the legions waiting at full strength to wreak measured vengeance. Now, from reports known to me alone, from Chester, Caerleon, Aldborough, York, I saw Fullofaudes' generals scudding round blazing countrysides seeking their own troops : centurions, instead of instructing professionals, rounding up mercenary deserters. Mostly German. My earlier suspicions were reinforced. For years, such soldiers had been more often seen lounging in the Baths than exercising on the Field of Mars. The Augustine Discipline was gone, no one trembled at the Emperor's name.

Supply trains were being ambushed by bacauds. Despite all those bizarre omens, and warnings from spies, Wall garrisons had been surprised. Several notable murders had occurred : at Caistor, the treasury chief was found at his own table, a knife in his groin.

The four Cantonal assemblies of Britain, which together with the Governor's Palace in London, should have been overseeing the crisis, could not function. Too many roads had been cut, canals and rivers were threatened, the great forests bristled with dangers.

People wondered at my composure, and still lacking Curial directions, welcomed it. Observing only the familiar, capable business man who knew more of their private affairs than they realized, they could not penetrate my seething expectations. More quickly than I dared hope, I might be approaching my meridian. Destiny was conditioned by blood and spirit, sometimes aided by luck, and my luck – aided by me – was interfering drastically but splendidly. I had been correct throughout. Each reverse only reminded me that Britain, compact and sea-girt, despite its ferocious neighbours, was an investment safer even than the Sacred Palace with its morbid synods, silken, waddling eunuchs with sidling voices and unhealthy, often horrible whispers. They offered me nothing, Britain lay in a fresher breeze.

To no one could I confide. Despite my position I had no recognizable following, no intimate amongst my contemporaries, idle sophisticates who gathered at Flavian and Flavia's ribald suppers, and applauded Metellus' small, sad verses about the tired roses of experience. They shrugged at life as if it were a sickness that, at best, afflicts others. They sniggered at me as 'Old Drusus', and hastened to agree with whatever I said, with smiles intended to make me feel half-witted. Sylviana had gone, perhaps irrevocably, perhaps setting one more crafty test. She had removed a peculiar taste, both joyous and stinging, and I was left wondering whether I was winner or loser.

She alone might have understood the longer range of my feelings. I was not some humble Dacian fisherman, Nilic peasant, Cretan liar, yet nowhere was I being awarded my due. My very wealth was at risk to the insatiable Roman State. Now the gambler hidden in so many of us was seeking release. By accepting the challenges, not of wild boar or absurd races – why endanger blood most precious? – but of enterprises, speculations, voyages, I had purchased ascendancy. Occasionally, embedded in files, letters, petitions, I entered another identity. I was the stark hero, holding the bridge, defending the citadel, spearing the monster. Also, unlike most heroes, I possessed principles.

Though enjoying dogs, provided they were not my own, I was sometimes disturbed by their tameness. Similarly, I suspected that men had become over-trained, too abject, though it suited my interests that they should be so. Yet I, so superior, would yearn for what I could not precisely name.

Here, as if tormented by archaic blood, I entered a boggy twilight. Probably most know it, only to recoil, that urge to defy the lightning, run naked, tell the Augustus that he was only a skin with seven holes.

I had had rare hints, sharp yet lingering, of existences not yet quite purchasable, contradicting, if only apparently, my own matter-of-fact course. They came not from the catchpenny wonders of a comet, flying horse or grotesque sibyl, but from upstart dreams and impulses, not least those stimulated by Sylviana. Odd folds of instinct, which, like debts forgotten or denied, occasionally envelop even a highly sensible being.

All students knew, or used to know, of Scipio Africanus contemplating the destruction of Carthage, the flames, crashes, agonies. 'It is all very beautiful : nevertheless, I feel that Rome will suffer the same fate.' I would try to imagine his voice, his face. Was he, perhaps, smiling? I would not care for that smile, yet never forget it. His spirit saw beauty in a smoking pile of blood. Yet it might have been a premonition of his own secret murder.

Daily, vainly, I awaited an emergency session of the Curia, which had not met since the March nones. Usually, the Villa magnates, though legally compelled to attend, made only token appearance, but at this threat, however distant, they were now condescending to arrive. My own intervention, though telling, would be unostentatious. I was essentially a committee man, knowing that oratory, so infectious to the mob, was negligible beside the quiet, irrefutable word in private. Success was won more by suggestions than blunt revelations, as women knew so well.

We have to assume that others know their own desires, but very few actually do. Most have to be talked into recognizing them. My speech, brief but expert, would convince the listeners that they themselves had written it.

# VI

Valentinus' orders finally arrived from the great garrison at York, where Fullofaudes, Duke of Britain, was eager to rush troops to the Wall. Valentinus was to join him with all available men.

Abroad, the Emperor himself was assisting Jovinus and Severus against the Alemans. With Saxons, Franks and rebels at his rear, he might find the loss of Britain no total disaster, despite its useful land tax. A rumour that an imperial galley had landed at Pevensey I disbelieved, correctly.

Though never mentioning it aloud, I continued my disbelief in the high military proclamations of the impending extermination of famished Painted Men and pitiful Vagrants. Least Romanized of all provinces, Britain had generals shamelessly misappropriating taxes, auctioning commissions, promoting useless favourites, selling exemptions, getting themselves hated by veterans and despised by conscripts and hirelings. Fullofaudes' remedy was merely to increase salaries, at public expense. Few officers now spoke the languages or dialects of their men, thus relying on interpreters, a mischievous brood. And the cavalry, irresistible against barbarians, save Scythians, Huns and perhaps Goths, was notoriously, even criminally, depleted.

Too many commanders, many secretly coveting the Diadem, or remembering Carausius, were cautious about giving orders, both dreading and welcoming the unruliness of their troops. The British were renowned for mockery and disobedience. They had almost killed the efficient Pertinax.

Three legions were stationed here, officially, but improbably, twenty thousand men. Exemptions apart, the losses incurred by the pretender Magnentius in 351 had been replaced only on paper. In half-empty garrisons, generals, my own clients, claimed supplies and pay for imaginary men. Or, scandalously, illegally, slaves were recruited, while youths of all classes mutilated themselves to escape military service.

A few reverses might rebuff staff-officers' arrogance, restore whatever professional pride still remained, evoke talents hitherto frustrated. I would recommend executions of rascally centurions and their civilian confederates.

Fullofaudes' border troops, once from a dozen lands, officered by Spaniards and Italians, would now be British regulars and German auxiliaries, Treaty Troops. Despite my reservations about Britons, I remembered that their forefathers had once sacked Rome, and, four centuries later under the Icenic queen, had slaughtered thousands of Romans in London, Colchester, Verulam. Give them but a leader!

I rehearsed my speech. I believed, though I would not yet declare, that the situation might demand a dictator, one with the nerves of the Divine, monstrously treated Probus, who awarded a gold coin for each barbarian head. I would have reminded Fullofaudes of this, had I not had to lend him the gold. And 'the Divine Fullofaudes' did not roll off the tongue with much solemnity.

Were the Augustus triumphant in Gaul, he might spare us the intrepid Jovinus, but that would frustrate my plans, and anyway the most recent news rendered this unlikely. Vandals and Arii were swarming west, supporting the Alemans.

Tacitus was discouraging about the Arii.

'Their shields are black, their bodies are painted black. For battle they choose the blackest time of night. Their host advances as if under funeral shrouds, and they seldom find an adversary capable of withstanding an apparition so strange and infernal.'

I was glad not to expect overnight a visitation from the Arii, superbly defeated though they had been by Probus.

Nothing was heard from the Governor. Actually, he was no real loss. Like his more recent predecessors, he was obstructed by the officials. We needed the strong arm, controlled by responsible experts.

Cicero loftily considered that the entire criminal and plague-smitten gang of dictators should be expelled, but, unless he trusted himself to overwhelm barbarians by rhetoric, or pleadings in language unknown to them, he might have thought differently in 367.

Dictators command the present, but seldom make terms with the future, though Caesar showed that this is possible. Meanwhile, alone save for trusty Aurelius, whose fortunes depended on my own, stealthily, with the tenacity in which I had no rival, I was moving grain, stockpiling wine and flour, adjusting prices, forestalling competitors. There would soon be no more absurd gibes at Old Drusus, or Septimuleius.

I was also making guarded inquiries about Silchester itself. Conditions were too slack, with latent perils. Squatters, occupying several mansions, were no bacauds, but well-spoken, well-dressed, with documents, unexplained influence at the Municipal offices, and no known loyalties.

To all this must be added the Julian Law, forbidding any but hunting weapons to almost all civilians, particularly slaves. Essential in secure times, it might now be a disadvantage, though I doubted it was being rigorously enforced.

Those days before the Curia were of rumours, counter-rumours, and the heavy, belauded activities of Valentinus. A lawyer, with interesting London connections, unaccountably vanished, setting many foolish tongues clacking that he had been transformed by some evil eye into his own dog, and indeed that animal's behaviour – listening judiciously to conversations, jumping on the master's stool for meals, sleeping in his bed – did somewhat suggest this.

This evil eye, connected by some physicians with women at the menopause, was frequently deemed influential, notoriously on the pregnant and, some maintained, on the last comet.

As soldiers tramped and horses filled the streets, people wondered, rather maliciously, whether Metellus, with his hankering for wild wagers and boar forays, would risk life and fortune with his hero, Valentinus. I, and, I suspected, Sylviana, knew the answer to that.

A letter reached me from Gaul. My brothers had raised a war band against truculent peasants. At Court, zealots prated about Jeheshua preparing to judge the world after turmoil and conflagration. Possibly true, though I would resist his judgement and be prepared to judge him. His British followers too were spinning fine words. These could be meaningless : for the question-begging 'Love your enemies', I would more intelligently, if not fervently, substitute 'Respect strangers'; or they were so imprecise or contradictory that Christians went crazed or bloodthirsty in efforts to interpret them.

Better-class Christians, while visibly respecting Plutus, god of riches, somehow believed that wealth was a material illusion, an obstruction to reality. They did not refuse my loans, and monks were surreptitiously begging me to fill their larders. Many amused me by, like their revered Constantine, conveniently postponing baptism until extreme old age. Their leaders now enforce infant baptism, ludicrous as it seems, against the licence and self-indulgence invited by Con-

65

stantine's sensible example. They even claim that the unbaptized scald in fires after death. A grotesque, though revealing, blackmail, a vicious aid to recruitment.

More worrying to me that week was the rapidly increasing failure of postal services, not only from the far north but, increasingly, further south; I wondered how the Bishop's intelligence service was faring. Oracles, priests, magicians, like myself, thrive on being better informed than their supplicants. Sporadic unrest was reported between Silchester and Readingas. A local wood, hitherto mere unused timber on which I had a claim, now assumed a breathing menace, hiding the unmentioned, and perhaps unmentionable.

I made ready for the Curia.

# VII

Deliberately, I departed for the Basilica in unusual state, on an old-fashioned chair above a procession of clients and brightly-clad slaves. We joined a considerable gathering of Curials, watched by a silent, curiously intent crowd. To my annoyance, we were once impeded by a flock of sheep, at which some oaf shouted that these would do better than all of us. Also, a dark, hook-nosed centurion began jabbing aside civilians, even Curials, which formerly would never have been tolerated.

In common with Christians and philosophers, I believed in hierarchies, though they should not be self-perpetuating deadweight. From its old tribal feuds, Britain retained egalitarian elements fiercer than elsewhere. Celts also hated each other even more than they did Romans; vendettas persisted beneath Roman towns and laws like their noxious, half-hearted gods crouching in forests and shadows.

A large, more orderly mob surrounded the Basilica, and soldiers shuffled on the broad steps, their metalled boots striking more sparks than their swords might against the invaders. They should have been in the north, already struggling for the Wall.

In the columned Plenum, blue-gowned lictors were awkwardly bearing the rods and double-headed axes. For the first time in years we filled the broad crescent of benches as, by law, we should always have done. A few carved faces smiled down at us, as if calculating our value, not very generously. Facing us, in antique, ceremonial toga, on his tall curule chair, the President sat beneath a bronze statue, nominally of the Augustus, more probably of Trajan. In this, we did our best to detect manly vestiges that might survive in Flavius Valentinian, Despot of the West.

I saw old Avitus, then Atticus, Cottanus, Metellus and his uncle . . . . Some could still speak a Latin which Vergil would have understood more readily than the Augustus. Others had muddy accents, rather too obviously German, mingling with quick British dialects.

Some had most questionable rights of admission, notably the Armenian, with his confidential grin and murmured stories, in a richly brocaded shawl drooped over the Curial robe to which he was entitled only through much-disputed land claims. The *agentes* would be about and I had often wondered whether the Armenian, his purses clearly unaffected by sustained work, was really an informer.

Behind a pillar lurked Sylviana's mock-lover, the police chief Brunnus. He had no constitutional right to be there, but none dared protest.

Avitus nodded, Metellus gave his vague, fragant smile, touched my hand, drifted away. Since the wedding his face, brown and crisp, though weak at the edges, had developed a few lines and shadows, as if, I considered rather glumly, from strenuous nights.

I was then saluted by Rufus 'Curses' Sabellinus, under obligation to me and anxious to be more so. Red-faced under hair prematurely white, angry-looking, he owned a dye works, so that few relished his touch. (He was said to test unusual tints on his female slaves' pudenda.) His nickname derived from a visit to Colchester on a municipal delegation. Addressing the Curia, he was reaching his resplendent peroration when his wife dropped dead beside him. Interrupted in mid-sentence, he swore loudly, 'Curses! Curses!'

The Bishop had come, doubtless to insist on proceedings opening with a prayer to the Three in One, a concept presumably cribbed from Egypt's Isis-Horus-Osiris, some speculations of Plato, and our own triple-goddesses. I preferred deities to keep their identities more under control.

The Bishop would do more than intone pretentious nonsense. Since Constantine, Christian officials had partaken in the imperial administrations. They were often competent, though in Britain quicker to refuse work than the titles and stipends accompanying it. The Bishop I had barely met. He was from Arles, had studied in cosmopolitan, intellectual Antioch, spoke Greek and Hebrew, and might prove useful. Meanwhile, fleshy, youngish, but somewhat matronly in wide, white drapings, he stood soundlessly suggesting he was conferring some inestimable bonus. He was also adorned with a tall silver headdress wich imitated, I knew, some Persian solar insignia. That his monks were vowed to complete pacificism would scarcely assist our deliberations. His own professional craftiness might avail us better.

There followed an invocation to the Augustus, Lord and Sacred Majesty, Most Noble Possessor of the Genius and Discipline, Protector of the World, Ever Victorious, to which the great statue, whoever it represented, seemed to listen with some satisfaction. After a wait, during which we heard a short scuffle, a breathless priest poured a libation, still legal, to Apollo, protector of Silchester. The acrimony was a reminder that the Christian concept of love owed much to barbarism.

The speeches, mostly in Latin, thus incomprehensible to the worried or sardonic onlookers in the shabby public seats, conveyed an elaborate pretence that nothing really untoward was occurring. The most urgent question concerned only the old temple of Janus. Should its gate be opened, as sign of war? Or would this acknowledge excessively the importance of barbarians? The Bishop remained diplomatically reserved, though presumably wanting to eliminate all temples save his own. His position had several, enviable options. I decided I had better make his acquaintance, without seeming in any haste to do so. The temple gate, I imagined, was too rusty to actually open.

'I have to say,' Cottanus mumbled into his sleeve, 'that is, I would prefer to state . . . in a word. I scarcely know.'

My own speech was folded in my gown. No haste, let their verbiage prepare for my entry, I would the more be greeted with relief, with thanksgiving. Only when events overwhelmingly proved me right would these men turn ungrateful.

A stranger might have thought the droning voices were celebrating Vacuna, goddess of leisure. Their owners were tirelessly self-important, yet without ambition. When legislators lose zest for gain, their root in society dwindles. More preferable would be government by slaves, who have rewards to strive for, than by those satiated with possessions, too weary or philosophic to crave more. Power, I could have told them, should not be endured but enjoyed.

Amongst the drowsy, sinking heads, only the Armenian would have enthusiastically agreed. During a recess, he greeted me elaborately, doubtless glad to be seen in my company, then said, too loudly, that the spectacle reminded him of a former acquaintance, Epimenides of Crete, a young shepherd who, guarding his father's flock, fell asleep for fifty-seven years. I did not bother to tell the fool that the story itself was a thousand years old. He added, more convincingly, that our old friend 'The Frontier', hitherto so boastful of his military prospects, had already galloped away, to the thick defensive walls of London.

Gradually the discussions veered towards some reality. The Bishop had gone, perhaps on some more purposeful negotiations, and I could no longer see Brunnus. From his chair, Sabellinus pompously announced that Jovinus had, once again, routed the Alemans. My own returns from Gaul were different, but I forbore to contradict. On principle, I waited for my views to be asked, my help besought, my advice given in unpublicized confabulations. Real authority may resemble theatre, but it is not, though it may contain drama. It was not for me to blow my own trumpet, when those of genuine merit so consistently did it for me. In reply to a bumbling question about imperial needs, I did, briefly, concisely, outline the urgency of guarding particular roads. Roads, I told them, in happy phrase, were the veins of the Empire.

Contemplating the cracked, tessellated floor, occasionally imagining Sylviana's caustic comments, I amused myself by noting the personal interests behind each proposal. Clinus, a rich building contractor, advocated renewal of the town walls. Verus, the vintner, demanded abnormal purchases of wine. The Villa magnates mostly sat in silence, as if with more in common with the August statue than with the rest of us.

Metellus deprecated public speaking as vulgar, but conceded that those like himself should set an example of social spirit. His airy, inconsequential manner seldom suggested this, though he now made an effort. Like a mathematician with a new theory, he stated that generosity and forbearance were the gifts of Rome, a claim at odds with the tax demands he had received from Hyacinthus, even more exorbitant and peremptory than my own.

Metellus twitched his elegant robe, examined his smart rings, encouraged by a spatter of applause, which was, perhaps, actually intended to stop him. 'This, do you know, I really believe. In certain circumstances money can be a meaningless symbol.'

This babble evoked some laughter from those to whom he owed considerable sums and, pleased, he sat down. Through personal attractions, he usually managed to be absurd without being openly ridiculed. Once, he had proposed that the sacrifice of a heifer to Plutus could cancel the municipal debt, and almost won the vote. I later wondered whether Sylviana had inspired this effort. I still remained in no hurry to close the proceedings with the unanswerable. Let them waste time and breath, then readily welcome deliverance.

A Cirencester delegate restored some gravity. Germans had been landing between Humber and Thames, where Germanic settlements were thickest. He did not mention Gaul, but might, as I did, know of Gallic coastlines in flames.

Alarm at last shook the heavy faces. Where was the Augustus? What forces could he spare? Should not Count Nectaridus and his ships be halting the landings? I did consider giving specialized information relating to naval garrisons, with a reminder that plunder motivates a barbarian raid, which is usually short-lived. Sabellinus, however, looking like a profiteering butcher peering out from the top of a tent, was already replying, unexpectedly meticulous and authoritative, somewhat aggrieving me.

'Friends and colleagues, Conscript Fathers. My sources are reliable, as they always are.' (This was sheer effrontery.) 'Were they not so, I would not have been awarded the most revered honours of this hallowed place.' (The hallowed place had witnessed more gibberish, crooked deals, specious deceits from mendacious presidents than even a temple of Isis.) 'I have worked many years for this town. You will tell me that my work has been ill-done.' He paused for dissent, which to our honour, did not come. None had such a record of political advance through fraudulent tenders and equivocal gifts, in the blatant manner which I always so avoided, the more greatly prospering. He had sold Germans slabs of wax, calling it marble. Metellus said that he owed his presidency only to his elaborate senatorial hair.

'Very well.' His expression grumbled. 'I can now repay your trust. I have news. Rich news. News of supreme value.' At last granted full attention, he waited, one hand raised, like a Jupiter badly carved, lictors and attendants straining to hear him, and Brunnus reappearing, like a hired man promised a jar of wine.

'Nectaridus arrived yesterday from Boulogne with a powerful squadron. He is now off Wight with ships guarding Dover, Lympne and Pevensey. Clearly troubles in Gaul are exaggerated, as usual. The Augustus, as some of us expected, has acted with promptitude, dispatch, deliberation and foresight.'

These last words must have been for the foxy ears of Brunnus.

General approbation, as if at a signal, was interrupted by cheers, hails, clatter from without, and I knew at once that my speech would remain undelivered. Angered, I sat motionless. The din loudened. Spears were grounded, the wide doors opened, and many jerked up, hands seeking knives or clubs illicitly concealed. Astounded, we saw, just possibly, Mars himself, clanking, covered with mail, until, as an

71

aide obsequiously removed the crested helm, we recognized Valentinus. Sweating, clumsy, and needing a bath.

Strictly, he was trespassing, as would be the Augustus himself, were he to appear not as Consul but as general.

'Honoured Fathers.' His tone was imperious, rough, his Latin execrable. 'I come only to bid you farewell. Tonight I march to join my great commander, Fullofaudes, and restore the frontier.' He invited a vision of grandeur, which I did not reciprocate, though Metellus at once glowed with admiration childishly sincere.

'I have have first a proposal. Nay, a demand. The enemies are pitiless, plunging far and wide. Every man must be armed. Whatever his calling. Even slaves.'

His glare challenged our tense silence. He had contravened Rome's most fundamental prohibition, the Julian Law. To allow weapons to slaves was a capital offence. Open disbelief touched the dried skins and smeared eyes of the Emperor's trusty and well-beloved advisers. Before it subsided, Valentinus resumed, surprisingly indifferent to Brunnus, whose sharp face expressed nothing.

'The Duke of Britain has requested land reinforcements from Gaul. Should the Augustus feel unable to respond, should he not be willing to....'

Even I was startled by this, but an officer had hurried in, with what appeared, or was made to appear, an urgent message. Valentinus turned his back on us and stamped back into the still noisy town, leaving behind prolonged uncertainty.

Avitus looked worried. The Armenian had gone, perhaps scuttling for some advantage from Valentinus, one which would not demand attendance on battlefields. While excited talk began, I remained silent and alone, partly for effect, partly to consider. If Valentinus intended treason, he was extraordinarily reckless, unless the military situation was worse than I knew. The *agentes*, Brunnus leading the pack, would be panting to denounce him, unless they too were implicated. Perhaps no appeal had been sent to Treves. Maybe the danger was being exaggerated, for the army's secret purposes. Fullofaudes was stolid and unenterprising, but young officers were susceptible to conspiracy. That they had not approached me needed more studious consideration.

Metellus joined me. His smile was faint, his yawn contrived, but his green eyes gleamed. 'Picts, people like that . . . but why call them people? No matter. Valentinus will throw his weight at them. He

72

wanted me on his staff, you know. But it wouldn't quite do. No rancour, but Sylviana wants us in Bath very soon, to display those new silks you so kindly got for her. Not that you exactly robbed your own pocket. Ah well! At Bath, of course, it's more a matter of taking them off. No one will be the loser for that. As for Valentinus, I can tell you he has quite extraordinary strategic notions, really beautiful. . . .' He fluttered on and on, allowing me no chance to remind him that generals' notions were mostly brag and appetite for windfalls.

Metellus hummed a silly tune, hesitated, looked at me with a solemnity he was unable to maintain. He had wanted to confide something, perhaps, what I most dreaded, Sylviana's pregnancy, but then retired into a small, shallow smile. 'Rufius was his normal self, never a position to be envied. Did I tell you that last month he sat completely speechless during supper gaping at Sylviana's upper parts, then, at the very end, complained that he found so few people with anything to say?'

Next morning, the Curials stood in formal ranks to watch Valentinus' departure. We were less enthusiastic than the cheering crowds. Armour and weapons were rusty, the marching was ragged, impervious to the centurions' anxious barks. The men, many with girls on their arms, shouted boasts and exchanged obscenities with the populace. If Fullofaudes knew his job he would be disgusted by their smell even before he saw them. And who else of my colleagues noticed that amongst sword, javelin, buckler, was no spade, no axe? The absence of supply carts suggested less Valentinus' urgency for battle than his intention to subsist on pillage. This was doubtless the bait : the men straggling before us fought for paymasters, nothing else.

Knowing myself observed, I applauded with the rest, but my own eyes were vigilant. I was astounded not only by the size of Valentinus' personal retinue – he was riding past with some fifty plated officers – but of the whole troop, several hundred men, mostly infantry, with two lumbering, dragon-like catapults. He must have conscripted or bribed every bucket-shop desperado, barber's nancy, ponce, in the valley. Were Germans to attack from the Thames or the coasts, or Scots penetrate the Severn, towards Cirencester, or the Picts hack through midland forests, we would be virtually defenceless. The very Basilica sentries had gone.

73

Only with Avitus could I share misgivings, and, in the town, the withdrawal of thieving, licentious soldiery was welcomed, particularly by storekeepers and mothers.

Only thirty miles away were Germanic villages, entrusted by the present Augustus to defend the upper river. They were men of passion rather than considered loyalty. I would scarcely insure myself with them. I was more glad of the town walls, erected, like many elsewhere, only in the last century, after the Carausian episode. Enclosing us octagonally, they were vital against barbarians, who could overwhelm an open town in a single, hysterical rush, but, like bacauds, would not sustain a siege. They lacked not only artillery, engineers, medicines – dysentery killed more than Mars at his most savage – but patience.

Avitus nodded. 'To cleave to our generals is most inauspicious. But to whom else? In any real danger, our rulers will find very urgent reasons to report to Strasbourg or Treves. They will rush to the ships, beseeching passage in tongues few of us understand, and still fewer wish to.'

His old eyes glowered, under tufted, untidy brows. Marulla, as ever, sat placid yet missing nothing. To neither, however, could I declare my real thoughts. Avitus was too old, too entrenched, too thoroughly Roman, to have real place in the Britain I might yet establish.

Neither Roman nor British, I was the new man, poised to restore life and light to a top-heavy world. Once the barbarians had been crushed or appeased, we might have to dispose of a Fullofaudes, a Nectaridus : certainly prevent the Governor's return. A Valentinus could conceivably be allowed sufficient women, then yoked and tamed. Seated in that quiet room, holding fine wine, quoting Livy, listening to Avitus telling me what I already knew, I again felt that small, quivering thrill, a barely expressed flicker of nerve, like the half-promise of adultery from a woman hitherto prim, the invitation to kick over routine, secure positions, stirred in me by threatened disaster on the Wall. I could not easily forget Tertius Manandus, enormously rich and popular, who nevertheless craved familiarity with his own common slaves, as if enchanted by them. Superiority in will, mentality, affluence, could be insufficient : a prolonged banquet quells the appetite. I remembered myself, long ago in Gaul, youngest of a large family, clasping slaves' fate-tales of glistening but ruthless heroes, savages with enchanted gifts. I only half-heard Ativus re-

74

plenishing his sententious melancholy with a citation from Plato.

'In democracies, drones control almost everything : leaders cast to the mob the money of the rich. Homes surrender to anarchy . . . the father fears his sons, the son feels no awe of his parents. The teacher is scared of his pupils, toadies to them, and they thumb noses at teachers and superiors, while the old copy the young, afraid of appearing hostile or dictatorial. Youths resent the least hint of obedience and refuse to tolerate it. They finally ignore the laws written and unwritten so that, Zeus protect us, they can escape all authority. From this fine and powerful root derives tyranny. The almost certain outcome of too much freedom is too much slavery, amongst the public, within the administration : from the summit of liberty they fall to the most ferocious extreme of serfdom.'

Though I hastened to agree, I simultaneously felt the most ferocious degree of tedium.

# VIII

---

Early summer hurried forward, whipped by rumour. Without much confidence, I continued arranging my annual trip to Gaul and compiled the daily dispatches, fretting at the delayed arrival of tiles, gold filings, timber. An order for northern pearls remained unacknowledged, most reliable agents were silent. What could the north be enduring? From Valentinus, nothing was heard.

Bacauds had wrecked a large villa beyond Readingas, before being driven off by a confederacy of smaller estates. Open assault on a villa was unusual, but this one had long been used only for stores, its owners preferring more defensible quarters further west.

To test opinions, I visited the Baths, despite my dislike of stripping in public, especially before the effeminate attendants. My legs were scrawny, my member small, like a cat's, Sylviana said, though allowing it a very capable range of repartee and sometimes dialogue. Secretly, I had once attached a stone in an effort to lengthen it, and once, to her unobtrusive glee, forgotten to remove it.

I learnt very little. Cottanus informed me that, from a wonder-worker asleep in a tree, a slave had overheard the prophecy of 'Grimmer, the Masked One', who could be expected at any hour. The foolish were identifying this figment with the British usurper Magnentius, returned from the dead, or benevolent Martinus, whose suicide had been feigned, or even 'Carausius II', totally unknown, despite his few ill-edged coins. The carved floweres held by a granite Ceres were said to have withered, but no one knew where. Flavia and Flavian had caused merriment at a hunt by hiring a beggar, painting him all over with birds' faces and serpents, then setting hounds on him, to train them against the Picts, in whose honour they also promised to give a banquet, if any survived Valentinus' heroism.

Shrugging, I prepared for a year of considerable losses, loudly grumbling to conceal my genuine self-assurance. With unquestioned credit and ample reserves, one can reap more than one sows.

Fullofaudes really should have been able to restore the Wall, which despite random breachings, was manned more fully than during the last troubles. Veterans settled around York, Chester, Lincoln, should stiffen the counter-measures. Abroad, Jovinus and the Augustus were accustomed to contain, then eliminate the Germans, and should have been able to put down ill-armed Gallic peasants, though I did not wish the Court to triumph too swiftly, too easily.

Thus occupied, often tired from the humidity of the river lands, with no time to bother about absurd masked ones and incontinent statues, I was neglecting Vesta and Junius, but wrote reassuring messages. Rumours were exaggerated. In any unrest, I would protect them. They should report any slave disobedience at once.

Sylviana remained silent. I had hoped that marriage would spice the delights of betrayal, but she disappointed me, and perhaps herself. I reflected, rather too vehemently, that I was too busy to care, but I missed her eyes, so quickly drooping and bored, her voice with its lights and shadows, amused complaints, sarcastic praises.

'Oh Drusus, you're so reliable, so reliable, so rich. And so few envy you. You are so adept at reconciling me to my lot. How wonderful to marry you, I would feel so much more solitary! How I love being alone! Only then can I know my friends.'

In bed, she had shown very little desire for solitude.

Business dealings, of course, had taught me that words can often conceal more than they reveal, but the unguarded glance, the involuntary frown, pause, tremble, open the other like a prospectus. Metellus laughed too readily, agreed too eagerly, plucked his sleeve too often. His invitations were bribes : for reassurance, for affection : insurances against anxiety.

Another invitation now came. He wanted to meet me, presumably to borrow yet again. He suggested the Legionnaire's Haven, a better-class taberna with private rooms.

Could he be Valentinus' agent? Was conspiracy afoot? To talk of plots, rather than partake in them, was his nature. Languid, idle, no longer a youth, he avoided all that demanded plans, forethought, decision. The brief madcap risks of hunting remained his meat. Conceivably, though, Sylviana had been taunting his prolonged toying with life, his uneventful rest in placid Silchester.

He embraced me in candlelight, exquisite in pearled cloak of oystershell patterns which I had procured for him in transactions that had evaded the scorpion eye of Hyacinthus.

Huge shadows streaked the smoky plastered walls and high crossed rafters; three pewter cups and a large flagon awaited us.

'Sylviana says we should be learning Pictish. But their words for what we most enjoy would probably make it sound foul. Imagine a world without books. I suppose it might shake the pool.'

I expected his plea, for credit, mortgage, even provender, but he only dangled his sleeves, examined his jewels, and spoke more seriously than usual.

'Yet the more I know of these illiterates, the more I distrust our own highly literate forebears. Particularly Cicero, especially Tacitus. Prose, prose !' From his cloak he produced a tablet.

'Tacitus actually believed this. "Primitive man lacked evil desires. Being blameless and innocent, his life had neither compulsions nor penalties. He also needed no reward, being by nature good." '

Metellus' laughter was girlish. 'There ! Now you know how to welcome Picts and Scots, let alone friend Brunnus. Well, you're now going to meet a bear. Watch him. He'll swig all the wine, steal the cups, turn up tomorrow and offer to sell them to you. Here we are !'

He opened the door, shouted, and with an unpleasant alacrity, a stranger stepped in. Short tunic over squat body, earth-coloured cloak, brown leggings, pointed cap in his belt. Bald, dirty, shaggily bearded, as though a bunch of hair had abandoned the top of his head and found refuge on his chin. His appearance annoyed me. He should first have visited the Baths. In Brigantine accent, broad but comprehensible, he told me with cheerful assurance that he peddled for the Servesius Brothers, of Lincoln. I knew them, they were reliable enough, though owing me a trifle which, with Lincoln in the fighting zone, I had better get Aurelius to recover.

Metellus withdrew into shadows; uninvited, the pedlar took a stool, handled a cup, indeed as if wondering whether to pocket it, but instead, filled it to the brim, began gulping too noisily, then explained himself in tones grossly familiar.

He worked amongst northerners, with a few packhorses laden with salt, cinnamon, cheap pottery and metals. I had begun using such as he, sending them down little-known roads and forest trails, yet still doubling my outlay.

'It was nine weeks back. I was at sea, taking animals to the Humber. It's got risky on shore, with thieves all over hills and moors, and armed tribes wandering about. Nothing that your Duke can't manage, but I hadn't been spotting a single legionary. Not one. What's happening to you, eh?'

I concealed my feelings. Even Metellus would not have brought me here to waste my time.

'Well then. Like this. I was blown off-course, swept out to sea, losing the cargo boat. Anyway, quite alone, I was carried over to Scania. The cold, the wind, my! A gulf ran between miles of rock, real fangs, and bleak, dark islands. As if the underworld had pushed up into the bad light. No fun at all, my good sirs. No. All unknown territory, but I've plunged about the world and trust my own salt. The gale dropped off, my tiller was unbroken. So I got into a quiet creek and rag-and-bone village. People like gaunt seals. Often they sacrifice strangers at once, to please the sea, who's lost a good meal. But I'd two cracked mirrors with me and was taken for a magician, and was soon sucking frozen beer and walrus fat. What then? Next day I was trudging through snow to hills, behind two fellows who looked old, but I couldn't tell. Steep cliffs, wild woods, stiff moonlight. I could understand some of their words. We were to meet Nameless. They seemed like long-lost Goths. Wooden shoes covered with fur, bearskin caps, wooden shields, iron spears I fancied stolen from your Rome, or betrayed to them. We pulled down to a milder valley, smoking roofs, cattle, very thin, their bones clicked. No matter. A very great god was going to favour me, were I loyal, chaste, brave, which, not quite to the letter, as you say, I claimed I was, to test the god's quality, though, gentlemen, I've always found gods knowing little and caring less about such matters. Anyway, I might get a message, which I must bring back to my own folk here in Britain. I wanted to know the god's name. A mistake. A bad silence. I learnt afterwards I'd risked having my head sliced off. Instead, they expected the god to blind me. He didn't, so they grinned through their whiskers, said his name couldn't be shown to a stranger but I'd be washed free in the temple. This was quite large, round, all wood. They kept me hungry all night, then with no by-your-leave pushed me inside. All empty. It was murky as a giant's privy. Before a long screen carved with ugly faces was a very thick block of oak. This was not the god but his son, Cheru, son of one-eyed Grimmer, the Mask. Traveller, Warrior, and Third. Yet Grimmer wasn't really his father at all.'

Almost invisible in the recess, Metellus giggled, then pretended to be coughing.

'I didn't understand, wasn't meant to. I was alone with Cheru, certainly felt myself under eyes. Then a voice began, behind the screen. I can't quite describe it, sirs. Not quite a man's, not exactly a woman's. But here was the message, plain as a nose. Three crones control the future. Without names, they seemed nameable. Needing, Living, Destined. Understand? Something like that. They'd seen Rome going down. Nothing left. Cheru had gathered his peoples together. Then it all ended in craziness. I didn't understand a word more.'

Metellus soon dismissed him, and briefly went to order a supper. I discredited most of this stuff. A general barbarian conspiracy would need arduous planning, infrequent even amongst Goths, and certainly unknown to wild northerners divided by stormy seas, fierce heights, vast forests. A single commanding genius was not impossible but I doubted his persistence.

Metellus returned and we sat pleasantly together, complaining about the food. A meal can be judged by its scallops. Tonight, these were missing.

From below, the shouts and laughter of roisterers recalled our student days, when we had often talked in such a bare, sparsely-lit room, rearranging the future.

Metellus' slightly scented voice tried to assume the gravity of a philosopher.

'Rome, in her pride, I suppose, displaced too much blood, not only her own. Now, she's having to pay. A million or so ghosts screeching retribution! Minerva's owls, actually worse! How does one slash a ghost to pieces? Like Valerius, I suppose.'

Valerius had been a fellow student, one of those loquacious upstarts who presume themselves already teachers. He had thrown pebbles at a ghost, scarcely heroically, being in no danger of them bouncing back.

Metellus' speech was now slurred, his hand trembled, spilling the wine, without him seeming to notice. 'Rome bleeds. I suppose we've come so far that we no longer care.'

One side of his soft face was insufficiently co-ordinated with the other, surely denoting a flawed nature. He had spoken wistfully, but now sat up, dispelling shadows, eating vigorously. Like many weaklings he had spasmodic fits of resolution. 'Drusus, we must keep watch. That fellow wasn't a scoundrel. I suppose he should have a ring

80

through his nose but he demanded very little. Listen, I'm going to distribute a few daggers amongst my slaves. Brunnus can do what he likes. Anyway, he knows we're friends and he won't dare offend you. He's probably a dog whose day is over.'

Again he slumped : too drunk, too tired, slightly spiteful, staring at the candle flames. 'Why is it, Drusus, that wherever you are, even with that Nestor of yours, Avitus, fit for Jupiter at his worst, you're always the oldest fellow present?'

I was certainly glad never to be the youngest. He was probably repeating Sylviana, and misunderstanding her.

Again he recovered, rumaging for gaiety as he might a love-potion, and looking theatrically contrite. 'Anyway, what was I saying? Oh, yes, Rome.' He giggled, rather falsely. 'Do you remember that ryhme they used to whip us with?

> Don't care was made to care,
> Don't care was hung,
> Don't care was put in a pot
> And stewed till he was done.

Let's finish the meat, awful as it is. The oil's rancid. Is there a short-age? Did I tell you about my cousin Varvilla? She was convinced that her cat could write verses. Fortunately, the little wretch died last week. The cat, of course. Doubtless suffocated by its own genius. On a blazing afternoon a woman had to dig a grave in unusually hard soil, the men heave over it an ornate memorial stone and a rather awful bust of the departed. That done, all utterly exhausted, Varvilla comes along like a fat Niobe, and says she's forgotten to place the creature's poems under its head, so everything has to start again.'

## IX

In the first week of June, with incredible haste, the air darkened over
Britain as if Cheru had indeed hurled a deadly hammer.

Directing, cancelling contracts, advising distracted clients, replacing lost vendors, I contrived time to be heard reciting Vergil's horror
over Troy :

> 'From some tall boulder the malignant Fury sees
> Chance for spiteful play; she flits to the roof of the
> High stable, from whose sheer heights she sounds the alarm
> That appals the shepherds. Through her curved horn rang
> Music of hell : the woods trembled. . . .'

Let them all see that I at least was in no panic, I who kept my foot
more firmly in real culture, real Roman grandeur, than did those
despairing at my door.

Reports had misled even me. Alemanic inroads had indeed been
exaggerated, but Saxons, Franks, were storming through Juteland,
Frisia, Batavia into north Gaul and, whatever Nectaridus was doing,
massing at ports and islands opposite Britain. Wight was overrun. In
Scania, tusked horrors were blasting war-horns, human sacrifices running red. Advancing south, already sailing towards Humber, they
had been reinforced by a fugitive Gothic king and a herd of Vandals.
These names meant little to me; wolves may differ from savage dogs,
but in ways insignificant were I lost in a forest, a situation suddenly
far from impossible.

All this was marginal, for, that dire week, while yelling, triumphant Picts smashed through almost the length of the Wall, boatloads
of Scots and Attacots were beaching on western shores. Durham was
burning, Corbridge's walls were broken – an exceptional barbarian
feat – villas demolished. Scots had penetrated deep as Wroxeter and
flooded the Dematic regions. My gold mines must suffer. The work-

ings would be destroyed but Hibernian savages had no skill in extracting metals. Bacauds were said to have seen Attacotic fires on hills, and had themselves burnt the temple of Minerva near Bath, before being driven off by cavalry from the most powerful villas in Britain.

I have never discovered whether these Attacots, 'Wizards', were a distinct people or merely splinters of the Celtic horde. Reputedly cannibals, they were certainly ruthless. Emperors had gladly enrolled them into their legions. I imagined enormous tongues and tiny genitals. The former could be sold as offal. Whatever it owed to a Cheru or Grimmer, here did seem a concerted barbarian effort, unknown since Marcus Aurelius, when Germans had forgone their feuds, giantly combined, and been bloodily repulsed, many of them being then deported to Britain, who proved ungrateful.

The barbarian world was no customer for me : at best it wanted bright rags, tawdry jewels, murderous weapons. But I now recalled, uneasily, some words of Junius :

'There are records of an earlier human type. Not very large, but exceptionally heavy in the jaw. Their tools were finely crafted. And their mathematics were superior to anything Claudius found here. Later, they lost all their sense of numbers, almost all their crafts. They became more or less animals, though less sensitive.'

With the dams breaking around Britain, I wondered about the shape of the Attacots' jaws. Again I cursed the absence of a strong arm, live Genius, focus of loyalty. Fullofaudes and Nectaridus, who disliked and might conceivably betray each other, possessed no legends by which men live.

I pulled out certain maps kept secret even from Aurelius. We, in inland Britain, were in a bag, cords tightening inexorably, unless the Unconquered Despot condescended to succour us. The far-western lands, only nominally Roman, would swiftly revert to rapine and bestiality, hooting away the tyrannical land tax. Yet unknown factors, like an errant number, could interfere. On the Plain the towering stones, the Titans' Dance, packed with queerness, might awe the Germans, then send them away howling. By some weird subterfuge, the stones cannot be counted. They were dedicated, Junius thought, to Diana, frozen and freezing moon huntress, and with some influence from Saturn, whatever that meant. It might mean more than enough to unstable Germans. The Roman Empire, seeking defence from a pile of rocks !

Around Silchester, the Thames, busy highway, was overnight the channel for Saxon cut-throats. Likewise the roads and canals. Hitherto radiating, they now converged. Valentinus had marched off our youth. To trust in remnants of barbarian Treaty Troops made one shudder, though fortunately the main Germanic attack was still withheld, conceivably by the imperial ships.

Valentinus had also commandeered all but our most decrepit horses, including those of the fire office.

Bad news piled up like tainted revenue. Cantonal post-houses were overturned or abandoned. Around Gwynchester, estates had been fled. The tax officials were facing that gigantic barbarian promise, corrosive, menacing, but thrilling, 'Moratorium on debts.' It also meant 'Moratorium on life.'

With no instructions from Court, Praetorian Prefect or Nectaridus, and only confused directions from Cirencester, I was forced into daily discussions with Curials, neighbours and many whom normally I was indisposed to meet. The Bishop I had still encountered only formally. We were not avoiding each other, we were like champion wrestlers, each feeling for a powerful grip. Otherwise, though I talked, I did not often listen. Outside my family, a few Gauls and Jews, Sylviana and Junius, people had marked stupidity, at best a venal cunning. The more I saw them, the less of them was there was to be seen. Many, like Metellus, relying too long on delicacy and grace, ruined themselves through inability to understand compound interest, which underpinned urban life, and was more commanding than bishop or despot. Admittedly, its effect on Picts would be negligible.

Usually I could control the agenda, select the right questions, but even to me, answers were not immediately to hand. Dare we arm the slaves? They were treated well enough. Masters' absolute rights had long been requisitioned by the State. Tacitus' story of four hundred slaves privately killed for not preventing their owner's murder was archaic. But I abruptly realized how little I knew my own. Most spoke only amongst themselves, and slyly, for a prudent householder employed spies. In my house and emporiums they were Atrebats, docile enough, but I did not care to envisage the ancient dreams and resentful godlings hovering behind faces trained to lack of expression. Sometimes slaves outnumbered citizens, and, in Silchester, their numbers were uncertain. Dangers simmered during those sunlit days. Despite promptings from Cirencester, the Curia mistrusted a census, fearing that too precise figures would invite further vile tax depredations. I had not yet armed my own slaves, but suspected that Metellus was not alone in doing so.

We now appealed for volunteers from any who had dodged Valentinus, requesting them to gather outside the amphitheatre. None came.

A small riot erupted in the Forum, against shortages, price rises, loss of jobs. I sent out some of my men, who deflected the bawlers by claiming to recognize certain of Brunnus' informers. One was fatally injured. The first death.

Brunnus, whatever his plans, was ostensibly at our orders, with none to whom to report save the declining authorities at Cirencester. The Armenian was still cadging minor favours and complaining of Julia.

'Valentinus, that porker, takes our men. We must arm the girls. I've known kings on islands with women guards, leaving the men to spin and hoe. It's proved that Gallic ladies wield a plucky sword. Merciless. Greeks tell me of Persian women leading the attack on Athens, I forget when. I've noticed that when women make them do the housework, men grow smaller, plump as partridges, get scared of going outside, and leave adventures to the wife. You'll see, the girls may save us yet.'

I insisted to all that the Pictish threat was more deadly than the Scanian and German. Perhaps from faculties discarded when we ourselves adopted horses and wheels, they moved very fast, though unpredictably, shying from our great roads.

The situation was worsening and from private messages I disclosed only what I thought fit.

With gaping incompetence, loss of nerve, misplaced guile, the State had planted settlements not only of veterans but of Scots, convicts and malcontents, paid to spy on barbarians on both sides of the Wall. I had received proofs that these 'Arcans' had been consistently betraying Wall secrets and encouraging Pictish attacks. Garrisons had now fled to Aldborough, the Brigantine capital. The whole Wall was lost. Brigantes would only support winners, though probably preferring Scanians to Picts. Elsewhere, Caernarvon was withstanding Scots and Attacots, likewise Buxton. Scanians had made beach-heads north of Berwick and around the Humber estuary.

I calculated that while the north-western Votads tribe around the Wall had prospered under Rome, their neighbours, the Selgovs, had not. They had been fleeced, for benefits they neither acknowledged nor understood, and had suffered confiscation of their best lands. Lithe Picts and heavy Scanians they would, however briefly, welcome as deliverers. Nor was this all. Everywhere, peasants, forbidden to leave the land by Diocletian decree, would revolt at any opportunity.

I could only remind people that despite Fullofaudes' reduced cavalry, our foes had none, and Pennine forts had recently been strengthened.

Two further details I did mention. Maponus and Bel Atacadrus, green-toothed northern gods, were seen riding amid Picts on gigantic horses or bears, also, more significantly, Sucellus, a midland hammer god. These did not alarm me, but more solid apparitions were to show fangs. Alarmed by multifold invaders, wild animals were plunging south : wolves, reindeer, bear, elk, becoming supernatural with the telling.

On June's last day, Rufinius Sabellinus hurried in, after dark, muffled like a conspirator. Impatient to speak, he waited until all slaves were beyond hearing, and even then spoke very low.

'Drusus. You must know it. This won't be announced till tomorrow. I've asked Brunnus to have every man he can get, to defend the Basilica. Anything may happen. And we'll need all you can give us.'

These querulous, small-town trademen, toadies and Villa magnates hated to admit that opulence does not derive merely from breathing. They had sneered at my industry, now they squawked for my protection.

'There's been a disaster. Utter collapse. I've got the news from Cirencester, their man's half dead on my own floor. The Duke of Britain. . . .'

'Fullofaudes ! Surely he's found his army at last ?'

'He's dead. Ambushed like a stoat in a trap. Two legions cut to bits north of York. You warned us, and you're right. The tribes followed the Painted Men like famished scavengers. They'd have eaten the Standards if they could. They've probably burnt them and swallowed the ashes in their filthy swillings. Anyway, only flood, or the gods, will stop the Picts. They'll ignore the towns and burn their way to London. Think of it, whole forests in flames. We'll be like fish in a net. Picts, Scots from the West, Germans from the east, and every foul rebel and degenerate you like, rushing in from the south. They may all tear out each other's throats, but after they've guzzled upon our carcases. Only Nectaridus . . . he's our last hope.'

I doubted it. Disaster it certainly was. All Britain was open for the great war between Celtic and German barbarians, which could engulf Rome, extinguish the Genius.

'What about Valentinus?'

'Probably dead with the rest.' Rufinius was suddenly old, parched with hopeless fears. 'May the gods honour him and all that, but I trusted him no more than a sottish bull.' Rufinius knew about sots, he was one himself.

I believed less readily in Valentinus' death than his desertion. He had always complained that only Court favouritism had promoted Fullofaudes. As for the latter, I blamed but scarcely mourned him; he had once shown me marked discourtesy at Cirencester.

To Rufinius I remained sufficiently politic to show more despondency than I yet felt, and to depreciate my own resources. These remained substantial, with reserves largely concealed. Dangers had undeniably increased, but, after sensational initial impetus, barbarian confederations invariably dissolved in tumult. Scanians, lurching, oversized, were unimaginable allies with the agile, malevolent Picts.

Unable to control his own teeth, Rufinius Sabellinus, President of the Curia, was stammering, 'Every grain of barley and wheat . . . every weapon you can grab. . . .'

# X

I swiftly faced, then dismissed, the ludicrous suggestion that I, potential restorer of Britain, fly enough to maintain contacts as far as Arabia, could be snuffed out by a tartarean war band whose breath stank as high as Olympus. But a page had been turned in a ledger, abruptly disclosing bankruptcy, illusionary profits, forged signatures, criminal contracts, reports ignored, sums wrongly added, deductions falsely inscribed.

The danger was unique. The Conquest had been no threat to civilization, had indeed been assisted by the advanced Celtic-Germanic Belgae. Now, perhaps heralding the gay-go-down of the West, we might be sinking into Pictland.

From London we learnt of Scots coracles pirating unmolested. Under Severn mountains, invaders would meet Silurians, doughty fighters, but who might recall helping the Briton, Caractacus, against Emperor Claudius. Further north, the Ordovics had no Roman loyalties. In the east, Scanians had fired Berwick.

Cantonal rule had collapsed, only in Cirencester did an *Ordo* survive, in permanent session. The Emperor's writ was barely alive in towns this side of Trent, by now dangerously swollen with disconsolate or mutinous refugees. Surrounded by ill-defended hill villages and plains, we could know nothing of the beleaguered cities. They might yet be safe, though, outside Chester, those vital salt pits would have gone. Unless soon recovered, this could prove drastic, more fatal than Pictish venom. Seeking easier prey, the painted swarm would scream at the walls for an hour or so, then hurtle on, raping and gorging until satiated like a vast python. Rural Brigantia would inevitably suffer horribly. I only wondered whether Queen Cartimandua's savages had been tamed by our Roman ways, or in bloody hopes joined the invaders. They would regret that. Contact with a Pict disfigures like a vampire's kiss. Germanic colonists were another matter.

Aurelius, very unhappy, fearing for his own property, reported missing not only a load of amber but three slaves, an omen more telling than any three-headed cow, baby born speaking fluent Greek, or abnormally large moon.

Inevitably, we had to use the loathsome Brunnus and his *agentes*. Already, the abject fugitives had straggled in, woeful about German marauders, though plainly implicit was their own cowardice. As I had foretold, the invaders had been welcomed by resident fellow-barbarians. Like sycamore roots stealthily coiling in a drain-pipe, forces, guaranteed by our own crassness, were working to drown us.

Food, however, still arrived, at fiercely contested prices, from villas, though I did not bemoan the lapsing of the State's fixing of maximum prices. With diminishing markets, pubescent riff-raff too young or diseased even for Valentinus, hangers-on of brothel, dram-shop, slaughterhouse, of wrestlers and bear-baiters, calling themselves Followers of Nero, until Brunnus intervened with whips and chains, roamed the streets singing obscene songs, threatening, pilfering and shouting wild promises to appease the Saxons with meat and slave girls.

The death of Fullofaudes caused less dismay than satisfaction at a rebuff to the officer class. Some of this I shared. I remained confident that Silchester, if sufficiently provisioned, could repel attack. Atrebatan farmers, with resilient Belgic strains mingling with tough but controllable Germanic, would defend their steadings. Their notables, stubborn as mastiffs, would follow a coherent plan. I did not fear treachery from them, whatever the confusions further north.

To appear over-conspicuous while going to the Basilica would have been unwise – there were murmurs against me as a monopolist – but once there I was hailed as natural leader, and saw to it that Brunnus, patently anxious to obey despite his hitherto barely concealed hatred of all Curials, conscripted refugees whatever their protests, and placed sentries at river-bends, against soundless, flat-bottomed Saxon boats. We were all alert for heads like yellow stubble, eyes grossly eager for raw meat and atrocious beer, and women with hides like pigs'. We joined with nearby towns in erecting beacons. The monastery, too near the river, was evacuated, the monks of Christopher, while preaching non-resistance, evincing no disposition to exemplify it. Hill forts could be used, if we could persuade villagers to man them.

Throughout Britain, imperial officials had fled, on specious pretexts, or been expelled. We ourselves had already determined on a day of reckoning; indictments of certain functionaries would be dispatched to the Augustus when his authority was restored. In this we had the Bishop's support, useful in the religious fashions prevailing at Court. After a most courteous letter from myself, he had at last issued a declaration, though it was scarcely resounding, announcing little more than that Jeheshua despised obvious means of protection and that to draw a cord through a needle was easier than for the rich to acquire supreme merit. Some magnates joined with me in a demand, slightly less courteous, whether he would thus still require tithes. His response was unsatisfactory.

Beneath bustle and intrigue, fear was insidious, poking. Sacrifices, dolorous and perhaps subversive, occurred in poorer quarters, to Gwyn, a confusion of sunlight and shades natural to a wilful and unsystematic people. Philosophers performed their useless antics. A Canterbury mountebank exhorted idlers and silenced even the Followers of Nero, expatiating on 367. 3 symbolized not the ancient triple Goddess but, absurdly, a magic reed carried by Jeheshua before execution; 6, Jeheshua's spirit; 7, green, the process of creation. Apparently, it all promised fulfilment of the god's lugubrious foretelling of disasters preceding the apocalyptic fire, cloud, judgment.

Brunnus soon disposed of that nuisance, though the teachings, unwelcome, were not wholly foolish. Numbers link the rhythms of the blood with those of the universe. The dictator Fabius Maximus was careful to finance religious rites against Hannibal in multiples of 3. Junius reminded me that a soothsayer warned Nero against 73. Nero chuckled, for he was still young, yet was soon overthrown by Galba, a man of 73. By my own power over numbers, I might yet oversee a throne. The throne itself I was too sane to covet.

Soothsayers were earning high prices. My own investments in the temple of Mars, long useless, recovered as adherents flocked back, doubtless fostering new and resounding legends about I myself being born of Venus and praised by Mars.

Prayers, auspices, concerned me little. The sensible man does not beseech gifts and signals from without, he uses his own gifts to extract treasures from within.

Holding my head over gloomy accounts, incredible reports, I kept a brave face to the world.

# XI

The real Followers of Nero were Flavian and Flavia – the two wives, the Armenian called them – who invited me to a 'Panic Party', celebrating not 367 but 69, when four emperors perished bloodily, the Empire shaking as if in an Alpine gale.

Crisis impels incongruous allies and I thought it best to go. By a stupid accident, for which I hope someone was soundly flogged, the invitation requested my wearing the costume of some previous era, and I took special care to rig myself, aptly enough, as the wise and admired King Numa Pompilius, with crown, sceptre, simple red cloak and bare legs.

Greeted with some hilarity with 'Hail the King', I was disgusted to see everyone else in usual party attire, forcing me to drop my regalia and beg a long robe from the grinning slaves.

The twins themselves in dress harked back earlier than Numa; they were nude save for wreaths and silky wisps bluish as Neptune. Their skins were dyed with bizarre leaves, wings, eyes, their genitals elaborately coiffed, and, welcoming us, they moved through clouds of rich perfume, inducing a lassitude dangerously pleasant and incoherent. To me they were respectful enough, until, smiling in oversimple friendliness, Flavia addressed me as 'Divine Majesty', at which I at once withdrew to another room. A voice was murmuring, 'When the Painted Ones arrive, stark naked . . . we'll see how they're built, eh! It's said. . . .' The obscenity made a girl giggle shrilly, and a slave, holding a basket of apricots, allowed himself a smile I at once mistrusted. But already much was indistinct, I felt dreamily heavy, slow, almost shackled, though able to see that the profusion of wine and sweetmeats was a flagrant, wasteful frippery. Also that I was the only notable present. I was enclosed by those debarred from decent households, greedy for free wine and vulgarity : temple nymphs, handsome barbers and worse, their hair often striped green, yellow, scarlet, or shaved completely, as if for an unwholesome cult.

Anxious to depart, I was detained by that putrid, sickly languor trailing everywhere. I dragged myself through packed, strident rooms, where each wall was bright with lewd hangings. Jeering through foliage, satyrs aimed tumescent cocks, dripping like honeycombs, at sportive buttocks, open vulvas, Priapus brandishing his so tensely that it seemed about to snap. To high flutes, girls slowly danced in Spartan chitons, revealing all. A teacher, middle-aged freedman, normally sedate, now faintly painted, stared at a blonde pubis and suddenly groaned, then, pretending not to recognize me, tweaked my sleeve familiarly, speaking loudly against the clamour. 'I can tell you this, old fellow. Caesar's lads besieged some town here, and saw on the walls not bows, javelins, stones, but, don't think I'm joking, women's breasts. Big ones. Hundreds. Ranged like melons, dangling for the warriors of the Divine Julius. We Romans were no Greeks, we saw things as they were, not as glistening symbols and ideal solutions. Forward, yelled the soldiers, Juno's with us, the girls want a fill-up from real men, Forward March! But Caesar got a raw nose, he'd forgotten that women's breasts are like torches, they can do more than glow. They produce invisible rays, they weaken the gloaters.'

Slaves, musicians, actors swapped raucous jokes, danced, even juggled. Actors I had never entertained, and disliked having to meet them now. People unable to accept their own selves, or with none to accept, thus having to borrow others, are shallow, grimacing, dishonest. That slaves should mingle with guests was even more outrageous, part of the degenerate vision through which Flavia and Flavian minced, waved, odiously embraced each other, then reached out to fondle a breast, a cheek. They now wore painted wigs, smooth gold, tousled blue, the fantasies daubed on their bodies dissolving in heat. Bemused, unsteady, already too much in wine, I myself had declined into an actor, even obeying when the Master of Ceremonies, a sweaty Silenus, ordered us to pair off and stare into each other's eyes. I took a girl in crimson sleeves, with wide eyes of a radiance scarcely healthy, which suddenly blinked incredulously. 'Why, it's old Drusus,' and she at once vanished in a wake of giggles, leaving me fooled, outsized, a little helpless. I could have sold up everyone here; yet, in this sticky, crawling dream, was unable to pull myself free.

I contrived to push through into a dome-like hall gaudily frescoed in mock-Corinthian : Bacchantes, as if joining the party, flowed naked down a hillside after their cruel, mysterious Asiatic and his green-eyed panthers. More dancing here, swifter, to wilder pipes, led by a kilted youth, bare torso unnaturally soft, caked with yellow, flaked with silver, his small head plumed with ostrich feathers that, under the torches, seemed about to blaze. When he paused, his raised hands, black gloved, hovered like bats. I watched, simultaneously almost touching him and at a great distance, repelled and enchanted, while as if from nowhere a voice drawled at two young men stroking each other so vacantly that they might have been seeing nothing but coloured air.

'You remember, dears, Dion's distinction between ourselves and these almighty barbarians? With us, farts are deliberate, discharged at someone special. Barbarians don't notice.'

I could have added, perhaps I did, the celebrated story of Hyacinthus escorting an important official. A horse grossly exploded, Hyacinthus apologized, the official smiled tolerantly, saying he often did the same after baked sturgeon and that the horse would probably outdo them both.

Then, as if speared, I awoke, realizing why I had lingered, why I had come. Sylviana, in green, shift-like tissue, face very white, hair and eyes very black; motionless, as if blind, impervious to the heated dancers and jabbering drinkers, was standing with a tall, hooded man, hearing but not listening, in the way I knew so well.

I moved, but could not reach her through the dancers, my drowsy limbs would not fully respond. I was massive, could break through like Hercules, yet was awash with the drifting and unreal, stifled by so much nakedness, so many graceful but nauseating gestures. Wealth, power, intelligence hung over me like a clown's jingles; I was some stupid senator in a Plautus farce mocked by his own servants, the beautiful girl glimmering endlessly just out of reach. Voices surrounded me like netting, very quiet, yet abnormally distinct beneath music, applause, outcries.

'He seemed to be saying, darling, that if I ate, actually devoured a rusty nail, I'd live forever.'

'You'd better eat a cartload. If your hams taste as delicious as they feel, our interfering friends the Attacots won't leave much of them for you to use.'

'Once you get any taste for human flesh, you want more. Real lust. Girls are sweeter than pork. Beef, venison, carp all become nasty as shavings. As fox.'

'I can tell you more. At the lawcourts, one of those hired witnesses, born and bred in a brothel, was complaining of stomach cramp, and a temple Magus gave him the formula to appease the demon. It was wrong, the fellow changed into a wolf and chewed off most of a slave girl. We managed to get the Magus sober, he juggled with the spells and restored things to normal, but the witness still craves red meat of the most irregular sort.'

'I would not call Scots people of refinement. My apothecary says they use menstrual blood as love potions. Swallow it, mulled, with vinegar, radish, fish scales, and you get Venus on top of you.'

Sylviana had dissolved into the blurred colours; a figure in only a waifish gold belt and green sandals, sharp breasted, was before me, boldly on offer, but someone was tugging my cloak from below, a repellent old witch in dirty scarlet cloth woven with *Roma Dea*, and squatting as if to urinate. Pushing them away, determined to find Sylviana, I was again obstructed. Green and silver baggy trousers, maroon jacket, jewelled belt . . . dark artful eyes and facetious manner . . . the Armenian, greeting me with a crowing insult. 'Ah, Drusus! Of course I expected to find you here.'

Very amiable, he touched my fingers. 'What a lot of interesting faces! I've counted at least three! Did I ever tell you I was once in Chester on a mission not unconnected with the Duke, I should say the late Duke of Britain, that grub, and met the priest of some god or other? He introduced himself as one of the treasures of Britain and boasted he knew the names of three thousand butterflies. I did not ask for more, though I did get a joke about Jeheshua's first cousin, a pilchard, which he had already from me! These Britons! I was staying in a most sumptuous villa. A freedman of very inferior quality, with what he called a sizzling prick, had a fit in the night and wrote himself eleven tragedies.'

Then he too receded into the fluctuating hues and outlines into which I plunged deeper, taunted by dim vestiges of Sylviana, a girl in a maze. Now I was becalmed amongst weird children in fawn-pelts, ivy at ears and throat, dancing around me hand in hand to claps and chirps. Wine, poppy-seed, flute-wails ravaged the night where the longboats silently glided towards us and the wild men crouched on the hills. The children sank into a mosaic and two women with vermilion nipples were embracing with caresses rapt and prolonged. I followed their movements, not with distaste, but with the intentness I would feel for those of a skilled craftsman, while aware of small twitches on my robe, sudden squeezes, faint salacious

94

whispers, until a familiar voice intervened too loudly.

'Drusus! How exceptionally pleasant to see you. My ever-respected benefactor!'

The Armenian again, now in rich sable cloak strewn with starfish, his face keener, swarthier, as if newly sooted, his brows astonished. 'What a surprise, I'd have imagined you on the Walls keeping watch. This music! Like girls' fingers separating silks and ready to explore further.'

His smile slanted mirthlessly, was lost like an arrow. 'I'll tell you how to arrest the Picts. By music. That gushing old stuff about Orpheus is true. Music makes us tingle in unexpected places. The more savage, the more thrills. Well then, we're getting too many dirty mouths to stuff. Let's spend some of your own magnificence and shove a slave orchestra into the north. Test sweet sounds against these offensive nothings. They'll at least hold up the Attacots, providing a cutlet or two.'

Descending, I saw, or thought I saw, a girl, smeared, naked, kneeling, gasping, as a man with long artificial breasts, nodding at his companions, thrust into her from behind, joylessly, as if paid, which he probably was. A streaky face, one of my creditors', pressed against my shoulder, then lapsed, and I saw instead a slave's coarse, pitted cheek, gashed, spurting. Coolly, challenging, he invited me to kiss it. The air was like that of plague, when despair loosens bonds, the sexual reek overpowering, as an ungainly Dido accosted some phantom Eneas.

'My precious . . . love makes the heart beat sideways.'

'The heart! Not much else, I hope!'

'Let's talk about Scanians. Their eyelashes cut you in half. They came from the Gorgon's head. They've got a shout, I hear, that blocks your earhole and paralyses you. But Fortune's seen to it that their brains are in the soles of their feet. A delicious prospect!'

I was parched in the drugged heat and, craving food, amongst naked figures, gently pubescent and pouring scented water over hands, then offering platters of thickly cut meat, strongly flavoured, unidentifiable. Could it be. . . .? Despite hunger, I thrust it away, and struggled through an arch, frantic for Sylviana. The entire mansion throbbed and resounded, ferociously shaken. I was foolhardy in remaining, risking poison, even the knife, an eagle mobbed by insolent starlings. In a gallery, the twins, sheathed in molten silver, were quarrelling, or pretending to. Flavia's eyes, huge, flowery, looked

95

troubled; Flavian viciously slapped her bare breasts : they seemed to
bruise, and, encouraged by applause from below, she laughed, hoarse
and cutting, like the cries of the young men splitting their girls behind
the wall. Turning away, surely I was not imagining Sylviana, smiling
sharply, drily, while a slave beside her made imploring gestures? Was
she too about to strip? Then, with that familiar, casual shrug, she
drifted away, voices loudened, echoes as if in a lead mine; I could
pursue her no further, I had to find some corner and sleep.

## XII

That undignified escapade was best forgotten, and hectic days made it easy to do so, though in the town it was favourably misinterpreted. That I, alone of the municipal dignitaries, had deigned to attend, was held as a subtle political realignment, a move towards the unruly and democratic (which, of course, were repugnant to me).

In the midst of my consultations, stockpiling, posting of look-outs, penning of animals, censoring, Hyacinthus suggested we should meet 'to discuss policy'.

The phrase glinted like scrolls in dusk, not quite decipherable. As always, I had to scrutinize words, probe ambiguities seeping through the ostensibly candid. *Discuss policy*. The language of that rotting, infamous system of compulsory free gifts . . . reverberating with the sinister *Promise of Imperial Favour*, which could imply secret execution.

I complied, knowing I need no longer do so, watching with some amusement his flattish, hairless, mendacious face. 'Most honoured Drusus. Drusus Antonius Muras. A name respected, celebrated. Jupiter protect you, Jeheshua bless you. To honour me with your presence in times so inopportune, indeed untimely! Do you enjoy ospreys? Allow me to offer you humble wine. No? Well. . . .,' he touched the rolled tax-parchment, 'our affair, small as it is, trivial, of so little inconvenience to either of us . . . yet it persists.' He leaned forward, in attempt to be masterful, 'I receive enquiries.' He was hinting that he was still in contact with London, Gaul, even Treves. I replied, unconcernedly, that his communications were indeed enviable. He went pouting, uneasy. 'We must not allow ourselves to be dismayed. Seven years ago, you remember, we had the same scares. They came to almost nothing. Life is long. We can escape the infernal.'

'No doubt. My own couriers, hitherto reliable, keep assuring me, however, that individual lives are proving uncommonly short.'

The office confirmed the tortured streak in his eyes. An entire recess, normally piled with files, was empty, many clerks were missing, the stone floor was dirty, and I suddenly imagined him crouching behind the table, moist, flabby, whimpering, trying to shield his throat.

He begged me to accept wine, then sagged. Curtly, I said that we must all await not only the decisions of the Augustus but his troops, if he still possessed any. He shivered perceptibly and, refusing the wine, I left him.

I myself had been calling in loans, and had received several rebuffs unthinkable only a month before. Threats were looming more immediate than Hyacinthus, making me examine unused depths of myself. To confront cannibals and Painted Men with disquisitions on compound interest and quotations from Livy would indeed be unimaginable as Hercules dropping his club and brandishing at the Hydra a well-argued treatise on the prevalence of bad behaviour.

Despite early interest in giants and heroes, I had no interest in courage, only its results. The brave were frequently tedious. Today, like the boom of some Stygian gong, invaders, disastrously heroic, were making Britain tremble. Four of Bath's seven hills were lost, Apollo's altar was gutted, at which Christians rejoiced, mischievously, foolishly, for Scottish victory would not be theirs. Warehouses were burning, ships were trapped, bales and casks abducted by bacauds.

I decided that, despite my private fears, I must emerge from opulent shelters and show myself, in one more effort to retrieve the hopes I had so long cherished. To assess the situation for myself, I would ride into the midlands, then, with heightened reputation, command the cantonal *Ordo*, even Nectaridus himself, could he and his fleet but be found.

I also had ordinary commercial reasons. My largest trade depot was at Leicester on the far side of Arden Forest. Nothing had arrived from it for a fortnight, and though I was pessimistic about reaching Leicester itself, to venture as near it as possible would dispense many surely absurd rumours, even fantasies. Also, I rather welcomed a few days' freedom from talkative but useless Curials, agitated women, restless streets.

Aurelius could do nothing but remain loyal to me, Avitus would watch my interests, if only to preserve his own. Silchester remained safe enough. Germans were still consolidating their beach-heads. I had no reports of Picts reaching Arden, Scanians had turned north, the Scots' passage of the wide Severn was still fiercely disputed.

My last night I spent with Vesta. Her pale, oval face smiled up at me, never quite losing the reserve or timidity that could often entice me when exhausted by Sylviana's flair for the unexpected.

She lacked Junius' education but was quiet when I was tired, absent when I needed repose, dutiful in bed but with that mixture of solicitude and muffled pleasure that sugared our minglings by making any unusual movement from her sharp and even daring. Her body, slightly plump, was incapable of swift gratification, and I fancied her grateful, in her barely articulate way, for experiments. She could now be surprised but not shocked.

From women I enjoyed, not their candid dependence, but small, spirited intimations of independence, spurts of minor challenge. Neither the insipid nor the overbearing were tolerable.

'Drusus, is it necessary to go yourself? The dangers! You worry us. If you meet those animals. . . .'

Always literal, she meant not barbarians, but the beasts fleeing south as the forests emptied and the flames curled.

'I must certainly go. Too few men risk taking a lead, and those that do are incompetent bankrupts.'

'I will think of you, very strong, on your horse.' I did not order her to undress, was content with the simple meal and the fine wine I allowed her, and with her presence, respectful but affectionate; her rather monotonous voice irritated me less than usual. On my departure, I left two slaves to guard her door unobtrusively in my absence.


I would ride with no slaves, only several freedmen, none in debt to me, and decided to risk the speedy Foss Way, from Cirencester. We set out, in clear sunlight, to much goodwill, for I had carefully publicized my venture as a dangerous undertaking for the common good, true in its way.

On the first day we saw little untoward, save some apprehension in villas where peasants had illegally deserted. Several post-houses were still manned, each giving ill news, none of it actually witnessed. A riot had been suppressed in London, Wroxeter was a ruin, Scanians had raided York, either colluding or fighting with the Picts.

Summer fields were in early crop, sinuous smoke rose from villages, where I was eagerly greeted as legate of recovery. Picts had been seen on horizons, some in chariots, naked warriors from obsolete medallions. I inspected conditions, renewed occasional business heritages, spoke optimistically, then rode on.

The trees began, but clearings were mostly preserved on either side of the clean highway, forty feet broad. The blue sky faded, a small but chilly breeze met us, rough clouds were always ahead, greyish or dun, hiding the sun. Several smashed bridges pushed us into detours and improvisations, but I felt well enough, exhilarated by the freshness, the speed, the escape from dreary, inconclusive gatherings.

After two days, landscapes had changed, as though summer processions had become funerals. Villages, though mostly intact, were abandoned, or filled only with squatters who stood silent, tense, as we galloped through. In lonely creeks, fugitives besought our protection, with tales of killings, dispossession by bacauds or small spectral raiders, slaughter on hillsides. They trembled incessantly, a fever coursed through them. Their subsistence was radishes, peas, unripe fruits and nuts. I could do nothing, save make useless promises. Further on, I saw a Germanic colony where polecat tribalists, as Tacitus described, still used caves and barrows roofed with turf, hay, refuse, so that they might be unnoticed. The suspicion that other such hide-outs existed, on treeless moors, stony hills, and by rivers, gave uncanny tinge to the air as it drooped around us, over flattish lands and the thick, darkening wedges of forest. I realized the powers of those nerve-ends by which officers detect ambush, or thieves know whether a house is empty.

We were not to reach Leicester.

Increasingly, the region was charred. Blackened hovels, treestumps, tumbled roofs, ashy shells of barn and village, a bright yellow pasture scorched at the edges, a smouldering tower. Bumpy fields seemed quilts covering the hideous. Birds were elsewhere, deepening a queer, ominous silence. The sky's grey was unnatural. Gods were either emphatically present or markedly absent, the world reverting to the primal. Only the stone road was inviolate, Rome at her most ruthless.

For hours our horses were fearfully loud, we met nothing live, the breeze had gone, leaving waters utterly still. The sky was thick, as if curdled.

Finally, on the outskirts of Rochlus Forest, a kneeling, distraught group halted us, gaunt, almost naked, eyes hanging dazed and unblinking. None spoke, but skinny arms stretched leftwards to the Fields of Light, sacred to British Lug.

The nose rather than eye led me. Without warning, our horses simultaneously stopped, whinneyed, then refused to stir. Dismounting, we felt our way forward through an acrid, enveloping smell. Then we saw them. Several hundred bodies felled by slingshot, sliced, transfixed, scalped, riven, all stripped and waxen, amongst them occasional darker flesh, bearded, painted. A child's terrible double-grin on the slashed throat, a baby staked to earth through her belly, lopped eyeless heads and limbs befouled in their own juices, dried rivulets of blood, sodden ribbons uncoiling from agonized skin, men patched with raw, oozing crimson, their genitals scattered and already blackening, petrified remnants of unimaginable pain that must have gorged Lug to stupefaction.

A keening, silent but inescapable, penetrated the carnage, which, further off, abruptly shuddered, as all the sky's birds rose like a dim coverlet, angry at our intrusion on their tearings and guzzlings. From the horses behind came a sound I had never heard, high, eerie, stretched.

We fled through a dusk sagging and evil, to rest miles south between ransacked walls. One fellow kept repeating, 'The bells, bells everywhere . . . ,' despite the horrid silence. None of us slept. A screech-owl ripped open a night reddish as if from the bleeding spirits. The moon had risen, cold and mineral. Once the ground slanted away and I vomited uncontrollably, noosed by the atrocious splinters, intestinal coils, castrations. (Joy-bags for sale, the Armenian had once chuckled.) Under that sky the women still lay with sharp twigs rammed between their legs, breasts swept away, eyes smashed by the contortions of their dying children. A fragment of verifiable Hades, which I wanted to present gratis to all traipsing, rowdy Followers of Nero.

Bats were flying, soundless, fidgety, black pus of the dark, and we heard the long howl of wolves, so agitating the horses that soon we were outside, galloping with the monstrous at our back, the moonlight itself waiting over the vague transparencies that cowled the Fields of Light.

# XIII

---

It was difficult to credit even ghosts surviving those glazed, emptied carcases. Ghosts themselves, lacking metabolism, are frail, though few relish their presence. I believe (one is never certain) that I had seen no complete ghost since a harmless childhood encounter with a Gallic warrior sweating black blood by the tombs.

The massacre was already a bestial norm by which to judge faction, history itself. Some madness had been simmering through centuries of barbarian blood. 'Everything is full of gods,' Thales taught, but gods and demons have roots perhaps identical.

I looked back with some incredulity to days of orderly mails, regular reports from Milan, Ravenna, Strasbourg, quiet arrivals from Gallic ports. Now before me, like the apparition of some dying Nero, hung terrified eyes, gaping mouths.

The fourfold invasion of Britain had suggested stupendous prospects. I had been like a woman fearing yet craving rape, but, scurrying like a felon through that damning night, I knew that I had been guilty of bad judgement. I myself.


London remained secure. Independent of Nectaridus, its flotillas still cruised the estuary. I received the unofficial mails, smuggled in by pedlars, farriers, equivocal *agentes*. The vanished postal officials had, of course, long been State spies.

All respected my purses and sought me from unmapped lanes that avoided the perilous valleys. However thick the forests, tribesmen knew immemorial tracks.

Joined by Selgovs, Orcadians, Hebrideans, the Picts now squatted on one-third of Britain, with certain walled towns, isolated towers, and some of Trajan's fortlets near the Stanegat Way still resisting. A junction had been achieved, however briefly, between Picts and the tempestuous Hibernians, but somewhere, remnants of Fullofaudes' legions were conceivably regrouping, perhaps under Valentinus. A reliable signature attested that, as I had expected, the tough Votads had mauled a Pictish horde in the western heights. Scanian longboats had landed at Humber-mouth, though some had been wrecked by an unexpectedly high tide.

Nectaridus had reputedly won a battle off Reculver, scores of Saxons now littering the Kentish sands. Jutish and Burgundian immigrants might thus hesitate to assail us.

Nearer home, the Severn landowners still withstood Attacots and Dressens, with desperate fighting in the streets of Bath. More Scots were floating across, weapons aglint above round, bullhide shields, their curled war-horns, tall as wattle huts, blasting the way ahead.

Abroad, Alemans, Vandals, Arii were either held or quiescent, but, further west, the Augustus was grappling with large-scale peasant revolts. I did not envy him. The alleged virtues of sturdy peasants included greed, envy, callousness. Ambushes, incessant on Gallic and Spanish roads, had murdered the Emperor's brother-in-law.

Mysteriously abstruse violence was being inflicted by parents on children, even in Silchester.

Christian monks were useful, preparing emergency hospitals, volunteering to help store my granaries, though somewhat complacent at the apparent fulfilment of their own glum prophecies. Despite increasing food deficiencies and endless lectures on the holiness of poverty, they remained sleek and healthy. Their professed assessments of human enterprise were as dangerous as tribal notions of equality, in which all share identical portions of squalor.

Sylviana I seldom saw, and never alone. At a distance she was unchanged, cool, only slightly curious about the intimations of catastrophe.

Only with Avitus could I speak freely. 'Wherever I go, I hear sham philosophy. That judge and criminal are the same, that lunatics are more sane and gifted than the rest of us.'

Avitus knew great slabs of Cicero, a gift for which I was ungrateful.

'You remember Cicero's words?' Wise, as always, he droned :

' "The armies ready to assault the State outnumber the defenders, for a single nod will incite the rash and desperate – indeed, they incite themselves against society without being summoned. The reliable elements rouse themselves more languidly : they disregard early signs of trouble and only at the very last are goaded into action by sheer

103

crisis : the pity is that, though they strain to keep themselves safe even at risk to their honour, their own delay and wavering often lose them both." '

His mildness changed, his old features drew together decisively. 'For the safety of us all, Drusus, you must, of course, represent us at this special assembly at Cirencester. Rufinius and I have nominated you, Brunnus will manage an escort.'

I pretended a gratified astonishment, but had naturally prepared for this. No other *Ordo* now survived, the other three might never meet again. Avitus' words had reminded me only of Cicero's head and writing hand nailed up in the Roman Forum by Antony. But now, from Cirencester, might emerge the post-Roman Britain. A tiller must be grasped by the exceptional man, whom Sylviana might at last gratefully acknowledge.

My pleasure was later dimmed when I fancied overhearing a slave muttering, 'Cheru'. When examined by Aurelius, he swore ignorance, and asked if this was a new horse. Torture was no longer permitted, and we had to let him go, though convinced he was lying.

I wondered whether the word was totally unknown to Aurelius himself.


Richly endowed and urban, the province of Britain yet secreted black impulses, long submerged, now thrusting up. Picts and Scots, like Avars, Scythians, Huns . . . used anything but their brains. We ourselves were becoming more aware of our bodies, experimenting with sword-grips, knee-armour, daggers, feeling strange sensations at throat and breast, odd tremors and flinchings. Lost animal skills must revive. Junius informed me that, by sniffing a tree, a fox could detect not only a prowling male but the very contents of its stomach. Useful, though, for me, unenviable. Avitus recalled Timoleon, tyrant of Syracuse, who, becoming blind, developed inner sensations and apprehensions, thereby enhancing his power.

My journeys had taught me a Britain known to no other Curial. Charcoal-burners' secret societies, proscribed Druids and warlocks; Celtic outlaws; bacauds; Roman renegades; underground forest temples; bear cults surviving where bears were extinct; a tiny shrine to Carausius on which flowers were reappearing; small, clustered villages invisible from roads, cherishing old tales of wolf and hare upright and tall as men, and, like stone, metal, tree, stored with the uncanny. It profited me to know this. Fathers, teachers, statesmen should likewise remember their infancy. Watch children, and listen, tiresome though it generally is.

Few children grow far; much political confusion derives from belief that most adults are mature; a Valentinus, a Metellus, even an Avitus, each in his own way vain, develop only some bit of themselves. By distancing myself, I saw them whole.

Tribal lore I respected, for its talking beasts, miracles, shrewd dwarfs, gave bright clues in darkness. They related to dreams, to fate, those old men droning riddles at crossroads, setting tests and warnings. Gods might not advise through dreams but a dream could measure one's situation and whittle it into shape. The mind expands at night. Before the mutiny that enthroned him, Julian dreamed of a great tree overthrown. I dreamed of a long key unlocking a small room in a wood and awoke moist with desire for Sylviana. Frequently lost deep in a dream forest, I simultaneously soared above trees. I had normal daytime visions, only apparently unnatural. A face glimmering on a cloud, leaves suddenly agitated by no wind. In Gaul, I had entered an unknown town and at once, correctly, foreknew the streets, the names of citizens, a bright cavalcade of riders.

Such minglings of real and potential Metellus explained, in tones flavoured with self-esteem, as the dismemberment of Minerva, symbol of moderated instincts. Perhaps. I would not deny that club-bearing heroes and divine archers, however refined by poets, were simple mental devices to ease the common lot.

My own knowledge of Britain astonished even me. For years, authoritities had disregarded signs that entrance barbarians and prefigure unrest. Boundary stones removed, cattle stolen, sacred trees injured or decorated. These were like the abrupt, ominous hush before storm. The children's legend of Britain terrorized by a travelling shriek was prophetic. Slaves' chatter that a woman's day contains more hours than a man's made more explicable Sylviana's smiles, gestures, pauses, silences. I no longer despised the belief that alongside each village was an invisible village of the dead, though I refused an exorbitant offer of their advice.

In instants of despondency, I saw Britain passing to mad children, barbarian butchers, and the dead. Like black columns stood facts inescapable : the savage vermin in skies above Leicester . . . the powdery shards of Carthage, of Troy.

# XIV

In Cirencester, second largest town in Britain, where I had many enterprises, I expected welcome from obsequious patricians, but was met by only two smaller traders, mutually suspicious. To the other's peevishness, Trivicus had rooms for me in his own house, where a meal was waiting. Not of the best; baked thrush was no delicacy and I surely deserved more than Gloucester cider but, seated under plain dark hangings at a rough table, I listened carefully.

Suitably glad of my patronage, Trivicus was small, with Spanish eyes and nose that looked as if sharpened to prise out trade secrets. Instead, he quickly lamented the food shortages, blocked markets, unpopular refugees, prominent disappearances, but then seemed nervous, hesitant. I waited, sensing more to come.

'There's dangerous talk about. It may sound absurd to you, sir, I scarcely dare mention it . . .'

'Nevertheless, tell me.'

'Have you, by chance, sir, heard the name Cheru?'

I kept my expression unchanged but was inwardly startled.

'Scanians, as you know well, worship metal in their sunless forests. They fear Cheru, god of weapons and battles. He's a god often convulsed by a sort of crazed rage.'

He was worried lest I thought him stupid, not in itself unreasonable. 'Cheru was once their chief god, we hear. The unappeasable. In love with his own pain. His metal creates a magic, though our Roman gods would scarcely use him as doorkeeper or ostler. Now, he's got a magic sword. It's named this.' He passed me a tablet inscribed *Sokwabeh,* outlandish, like pigs' grunts. 'Dwarfs in a pit made it. The usual stuff's told of it. It flashes mysterious lights, flames and so on. But here's the point. It vanished from Cheru's temple. In despair, the war-chiefs consulted a shaman.'

'No surprise in that, though I've never found an oracle that speaks plain language. They always tell me such useful matter as that a sterile tree might very probably bear the best fruit.'

Trivicus' laugh was forced. 'The shaman declared that Cheru had withdrawn the sword, that he would present it to the master of the world to his own injury.'

'So! You've taken your time telling me that. Haven't you more?'

'It's the date, sir. This happened in 69. The dreadful year of the four emperors.'

I dislike being instructed in history. He said hastily, 'Before the Divine Vespasian soothed the Empire, he had to overcome Vitellius.'

'A particularly lazy, improvident and gluttonous incompetent.'

'Yes. Of course. Without doubt. Perfectly put. But he was once, as Prefect of the Lower Rhine, feasting with his staff. A messenger staggered in from the frontier. Vitellius hated being disturbed at the trough, but the messenger breathlessly implored him to go at once to a barbarian who refused to let his shadow touch the walls. Vitellius, ill-pleased, strode out. Outside was an immense fellow, a savage Mars, not to be rebuffed. Silently he handed the Prefect a sheathed sword. Drawn, it showed unknown runes, queer designs . . . snakes biting their tails, a one-eyed lord hanging from a branch, another half-devoured by a wolf. The stranger declared that, for as long as Vitellius held the sword, he was lord of the world. Then vanished, as if in mist. But for the massive sword in his hand, Vitellius would have thought him due only to the wine he'd swilled. Then from somewhere, an unknown voice boomed, "Hail Vitellius Augustus." The officers, the entire Cologne garrison repeated it. So Vitellius made for Rome, against Emperor Otho, and won. He climbed the Capitol holding the sword aloft, but dared not risk all by depositing it in Jupiter's temple. Well, we all know that his mastery of the world meant only mastery of the banquets. There, he forgot Rome, the Praetorians, the gods. He forgot General Vespasian in Judaea. And forgot the sword. In a hurry for his roasted larks, nightingales' tongues, truffles in saffron sauce, he left it in the peristylum. A Praetorian sergeant saw it, exchanging it for his own sorry blade. What then? My esteemed master knows. Vitellius continued his labours . . . meats, wines, boys, wenches. Ignoring the Senate, he pretended not to hear rumbles from Asia. Vespasian was leaving his hills, Vespasian was at sea, Vespasian was in Italy. Provinces were falling away, generals were missing. Still our emperor munched, chewed, gulped, sicked it all up and began again. Had he not the sword? Well, of course, he hadn't. Rome's gates swung open to Vespasian. At last Vitellius bestirred himself. He lumbered out, drew at his belt and found only the sergeant's rusty thing. He was now quite deserted. In panic, he threw away the purple and, in a filthy cloak, staggered into the roaring streets. The mob recognized him. Hooting, jeering, they dragged him to the Gemoniae Palace, where, with Cheru's sword, the sergeant cut him to bits.'

'A good story, Trivicus. What happened though to the sergeant? He couldn't be called Trajan?'

'No. He ended up in Pannonia. He served the army well, Sokwabeh bore him scatheless through all battles, but in old age he found it too heavy to hold. For some reason, he grew afraid and, alone in a hut on the Danube, he buried it. He'd no ambitions beyond a veteran's pension, so Cheru didn't bother about him.'

Trivicus had gone hoarse, his nose even sharper. 'There's a rumour humming round the barbarian north. The sword's been found.'

I had heard sufficient. I believed neither in Cheru nor Sokwabeh, but deceits and fables inspire multitudes, and any mountebank with dirty peplum and ragged claws, calling himself Dionysus, Nero, Carausius, flashing a hired trident and running his tongue into the universe, could inflame the world.

I set out for the *Ordo* in a litter, alert for any changes.

Most temples were brothels, noisy and crowded, save that of the Triad, Jupiter, Juno, Minerva, with its columns of hyacinth richness, allegedly Tyrian, and the small shrine, darkly timbered, to the Celtic forest god Cernunnus, horned, holding ram-headed snakes. Sacrifices, becoming too costly, were now rare. Many statues of gods had been mutilated, but only in riots. The homicidal disputes between Christian sects were forbidden in Britain, never celebrated for religious fanaticism or even conventional piety. Above his own forum, which now showed few stalls, graceful Mercury, floating above cock and ram, had lost both arms.

From crowded, raucous streets I received no salutations, and only with blows and curses did my slaves manage a path through the jostling, aimless multitude. From an ancient podium a zealot harangued an abject mass in vile barbarian accent. His stuff was scarcely a call against howling Picts, fanged, scourging Attacots, huge wilful Scanians and Germans.

'These are the last days, the pangs of the Messiah. The Day of the Lord will come as a thief in the night, when the heavens crumble in loud din and the elements melt in fiercest heat, the earth as well, and all will be consumed.'

It was drearily familiar. I could have thrown this barnyard ranter the words of Euripides : the gods are cunning, planting long-set ambush for the impious.

In the Basilica, lately repaired with imitation marble (supplied by myself with insufficient profit), many faces were missing, notably those of the magnates from further west. The hall was only half-filled, but I was greeted with fervid relief, at last receiving the honours due to me, the sub-prefect, a sensible man, announcing that my presence was worthy of a relief army.

I seated myself, modestly enough, not near him but by Clisus, a banker, so mean that he would dress cooks, barbers, dentists, porters, to double as his guards, even as his retinue of clients.

We began with an oath to Valentinian, rather perfunctory, while holding the customary packets of flour and tiny wine casks. I was probably not alone in wondering whether the Augustus still lived; perhaps he was being nagged by Juno, or seduced by Maia in a Christian sky. The prayer to Jeheshua was barely audible above the chatter, and Clisus confided some nonsense about the sick being cured by sacred scrolls placed under the head. My own physician, old Scaevus, advised against this, instancing the usual holy dirt on sacerdotal hands.

A magnate, assured, incisive, then outlined the general situation, confirming my own assessments, though omitting Cheru and the pangs of the Messiah.

Caerwent, guarding the Severn, and its sister fortress, Caerleon, still held out, helped by colonies of veterans, sometimes counter-attacking, but, further north, almost all marcher-lands, so freely planted with barbarian Treaty Troops, had dissolved. Pitiless skirmishes were raging scarcely twenty miles away as the Scots advanced across the upper Severn, delayed only by quarrels with Attacots over the spoils, as indeed, far to the east, Vandals were fighting Roman, Saxon, Briton alike. He reminded us that, though to trust in barbarian dissensions would be extreme pessimism, the Scots especially lived upon impulse, losing all courage if but one turned tail.

Never myself absolutely convinced of the Barbarian Conspiracy, I was more alarmed by conditions here. Slave attendants, rather drunk, were ignoring orders, leering at timid requests. Trivicus had mentioned a convict labour-gang revolting at Lydney, where the Lug cult had revived. No troops were available to arrest them.

109

Another speaker was orating: 'We cannot lay down our heads at night without counting the hazards. But barbarians exist in order to be thrashed. When they're treated as allies or fellow-citizens, we're doomed. Of what's happening amongst the Villa slaves we still know little. Meanwhile, we must act, while time remains, and in the most obvious way.'

I sat up. When people propose the most obvious way, they can mean either something feasible or the most reckless absurdity. His voice tolled through the stone pillars and heavy rafters as if he were an attempt to revive Scipio.

'It's necessary, essential, vital, to touch the heart and resolution of the Eternal Emperor. The seas are not yet entirely lost. We must dare them in a final, spectacular effort. We ourselves, the last free canton of Britain. We will be remembered by the gods, by the golden pages of history. Hear me. On behalf of imperial Britain we must dispatch a most solemn embassy, at whatever risk, to Treves. The wisest and most experienced here amongst us must make this sacrifice, in the manner which so often has saved Rome, for the world's salvation. They will convey not only our humiliation and agony, but our demands. The Empire is threatened with the loss of not the least of its jewels. We must not perish unheard.'

To shouts of encouragement he burbled on about the eyes of posterity, the insulted majesty of the gods, but I was silently considering. The Saxon Sea would be thronged with June pirates and invaders. Nectaridus' navy must be dangerously dispersed, attempting to defend all coasts against unlimited scum, though Dover and Boulogne certainly survived.

The risks were dire, but alternatives were worse.

I did not have to secure my berth personally. Inevitably, I was soon hearing, without affected embarrassment, the call to 'Our most respected brother and colleague, the renowned Drusus Antonius Muras'.

In secret conclave, the plans were formulated. Nothing would be openly proclaimed, to diminish traps and intrigues. Leading four rich Cirencester nonentities with resounding names, I would speak for all Britain save London. London was London, perhaps able to beat off all assaults and continue as an independent unit, with which, should the Augustus fail us, we might later have to negotiate, claiming equal terms.

Returning to Silchester, Brunnus' men clattering around me with naked weapons, my elation was not yet whole-hearted. Dangers were not only from storm and German. Dealing with the imperial secretariat, doubtless with the Augustus himself, would demand more than boldness.

I at at once discovered Metellus, alone in my atrium, strained, indeed haggard, bright hair tarnished. Had Sylviana. . .? He held my hands for support, a silky house dog lost in a jungle, our Metellus.

'Nectaridus is dead !'

Cheru's sword had glittered, then struck, off-shore from Reculver. The fleet was smashed, and, outside Canterbury, a small volunteer army broken by the Saxon ruse of the charge, straight and uproarious, at the enemy chief, gambling on his fall, on which panic almost always ensued. Metellus stammered, began weeping. I reminded him that he was entangled with Hyacinthus, had borrowed too much from Valentinus : one was helpless, the other dead, he was by that much freed. Then I announced my mission to Treves, though wondering if Dover and Pevensey were now lost.

He refilled his cup uninvited, then smiled as if touched by a god. 'You're right, of course. You'll manage everything. I feel better already. What else is there? Oh yes, little Hestia is getting herself married while there's still time. To Tullus Torquatus. She went to that parcel of rot, her father, informing him she needed nuptials. Quite right, quoth he, admirable, couldn't be finer, excellent, very much to be desired. She could marry whomever she wanted. Not a plebeian, of course, not a freedman, not an artist, and preferably not an aboriginal Briton. The joke is that Tullus is all four.'

Unknown to me, however, not only Hestia's father had suffered affront. The Armenian told me, and I was outraged by the new inadequacy of my own sources. Treves had acted.

At the urging of the great cavalry leader Jovinus, victor at Metz and Chalons over the Alemans, Severus, the master general of infantry, had gathered warships, filling them with men and horses to relieve Britain. Severus was no flabby court favourite, he had trained young Caesar Julian in tactics, loyally served him in Persia, and several times swept back the Germans.

My embassy was ruined. I awaited my reactions. (They were seldom spontaneous, for this induces folly.)

111

I was relieved, I was frustrated. The naval dangers I had dreaded. To depend on an envelope frail as the body, dodging bandit knives and rams on the wilful sea, was abominable. Amid waves, superstitions revive : I had once cast jewels to Neptune. Yet a place at court, long overdue, could have transformed all.

The Armenian's grin was supercilious. 'I've read – was it in Suetonius? – that poets dwindle to grasshoppers. For my ear, I can do without the first stage.'

I always doubted whether he ever read anything, but could, as it were, sniff the essence of books, dialogues, treatises, so that he could sometimes appear scholarly, especially to women. His garments probably concealed tablets on which he surreptitiously recorded the remarks of others, not least of myself.

He nodded, with new, insolent familiarity. 'Severus, eh! That will halt your little adventure. A pity, for both of us.'

I repaired to Vesta's. She was at market, but Junius received me, deft, slender, eyes grave, slightly withdrawn. I soon made a certain gesture indicating my sexual desire, but, as so often, he only smiled remotely. Though dependent on my favour, he had curious power, a friendly but obstinate independence. He gave another, more concerned smile, and pointed to an ant on my sleeve.

'An insect . . . a bee, aphid, that little ant, once it gets lost or abandoned by the swarm, loses all intelligence. Its capacities wither, and it dies very quickly. But the swarm itself, can it but keep intact, performs astonishingly perfect structures of organization. Campaigns, architecture, social hierarchies. Intricate patterns that Pythagoras himself could not better.'

His enthusiasm was scarcely infectious, yet I would enjoy his talk. Philosophical and doctrinal disputes were futile. Fat do-nothings maundered about the problems caused by levitation, before ascertaining whether levitation actually occurs. Young Junius, however, always produced unexpected facts, and now informed me that Pictish bestiality could be caused by mental derangement, revealed in unusual lines on their hands.

He had the lover's knack of making me feel inferior, and I was always glad when I could enlarge on his revelations.

'I've a symbol for barbarism, my Junius. In Dacia, a single centurion, L. Calpurnius Muca, was in charge of fifty dangerous prisoners. He had no sentries available, so he painted on their cell an immense eye, and slept by day quite peacefully, knowing that none

112

would risk an escape. At night, he kept awake, the brutes believing that the eye evaporated in the dark.'

The trouble with clever Junius was that he might then tell me who had provided the paint, but we were unexpectedly disturbed. From the street below, like a sudden call of cracked bells, outcries began, and, despite my reluctance to be seen in such a quarter, I hastily leaned from the window.

Faces like leaves in wind, voices in shrill alarm. At first all was confused, incomprehensible, but finally I learnt the cause. The Supreme Despot had already countermanded Severus' appointment. I had no more time for Junius, let alone Vesta. Back home, Aurelius had news for myself alone. Jovinus, mighty Jovinus, would replace Severus, but only after both had utterly pacified Gaul and Germania.

I was not much of a hero, but, again, must accept the chance to behave like one. And I seldom prayed, but did so now, to Mars, our family protector. Deliver me, O Lord, from the perils of this journey. From the sword of Cheru and the machinations of courtiers. From Valentinian himself, sanguinary and arbitrary.

# XV

Palaces fascinated me, for even I had known very few. Like a rich man's ledger a palace reveals many layers of existence, within a huge account supported by irrefutable numbers and extraordinary credit.

Less enticing, within the clamour, lies the stealthy menace of a snake-pit. The intruder instinctively avoids shadows, recesses, pillars, balustrades, and, on steps, keeps close to the wall.

In alcoves alongside the wide, brightly tessellated aisle, methodical above gilded Nilic pens and cloudy hour-glasses, continually moving, moving, were secretaries, accountants, scribes, advocates, money-changers, mostly Cretans and Ephesians, closed-up, expressionless, with pointed hoods thrown back onto short Gallic cloaks. Their light breeks and short boots were of unmistakably poor quality. Stiffly robed notaries in small, lamped cells, softly, importantly interviewed courtiers. Alexandrians with enigmatic smiles, Dacian exiles, Spaniards, Italians, Samarthians, dark Numidians, languid Asiatics with eyes bright and unnaturally still. Everywhere were ruddy, blunt-faced Germans, who dominated the military commands.

One notary, under a *clepsydra*, water clock, head pumiced clean of hair but with a red stripe painted across it, fondled a brown cat to which, as if from habit, he seemed to be giving expensive advice.

Ceilings, dark, decorations messy, were of exaggerated height, as though for giants scared of damaging their heads, so that the people beneath seemed small, dollish suppliants, save for mailed Palatine Guards and Targeteers fixed at all corners, under every thick rounded arch, column, stairway, with long naked swords. Taken from diverse races, mostly barbarian, they were thus loyal not to particular generals but, for as long as he could over-pay them, to the Augustus alone. Visors half-concealed their faces, their eyes saw all directions, all entries. Either from towering casques, or long hair bunched on the crown, they were abnormally tall. Sun shafts lit their scales (brass passing for gold) and the rigid lines of buckler, shield, greaves. The atmosphere was that of a camp.

Bundles of arrows and herbs lay on niches, on ledges beneath apertures oval or slitted, a few of them glazed. New markings showed that many furnishings had been lately removed, perhaps nervously before the latest victory, perhaps after. The mendacity of dispatches was notorious.

Processions continually passed. The Prefect of the Sacred Bedchamber, the Advocate of the Treasury, the Grand Chamberlain, Master of Offices, Quaestor, Count of the Sacred Largesse, each with his priests, sophists, lawyers, and other parasites. In outer courtyards, litters emitted perfumed, daubed, ostentatiously clad women clutching dogs, tiny, with sparkling collars, scarcely breathing, as if prepared to be eaten. They and their heavy, brocaded men were meticulously searched at the Imperial Gates, which seemed stronger than the walls flanking them. Horsemen galloped in, dusty, hot, shouting for towels and wine.

Metellus declared that a Roman gentleman has fifty ways of assenting, thirty of denying. Certainly, Valentinian's courtiers thought very carefully before committing themselves to the most trivial. A small grandee did assure me, directly, that the day was fine, then, with alarm, almost terror, saw that rain was falling, and stuttered, 'That is to say, not precisely fine, by no means anything very much. It depends on His Sacred Majesty's pleasure.' He shivered when a black, half-naked slave, hands aloft, painted gold, paced through the resplendent group which mysteriously divided for him as if by suction, heads devoutly lowered.

My room, lemon coloured, both damp and too warm, was evidently not of the best. Truckle bed, trestle table, brazier, Greek amphora, birdcage with golden wires, fortunately empty. I could calculate its cost in several markets, a most healthy exercise. A one-eyed Sardinian mute attended me. I overlooked a colonnaded parade ground and was glad to see serious drill for yellow-headed, moustached Frankish stalwarts, with wolf and mastiff heads instead of caps, and bearskins over cuirasses.

The incessant stir on all levels of the Palace made sleep difficult, and I moved between dreams intense but broken, keeping pace with the complications without, and in which I wandered through an interminable theatre, actors and spectators identical. Veiled shadows could be mystics or conspirators, dwarfs were secret giants : a priest, resembling the Silchester bishop, cat-mouthed and smooth, with towering cross and smirking acolytes, whispered to women painted so thick that they seemed permanently stupefied. Further off, young eunuchs, surely far less numerous than in Constantinople, twittered and swayed, watched by children with old, drowsy faces.

After three days we had yet to see the imperial visage, either through Valentinian's own policy or that of his inner consistory. The Empress was at Milan. At least we were not expected to fast, in servile preparation for an audience; indeed, we fed so lavishly that, unusually tactless, I suggested to an official that we were being deliberately fattened. His silence was unfavourable. Actually, unlike my four colleagues, well-bred flunkeys, I had little wish personally to encounter the formidable soldier-Emperor, but merely to influence his decisions. Diocletian's legacy of intricate ceremonials, prostrations, flatteries, was not only despicable but easy to mishandle, and to wait daylong in vestibules crammed with malodorous place-seekers, monks, toadies, was undignified.

Patiently, quelling upstart fears, I noted, watched, committing nothing to paper, presenting myself as cool, confident, professionally aloof, smiling away women paid to waylay me, ignoring the Sardinian's suggestive gestures, feigning courteous satisfaction with all arrangements, or lack of them.

The Palace, too large to be minutely explored, was a sequence of arched halls, sparsely decorated save where the sacred monarch condescended to appear. Painted stools, screens, tables, followed him, rather forlornly. I advised, no, ordered, my companions against being seen talking, save in a crowd. Spies were certainly trailing us.

Contrasts were startling : the luminous and shrouded, the exotic and cheap. The Prince of this World might be secluded here, or in arms on some distant frontier, he was never mentioned save in most oblique phrases, yet I sensed him always about to emerge : the motionless Targeteers seemed intently listening, his reach was boundless.

Meanwhile, I observed white-robed Pythagoreans mumbling about transmigrations and mutations of 7, eliciting jealous frowns from Christian priests. Once I was suddenly encircled by turbaned, bandy-legged midgets attached to large cats by silken cords, speaking unknown words in mocking tones, then vanishing into a pall of dark. Councillors, Companions, Ministers, continuously paraded, as if in anxiety to be seen, their gemmed hands holding onions to chew

116

against dysentery. They, like the Guards, were elongated above the rest of us, by high-heeled scarlet buskins, and long straight robes with stripes of rank, sumptuous titles matching curled wigs, lengthy, tinted finger-nails, nodding ear-rings.

Soon I was leaving the great crowded halls for the long galleries of carved cedar and the narrow stone passages, darkened corridors, remoter stairways. There I would stand, as if pausing on some mission, apparently casual, yet disregarding none of the fleeting murmurs between rigid lips, the furtive signs exchanged without formal salutations, the cowardly glances, the chilly laughter from behind a wall that ceased so quickly. I suspected that within fine mantles and peaked head-gear were *silentiari*, police. Continuously I had to seek connections between imperial Treves and Britain with towns and forests in flames, the traitors and invaders, the broken walls and skewered bodies. Of none of this I had yet heard mention, though it must be known. Somewhere, in over-heated apartments, Britain must be being pondered, myself and my party being assessed by those whose reputation for trained administration was by no means ill-earned.

More days went by. I was being acknowledged respectfully enough as I made my small explorings. I could now distinguish certain clues within the bells, proclamations, chantings, and the futile chatter of ornate figures separating and then reforming as if for protection and with no obvious function; also the bays and snarls of animals. The Augustus' private quarters were guarded by his two bears. In Britain he was reputed to enjoy them mauling the condemned, but I could scarcely repeat this here. In one corner of a small throne-room, shiny with artificial stones, green and white marble – the throne itself alabaster, probably British – bars restrained a Syrian lion, shabby and stinking, usually inert on fouled straw, together with an uneasy Nubian continually rubbing a pink leg blain, and whose face, squashed, blubbery, suggested a dusky Valentinus.

Jeheshua had a lofty, incense-drenched chapel of Synnadon porphyry, white flecked with purple, which alternately glistened and darkened in draughty candle-light. Copper glimmered from shadows. All was dominated by the towering mural of a staring round-eyed face, surmounted by rich diadem, beneath which, grotesquely small, knelt his eleven favourite judges. Here was not the puny, cross-eyed god known in Britain, querulous, tantrumy, mischievous, but a tyrant akin to the Unconquered Sun. There was some nonsense about this

117

visage having been clamped on the wall by mental transference, from a priest's dream, vision, even prayer. I believe something of the sort did once occur at an Ephesian monastery, producing a picture rather too obviously phallic – scarcely unbelievable, given the nature of monks. I also witnessed priests baptizing a bell in magic waters, their chants like low, regular waves in a cavern. Niches held figurines, clearly refurbished Olympians : milky-blue Mercury with cadenus, vermilion Bacchus, his thyrus glumly, crudely, transformed to a cross.

Listening to a monk's exhortation, I reflected that his creed should appeal to me, analogous as it was to Jewish accountancy. Piety was correct auditing. Do *this*, and *that* follows. Or else !

Nothing is unique. A bargain struck in Colchester provokes a replica in Norwich. Diverse, even contradictory elements in ancient gods coalesce in Jeheshua – Apollo's radiance, Apollo's coldness, Jupiter's mastery, Mercury's agile wits and mystic inclinations.

My British associates, unused to foreign splendours, were astonished by the mincing catamites and enigmatic eunuchs, the artificial eyebrows and beards, jewelled hair-styles and ochred eyes, the perfumes, the affected idioms, the flatteries extravagant yet vague as water. Seeing me drawing on my sceptical, cautious adroitness they gladly lapsed into my personal secretaries, surrendering all pretence of diplomacy. I let them infer my partaking in secret conferences, nocturnal audiences, reforging the links of Empire. This would ennoble or damn me, half-measures were useless.

I was accepting the compliments due to me from chamberlains, subaltern ministers, officers, their requests for my opinions, estimates, appraisals, not of Britain but of Gaul, where my family was respected, solid amongst so much flimsiness and religion.

From my father I had learnt not to adorn but to construct, not to lecture but to demonstrate. I was able, even encouraged, to use the couriers, sending him news from Britain in language comprehensible to him alone, though outwardly profuse in admiration of the Augustus. The *silentiari* would show them to the Consistory within the hour.

With no definite summons, I settled in amongst the functionaries. Elaborate self-esteem seeped through their embroidered exteriors. Even the most bovine contrived some military insignia for their court brocades, sashes, ribbons, bracelets, their tasselled sleeves. The very emeralds proudly upheld against eye-strain were fashioned into tiny shields fixed to gilded lances. Prolonged bows, smart greetings, soft

118

embraces meant nothing. To judge a smile was like dividing snakes. My mission remained unexpressed, probably unmentionable. A reference to Britain received an expression of studied deafness, the considered silence evoked by a fart.

As a test more subtle I carelessly uttered 'Cheru', but occasioned only a rustle of gowns, a wearily polite smile as if at the witless joke of a friend's child, and indeed, amid the leisured gaits of magnificent, and perhaps useless hierarchies, the spies concealed in hollow pillars and the confessional, Cheru seemed the phantom hero of a crone's fable, which doubtless he was.

Real power remained hidden, within earshot of the Augustus alone. I already felt far superior to those whose daily expressions reminded me of Hyacinthus. Like all court language, theirs was repetitive and devoid of substance. 'Faithless as a termite,' an Imperial Companion enjoyed saying, with the satisfaction of a sophist. I could have instructed him. In circumstances for which conventional Avitus might have reproached me, Junius had cited these organisms as more sexually loyal than most humans. At Treves, neither loyalty nor affection were imaginable.

I attended constant banquets, not reclining, but upright on stools, gilded but unsteady, at a jasper-studded *stibadium*, at its horns presiding grander Household domestics, the Vice-Chamberlain, Deputy Masters of Offices, Requests, the Horse, or the Imperial Confessor. The atmosphere was womanish, though women were seldom present, appearing later for planned assignments. Reluctantly, I still forwent them. Through wine, lust, fatigue, they were immeasurably dangerous. My abstinence doubtless procured me a reputation for extreme perversion, which might, finally, increase my standing.

Furnishings were richer than the actual fare, at which seated between dying nosegays I met garlanded rhetoricians and teachers, for the Emperor, himself an uncultured soldier, valued education, and ordained numerous colleges and reforms. The teachers, like most State dignitaries, were mostly freedmen, often barbarian. All were outnumbered by the military, whose deference to them was perfunctory, and whose table manners were worse. I wondered how many earned their keep : few would have graced my payroll. They were always polishing torques and brooches, examining themselves in silver hand-mirrors, and the Saviour of Spain, a skinny youth of twenty, with crimson ankle-bracelets, wore an ebony comb in his green wig. Would the Augustus himself, Triumphant, Orthodox,

Father of Peoples, Shadow of the West, reveal himself in a guise more encouraging?

I remained alert for tell-tale gestures, verbal slips, listless errors, that paralleled the imitation jewels, mock-Parthian leather, garments spectacular but tawdry. The imperial palace more resembled a debased stoa. Table talk, though incessant, dared to be no more than highly coloured and neutral. Rhine battles, Gothic threats, the collapse of Britain, were scrupulously avoided. I did hear whispers of a great battle somewhere, which may not have occurred. That I had encountered no Briton here, might save me from malicious talk of conspiracy.

Conversations often began in Latin, then faltered, scattering into dog Greek, and Gallic and Germanic dialects, of which I feigned ignorance, together with an appearance of stupidity, not in itself easy. I learnt little of significance. Topics would start, then trail away like the efforts of athletes badly prepared.

'I understand, my very esteemed, that Jews living in conditions similar to racially-connected neighbours, develop dissimilar outlooks. How so?'

'I am forbidden to say, but can disclose this. Wars increase the size of our brains, and diminish those of women.'

'Would you say, Sextus, that women have much to develop in that quarter? What we require from them is surely perfected already?'

'That reminds me that the late Marcellinus gave his wife a special feast after each unfaithfulness to her. She was the fattest lady one's likely to see, unless our friend Dunius sees fit to marry on such terms.'

'It may be, it may be. Meanwhile, let me say that under the great Antonines, so just, so law-loving, as many people killed themselves as under the criminals. Is that not worth considering?'

Evidently not. Consternation ravaged all faces, which then at once closed up, before someone resumed as if nothing had been uttered, 'Days were once shorter, so I'm told.'

'Thanks to our Saviour, Gallus my friend. We are exploring our natures further than ever before. This is an era the greatest yet known, not forgetting the Medes and Babylonians.'

'Dreams, now. They come into their own, now that the oracles are sulking. I hear that some Etruscan diviners are expected. In China, a sage never revealed, even to himself, his fears of ghosts, rebellions, mighty events, yet his dreams were such that frequently he could neither eat nor drink, and he died of starvation.'

'It's said, I forget by whom, that our knowledge of dreams is about a thousand years behind our knowledge of physics and numbers.'

'Women can now count.'

'Journeys, journeys! Up, down, and across. Very grotesque. Towards what? I tell my children fate-tales. Seed falls, heroes conquer, riddles are answered, magic hills are climbed, until we meet our real selves.'

Despite my dislike of gardens, I gladly escaped to them from these cliques, anxieties, fevers, the beheadings in well-drained cells, unacknowledged but recognized. I envisaged the executioner's expression as he shaved the doomed neck of a minister hitherto loaded with exceptional favours.

The imperial park, very green, well-watered from the river, was usually empty, or appeared so. I wandered through still trees and flowers, towards the *palestra* where racers competed without visible disposition to win. I inspected opulent though ill-made pavilions on artificial islands, deserted amongst bushes cut into fawns, satyrs, trees planted fully grown, many wilting, and little skiffs waiting very bright and empty. Reflecting, I wanted not Vesta, like a garden flower too dependent, but Sylviana's acute sense.

Conscious of spies I visited the Baths. In *frigidarium,* in *sudatorium,* naked, hairy, paunched, on terraced marble reclined the West's leaders – Gauls, Franks, Africans. Grossly storeyed bellies overwhelmed the tools beneath, were hour-glasses arrested in hideous time. They sweated and grunted as masseurs pummelled them, or lay smiling, to be fanned and oiled, scraped, perfumed, coiffed. I heard of chariot races at Antioch, Christian Orthodox pledges to extirpate Christian Arians who had once caused so much frenzied bloodshed at Rimini, Emperor Constantius watching, surely sardonically, the holy ones entangling themselves with formulae that resisted meaning.

Nothing about the soaring prices of Egyptian wheat, Spanish oil, the cornering of Parian marble by imperial favourites.

In a sunlit, unroofed courtyard I unexpectedly saw, standing up to her thighs in dark blue water, framed between tall, scented alabaster vases, a naked girl, her pubis, in the Tyrrhenian mode, bare, like polished stone and floating like a faintly cracked shell, her head golden with lustrous hair worth two slaves to the Arras wig-makers.

Her eyes looked through me, or were blind, then a flock of birds swept over the sky, like a curtain being drawn, and, soundlessly, she had gone.

121

She was inescapable as, later, I paced the streets, the moon lighting rampart and tower, dome, column, statues, fretted balustrades, and the stark cross above the Palace.

# XVI

Before our sailing to Gaul, Britain became a fierce collateral of defeat. Lawcourts emptied : criminals, absconding prisoners, rebellious children roamed at will, avoiding the barbarians but often joining bacauds hovering outside towns. Post stations finally ceased, as the Picts surged towards London.

Even educated men were regarding the Conspiracy as nexus between forest and nerve, bog and dank temple. One heard plausible evidence, less of Cheru than of ancient Titans, driven far north by the gods, and surviving through gaunt, frozen centuries, monstrous growths gradually flaking away into ogrish tales, neither human nor wholly animal, with queer interbreedings that fined down empty faces to merciless, unblinking stares of Painted Men, Vagrants, Wizards, delirious for gaudy colours, raw, huge buttocks, infinite gorgings, the primeval conceptions of beauty.

I was not superstitious, but sensed the invisible manifestly at work, and no longer wholly despised popular beliefs that the long decline of the sacrifices had rendered gods eager for blood not their own. Quite possibly, the dead communicate more freely with barbarians, who are thereby confused by dictions, quarrels, disorders, from the half-seen or forgotten.

What remained of Roman Britain was helpless and bewildered. The prescribed, the usual, were rendered useless overnight. Parleying was incomprehensible to Picts : Attacots would accept hostages only as a free feast.

Watchfires on hills were closing in on London, generations of toil, planning, restraint to be wasted in a few months of harridan fury.

Britain needed a scalding summons to the last, demoralized troops, then measured withdrawal to walls, as preparation to counter-attack. But we were hopelessly dispersed. Western heights, the defenders hampered by refugees, were ringed by Scots : eastern sea forts by Scanians and Saxons. Aldborough was wrecked as all Brigantia succumbed. Word was spread, though by the Armenian, that Picts now deployed unknown metals which, if grasped tight, not only stabbed deep but inflicted nervous shocks on enemies still invisible. Was such stuff implicit in that tale of Cheru's sword?

With life pared to stark alternatives, even those most jealous and resentful agreed that rescue depended on my mission over bandit seas, through a Gaul that had become unknown. Praises fell over me from all sides; Sylviana's silence, though hurtful, was the more powerful, containing so many variations, at odds with Vesta's mournful admiration.

The Cirencester worthies joined me. We travelled to the coast, not in ambassadorial splendours but in clothing, like our escort, humiliatingly mean. Avoiding the great Stone Street, I chose the chalk ridgeway over the hills, often looking down on recently fired villas and cottages, and occasional groups of the ragged but armed, against a distant sky. On one scarp, an ancient henge, grey tall stones, in heat haze, suggested the dead : silenced, stylized, brooding. There I tightened my gear, for such stones, if approached too carelessly, can dislodge a brooch, ring, dagger, through a potency insufficiently analysed.

We had no adventures. Nearer the sea, horsemen still guarded villas, though country folk scuttled from us. I insisted we slept in the open, partly for haste and strategy, partly to early assert authority. These magnates were more at home in Villa society than myself; my interests demanded that they should be restricted to the unfamiliar, even alien, thus absolutely dependent on me.

Dover was free, thanks to prolonged native resistance, a few cool officers, and barbarian disunity, though the green, reassuring patrol boats had disappeared. A swift, well-armed brigantine awaited us, and, with our horses, we sailed at dawn into the grey sea. Twice we sighted long, ominous ships; I trembled at drowning, at my throat hooked out by vast hands under blue, pebbled eyes, but, deftly tacking, we reached land.

Roadways were mostly clear, with few signs of violence; round, wattle huts, clustering behind freshly-built stockades, were utterly soundless, though thin smoke indicated watching eyes. Bridges and crossroads, usually so crowded, though intact, were often empty; isolated mills were silent. Probably I alone noticed, scratched on walls, limed on gates, cut into trees, a rake, emblem of peasant radicalism. Yet Gallic peasants were not anarchic, they revolted for old independent Gallia.

Nearer Treves, communities were more open. Asses, slaves, decrepit horses, turned mill-wheels. Oxen drew carts and ploughs, villages of reed and daub, plaster and timber, though impoverished, were noisy. Several times I observed bales with my seal on them, and made sure my followers saw them too. Penned under ancient fortresses were Gothic prisoners, with long bodies but weak legs.

We were greeted pleasantly enough in taverns. Most trouble apparently came from the Emperor's mercenaries.

Fertile Moselle valleys, vine-covered slopes, showed continuing prosperity. We were joining files of mules with loaded panniers, lordly litters, opulent retinues, huge, decorated wagons, orderly slave-gangs and soldiers, barbarian captives. We had a long wait before passing through the Porta Nigra.

Treves is large, comparable to London, Cologne, Paris, Strasbourg. Ionic Baths, Basilica, Amphitheatre, Hippodrome, temples, churches, dazzled at the noon. Much, in white smooth coils, dated from Constantine, and was very bare, with a starkness that cowed. Many sculptors must be jobless, and I regretted the departure of gods, winged spirits, dolphins, enchanted foliage, from the frieze, portico, podium. The inessential fills many purses.

A gigantic, flowing Roma Dea confronted the Palace in a square dense with market stalls, donkey vendors, slow mannered officials, hustling messengers, itinerant hucksters, and the usual quacks screeching cosmic secrets, the buffoons, conjurors, religious processions.

High Priest of Jupiter, Emperor Flavius Valentinian was also a Christian, though, as a tough soldier, impatient with bullying or abstruse theological arguments. In the first courtyard a tall column was surmounted by a black cross, and, trying to embrace it, huddled cripples, madmen, shaven, dilapidated lepers.


After six weeks without one glimpse of Valentinian, the Consistory invited us to the Field of Mars, for the investiture of the Augustus' eldest son, Gratian, aged nine, brother of a younger Valentinian, as Caesar, heir to the Western Empire, an unenviable award, less grotesque than it sounds. As precaution against succession disputes, it was logical, though few legally-born sons had actually reigned.

The invitation was diplomatic, tricky, issued on behalf of the Senate and People of Rome, though the first was an insignificant curia of Christian zealots and the second a multitude of paid idlers, Italy itself sheltering behind legends from the Goths

In legatal collar and jewelled mantle, I had excellent position in a stand for distinguished *equestrians*. Long lines and squares of soldiers – Illyrians, Ligurian Highlanders, Syrians, Gauls, Macedonians, Thessalanians, Germans, Spaniards, all in pale shimmering surcoats and plumed helms, silver lances aloft – were stationed behind the mounted, visored Count of the Domestics and the Master of the Horse, and radiating from the Standards, bronze, or painted to resemble bronze. (Little was genuine unless provided by oneself, and not always then.)

The army gazed beyond its officers to a high, gilded platform and empty throne, *Sella Aurea*, with its gold and ivory slats, arm-rests ending in claws, legs fashioned into dolphins, and flanked by six giant Targeteers, encased in iron, with slanted javelins, sham-gold shields. Beneath hung a dense golden plate, the Unconquered Sun, under which pallid flames rose from bronze, spiralled bowls.

Massed in seven stands were magnates and their women, in sparkling tiaras, flowered robes, all murmuring like a vast concourse of doves, and from whom drifted aromatic clouds, while turbaned dwarfs gestured importantly amongst the richly decorated children, sallow and senile. On a special dais, shaded from the hot sky, were ranged the Master of Offices, Ursacius, and the Grand Chamberlain, both in sumptuous brocades and stored with secrets probably unwholesome. Circling them was the entire Consistory, repository of imperial will, together with the Bishop in blue and gold cape, a gemmed cross upheld before him by the Grand Keeper, all with flashing servitors. Here too, formalities were exact : a nod carefully affecting infinity, each bow, each inclination, reflecting some pattern of stars, the sun's course, degrees of divinity. The display was Asiatic, second-hand splendour stylized by Diocletian to overawe the army. Whoever ruled, the mangled spirits of slaughtered predecessors tinged the air he breathed, lay in the cup raised to dry lips, in the eyes of menials, in the soldiers roaring loyalty to his Eternity. Not for an instant would Flavius Valentinian Augustus, Regent of the Divine, forget them.

We had waited an hour, noisily expectant until, without warning, stilling a sudden, dangerous impatience, trumpets blasted and there unfurled the *Labarum*, white, with Jeheshua's blue *chi-rhu*, the standard of Constantine the Great.

126

By a shuddering clash of spears or smiting of sword on shield the troops could show fatal displeasure, but, that day, appeased by an enormous donative wrenched from taxpayers by the Warrior Emperor, they were cheerful, clanging shields against knee-plates and emitting a long acclamation for the Ever Devout, Ever Augustus, Fortunate, Invincible, Son of the Consecrated Sun, titles like lions mating.

He stood, very briefly, high above even the tallest stand, dazzling, inhuman, in purple chlamys thick with roughly cut emeralds, purple slippers, turban-shaped diadem crusted with pearls, golden oak leaves of Jupiter on his shoulders, balancing the golden cross at his breast. A prudent fellow, Valentinian.

The silence was now profound, like sea on the eve of a tidal wave, until, without seeming to move, he was seated, new shouts rolling up to him with the shrill cries of court ladies, while, utterly motionless, he received the sceptre and the orb of the world topped by a sparkling cross, ensigns and eagles streaming behind him.

With the resounding, regular surge of greeting in full flood, he stood up; it receded and died and, harsh, metallic, he addressed the legions in an oration majestic though clearly much rehearsed. Then, very slowly, not warily but as if matching a supernatural rhythm, he invested his boy with the purple surcoat and bright coronet, the massed ranks intoning : 'Hail Caesar Gratian. Immortality to Flavius Valentinian, Father and Protector.'

Fair, tall for his age, Gratian was too plump, his face too ingratiating, grateful not to his father but to these barbarian troops. He should have learnt from Valentinian, who stared into the sky, stern, impervious, as if deaf. Gratian merely grinned, perhaps forgetting what to do next. His jewelled ears and golden sandals seemed hired for the occasion, and I remembered with some foreboding those ambitious master-generals, Jovinus and Severus, and at once saw a hand near me pointing at a squad of shaggy cross-bowmen, and heard a jeer :

'Hail Gratian of blessed memory.'

Afterwards, I discerned the investiture more precisely. Its many unplanned allusions were not reassuring. Some years previously, Constantius, having murdered Julian's father, uncles, brother, forced him to exchange the philosopher's gown for a Caesar's purple in just such an ornate ceremony, then, hoping to get him killed, dispatched him against the Germans.

127

I had reason to suspect the quality of weapons and armour on parade. Leather shields painted iron grey, antique breast-plates inadequately scraped of rust. Only that motionless enlustred idol under the Diadem retained *aura*. 'Emperor of Rome' could still be more implacable, more commanding, than any Masked One, Mysterious Stranger, Cheru. The Emperor's gaze, that of a lion tamer notorious for fits of ungoverned rage, leashed his brutes inflexibly, though, should it falter, should his outbursts be ill-timed, a new Despot would be promising donatives and raising the long-poisoned chalice.

Before descending to an honourable station at the banquet, I imagined Valentinian as a child, bewildered by changes in the sky, and by silky adults withholding secrets that might destroy all.

Henceforward, I felt that the Palace, despite fawning grimaces from the resplendent officials and prim spies, survivors from so many reigns, was haunted, stricken, sheltering half-formed, broken-backed plottings, and, for my mission, useless. While Britain might have been totally consumed – those moonwashed cadavers stacked in the Fields of Light – I was stranded amongst presences seemingly disembodied. Yellow wigs passed above green marble; superbly pearled legs stood behind a black grille; from a curtain a silver glove, starry with trinkets, clutched a slim jade stick. Theatrical make-believe hung like gauze, distorting the movements behind it. Resonant titles deceived. An old lady in brilliant shawl and general's bracelets, eyes burning crazily on depleted skin, crouched on a stairhead praising dead Julian. An unseen man groaned that the Three in One had transformed his beloved into an ugly table. Courtyards sprouted 'the Essentials of the Empire', tired catamites, pink and fumbling, rancid with perfume, their buttocks puffy, their faces under floppy caps stained as if with faint plum juice.

I was not to meet the Augustus, but developed my style, not as beggarly provincial but reserved, polymathic, consequential ambassador, willing to advise the Empire on request. My professional instincts soon told me whom to ignore, whom to salute, and in what manner. I had, of course, made certain presentations from family depots : Palestinian balsam, Persian myrrh, Tuscan oil, Silurian gold.

I wished to inspect the celebrated Mint, its gold, its craft mysteries; my desire was applauded, arrangements were always about to be completed, but as the days passed, through wheedling smiles and attentive gestures I realized an obdurate, perhaps threatening refusal.

Autumn approached, though, within the Palace, seasons were anulled into airless monotony, while without, troops departed for Rhine and Danube, or clanked back with peasant heads on lances. Gallic revolts had been exceptionally violent. Gratian left in state for Milan : doubtless a Triumph would be celebrated in his name for shaking earth and sky, overcoming the Goths threatening even Uncle Valens, in Constantinople.

My own mails from Britain were presumably intercepted; I heard only stealthy whispers of marauders roving unchecked, Saxons beaching twenty miles up-river, near London, within catapult range of Painted Men.

Then, as I inwardly fretted, we were unexpectedly invited to a privy conference with the Consistory itself. My unrivalled chance, for I had continued tempting my colleagues into over-indulgence at table, so that they were now supine, befuddled, timid as corncrakes, in Junius' phrase. By enlarging on the dangers and responsibilities ahead, I manipulated them into imploring me to confront the crafty ministers alone, and, with a show of reluctance, I submitted.

In the square room of black and red marble in a secluded turret, I was, again, swiftly aware of the confusion of cheap and splendid. Hangings, depicting Hercules clubbing Cacus, were so clumsy that the bruisers were identical : from an atrociously painted amphora filtered an extravagant and rare perfume, the bright matting was trashy but the god or saint above us was masked with authentic gold. The wine, excellent, stood on a wretched table.

The ministers were headed by the Illustrious, Ursacius, Count of the Offices, bald, fleshy, gracious, wrapped as if against cold in suave turquoise, a thick silver chain at his neck. The stones on his broad, official belt seemed flawless, cut in fine old Bythinian style, and in such array that they might have been his whole collection, worn constantly, against theft. I then realized that his sleeves, sumptuous Indian silk, had been sewn onto coarser, Gallic stuff, embroidered with awkward birds and petals.

His movements, though ample, were slow, as though the robe concealed a metal vest.

The Illustrious, Most Intimate Friend, his grey eyes shrewd, led the talk in Latin, very bad, though with wondrous affectation. The others, a formal group of wigs, stripes, badged ribbons, each with golden stylus, waxen tablets, sat at varying distances from him, assenting, nodding, winking to order, following each intonation as they

129

might the result of a wager. They were more easily imaginable as petty intriguers than statesmen. Eyes like live currants in dough, a nose beaked like a snipe, hands exquisitely manicured, a mouth continually open, as if fear or boredom had exacted extreme revenge. Save for Ursacius, all wore some martial detail – sword-belt, hand-guard, dagger – as if convincing themselves that they were really in camp, holding the frontier.

Along the walls, on benches, behind small stools, tallowy monks had quills raised above papyrus.

Preliminary compliments were well-oiled. I was honoured kinglet, my abilities were praised from Caledonia to the Sacred Palace, few indeed spoke of anything else. Britain was renowned only for my sojourn there, my least breath was a precious gift to the world.

Finally, from those delicious sleeves, Ursacius deftly produced some parchments, smiling even more comfortably, as if about to announce an infallible cure to King Midas.

'Now, my dear friend, revered and most truly respected, the Augustus is distressed . . . I say further, he permits himself to be mortified by the failure of food supplies and fiscal dues from Britain. An irregularity. I could put it more strongly.'

So could I. Though my fixed equanimity may have challenged him to do so, I was astounded. Evidently, however, this too was decorative embellishment, for he at once resumed, his flowing tones occasionally betraying a harsher glint, an involuntary signal to beware. I was probably more sophisticated than he had expected, though, with his own eloquence so capricious, so profuse, I hoped that the nearby Master of Rhetoric would remain silent.

'Fortunately, times have never been more gracious, ordered, beneficent. I use the term "quiescent". It follows that the small, I should say trifling contributions from your rebellious province have yet to seriously inconvenience the Treasury, insulting, indeed worse, as it necessarily is to the person of our most holy Lord.'

I braced myself myself for the worst. Rulers make invasions an excuse for crushing levies, which officials spend on themselves. They sometimes invent invasions.

The monks wrote, the ministers sighed, the principle on which the Augustus selected them seemed uninviting. A sleeve permanently covered Ursacius' left hand, if it existed; the Master of Rhetoric was one-eyed, the rest were lop-shouldered, twitching as if helplessly fatigued, or with scars beneath their paint; as if they were freedmen,

130

lately released by brutal masters.

Ursacius' manner had insinuated that I represented rebellion. Quietly I intervened, concisely describing the situation with which he must have been well enough familiar. Calamity was from Hibernia and Caledonia, Scanians might soon exhaust their tempestuous impetus. The Germans, horseless, tactically stupid, raw in organization, could be outwitted, outpaced, outfought, by cavalry, and by the intelligence and initiative displayed by Emperor Julian but ten years back. Julian, who had desired a professional, well-paid peasant army, trained and mobile. Who (my smile was as persuasive as his own) could doubt that the Augustus, an inspired survivor of Julian's staff, could by his usual wise adaptation, and by his very name, quickly restore Britain to her allegiance, with the dispatch of a mere troop of regulars? With the barbarians routed, bacauds would helplessly subside.

I mentioned, as if it were of no importance, that in recognition of the diligence, assiduity, generosity of the Augustus and his munificent advisers, I could provide some Baltic amber, and further gold.

Then I paused. The monks desisted, in unpleasant stillness the bleached, ranked faces remained expressionless. Silence had many voices. All was too far from dogs barking, hucksters calling, from bells and dice, the stir of petitioners, of life; I could have been in a condemned cell, and perhaps I was. The cunning were visibly inheriting the world.

Ursacius maintained his agreeable manner. 'The Augustus Eternal has condescended to incline his ear.'

I could only envisage Sylviana's disrespectful wonder at the Augustus doing anything so commonplace, though Ursacius' minute shrug suggested that Britain, even in distress, made too small a noise to attract an ear so almighty.

'First . . . ,' the delicate fingers on the only hand available dismissed the matter as barely sufferable, 'the treasury is authorized temporarily to forgo your taxes, as an expression of magnanimity commensurate with available funds, the substantiality of which is destined for the rigour, the glory, of the Empire, and to bind it still closer in the affections of His Eternity. It is further authorized to dispense two talents of silver to whatever force is considered for the pacification of Britain.'

Two talents! In a time of stable currency, Julius Caesar's debts

131

were once eight hundred, of gold : to win over Spanish magnates he spent three hundred. This I did not mention, nor that Valentinian's mean gifts to the Alemans had earlier ensured a serious war. At home, my reputation demanded more than this suggestion that Britain was little more than a liability, easily written off, dumped in a Saxon sea.

To speak of the abortive appointment of Severus would have been an aspersion on imperial resolution. Ursacius' polite incredulity would deny any such appointment. Severus was preoccupied in Africa, Asia, Illyria, Severus did not exist.

Ursacius had retired into his voluminous self, yet the conclave was unfinished, perhaps scarcely begun. I waited, after professing requisite gratitude. The monks still bent over their papers. There followed a nod, barely perceptible, from the Quaestor, thin, morose, and the dry voice of the Master of Rhetoric, dripping from a bubble-face under bright, yellow, artificial curls.

Glancing at the Illustrious, like an actor reassuring the prompter, he clenched his hand, blinked his solitary eye, then said, as though he had already been speaking and was now providing a minor codicil, 'The legions have never been more victorious. At present they are undergoing extensive manoeuvres, revising strategic maxims and drill under Jovinus, Jovinus himself. These are guaranteed overwhelming success against Alemans, Vandals, Burgundians, which is already assured by the Augustus now finding time to take back the command into his own hands. He is, you appreciate, the foremost military engineer of our age, and has planned complete refortification of the eastern riparian frontiers, on a scale without precedent. This will secure peace for ever, of which you in Britain will share the benefits and will be eager to help pay the costs.'

The imperial ear, the imperial hands! I affected his own indifferent accent. 'Nevertheless, Britain would still welcome a gracious application of tactics, employed by what the Illustrious has so neatly, so perfectly, described as a force for pacification.'

The Quaestor's very nose looked aggrieved, but Ursacius returned, leaning very slightly towards me. The chain, slowly magnifying, briefly glittered, reminding me of some sharp, distorted grin which had escaped the smooth face and shark's eye.

'My honoured friend . . . to speak precipitately and thanklessly is against your nature, the remarkable and boundless sense by which you make such admired progress throughout the Empire. It is not too much to declare that the Augustus numbers you amongst those he most gravely trusts.'

In his fulsome grandiloquence, the man was a superb performer, a Professor of Dignity, though one I would at once match. 'Your Noblissimus, at least, would understand in his signal profundity that, despite certain internal dislocations and irregularities, we in Britain, already on our knees before the extravagantly awarded talents of silver, would be gratified, and are indeed prepared, to provide ground for the manoeuvres and drill, and indeed targets for the most elaborate exercises, not forgetting any refortifications that the Augustus, so rightly acclaimed for his engineering skills, I should properly say genius, can allow us.'

'Beautifully spoken, Drusus. Now do me the pleasure of hearing that, by next year, let us say a twelfth month, the Emperor's extraordinary projects in Gaul will have been completed. Almost certainly so.'

He could have spat in my face, I restrained myself from doing so in his. He had doomed Britain. To endure another year, quite alone, amid subject races deliberately kept unarmed and untrained by the jealous State, assailed by Europe's most monstrous stock, our commanders dead, half the island lost . . . such was the imperial offer. Ruined pretenders, crouching in twilight, would greet me in ghostly desolation.

Did any of these flabby, fishblooded creatures remember the words of Marcus Aurelius? 'For all its pomp, the Senator's purple robe is but sheep's wool dyed from shellfish.'

The washy smiles, thin congratulations now broken over me from these farceurs, sickened and mocked.

'As a very particular favour, most admirable Drusus, the Lord and Despot, with his own hand, in the sacred ink, purple ink, no less, has already instructed the most truly exalted of the Companions to attend, in full time, to remedy our useful Britain, to restore the gainful and exact retribution for all insults to the imperial Name. The Emperor is not unmindful of your people's own responsibility, some of it dire, most of it condign, for errors, losses, tribulations, but has not allowed this to detract from his grieved and paternal concern. He has commissioned our Spanish wonder-worker, Count Flavius Theodosius, descendant of Trajan, the divine Trajan himself, to visit Britain at the season aforementioned.'

He sat back, as if he already saw Jeheshua in fire and cloud transforming the world.

That night I reported a suitable version to my fellows, whose eyes started in abject wonder, whose tongues stuttered my praises. I had secured them earth-sung Theodosius, of whom none of them had heard and for whom, I suspected, Britain might well signify ignominious exile. Mustering all my powers of persuasion, I asserted that he would come when recovered from a heroic wound not yet to be divulged even to to them. Jovinus' Triumph, Severus' victories were rightly his.

Their relief was heartfelt, they embraced me, a most superior magnate knelt, slobbered over my hand, mumbling that, but for me, Britain would verily be Pictland, a gruesome catacomb.

True, but I needed to depart. Palaces might be my proper station but Treves' foundations were gangrenous. The very sea was safer, I had been dared into a capital danger. If Theodosius was real, he might never reach Britain, might vanish overnight. A favourite, even a master general, lives precarious as any lover.

Yet I had failed neither Britain nor myself. My say was heard in the West, had achieved whatever was possible could our canton but endure a year, at costs however drastic, old Drusus must be patron, guardian, even inventor of Theodosius.

## XVII

'Excellent, of course, very busy! Inspired behaviour! Do you consider it of serious importance?'

'Sylviana, don't play. The pattern, the nature of Britain will change. You will see the return of the gods.'

'You speak as if either is really desirable.'

She was unchanged, lolling in pretty clothes on a blue hot afternoon as she murmured, 'You see yourself as the wise, hoary centaur, and indeed there's a bit of the horse about you, though sometimes I seem to hear more of the cow. Yet you do spoil it when you start neighing. I can only think of you as rich, and I suppose you don't always consider yourself absolutely adult.'

Silly, teasing, she had always to be envious. Her husband, her clever friends, depended on me. They stole to my door for loans, credit, a word in certain quarters, letters of transit. They might sneer at my indifference to satirical fireworks, allusive jests, but they misquoted Ovid and got their sums wrong. The Armenian had proclaimed himself greater than Vergil and no one dissented. With greater justice, I could have done so myself. I was not only worldly-wise, I had wisdom.

Wearing the jewelled bracelet awarded me in the Emperor's name, I had first visited Metellus. Sylviana, as I had hoped, was present. Their wine was almost rancid, surely none of my own, but neither, usually so fastidious, seemed to notice. Doubtless, my arrival had over-excited them. The revelation that I was friend and confidante of Theodosius, putative saviour, elicted from Metellus a few tired compliments, decidedly irrelevant, then he wandered away.

Sylviana, with a fine display of hospitality, poured more wine, but still said nothing. Faint lines were traced under her eyes, her dark fringe hinted at grey, though her manner was as ever, drily amused as if at dullish but inexpensive entertainment.

'What a very boring man you are!' She smiled in unexpected

friendliness, rising, crossing, seating herself beside me in ribald respect, as if she had glimpsed the imperial officials at Treves, their stately titles, serpentine voices. 'And what a nasty bracelet! You've been buying from people with worse taste even than yours!'

Like men of all ranks, I was now wearing Celtic dress : breeches, short tunic, cloak, useful for sudden mobility; coolly, she touched my loins, then nodded, in our former complicity, 'It's still there,' adding as if to her steward, 'keep it tight.' She repeated an indecent line of Ovid's, as he reflected on a bodily response embarrassingly lukewarm.

I was glad she was still not pregnant, and might be confiding that my tireless vitality might yet serve her better than anything else in these epicene surroundings. She would do all save declare herself direct, perhaps testing my need for her.

'You're no September swimmer, Drusus.'

She did not explain but seemed disposed to begin our first intimate talk since her marriage. Her smile was more natural, so, to prolong her mood by frustrating it, fanning her discontents and desire, I pleaded business and left her, rather pleased with my own restraint, and was soon thinking, not of her naked body, but of Metellus, my oldest friend, and the divergence of our careers. Enervated, his dragonfly graces were soiled. For too long he had hunted boar recklessly, drunk and wagered, while debts accumulated and interest mounted. He still sauntered towards nowhere, with too much *placebo,* and nothing into which to change; even his courage, which might now have served us well, had chilled, whereas I . . . just so. I had claims on the world, with no archaic dreams of retiring to a Sabine farm in small, rough hills, or watching sunsets in Bath or Baia, sipping Salernian, or joining Thracian or Egyptian cenobites to study unreadables, or freeze in Scythia amongst hideous Alans, perfecting my spirit through consolations of squalor.

That night I bedded Vesta, though with thoughts elsewhere, masterfully reaching the target, relishing her cries as much as my own surges, glad of her greeting of me as a historical figure.

# XVIII

We had landed furtively at an inconspicuous Kentish islet, autumn storms having scattered Franks and Saxons. Inland, we at once met blackened trees, gashed and scalded fields, general devastation, a singed emptiness beyond which hovered wolves, wild cats, the night thick with underworld grunts and ringed with fire. Most of the Haestingi and Cantiaci had fled to the huge Anderida forest, and only by chilly detours in search of Thames fords, hours of crouching in undergrowth, did we reach Silchester, many days overdue.

Outlying copses, vineyards, even shrubs were fouled or destroyed. A *vallum*, six feet deep, now surrounded the town, the excavated earth, turfed and stoned, forming a rampart. In my absence, had Brunnus grabbed dictatorship to achieve a feat so considerable?

All gates were guarded, elderly watchmen ranged the walls, and we were admitted by ragged boys with drawn daggers.

Like most Roman towns, Silchester was built on a draught-board plan, the right-angled, slightly sloping streets easy to barricade. Grass now flourished on cracked pavings. In arcades, at corners, stood hang-dog figures, obviously refugees.

All had to be reconsidered, one must be a strategist, seeking not gods smiling disdainfully from the ether, but fully paid police, perhaps with a change of leadership.

(When you, you and you hear that the police have abandoned you, does your spirit soar, like Pegasus, chanting 'Freedom at last!', or do you huddle in your bed, praying that doors will hold?)

Aurelius, the clerks, barbers, cooks and the rest, welcomed me with gladness and relief. Fresh leaves garlanded the small, grave, household gods, pleasing me, though their powers were feeble, their reality probably void.

I wasted no time in getting reports, inevitably bad. Sums owed me were unpaid, scores of packhorses lost, Aurelius' accounts were in strict order but his own riverside holding had been burnt, his slaves killed or deserting. I guaranteed compensation but was not displeased. His considerable investments in my concerns would make him labour more thoroughly.

My garden had suffered in some disturbances, the cherry trees were slashed. With many walls demolished to provide bricks, gardens were dangerous.

Life was adapting to the instinctive through headlong events, but Silchester had had no external attack. A defence committee ruled each street, responsible to Brunnus, who was executing thieves, enforcing edicts against hoarders and profiteers. Famine threatened, unknown since the Conquest, save during plague.

No Brunnus, however, had ordained the *vallum* and the new regulations. Valentinus was back with some scores of infantry, and had got himself appointed Praetor, with total powers. Illegal, but what did that now mean? He had also added to himself the ancient office of Censor, inquisitorial, all-seeing. Similar revolutions had occurred elsewhere. None had withstood him, Brunnus was his creature. Until Theodosius came.

Already, Theodosius, even the Augustus, like my own plans seemed thin, even wraithish, though I determined to keep a bold face.

I listened intently to Aurelius. From outlying districts, Valentinus was rounding up gladiators, brutes without hair or wits, with swollen limbs and glazed eyes: wrestlers with bitten cheeks and necks: all mostly jobless for years and willing enough. The amphitheatre, outside the walls, was again in use, for drill and executions. Boy conscripts collected taxes, supervised slaves on the new defences, reinforced Brunnus.

That night, Valentinus summoned me, sending a special pass, for streets were now kept empty after dusk.

In poor lamplight, the Basilica glinted with soldiery. The clank of metal was everywhere, side aisles were crammed with weapons. Deep in the interior, red, bulbous, sweating, in rough, pigskin cloak, Valentinus received me at a refectory table, looking like a hog and eating like one, rootling, grubbing, scattering, plunging back in hurry to fill himself further, fat morsels dripping from his lips. He was more than a pig, he was a flat-cheeked Hun, a rebel slave, sacking a city.

Uninvited to sit down, I deliberately did so. Above the soiled, brutal nose, small eyes noted my imperial bracelet.

Without waiting for him to speak, I carefully built up for him my grand reception at Treves, my procurement of Theodosius and, touching my bracelet, my intimacy with the Augustus.

He seemed not best pleased, but professed curiosity about the Court. Naturally, I said, I had told them all, the Emperor himself, about Valentinus' prowess in beleagured Britain, at which he grinned like a schoolboy, then nodded ominously at my description of Caesar Gratian.

I left without permission, though not before he had demanded that I join his military council. This I had the right to expect.

Inescapably, Cheru would be rejoicing, the prongs of his attack were deep into Britain, which lay stuck like a Cretan bull, expiring in bloody dust.

Picts were everywhere, yet nowhere in particular, flitting down rivers, poisoning Kentish wells, castrating prisoners near Wroxeter. One town offered surrender without being summoned, only to find them vanished. Brigantine resistance was negligible, few spies returned, thermal Buxton was ravaged. Louth was in flames. London suffered fire darts from land and water, though Saxons had withdrawn a few miles, the broad fierce warriors apparently wary of Picts. All mints had ceased, the largest sea forts were emptied, Germans held most of the eastern coast, and, in the south, were nearing Gwynchester, encroaching on Pevensey's great towers. Other towns remained unmolested, scattered outposts stranded amid waves of frightfulness. Children nailed to trees, older women buried alive.

Messages crept in from quarters hitherto unknown, probably treacherous. Scots were deep up Severn, side-stepping Caerleon and Caerwent, falling back before Bath, not yet endangering Cirencester, but flooding smaller places, thronging plains and valleys, stabbing, crucifying, piling coracles and wagons with plunder, then separating into blood groups. Around Silchester, old Atrebatan resentment of the haughty Belgics might yet entail disaster. The defeated, particularly if illiterate, are sustained by memories. Belgic collaboration with Rome, three centuries back, was unforgiven.

Bacauds swarmed, but our slaves remained docile, after several, belonging to Manlius, a grain contractor, had fled by night, to be found still close to the *vallum*, naked, gnawed, their stomachs gaping, throats torn out : by wolves? by Attacots?

I had always been careful with slaves. Even emperors can fatally offend them. In bed, at table, one was at their mercy. Never familiar with them, I was even-tempered, knowing when to pretend anger or generosity, and, as others had done, I decided to risk arming certain of them, though even in my presence they now chattered with a license that Aurelius and I were too busy to check; I overheard unlawful prayers, queer curses, scraps of unknown speech hitherto unuttered, and invocations to Annyn, the Celtic underworld.

Avitus looked strained when at last I could go to him. Marulla was absent, I wondered if she lay sick, perhaps under-nourished, with Avitus too proud to admit it. Undeniably, all had worsened. Or she might be in darkness, communing with powers known only to women.

I questioned the old man about Valentinus.

'He arrived a week after your departure. Very dirty, I would call it woebegone, his men exhausted. Yet he was soon praising himself for incredible rearguard actions, god-smitten upheavals against odds insurmountable. Oh indeed, with Picts tireless as hydra heads! Our new Hercules, though more likely Commodus. So be it! My observations suggest that he objects to the lies of others, without himself possessing much love of truth. He is, of course, a general!'

His voice, always low, diminished further, against slaves, against spies. 'Women, of course, flock to offer themselves. Disgraceful abundance adorns his table. The Curia's an officers' club, the Council exists on Valentinus' say, and controls everything. Brunnus reports to him alone. This is interesting, and I advise you to watch it closely. He gives Brunnus much credit for the town's survival, but gives it too loudly, shifting some of the responsibility. Such people tend to shout when uneasy about their position, and Valentinus always seems to be addressing a mob, even when he is not. He managed to get troops from Cirencester, and a few veterans to whom he is Hector in person, leaving the place under-manned, and with one of his creatures installed as governor. I rate him undisputed master of anything left between Thames and Severn, whatever they may be doing in London. We have no option. He is energetic, without pity, without morality. Even you and I will have to defer, until he gets himself destroyed. If Homer is to be believed, Mars is liable to setbacks. Valentinus is no Carausius. Necessity breeds such earth giants. We should be grateful,' Avitus' smile was grey, 'glad that he has not bowed to the barbarian gale and defaulted. Now he ejects squatters, charges our great ones handsomely for the privilege of re-entering their own habitations, those he has not distributed to his favourites. Well!' His wrinkled hands moved painfully. 'You may find worse than he. Readingas has already had two conflagrations. Rioters, you know. Hungry misfits. Even here, they are starting to demand more than can be had. Of Rome, Valentinus knows nothing. To him, the world is no more than a farmyard, controlled by a dung-hill cock.'

I said that I preferred Mars, my ancestor, to Jeheshua, to whom the defence of our homes would be only the defence of what we had no right to possess.

'Our young Bishop will answer that for you. He urges us to remain awake for what he calls *Cledon*, a prophetic sign. Marulla has told me that a bright circle has indeed been seen round the sun, the same as Antony saw before Actium. Not, perhaps, auspicious, unless we agree to call each other Octavian.'

I enjoyed the occupational routine, ransacking for food, cloth, oil, weapons, medical stores. I arranged the future as thoroughly as any Valentinus or Brunnus, though no better than them able to guarantee success. Theodosius lay like a talisman not yet available, perhaps mislaid. My cells were stuffed with useless coin. Only debtors were truly solvent. The more they owed, the more their creditors had to ensure their survival. I myself had to trust the goodwill of those hitherto my reluctant dependants. With the ruling class existing on sufferance, I was compelled to rely on loyalty, affection, love, which I commanded less than a Metellus, Avitus, even Valentinus.

Hyacinthus still remained, crouching behind his door like a scorpion short of blood, debarred from his London protectors. Needing security, he had joined the Christians, only to be confronted with his name chalked, in fish shape, amongst the rather specialized inscriptions in latrines. Compassion for such a man would shame my moral principles.

External trade was extinguished. No convoy was safe, barter was replacing finance, and I dispatched Hyacinthus some inferior cabbage and useless malt. His gratitude was servile.

Curiosity was perhaps the largest of my own many gifts, and I watched for new personalities to emerge. Now, even timid Vesta had joined a street committee, without, of course, shedding her duties to myself.

Lying on her, I occasionally failed, though the responsibility was largely hers.

'Drusus, you are so tired. You do too much. You uphold us all.'

'Yes, I am tired.'

Though actually, between spasms of doubt, sometimes fear, I

141

thrived on the drama of our shrinking Britain. Sylviana was wrong in saying, long ago, that one is what one is. No, I retorted, very aptly, we are what we choose to be. Metellus had chosen to be only Metellus.

The Armenian had vanished, perhaps murdered, more likely deserting. His sniggering anecdotes were not lamented. Flavia and Flavian, 'the two wives', were unseen, reputedly indulging in obscene mimes, and worse.

Temples were crowded not only with fugitives and the sick, but those needing propitious dreams and omens, immersion in sacred pools, expensive lustrations, spiritual quicksilver. Sacrifices, though forbidden by new food edicts, increased surreptitiously. Rumours began of children and virgins slitted in alleys, gardens, drains.

Autumn displayed unusual tints and blurs, as if from the stark growth of mortality. I disbelieved that ghosts often pushed open urns and graves, but something of spirit did seem to affect the air, more than exhalation of the putrid. Christians prated about Alban, their anti-Roman magus. Martyr cults flourish on human credulity, and I had sometimes considered promoting one, to develop civic trade.

Demented sectaries raided rival shrines unchecked, while the British populace brooded sullenly on unsavoury nature gods fed by dank woods, diseased soil, bitter fruits. Not for them our southern apricot, cherry, fragrant wine. Monsters, plated, tusked, long thought extinct, were said to be lumbering from the depths of the burning forests. Rufinius 'Curses' Sabellinus, in charge of morals, had peasant refugees expelled for yelling about the revenge of Nodens, Light in Dark. Those who should have known better were whispering of Llew Llawr, with magic hair kept unshorn; survivors of the Followers of Nero were transferring to him, with matted knee-length locks, brandishing daubs of him dressed as a shepherd, seated in an osier-basket, and resembling a hirsute beehive. Streets were thronged as if by gibbering satyrs. From the slum fane, for long almost derelict, of the bear-god Artos, with its ikons of a tree stuck with a sword, sounded dreary pipings and, allegedly drunk on bull's blood, a naked fool promised redemption by a wise child, a talkative demagogic demigod, even Marulla's bright circle.

I retained enough acumen not to wholly despise the despicable, and agreed with Junius that, throughout Britain, the smashing of so many sacred and ancestral abodes might be releasing energies wayward and electric, vulgarly related to magic, thus magnifying the chaos. Even

142

Christians feared gods left homeless, and, helpless against Pict and sky, people undeniably felt jostled by the invisible. Yet I had a keen nose for charlatans, and drove them off wholesale. To repel demons, I was offered a most rare repast, apparently ear-wax and pigeon dung. A certain Antiochus proposed to improve my own shadow, protecting me not only from weapons but spells. Nevertheless, I once found myself, quite sober, staring at a slab of stone and expecting it to move. I was back in childhood, seeing a slave gaze at me from over a wall, then disappear, convincing me that a head had been placed on the ledge and, meeting my eye, had fallen off.

A sortie to protect a food convoy was ambushed by bacauds. Valentinus himself led cavalry against a Saxon camp, capturing javelins and hides, admitting no losses. At night, the town throbbed with uneasy shadows : all cressets were unlit to save oil, all windows shuttered. Once, from the blackness, flaming arrows sped over the walls, firing thatch and timber. Slaves murmured about the Icenic queen burning London, Colchester, Verulam, long ago. Nothing was extraordinary. We were the blind, receiving signals through ear-lobes, fingertips, foreskins.

Poison was feared more than arrows. From Pictish elk-horn darts, from wells and conduits. I myself was more perturbed by informers, now called *delators*, from those used by the wicked yet nervous Emperor Commodus, and who had denounced and murdered with impunity. Valentinus scarcely reassured me by grunting that justice could no longer be a matter of debate, only a matter of decree. I felt he was quoting, from a source distinctly lurid.

If Theodosius never came, and if the barbarians receded, each region might have spawned a Valentinus, thrusting towards a deadly prize, the Diadem of Britain.

Late in November I found sentries outside my own warehouses and granaries, forbidding even me entry without Council permission counter-signed by the Praetor. A lesser man would have submitted, but I at once set off to protest, and was kept waiting while women, lutists, jugglers, took precedence.

When at last he received me, his tufted eyebrows and rough mouth were unfriendly.

'Our friend Brunnus will know all about that. He may have been too eager to look after you. But you'll lose nothing. The fellows protect it. You alone are free from requisitions. Your fine stuff's safe.'

The implications about my personal luxuries was a threat, and I could only assent. Valentinus and Brunnus, pig and snake. The pig needed handling with metal gloves, for he had crude popularity as fighting man. Brunnus would stand or fall with him. I could only wait, for what might never happen.

Junius suggested that a prolonged stare would appease most animals : experience had taught me that barbarians could be restrained for as long as you could keep smiling. With Valentinus I maintained an idiot smile, remembering the Augustus himself, enthroned above seething crowd and ferocious Guards, surely holding himself rigid only by prodigious will.

With roads so often barred, shortages inexorably increased and, at last, I welcomed those sentries against incipient unrest. I had very considerable stores. I might die, but not of starvation. Without Theodosius, others probably would.

Earlier, I had been constantly questioned about Theodosius. My replies were vague, hinting at supreme secrets, intimacies necessarily undisclosed, and at last the questions lapsed into a respect sometimes, as the weeks passed, touched with the scepticism I myself so often felt.

Citing an emergency provision of Constantius the Pale, Brunnus ordered three looters to be beaten to death in the Forum, and announced that others would be flayed. A butcher's slave was said to have cooked and devoured his own hand.

Some of my hidden regional agents still remained secure and loyal, though at fearful cost. A big load of malt and oatmeal, destined for London, was ambushed on my behalf, some of which I dispatched to Valentinus and Brunnus as Protectors of the Poor. No signs emerged of the poor having reason for gratitude.

With winter becoming exceptionally cold, famished packs of men and beasts would suffer worse, roving icy valleys, huddled in bleak woods, on moors and slopes in cutting winds, nerving themselves for agonized raids.

Midwinter saw fire rites both for Jeheshua and the Unconquered Sun; solar disks raised on spears, a tree trunk burnt to alien chants which were now accepted without query. At the January Kalends, older ceremonies, were large crowds, guilty for the religious neglect of recent years, which had helped the barbarian victories. Valentinus and all his Council attended, old Avitus stood bareheaded in snowy winds, shivering but upright. The annual altar of Jupiter Optimus Maximus was buried as before, images were upheld painted to resemble the All Loving, Son of the West, Hero of Heroes, Ever

Victorious, Undoubted, Undisputed Joint Father of Nations. Libations were poured to all gods (wine we could ill afford; I hoped the priests had watered it). Solemn oaths were renewed to Valentinian and Valens, led by the Praetor, braying promises of no more significance than a parrot clacking, 'All is atoms.'

That night the regulations were relaxed, a mob rushed through streets waving torches and bull-roarers, wearing horns, wings, skins, their gestures and imprecations licentious, their high, rather eerie cries wrenched from bodies already streaked with intimations of famine.

As a relief from strategies I occasionally mused over the lost peace, so recent, yet distant as Byzantium. Odd, concise instants of brightness. Evening roofs after an arduous journey, dawn in Vesta's bed, Junius in a meadow, showing me that grasses were far from identical and explaining the love of a particular bird for a red rock, a sudden halcyon smile from a stranger. Goldsmiths beating out the pure line. Those short nights, long afternoons with Sylviana. Sunny days, she said, lack history.

Now the sun seemed irredeemably lost and there was too much history. I myself was dangerously exposed, my prime weapon no longer my storehouses but fabled Theodosius, Lord of Reconquest. Was he a grizzled veteran, beardless novice, another Valentinus? He might never come. With Britain battered into gristle, Valentinus, Praetor, Censor, Dictator, might betray us, at best leading Germans and Scanians against the worst.

He was unimaginable weeping for a lost girl, enjoying evening lights, toying with the past as game or daydream : all that makes the superior man. Protector against barbarians, he himself was a barbarian, the headstrong tempered by cunning, with plenty to do but nothing to say. He might salvage the canton like an illiterate child rescuing a book from the marsh, then, puzzled, lighting a fire with it. He and Brunnus, I heard, had been compared by Flavian to nostrils reared exclusively in privies. I could not have expressed it better, and, forced to associate with them, I did not try to.

Throughout that iron winter, 'When Theodosius comes' was everywhere; hopeful, resigned, incredulous or, even in my presence, sarcastic.

On my outer wall, urchin malice had scrawled an overweight senator swallowing coins dropped by a mailed and crested rider. A kite flying into rain and wind was hailed 'Theodosius', premonition of some Roman Cheru. The debt-ridden, defaulting and harassed conceived all bonds, all bargains grandly cancelled, the streets awaited a Deliverer proclaiming the new and wondrous, the more preposterous the more believable. Tattered children moaned 'Theodosius' and asked if he could really fly.

Misfortunes were falling like nets over shredded Britain; toil and virtue might avail nothing, but let this be once admitted and we were utterly ruined. In spring, the Barbarian Conspiracy might tear down London, the smouldering peasants again fire Gaul, the Germans drive towards Strasbourg, Sens, Treves itself, towards Paris, Marseilles, towards Italy, there to link with Goths, strangle the West, isolate Valens in his Sacred Palace.

## XIX

February, 368, sky and stars frozen hard as the earth. By day I was allotting favours, registering supplies, revising rations, receiving deputations, reporting to Valentinus. During long, drooping nights, when the town filled with charnel gloom, I was usually alone. My spirit too often slumped, to be concealed even from Vesta and Junius. Save for ancestral busts, my possessions were barren, without associations. At Sens, my family could be permanently lost. Like some barbaric tatterdemalion I would start at a shadow, a crack on the wall. My nails had turned bright pink. Wine comforted, but I needed my wits. A thin vapour pervaded the house, felt rather than seen, in which domestics seemed leaner, very apathetic, too akin to the derelicts outside withering through lack of salt. Skins were patchy, eyes sunk, limbs trembled, we might soon be hunted nomads.

Valentinus had placed two guards at my door, sometimes I thought them gaolers. His edicts continued. Moss must be gathered to staunch wounds, little linen being now available : dogs be killed for food, householders report all suspect activities to the Censors. Only Valentinus' wolfhounds were immune, as gifts from the Emperor's Companion, Fullofaudes, though I recalled him buying them at a Cirencester fair.

Then, one windy oppressive night, all Silchester shook at an immense pounding, then shrill, owlish cries. Despite myself, I was at once fantastical. Cheru, Grimmer, Caurasius II, were striding from a baleful planet to finish us. My blood seemed to stop. My household stood trembling, like Asiatics at the roar of flames as the sun rises.

Recovering, I traced the blows down to the Julian Gate and, grabbing a spear, was swiftly out with my guards, joining soldiers and random neighbours. The Gate was already down; in dust and uproar, a wild company of kilted, bare breasted Scots *Dalriads,* knives raised, Germans with raw hide shields, short swords, straps on huge bare knees, and a horde of bacauds, bright-eyed from hunger, streamed forward, hurling rocks, torches, darts, yelling war cries. Infernal, writhing and thrusting in the blown glare, they had already fired some houses, striving to slash through defenders now massing across the narrow ways. The Dacian dye-quarter was quickly aflame, sooty smoke tumbling from stacks and vats, throwing acrid green over the struggles. Valentinus had come, shouting above the din. We swung whatever we could – clubs, stools, planks, axes, poles, hearthstones. Arrows and tiles were shot from windows, fountains and benches thrown up as barricades, strenuous grunts and challenges mingling with whines and yelps in the wind. Steamy air was rank with death. One big fellow with tribal curses rushed from Valentinus' side into the assailants, who briefly gave ground. I myself, slowly pushed forward by surging pressures, was dazedly lunging, warding off, flailing, part of incoherent sensations from an outsize pulse, breathless, yet quickened into a tireless, exhilarated anger. An eye, a hand, swelled then vanished, a blade swerved, a torso crumbled with a hollow wheeze as if its skeleton had groaned. A dead mouth sank into its own crimson pool. I slipped in blood, breathlessly saving myself from the dart quivering behind me; my spear jarred on a breast bone, I was spattered, then drenched; the Scots retreated downhill, then were back, all around us, screaming and crazed. Again I stumbled, but the two guards were suddenly flanking me and together we cleared a gap, Valentinus near us, swording with gigantic cleaving movements, supernatural in smoke and flame. We had no strategy, could only stab, gouge, kick at the genitals. More defenders rushed in, wielding heavy sconces, archaic weapons, kitchen tools, slogging and tearing. There was no time for fear, only passions. Some invisible presence lay between me and the blades, while my own spear sent reeling something fanged and vulpine. I, Old Drusus, cumbersome, badly conditioned, had dancer's ability, boxer's fibre, blooded appetites, a Roman stance.

The advantage of surprise was lost. The straight, tilted streets facilitated counter-attack as swiftly as they had assault. The unearthly light also helped us. Few Scots could ever have dared a Roman town, its columns and friezes, heights and depths. Caryatids, bent and tortured, may now have deranged them, their fury slackened. A stone god, posed and glaring, in hues of the dying, could yet be live, about to pounce; windows have dim spectral menace, filling, emptying; steps were uncanny lures into abysses. I wondered afterwards whether dead Hector had been dragged round Troy in some barbarian rite to appease vanquished gods and angry ghosts.

We were relieved by a company of archers and, from an arch, recovering breath, I watched bodies fall with stunned, elongated motions, a leg buckling, an arm collapsing, a head lolling, eyes astonished : or swiftly, all bones weakening together, leaving only a foul, draining heap of skin. Rich flesh, rich meat.

By a deft manoeuvre from the Constantine Gate down the rearguard walls, then an enveloping sweep, the Julian Gate was recaptured from without. Valentinus called for a last effort; the invaders, trapped as if in a murderous circus, were petrified as a wall toppled, then impelled down one street, still resisting, but soon to be slaughtered in another, the last few, agonized, defiantly swaying in red mire, sinking, struggling to dodge axes, sickles, scythes, hammers above them. They died at the corner where arcades met the Basilican colonnade, hacked to bits, the whole area awash, the night clamouring, Valentinus heavy, stentorian, implacable, garish from beheading a score of captives in triumphant, bloodshot leadership.

Flames still lit all sides, some, I soon knew, started by subversives, and later many archives were found missing, many mansions left unscathed by the Scots were pillaged. Bacauds had swarmed into the sewers where, blocked, they met atrocious ends, still being pulled out weeks later. The dyers' and cobblers' quarters were stiff with dead, many children amongst them. Children had either scuttled for safety or zestfully joined the fights, moths before fire, recklessly thrilled by carnage. Hercules' column had fallen, killing and maiming the frenzied Germans, starting the legend of the god intervening to save the town. My water-mill was ruined. Scratched, torn, I had nevertheless won through : Sylviana might even call me a September swimmer. Metellus, despite his ardour for Valentinus, had not been seen. I rejoiced in my valour. When the guards touched my bloody spear, smacked my back, I felt absurdly affectionate, ready to embrace a common salter who had fought alongside me. To kill earns peculiar freedom, and I at last understood the ecstacies of hunting. 'Hail Drusus !' a voice cried, was echoed (let my women hear it !). I was surrounded by bleeding, exuberant faces; we were all young, all equals, swapping adventures. Rufinius, I was told, had lost an arm, then died on blackened hay, a useful, uninteresting man, bravely gasping his life away amongst filth.

All Silchester applauded as we at last trudged to the Basilica. I may have shed tears. There was singing. In the ashen, paling night, stars

149

glistened for us alone.

Valentinus was already at the Basilica, in pompous vainglory, bristly, the veins around his twisted snout very blue, his eyes, as if affected by the killings, oddly yellow. The Pannonian blood showed in eye and jowls, now glowing, now fading, his retinue cringing as though he had shaken Olympus. He greeted me genially enough, and I took his hand. Whatever his actual talents, in brute attack he had not failed us. He had repelled onrushes, rushed lop-sidedly forward where knives were cruellest, and now swaggered in victory assuredly his, to uncouth British shouts of 'Pen Dragon, Pen Dragon,' some sort of sovereignty.

Beckoning Cottanus like a servant, he handed him a paper. Antony and Lepidus! (Do any of you recall the story of Antony condemning Verres because he coveted his set of Corinthian silver? The morals of dictatorship!) And indeed the roll was a proscription. A magistrate had quailed in mid-fight, some conscripts had fled, slaves had disobeyed. All must die. I dreaded lest Junius be amongst them, too intent on insects to regard a town in flames. None dared dissent. One fool pleaded that the town be re-named after the blazing Praetor, though at this, Avitus, who had manfully, wearily stood to arms throughout, made resolute intervention.

'My lord will remember that great deeds invite great discussion. Such civic approbation, deeply merited, might yet, on a further occasion, be construed as disrespect.' *Theodosius, Treason*, must have fluttered through all heads. Valentinus, if scarcely gracious, nodded, then pulled me aside, his speech slurred, his breath heavy, the little eyes still stained.

They went confidential. 'You fought like a prince. But they weren't lions, only wild cats.' He parted lips in his cumbersome way, then scowled. 'Now listen. Don't make any noise about this, but you civilians did most of the work. I was ashamed of some of my own men. Professionals, and they hung back. They won't do it again.'

Sobered, I was soon home, passing slowly through the atrium, partly through exhaustion, partly for benefit of the family busts. Headed by Aurelius, under flaring torches, the domestics awaited me in ceremonial order, intoning praises. They were very distinct, the vapour had cleared, even my fingernails had recovered. Yet my fervour was lost. Dismissing them with an involuntary military salute, too tired for easy sleep, I considered Valentinus' words. He had done more than grumble.

150

We have Sallust's word that early Roman soldiers were more often punished for over-eagerness in attack, over-reluctance to retreat, than for giving ground. Such ardour was forgotten, yet tonight I had seen no cowardice. Could Valentinus be plotting against his own men? Did he suspect a conspiracy?

Perhaps a dream would reveal more. Dreams present the familiar in unexpected guise. Once I dreamed of poor 'Curses' Sabellinus, so stately, lavish with senatorial dignity, but dressed as a woman. Curious, I hired a spy and discovered that indeed he sometimes did so.

No Valentinus, however, paraded before me that night. I was back in the struggle, scalded, exultant as the spear thrust and the flesh gave, as if I myself was Valentinus, butcher-boy emperor.

## XX

Vesta had tended my gashes, Sylviana sent me a quotation from Homer. 'So you were desperate to grab the horses of that valiant lord, Achilles!' And I had the apprehension that Valentinus had noted Metellus' absence from battles. Perhaps sensing this himself, Metellus attended him daily; though not on the Council, he accepted jobs however indifferent, with a delight that Sylviana must have seen with misgivings.

Frost and snow killed many children and the old. Youngish people were often stooping, the winds blighting them early. Wolves left the hills, bears were said to be mauling deserters, stragglers, bacauds. Despite prohibitions, witches sold the usual elixirs aginst cold, sickness, death itself. It never appeared important that they themselves were helpless even against thieving urchins. A slave was tempted into buying a pubic hair of Venus in a dirty jar.

Barbarian fury had subsided to sporadic hunts for food, and perhaps a few victims for shivering gods. Spring would whip it back. Information trickled in, late and unreliable. Lincoln on its hill was almost deserted, entire hosts lay under snow, starving Picts had clambered into Uttoxeter, Scanians camped along the Wall, 'a stare' paralysed some western valley. Dead fish, dead eels, floated on rivers now deadly. Rapine, peggings, boilings persisted. To be raped by a Pict . . . Flavia would giggle, Sylviana sigh, as if hearing a ghost story from a child.

No British winter, however livid, however baleful, would overwhelm Scanians. We heard that they were periodically stung to insensate rage by a fiery-spotted plant, eaten or inhaled, though, fortunately, they were too stupid to cultivate it. Thus intoxicated, seeing foes as dwarfs and shrubs, fire as dragons, they could be outwitted but, while the delirium lasted, never overcome; yet, when the plant's vigour dwindled, they were left helpless, bewildered, like orphans waking in a strange house. Their gods periodically died, clutching the last red petals. Junius averred that Scanians had evolved very few words, so that their blood powers, not weakened by regular speech, then strengthened by sudden outbursts of song, could be irresistible. Rome had collected too many words, thereby losing more primitive powers, such as Pictish ability to exchange thoughts by remaining silent, and move objects by keeping still. (I should add that, in Ravenna, Antioch and Alexandria, thinkers are currently teaching that the successes of the Barbarian Conspiracy were due less to battles than to the concentration of such powers during particular phases of the moon. I do not really credit this, notwithstanding that certain strongholds east of Humber were abandoned, and their trained cohorts fled inexplicably, with no enemy visible.)

That winter was, I was beginning to feel, hopeless. Pipelines had been cut from within Silchester, the Baths had dried. Women and slaves, escorted by armed muleteers, had to venture with buckets to the river, and not all returned. The poor were chewing leather. For barracks and Basilica, I provided from smaller stocks of meal, barley, soused fish. Squatters moved into the ground floors of rich mansions, threatening the landlords.

My position was uneasy. Valentinus, if only with the ferocity of a cornered rat, was still the bluff, volcanic hero defending the people not merely from wild men but from crafty officials like myself and Brunnus, association with whom was an infection. Valentinus' very baldness shone like a helmet, his wolfhounds gave him *aura*. Such is human perversity that his votaries blamed me for the shortages, though less than I feared. My prowess in the street battle had won respect in some quarters usually ill-disposed, and fear in others. My professed intimacy with Theodosius retained considerable force, though I could scarcely rely overmuch on it. Villa magnates, themselves unpopular for their large, greedy households, formerly so pleased to deny me hospitality, now pleaded for extra rations, extra credit, which I occasionally allowed, while disdaining the small, patrician houses, sometimes owned by their freedmen, to which they had fled.

Throughout the Empire, it had long been observed that, in crisis, aliens, immigrants, destitutes, are, like witches, both despised and believed capable of malign plots to control the world. Bad harvests of the last decade had been ascribed to Jews, Levantines, Numidians, though these perished as frequently as others. Blacks were deemed of unlucky planetary influence, for Alexandria had established that colours contained the numinous and magnetic, often undesirable.

Such beliefs were causing many denunciations of hoarders, profiteers, traitors.

Trees were felled for gallows and firewood, weeds pulled from the streets and, when possible, baked. Birds were eaten raw, Junius reporting the total disappearance of rooks, larks, pigeons. Fugitives, creeping through snow-bound forest and marsh, spoke of plague in the midlands. From my litter, now always closed and anonymous, I saw a bony child kneeling over a severed hand, trying to rearrange the fingers. Indignation gathered against women accused of overfeeding those refugees and slaves claiming to be too ill to work as scavengers and on defences. Rebuking them, a priest explained that Jeheshua divided mankind into sheep and goats, the latter deserving death everlasting. Youths at once hee-hawed, with lascivious gestures, like rope dancers fondling invisible ropes.

Christian humility was spurious, covering an inward chuckle : We have Truth, You have Not.

In prolonged twilight, the dead besieged the living, women seeing them raising dry, rancid cups above impoverished tables. Women's vision was more intense as death threatened. They feared Vagrants and Painted Men, but Germans, those wide blue eyes, bright litter of hair, huge dangling members, could spin them into giddy desires. At the rumour of Franks hiding near Readingas, some whores, and even respectable matrons, bribed the sentries and stole away from the town, to finish none knew where.

Even Valentinus could not enforce maximum prices, and I did not try. Small street markets cropped up everywhere, offering plates, chairs, parchments, household gods, together with roots, bark, birds' legs. Rats were gratefully accepted as 'hard-water fish'.

Valentinus, now styling himself Prefect, had arrested and executed certain officers and promoted a number of those gladiators loyal to himself alone. His henchmen were largely these, sutlers, saddlers, and other such plebeians. Giving an order, he would jab the air as if to strike sparks, and wore the golden belt allowed only by imperial permission. Music he thoroughly discountenanced; only on the march should troops be allowed to sing, and even then he probably feared the words. I could sympathize. Music obeyed no military law, it made people grateful to the incomprehensible, encouraged disrespect, fortified the cowardly assassin or mutineer. A mob in full song can demolish a throne.

Never quite sober, seldom as drunk as he seemed, Valentinus was not sociable but suspicious. Like a sweaty pugilist, he fouled the air and I was ever expecting him to foul the floor; I wondered whether to risk presenting him with a jar of perfume. He would scratch himself so furiously that he could have been always itching from nettle-rash. For his edicts he used no personal seal and signed nothing, perhaps unable to write. All was published by Brunnus. Valentinus was dirty, Brunnus was unclean (I was rather proud of this distinction). At night, the Prefect doubtless dreamed of Sulla and Marius, the dictators, thumping Italy like a mule.

I had noticed that for so bulky a man, despite legs slightly crooked, with such a full, arrogant stride, his tread was curiously light, hinting at some irresolution. As for Brunnus, small, smooth, secretive, he was almost always on the balls of his feet, prepared to flee. His expression suggested the fatalism of a bad loser.

Our Prefect induced recollections of the logic of Emperor Caracalla. 'Clearly, if you seek no favours from me, you do not trust me. Therefore you suspect me. This means you fear me. And fear of me means your hatred.'

Valentinus was gambling deep. I did not fancy his chances with Ursacius and that crew. I scarcely hated him, but to exist at his whim was shameful. His minions sat in the Curia, lurked in tabernas and privies, wore priestly garb. Food privileges were granted to whoever brought him an enemy head or right hand, and he laughed outright when told how this was abused. An unpopular storekeeper had his severed head placed on his own stall.

Stories were being carefully circulated about Valentinus' earlier valour against Picts. We listened patiently, though a testy old magnate, aggrieved by hunger and lack of deference, grumbled that to be born of a temple whore only occasionally meant that one was son of a god. Much was made of Valentinus' refusal to have the town renamed. He had announced that were the unequalled Theodosius to show himself, he, the Prefect would be honoured to be his slave. It implied doubts and I myself no longer referred to Theodosius. Nothing was more frequent than eminent generals inviting murderous Court jealousies. I was now apt to declare that events were more important than people, though the Prefect of course was indispensable. Like a ferret, I thought, sent against polecats, and several times blessed by the wily Bishop.

Let him flourish bespoke Standards, if Valentinus earned them he would salvage half Britain. Instinct prevented me seriously investing in him. He had function, no real being. Exceptional people contain a multitude of unfinished selves, he had but one, all too drastically completed. Should he recover the frontiers, he could be pushed back into the farmyard; civilian skills were beyond his reach. When I talked of co-ordinants and variables, he was helpless.

I sometimes presented him with best wine in a finely chased Ephesian cup; he would gulp it too fast, splutter out thanks, with no knowledge of what he had so coarsely swallowed.

Metellus? The athlete, bright hunter, no longer won prizes. More than deprivation was smudging his blonde hair, dulling his eyes. He was trapped in the Prefect's ponderous gaze. Valentinus amiably taunted his lack of military spirit, and perhaps had some interest in Sylviana, which would both disgust and amuse her. She behaved to him as to everyone, lightly scorning his pleasures, mildly approving his social blunders. When he split my most delicate wine with plum juice, she told him this was the only way to treat such rubbish. She also assured him that Orpheus' songs were copied by jackdaws, and that the Muses had been exiled from Olympus as promoters of most exacting boredom. He was pleased.

He must have enjoyed having a Metellus in his grip; mannered aristocratic weaklings yet had singularity, envied by the blustering Pannonian, who might have sought the husband's praise almost as he did the wife's body.

Metellus' old smile strove to break through nervous agitation.

'Drusus, it's absurd. He insists I accept a command. I'm useless at such things, but he won't listen, or won't believe it. He looks at me and sees someone else. Me, giving orders! We've always had too many generals. Caesar and Pompey would have done better to cultivate roses. "Oh, the lilt of the wild rose, the play of the tender sun!"'

I remembered the Armenian meeting a poet liable to faint whenever a cloud crossed the sun, and having to move to Africa. Metellus heard nothing. 'I suppose if anyone shoves away the Picts, he could be me; they'd think me so incredible they'd lie down and worship.'

His laugh was bright but empty, he drooped, was lost. 'I wish . . . ,' he murmured, then ' "Ah, the frail rains, Helen; oh, the moon!" ' Then stiffened, his shapely eyes attempting defiance. 'Mind, he's plenty to learn. Women keep giving him shoes, and because he imagines that shoes, like books, improve by being kept waiting, he never uses them. Those awful sandals, those hideous feet! With the women themselves, of course . . . well, yes!' But he faltered again. Like a child confiding a momentous secret, he said hoarsely :

'He only wants to get me done in.'

At others' bad behaviour, Metellus had always retreated into a superior shrug or mock-dejected verse, but now he was cut down to the raw and begging. As colleague of Valentinus, I was expected to intervene, but I was unsympathetic. An artist at very least has the the duty to resist forces that will destroy the world and all its art : also, I could scarcely endanger my projects, my very life, in a direction so flimsy. I reassured him as best I could, with some expectation that he might finally kill himself. Still no subtle invitation came from Sylviana. I suspected she wanted me to help Metellus, but her dislike of candour prevented her asking.

She and I met only publicly, often with Valentinus wearing grime like a livery, never washing, only adding another layer of cheap oil. Our play would have baffled the spies : our words were formal, our gestures negligible. We spoke as if Rufinius was still alive, Picts merely had bad table-manners, Theodosius was a circus performer, and summer still prevailed.

'Shall we soon ride out, do not the horses need exercise? A long day in the hills. Metellus will lead us.'

The dark eyes under the trimmed, enticing fringe lowered in dutiful, exaggerated plea.

'To the hills . . . yes. . . . .'

No limner could achieve her true likeness, she always eluded. I remember not her appearance but a particular edge in her voice, an indescribable shade of light.

To the watchers I could have been mistaken for her banker, or an older cousin from whom she demurely concealed the mischief of girlhood. We parted so that they could hear. Her eyes, though motionless, yet seemed to shrug.

'Would you say, Drusus, that the danger is easing?'

'Thanks to our most spirited Prefect, there is no danger.'

'And Vergil has said. . . .'

'Vergil has indeed said, and at great length.'


Vesta I still enjoyed undressing. She was loving and simple, and, though this could be unwelcome, it was now gratifying.

She told me that Nodens' oracle at Lydney had foretold an evil conjunction of forces, scarcely a difficult proposition. I myself could have organized a most profitable oracle with my early news of markets and politics, with Sylviana's wit and Metellus' verses, selling the half-truths by which customers live. For a millennium, the priests of Dodona, Eleusis, Delphi had lived well, thanks less to the gods than to well-paid information.

We were lying in her small room. Almost naked, a little nervous, fearing to bore me, Vesta touched my cheek, then whispered :

> 'Go, man, and tell the Emperor
> That the sanctuary carvings are thrown to earth,
> The god of the place is now homeless.'

I was curious, the words seemed more than the contrived silliness of professional verse.

She raised herself, her breasts, small and sharp, instantly roused me, but, for once, I encouraged her to continue. She said, a little louder, her fingers not forgetting I also required love :

> 'Withered is his prophetic laurel,
> The tongued waters are dry.'

I could see her blue eyes moist, stricken by something far outside a sorry room in a falling town. 'The Emperor Julian. . . .' she hesitated, but, as I touched her with some gentleness, went on, 'That was his last message from Apollo? Did Apollo never speak again?'

I had told her of Julian, the great soldier, throwing his life away, risking the Empire, losing five great provinces by his doomed and unnecessary Persian War.

Turning away, she surprised me. 'He must have understood loneliness. I think he really wanted the sun.'

'He understood rather more. He knew that deceit, slyness, extreme patience, could win him the sun.'

I liked teaching her, and repeated Julian's own words that, without knowing why, I had ordered Aurelius to transcribe. He had looked at me in unexplained surprise.

'Shall I now proceed to tell you how Apollo took thought for the health and safety of all men by begetting Asclepius to be the saviour of the world? . . . . Even before the world's beginning I had him at my side.'

She wanted more, but I had had sufficient of Julian and Apollo, and she submitted with pleasure no longer disguised, frankly guiding my hands, moving beneath me, slowly, deliciously, so that, deep within her, I needed not to master but share her clutch, shudders, little cries. So often copulation swiftly repelled me from the flesh I was occupying. Emerging, stilled and freshened, I kissed her with sudden and sincere affection.

Afterwards, Junius returned from duty on the walls, reporting small, surreptitious movements beyond the ditch. As always, he was courteous, respectful, somewhat reserved, forestalling anything more personal with bits of knowledge unexpected and seldom trivial. During wars, he informed us, more boys than girls are born.

## XXI

Valentinus was undisputed, even in Cirencester, though dependent on what only I could supply : food and regional knowledge. I then accepted a belated invitation from the Bishop, to partake of what he called his humility and indigence.

The self-styled Prefect was treating him with the caution due to one whose insights were woven with the uncanny, and possessed, furthermore, a considerable following. He inhabited a stuccoed mansion, with narrow windows, rounded turrets, steep steps, and portico inappropriately crusted with nymphs and tritons. The greenish atrium glimmered with scallop shells; unobtrusively, a squat cross was added as if in afterthought.

He received me in a warm, circular room, professing extraordinary gratitude, praising my handling of affairs at Treves. Two small lamps gave not quite sufficient light for me to examine him closely. Several female images were hung, jumbled together, like merchandise. Indistinct aromatics mingled with odours of peat and woodsmoke. Two monks, shaven, white-smocked, apparently mutes, moved between outer shadows. They laid down wine and breadcakes, then left.

Of indeterminate age, in dark blue robe, he referred to his own sojourns in Gaul and Lusitania, mentioning names known to me. The perils around us he alluded to only carelessly. 'Perhaps we should train ourselves to win over our adversaries' wives, if wives they have ! Did not the Divine Julius achieve something in that way? Well, we hear the Painted Men are peevish brutes.'

He seemed anxious to prove himself a man of the world, like myself, and smoothly refilled my cup.

'You know more of these things than I do. I myself subscribe to Seneca. I hardly need remind you. "Dead, we become earthly rubbish." And that hells are invented by scoundrels and dreaded by half-wits. This, of course, is only the beginning of wisdom and, small as it sounds to a man like yourself, in my insignificant way I may sometimes improve on it.'

'Did not Jeheshua promise worlds beyond the grave?'

'Figuratively, of course. He symbolizes movement, transformation, spiritual enlargement. He taught lasting illuminations, open to the wise. Rising from the dead is victory over spiritual inertia. For the stupid, this is trivialized into physical survival. Such folk scarcely know that their own Jupiter originated in a lump of flint. Why, at Readingas they've been dragging out temple statues, wrapping them in scarlet gowns from whorehouses, gabbling out nonsense they scarcely remember, seating them over almost their last viands, leaving them to feast. By dawn, you won't be surprised to learn that everything's utterly consumed.'

He laughed softly. Priests seldom laugh outright, treating laughter as a rival, like Valentinus did music. I was interested, in an unimportant way.

'You call Jeheshua Lord, yet he does not appear lordly. A refinement of Jewish beliefs. Is there more?'

'A man of your experience will recognize that his teachings lack practical significance. He is a metaphor for the overcoming of ignorance by radiant understanding. In your own field, coin becomes land, then dwelling, family, new life, high thoughts. There are grounds, I may admit, for Jeheshua's physical existence, born of her we term the young woman. Some are claiming she was eternally virgin, but this is not very important, and what indeed constitutes importance? Pythagoras was virgin-born, though I have heard this disputed. Jeheshua, a blessed man of course, may have been related to Immaculate Isis, and Horus the Light of the World. His gifts would not have been impaired were he not.'

His sigh was what Metellus once called elegiac, perhaps suggesting that he not only understood but by some priestcraft had actually known Pythagoras centuries ago, with no very great admiration.

'You very correctly ascribe some of our beliefs to Jews,' he went on, 'but I myself would add several Alexandrians, and others further east. I regard Jeheshua as primarily Magian, with his obsession with conflagration. I forbear, I have to repeat, to credit his physical resurrection, we can leave that to poor Hercules on his hill, borne away on a cloud. At his last meal, he probably drank poplar juice mingled with hemlock and soot, which, you remember, induces sensations of levitation, also immunity from ill-health. Jeheshua was never once ill. He may have distributed the Syrian leaf, most effective, you may

161

perhaps have found, when taken already half-masticated by a red-haired or squinting child. Placed in a spiralled dish, hung from an elder tree, then swallowed, it gives visions that would entertain Nero himself. Jews have tales of a red man losing his wits by eating it, mistaking it for a snake on a branch. There may be some truth in it. Ideas, I feel, are influential only when they are misunderstood. Our own beliefs are in a single sentence – the onus of incessant self-renewal. He who loses his life shall save it, as I sometimes enjoy saying.'

He was evidently pleased with the words, presumably his own high-flown nonsense of course!

The firelight showed him smiling, as if at a joke not quite in the best of taste, to be shared only between us. 'We get too many converts from the stupid, lazy or the wilfully ignorant whom Jeheshua very properly damned. As a teacher he lacked patience, a grave fault. They think we offer them mere physical immortality, instead of a greater intensity of what they may already possess. Expansion of vision and understanding after the death of the primal self, which I always think of as a wounded snake. Thus we die in order to live. Knowledge of one's own nature is the true Kingdom, the term Jeheshua uses, slightly crudely. He was a teacher who despised education as rendered useless by the approaching destruction of existing institutions. Our emperors may have averted this by acknowledging his suzerainity, though he seems to have forgotten the poor Britons. When bothering to perform miracles, he demonstrated, like you yourself, that obstacles can be overcome by will. Yet already his very simple propositions, you may find them too simple, are becoming entangled, quite unnecessarily, with metaphysical poetry concerning the Third Principle, Alexandrine astrology and philosophy, Aryan symbols of light and so on. We men!'

In comfort, with wine and fire, we were two serious leaders concerned with the unearthly, while trapped by roving killers and beasts, by famine and wrath, the glare of blazing libraries and lawcourts, the destruction of time. Few would have thought of it, but books, I considered, were the frail, slackening links with the ever-diminishing world of gods and plenty. Yet he could not have invited me only to discuss Jeheshua. He might soon be pleading for new tithes, extra rations, or sounding me for secrets.

His tones, sinuous, plausible, would have suited a moneylender. Ursacius would have found him a useful clerk.

162

'I do beg forgiveness for saying what you must know much more profoundly than I do. Yet I too have my duties. We should not denigrate the force of prayer upon knaves. Prayer must, don't you think, be uttered very slowly and monotonously, the controlled breathing ensuring full concentration. There is more within some of us than we may know. General, yet personal, like a flower. You remember Plato delineating it. My chaplain claims to be able to recite all that Plato ever wrote. I do not encourage him to do so.'

He crossed his legs, leaned back, seemed to stroke the firelight, then intoned with the monotony he had recommended : 'An immortal soul always learning and forgetting in successive periods of existence, having seen and known all things at one time or another, and, by association with one thing, capable of recovering all.'

I took the opportunity of remarking that Plato at least had some appreciation of civic responsibilities. He seemed grateful to be reminded, or instructed.

'You ask me how my doubtless commonplace conceptions relate to the present hazards?'

I had not done so, but allowed him to explain.

'The Greeks spoke of aeons, the recurrence of Grand Years, exceptional interludes, preludes to social change, symbolized by an individual, not always heroic. I see society as Prometheus, bound, but periodically released. He instigates an era of creation, until destructive elements slowly reassemble, demonically inspired, until again superseded.

Prometheus, Carausius, Cheru. 'You can see a Prometheus?' I betrayed nothing, appeared politely indifferent.

'The excellent Valentinus. . . .' His pause, very slightly dismissive, was sufficient. I sensed that he saw the real Prometheus in myself, and he then confirmed it, more gravely. 'Your intimacy with this Theodosius might suggest that our good friend Brunnus. . . .'

He had finished, but his allegiances were clear. I kept silent. Then he kicked up the logs, flames rushed up, the shadows fell away, leaving us convivial associates in post-prandial peace.

'Admirable Drusus has disposed of the most urgent and pressing, what the Greeks call *kairos*. In return, I will tell you the sad tale of a Scanian island. Some Spanish Christians fled there, from Diocletian. They overcame savages, struggled for years against cold, gale, famine. Splendid! They flourished, built a church, honoured God, were enlightened and so on. But, alas!' he unexpectedly chuckled,

163

'there are always busybodies. A Church Council dispatched a legate, he was received with reverence, feasted, blessed. So, so. But then . . . fatal mischance!'

I suddenly thought the priest was choking, but the noise was laughter, his dignity dropped like a towel. 'The delegate discovered that their sacred rite used not the ordained, consecrated wine, but local berry juice. The savage conditions forbade imports of wine more suitable to be hallowed, so surely, all would be forgiven? But the delegate was very angry. Nothing was forgivable, the juice was disgraceful, blasphemous, they had been living in hopeless sin, all souls were lost. And our worthy settlers, dismayed, renounced the struggle; they ceased to plough, let the roof fall off the church, submitted to Scanians without a fight, and perished utterly.'

## XXII

My nerves clamoured for Theodosius as winter dragged on, torn by snow winds. Throughout the canton, shivering troops scavenged for meagre supplies and hanged starving bacauds. A yellow sulphurous gloom crept along streets, dimming the slow figures, while, in barracks, in pest-house, dicers played for stakes huge but imaginary. Child prostitutes were maimed, even rich men, sometimes assisted by their wives, violated their daughters. Astrologers prospered, votive offerings were stolen, assaults were common in the frenzy for meat and wine. Borne on the western gales were Pictish howls, the steady killing of Britain, though I still doubted barbarian unity. No ordered campaign was stamping the province flat, only those piracies, hideous but random. Saxons still avoided towns.

In Silchester, those who resented police now flinched from unscrupulous vigilantes. Cryptic marks, slanting and upright lines, allegedly Pictish, were found cut into doors, pavings, monuments. Word went round that the absence of visible Picts and Scots was because they were digging beneath the town and would soon emerge, terribly.

No March taxes would be paid to Treves, one less sackful of blood for the Count of the Gifts. No Roman vessel was known to survive. Barbarian bridgeheads were extending everywhere. Famished, mutilated refugees, dying outside walls, gasped that Thunor and Wut, northern war gods, had built magic halls on wild fastnesses and bleak headlands.

The winds slackened, spring showed tentative signs, and I read them like an inventory. Stirrings in loins, buds on a last tree, a round, smeared sun, a breeze filled with tiresome cuckoos, whose voices should never leave Africa. Birds were said to have grown slow and fat, and starveling sellers of crane and partridge were themselves plumper as they fed the public kettles. Much worse fetched extravagant prices. Shrews, apparently, were too bitter even for cats, themselves sold as fowl. Though still living well enough, I considered it politic to be seen over black bread and inferior wine, shabbily clad. Outside, the rabble chanted to its raggle-taggle spring god, Gwyn or Gawain, his white hand clutching a hawk, and moaned that a boulder had exploded. My slaves were calmed only when I said that I would have been astonished if it had not. There were fears (and jokes) of pregnant women transforming to animals, usually hares.

I warned Valentinus and Brunnus to expect worse. Despite my promptings, autumn sowing had been neglected, the few surviving farmers unwilling to sow for others to reap. But more hopeful messages continued. Verulam, Canterbury, Colchester, Gwynchester, Pevensey, remained, amid ravaged environs, though upper hamlets, moorland crofts, made a sickening tale, and several-score minor towns had been sacked by their own inhabitants. Aqueducts had been broken, sacred groves burnt, canals and rivers were choked with flesh; men had been buried alive near the fens, and, the informant added, near Norwich, a brazen giant had probably devoured nineteen children. (Perhaps some version of a desperate sacrifice.) By Severn, Caerleon and Caerwent endured above devastated valleys. Bath was stormed; alternatively, it was intact. The great roads retained their powers, the very sight of the Watling Street had routed Attacots.

I displayed my maps to Valentinus, then explained very slowly the continuing pattern. Winter seas had obstructed Scanian and Germanic influx. Scots had proved reluctant to settle, only eager to hustle west their captured animals, girls, pottery, weapons. Picts were besieging London, Franks and Saxons blocked the estuary, but the big cosmopolitan population could probably defend itself, not having to rely on sly, pleasure-loving, distrustful Britons.

For a military man, Valentinus had signal lack of curiosity; he was more interested in a foolish allegation that a sacred ditch had once surrounded Silchester, further out than the new *vallum*, in days of larger population. From it, divine rays and tremors protected the place. The Prefect actually conscripted slaves and malcontents to dig up frozen mud beyond the walls, many then falling from enemy darts. I heard of the hungry accidentally discovering a root, by which they lost memory, or found a new one, getting obsessed with bricks, plates, toys, endlessly examining them as if for treasure or runes.

Nevertheless Valentinus was not neglecting his own hopes. He had ceased to refer to Theodosius, was himself riding into history. Venal lawyers had encouraged him to abolish traditional municipal and artisans' associations, even drinking clubs, declaring that but one authority was now needed. From my own sources, and an oblique hint from the Bishop, I heard that he had risked dispatching his most trusted confidants as far as Canterbury. From refugee magnates he collected taxes, on lands lost, on fields derelict, to appease his troops. This showed faith in the future, for shops were empty and many tabernas were offering only boiled nettles and baked dung. Those magnates, unemployed, disregarded, would be praying heartily for Theodosius, as the Bishop must have known. We could rely on them to a man.

Meanwhile, Valentinus, that swollen face, that peachstone head! The cantonal treasury was now transferred from Cirencester to his private quarters. Coins, of course, already disgraceful in quality, were vanishing. When a man was tried for looting, for 'plotting', Valentinus might judge him in person and force him to wager on his chances of acquittal. A condemned lawyer, with nothing to lose, roundly abused him as 'Tarquin', which, in his ignorance, Valentinus accepted as praise, Tarquin being the name of his favourite charioteer. The lawyer was at once pardoned. The reassuring phrase, 'At Valentinus' discretion', still current in Britain, was dropped with many caustic jokes about the Prefect's arbitrary judgments, briefly amusing the scoundrel himself until even his blunt wits penetrated the meaning. In impertinent taste, he invited my subscription for a brass statue of myself, rudely suspicious when I reported that no materials existed.

His greed was insatiable, though his policy, to be ruthless with a smile, was effective, and resentments invariably fell on Brunnus. Tacitus has recorded that Britons were docile taxpayers unless exasperated by official insolence, and Valentinus, jovial, flamboyant, knew his Britons.

I continued my gifts, and his broad face leered over them. 'Drusus the all-provider! He smells the wind. He has a care,' evoking evil grins. With no news of Theodosius, my brief popularity had ebbed, the old libel about Sepitimuleius had revived. Like them all, I survived on the Prefect's caprice, though for as long as I fed his troops, maintained their privileges, I was safe.

Deep beneath my house still remained hidden considerable stores to which Aurelius alone had access.

Blustery, strutting Valentinus, how he enjoyed girls and swillings, his own jests and declamations, the obedience, salutes, the clamour!

Entreaties reached him from half Britain, his name reached towns unknown to him, his Standards alone persisted, the very dangers thrilled him, challenging him to glory, to vainglory as he sat higher than Governor, Praetorian Prefect, the Augustus himself, though in a realm still dwindling, by now indeed impossible to chart.

The Bishop and I would exchange no private word, even glance, but our silence was a pact in which I knew myself the senior.

I had learnt to appreciate degrees of silence, the many faces of the goddess Tacita, and was thus more of a poet than Metellus with his elegant but passive verses. Silence is the active man's sustenance, unknown to loud Valentinus. Proposals, deals, bargains, risks, are wrapped in pauses, stealth, feigned reflections, more pronounced than oratory. Degrees of silence. (Happy phrase.) I imagined them docketed, packaged, displayed. The silences of a cold and suffering town are manifold, so different from those between lovers, after quarrel, before bed. Daily, I moved through the pauper silences of funerals, verdicts of tribunal and astrologer, the famished.

Never await opportunities, create them. A true Roman, I did not surrender to the times but strove to master them. For decades, the citizenry had relapsed into children, to be fed, punished, manipulated. The State expanded, the common strength shrunk. Here, in contrast, under borrowed names of freedmen, despairing clients, Aurelius, I was still bartering for gutted sites, damaged houses, the temple of Mercury wrecked by squatters or Christians. Valentinus probably knew something of this : he had his own way of telling me, demanding I counter-sign yet another edict from Brunnus, promising amputation, blinding, crucifixion for profiteers. But, if we endured, society would applaud my foresight. Property, I could not repeat it often enough, entails care, order, public spirit.


Spring, but we had not reached the limits of disaster. The sun would unfreeze the barbarian enclaves and the warships from Scania, Frisia, Jutland, Batavia. Valentinus was stupidly mirthful, hearing of Saxons massing to advance west, heads dyed bright red, honouring their thunder god. I, more properly, saw Britain as a failing, retching gladiator. Could it be true that human elements were permanently ill-balanced, to prevent stagnation? Or that some false quantity in the membranes ordained that life must always worsen, however often deceived by bright dawns? Crete, with shining cities, delicate artifacts, expensive fleets, had been toppled, blown apart, great Babylon was now a dusty village. Rome! Flies and vegetation were smothering huge stones finely chiselled, exactly laid. I was developing new sensitivities, hyper-perceptions not only of silence but of shadows, mutters, glances, and always kept a knife to hand. I tried never to turn my back on a slave.

Slaves. Read closely. I agreed with Aristotle that many, by nature, by blood, ignorant and mechanical, deserve slavery, but the gigantic growth of the Empire, its conquests, upheavals, crises, had complicated the slave factor. Equality, of course, was unnatural. Even rats, Junius assured me, had chiefs, hierarchies, sexual and food privileges. Tribal Britain was always grumbling, always demanding rights, singing absurd notions of equality. (Too many radical zealots demand the equality fancied by savages, who will shatter a precious Tuscan vase, then evenly distribute the fragments, coloured but useless.) The tribes disliked laws, though absence of law would of course breed tensions, like flames under a floor. I myself opposed that desperate remedy of Diocletian and Constantine : to arrest all change – of prices, wages, occupation, class – so that talented men dreaded achievement, the promotion that would decrease their income and double their liabilities. Class was unimportant, rank was all-important, were it rightly earned. Merit must climb, stupidity sink. The Mantuan potter's son became Vergil. A slave, like Aurelius, could end freer, richer, more useful than Metellus and Flavian. Gods themselves, lacking ambition, can get stuck in mediocrity.

Evidently, something was afoot among the slaves. Rural slavery had been in decline even on the imperial estates, and now many slaves gladly fled to the towns rather than defend the villas or continue working in salt pits alongside criminals. All work on roads, bridges, lighthouses was, of course, suspended. Valentinus had conscripted many, illegally but, I believed, justifiably, displeasing though it was to see tribal runaways and domestic renegades swaggering as Roman legionaries, and the ultimate prospect of Valentinus controlling Britain with a slave army was hideous, though realistic. Already these newcomers made small streets dangerous, particularly when allowed extra drink rations. A rough crowd, they cheerfully shared lot with the gladiators, pugilists, executioners, and, if Valentinus failed, if Theodosius evaporated, all would join the bacauds, who looked back to Boudiga's burning of Roman towns, and to the Celtic sack of Rome itself.

169

Domestic slaves were different. Mostly barbarian, they had long been tamed : wolves transformed to housedogs. They were no peasants. A peasant fears libraries as he does title deeds, but urban slaves were tutors, architects, mathematicians, Greek scholars, scientists, overseers. The poets Horace and Phaedras, the playwright Terence, were slave-born. Such men, like Aurelius, dread anarchy, revere property, seek manumission not to overthrow but to join their ex-masters. To seduce and marry their owner's widow was preferable to rape and murder. That Spartacus himself finally resorted to privilege and executions would seem to them sensible. Many were Christians, but Jeheshua had showed no disposition to overturn the Empire. Exceptional himself, he disliked the exceptional in others, as zealots usually do. If the slaves believed in some spiritual brotherhood, in practice it meant little this side of death (which, the Bishop seemed to admit, was probably the only side).

Such was the situation behind the British slave revolt in April 368.

Some still claim that agitators landed from Gaul with Saxon connivance, and one Gaul was indeed captured, hustled before Brunnus, then strangled, for spreading sedition disguised as history. He admitted informing certain slaves that Diocletian had been slave-born, that Artaxerxes, Persian King of Kings, had sprung from a common soldier and a tanner's wife.

Whatever the truth, even domestic slaves were now missing, those remaining showed insolence and disobedience, and stewards feared to inflict penalties. There was fear of hair sprinkled with poison, which, dropped into masters' favourite dishes, would take three weeks to kill. The slaves of my neighbour, Publius Verrus, demanded manumission, and, refused, instantly decamped. The effect was more sensational than a cracked hypocaust or pillaged granary. Households were transformed overnight, abandoned by slaves hitherto so conservative and loyal. Elderly Curials were seen honing blades, manipulating hand querns and spindles, oiling lamps, even cooking. Adultery was rife, with women forced to remain more often at home. All slave barbers were necessarily dismissed.

Queer tablets were discovered on suspects. 'The 12 greet the 20.' Before execution, a slave, a well-spoken grammarian, confessed that aboriginal oak-priests, tonsured, with golden sickles proscribed at the Conquest, had reappeared. In my own bed I found a dirty scroll.

'Whoever eats my flesh and drinks my blood has immortality and I will restore him on the Last Day. My flesh is actual food, my blood is

170

real drink. Whoever eats and drinks me lives forever in me, and I in him.'

This would surely have appealed to the Attacots, of whom little was now heard.

There followed further scandal, the theft of the hallowed Genius, municipal statue and guardian. Ferment increased, half my own domestics deserted, Aurelius wept, and by mid-April we knew that a slave force, the Genius in its midst, was camped by the river at Clewer, ten miles away. Their proclamation reached as far as Gwynchester, besieged by Jutes, and hailed Jeheshua as a vengeful fire god ready to burn the world on behalf of the needy.

On orders from Valentinus, the Bishop carefully explained to the crowded Basilica that such beliefs derived from ignorance of Greek. Jeheshua's fire was immaterial, the brightly particled dance of the aeons that quicken or destroy the soul. He spoke like a lawyer, but I doubted whether Valentinus was more satisfied than the rest of us.

From Lydney filtered accounts of another slave outbreak, pledged to the god Nodens.

Valentinus himself behaved like an old-style Antony. With Brunnus beside him he climbed to the rostra and harangued a huge despondent mob. I was carrying the spear that had already served so well, a reminder that I too had killed, and indeed (why not?) enjoyed it.

Amongst his staff was Metellus, absurdly in general's rig, crested, pelted, mailed, yet visibly servile, indeed pitiable.

The rags, sunken faces, fragile limbs reminded me of a host of worms wriggling in the April sun. Another such winter would leave Silchester as if picked clean by harpies.

Someone handed Valentinus the oration, which he declaimed as he might the orders for the day, the muddy voice rolling out, apelike in ferocity, grotesquely mouthing Vergil, as he imagined himself simultaneously Eneas and Turnus, without knowing the difference. Perhaps Metellus had at least supplied the quotation.

'Do not surrender to troubles, but go forward without pity, and boldly.'

Valentinus, Pannonian savage, was like the great surgeon whose operations were invariably successful though his patients always died. I could have lent him another Vergilian tag : that nothing can save the defeated except the knowledge that rescue is impossible.

I was surrounded by old patricians endeavouring to keep respectful

171

as his heroics hammered the sky. Like some bawling actor he was ignoble yet effective, the cowed multitude began to recover, streaks of colour glimmering within the greyness.

'They say the Empire's doomed. That Rome's shed too much blood and must now spill her own. Such talk is filth. Julius Caesar killed two million enemies and, I tell you, he didn't kill enough.'

Cheers began, feeble stampings, and I remembered Gratian, the boy Caesar, aloft and emblazoned and unenviable. Valentinus then began denouncing Christian slaves for refusing to join defence battalions on plea that enemies should be embraced in love. Quite rightly, he threatened murderous penalties.

He soon instituted an elaborate system, Brunnus' invention, by which masters informed on their last slaves and were themselves fined for each desertion. An onslaught on the slave camp was planned, to recover the Genius and overwhelm the rebels before reinforcements reached them. During these preparations, Hyacinthus was found in his office, naked, ripped as if by gigantic, even supernatural claws. The room was windowless and bolted from within, inviting a whisper that Artos the Bear-god had destroyed him.

I rejoiced, though it too easily matched the morbid oppression in which one saw, through twilight, blood-sodden figures linking hands in a ring, a sign from Hecate, nocturnal witch, whose copulation with demons originated the blood of Huns.

There followed worse.

Flavia and Flavian had long remained concealed, though satirical gibes were traced to them. One such praised the Prefect entering the 'Porta Valentinus' in a gilded cart, holding an onion enscribed 'Thunderbolt', while children brandished cabbage leaves which they named 'Sacred Bulls,' '100 white oxen'. They capered, threw dirt, screeched salacious rhymes, while soldiers, masquerading as captives, by mistake sacrificed to Jupiter, Giver of Blows, adding a holocaust of goods plundered from Valentinus' creditors. From Valentinus, laurelled, empurpled, bloated, about to burst, hung a priapic parsnip.

I did not envy Brunnus reporting this, for Valentinus would never admit that the fouler the joke, the more rough affection beneath it, as towards bawdy old Jupiter. Valentinus rated all laughter but his own on a level with music, though he would scarcely have known what Aurelius informed me, that Aristotle held it ill-bred, an impediment to self-control, best left to underlings. It is interesting that mirth, like concupiscence, is felt at executions, blindings of birds and elephants, flogging of children, maiming of tumblers and the marvellously varied torture of eunuchs. In a dream I heard a snake laugh, like the cries of Carthage at the end. Certainly, at the real Triumph, comedians obscenely mimed the Victor, cursing him, mobs roaring the sallies back at him. Obscenity protects against demons; I once paid a Mede to explain why; he took my money, vilely insulted me, and vanished. Jokes undoubtedly conceal ambush, disease, despair. The callous bellow of Ajax, feline wit of Achilles, smooth sniggers of Mercury, silent hoots of Nero in bed alone, if he ever was. Imperial jocularity chills. Caracalla, painted, silken, mincing over floors strewn with flowers; Domitian feasting his nobles, all decorations black, the food only funeral bakemeats, guests reading their names on charnel-house urns, the Emperor himself dressed as a ghost; Commodus parading in female dress, changing to his own name the months and seasons, boxers, citizens' wives, and Rome itself; Gallienus shouting 'Peace, I bring you Peace' while the Empire caved in, crushed by usurpations, civil war, barbarians. They all provoke most uneasy laughter. Caesar's smile, delicious in restraint, was more dangerous than Pompey's, too loud, too candid. Jeheshua was a clown uttering the preposterous, solemn only when joking, a gadfly feeding on a bewildered or outraged audience. When Xerxes had thrashed the disobedient sea, courtiers must have risked impalement for a laugh, their only defence. Did Egyptian kings ever laugh? Surely not. Remember Constantius, that frozen poise, more deadly than knives. Valentinus' own laughter was a warning, and when his army joked he must have shivered.

From Flavia and Flavian issued a final joke, at a saturnalia given on a deliberately chosen unlucky day to honour their slaves and dedicated to the murdered Lord and God Domitian, whose image, draped with grass, stood on a jewelled altar flanked by Roman deities. He was especially praised, that awful night, for his scheme, brilliantly unsuccessful, for suppressing a rebellion of the Nasamones, in which he pronounced, to grave trumpets: 'I, *I myself*, forbid the Nasamones to continue to exist.'

Few survived that feast, which retains gruesome charms, like temptations to be massaged by an executioner or stare into a snake-pit. Guests dressed as children in tiny tunics, drooling infantile rhymes and riddles in small high voices, fondling dolls and ribbons, toasted and flattered the slaves, waiting on them as they lolled at table or danced in bacchic frolic through rooms dense with perfumes. They entered

173

left feet foremost, to aggravate ill-fortune. A prolonged spasm of lust, satyr's breath, armpit images. Marvellous wines were splashed over a new floor-mosaic of Flavia, posed as naked Venus fingering myrtle sprigs, and surrounded by Miletan girls pleasuring themselves with fir-cones. Torchlit mimes depicted unnatural couplings – the divine swans and bulls, the screaming girls, the hermaphrodites. Real children stood stiff and naked, scarcely able to breathe, gilded all over, this safe in view of their intended fate. To flutes and shawms, slaves were heralded, crowned, all joining in an ovation for the shrew mouse that had squeaked at the instant when the dictator Minucius appointed his Master of the Horse, priestly regulations compelling both to resign at once. Insensate swillings hailed Manilius, expelled from the Senate by Cato the Censor for embracing his wife by daylight, in front of their daughter. After intercourse on floors, tables, couches, bodies were washed in wine, then stuffed again with superb foods illegally hoarded. As the music surged more wildly, a girl in nothing but a bracelet was casually stabbed so that sardonic Domitian could watch her bleed but not yet die. On a wide satin coverlet lay 'the two wives', bare even of pubic hair, as if each had fiercely sucked each other, embracing to shrill songs until at the last penetration, Flavia cried for all doors to be barred. Signals were given throughout the house, the torches were flung, firing the hangings, the gaudy erotic trappings, carpets and mats already tarred underneath. Flames swiftly leapt to sickening heights. A dancer was transformed to a red-petalled blossom, lovers blazed as they rose gasping or lay intoxicated, smiling as ceilings, floors, pillars extinguished them. Seen for miles, the giant flame would have gladdened those other slaves dreaming of conquest, mocking the Genius.

Many more slaves – secretaries, chief clerks, teachers – alongside cooks and porters, had deserted families that had sheltered them for years, and were soon assisting abominable deeds, emulating Emperor Maximum who suffocated prisoners within animal skins. A very sedate slave was seen superintending a disembowelling, a mutilation of tongues.

The slaves were not defeated by Valentinus or submerged in the massive convulsions of Britain; they were victims of an event as typical of this fevered era as Flavian's farewell. Accidents occur, or appear to. (Livy, Aurelius told me, describes Marcus Valeris winning a single

174

combat, against all odds, when an eagle alighted on his foe and pecked his eyes. A Caesar unexpectedly quells roaring mutiny with a jesting or contemptuous epithet. Ancient Senators had over-awed invading Gauls so long as they sat, robed, bearded, utterly still, holding ivory sceptres.) A stranger now mysteriously compelled our slaves to release their prisoners and surrender the Genius, yet addressing them in an unknown tongue, and garbed in very bright green which, backed by sunset, gave him fearsome hues. By night, the slaves had dispersed; they were easily rounded up and perished in scores. The green man was never seen again.

Aurelius' culture was becoming tiresome. (Under the first Augustus, a slave had been drowned for correcting his master.) He again referred to Livy, who had mentioned early historians describing gods mingling with men, to make more impressive the founding of cities. Could the green stranger, for all his usefulness, have been a sinister god, by a *cledon* foretelling a new Silchester?

# XXIII

Deep summer blue covered Britain, but, reaching earth, the light faltered, then died. Heat lay under the hills and along the river. Foragers saw the starved and gnawed, distant metal, weird fingers of smoke, unknown footprints.

Spontaneously, particularly on plains, emerged a cult of man-eating rats, allegedly breeding fast in wrecked sewers, aqueducts, hypocausts, mills. People tried to appease them with shavings painted to resemble flesh. Doubtless, much reddish meat offered me was rat.

Jackdaw voices squawked of the soul being reborn as animal or plant, fostering talk of Picts and Scots bearing souls not only of monsters but of victims of the Conquest, fervid for revenge. The Bishop was greeted with yells that he should select a child or virgin, both now rare, to bury alive, a tribute to Ceres, to replenish the fields. Notably in London, children were ritually stabbed, amid grumbles that they were invariably taken from the poor, though this was sensible enough. Every town, fitfully besieged or raided, depleted further by loss of slaves, endured the unkempt and dirty, beards worn to the knees. To be unwashed and tattered was to be virtuous. Unlikely people proclaimed contempt for wealth, though unwilling to cancel sums owed them. Magnates used cheap wooden cups and platters. Feverish cravings for nakedness caused indecent outbursts on the streets from sick and healthy alike. Valentinus himself was always stained and patched, obsequiously praised for imitating Jeheshua's scorn of appearances, and for scattering a rowdy, bedraggled procession honouring the bearded Llew Llawr. Then he executed a useful officer, Clinus, on pretext that, entering his presence, Clinus had touched the threshold with his left foot.

Rations had slightly increased as the birds returned. Like Picts, we dug animal traps. A surveyor, hitherto popular and respected, broke his neck in one, was swiftly robbed of clothes and ornaments, an outrage accepted as commonplace. Matricide infected Silchester,

Colchester, Gloucester. Near my house a patrician girl, prematurely grey, stabbed her mother, from whom she had been inseparable. In the streets, many of all ages dropped and died for no obvious cause, less in Silchester, more in London and Verulam : fewer such deaths occurred in towns most vehemently, and horrifyingly, besieged. Funerals were perfunctory and, displeasing the priests, I saw to it that all remaining incense was used to reduce the prevailing stench. Concerned only with military defence, Valentinus neglected hygiene. The statue of Janus was shedding tears, causing much agitation, though probably due only to sunlight melting its grease.

The Genius was restored, as much as it ever could be. (Restorations never wholly convince.) Complaints about rations, evictions, arrests, could earn an accusation for slander or blasphemy. One edict had some comic results. The Prefect, unmarried himself, forced others, irrespective of age, almost irrespective of sex, into matrimony, then collected the marriage tax. Due to exhausted, barely literate, novice officials, a youth had to exchange vows with an ancient priest, another with her own daughter or dog, both possessing the same name. Valentinus was amused, saying that one or the other had better be eaten, and collected an extra fine for the dog being still alive, illegally.

Despite the warmth, I was often cold, even shivery, and Vesta told me I looked very unwell. I had begun fearing to pass others, always sensing, without turning round, that they had halted to gaze after me. Previously, of course, this would have denoted respect, but I could no longer be certain of that.


'I have always seen, in Numidia and such nasty places, that a lioness, finding a herd of game, stares at the particular animal she has selected to devour. The rest, quite understanding, isolate the unfortunate and go on grazing unperturbed.'

The Armenian was back, sashed, ringed, fleshier, eyes gleaming like polished tin, beard bushier, hair damper. As ever, he was complaining of Julia. His return was propitious; his like scent the future, less thoroughly but more rapidly than I did myself. The fellow was unusual but by no means unique. Possessing nothing, himself little more than nothing, he survived. I had rewarded him, received very little, yet his manner would slyly rate me as a fool, unlikely though that may sound.

Such creatures are, I say, unarmed yet curiously protected. Con-

177

demned to death in Cappadocia, they are encountered in Antioch. Accused of peculation, they start chuckling. They flaunt splendid cloaks with empty pockets, indiscriminately strewn with stones false and genuine.

'My delightful and omnipotent Drusus, what a patriarch you've become! We are all most grateful. Silchester is the Horatius of Britain.'

I demanded from where he had come. He winked, lifted a finger loaded with a dirty beryl. 'Duties, dear sir, duties. Terrible sights everywhere, believe me. Thousands of beastly Picts all round London, Painted Men, naked as rain. The bridge smashed. Saxon longboats in sight. Angles in Thanet, like locusts. Orphans there sold as veal, pretty horrid too. German gods on the make, beer-sodden and disreputable, one lame oaf pretends to be Vulcan. No more of that. Let's hear of brighter things. The old days you and I remember. Corinth, Rome. It's a mistake to judge cities only by their amenities. But I should tell you that, only last month, up north, doing my job amongst the poor wretches crouching in caves and ditches, I met who else than the Lady Octavia, sister-in-law of that lost Governor of ours. She believed the universe rests on a tortoise. Well, it must rest on something. She's thousands of years old, to imagine her undraped is to see prickles. Squatting in a cellar, with Scanians lying around outside, drunk, she claimed to remember Marcus Aurelius, and none of us doubted it. She always wears rubies, to improve her liver . . . very superstitious . . . it should have been diamonds. Her cat was reputed to understand the philosopher Phissipus. Nobody else does.'

Clearly, while retaining his options, he was some sort of spy for Valentinus, and had perhaps ranged as far as Cirencester. His smile glistened as he strove to assess my standing. Fidgety, he seemed to have a mouse loose in his tawdry clothes, his imagination or wiliness breeding tortoises and Octavias.

'Crossing water, I once encountered the chief decurion of Arras, a very thoughtful person, thinking only of himself, doing all that he was asked, and plenty that he wasn't. A lot was always going on in what he called his thatched cottage – it had sixty-three rooms. An old nurse complaining, clerks robbing the poor, the wife departing because of demons in the loggia. His secretary was some type of Asiatic. He himself insisted on standing on his head before pleading a case. He kept saying that blind concentration solves all, and that he once strode through a wall, cool and upright as a crane. More probably, he stunned himself. He once complained to us for three hours in the garden, in heavy rain, about lustful imaginings and vain conceits, all that makes life enjoyable.

'So I went on, to Marseilles, to deliver a very important package. After a chance encounter with a sty-full of Germans, I travelled with an ex-aedile, pale as Phrygian marble. We were greeted by the town musicians, dreadful row, and no one knew the formula to stop it; whenever we uttered a protest, they went louder. His lineage was traceable to Regulus, through a connection rather blatantly unseemly. In his cups, he boasted of a grandmother murdered by Parthians for her collection of bears' paws, though history, unusually sober, prefers her dying in Neapolis, over prawns of inferior quality. The aedile, chief patron of Juno's temple, called himself a farmer, which meant part-ownership of a beehive stacked in a distant field belonging to monks favoured by the late, rather beastly Constantius. Well, a poem, they say, needs not gulping but savouring.'

Beneath his fine show, he was suggesting, indeed begging, for employment. Julia, he said, suddenly glum, was living with a diseased boxer. They deserved each other. I myself felt warmer.


The Armenian's return did betoken change, a light behind the gleaming summer, despite Saxon massacre, renewed Scotish assaults across the Severn, silence from Gaul. Public rejoicings were spontaneous when earth tremors in Brigantia caused Scanian disorder. Augurs were delighted when swallows encircled the temple of Jupiter, though they themselves had probably released them.

Unprecedented, Brunnus sent me an invitation to sup with him privately. I refused, not only through personal disgust but from suspicion that he was losing nerve, then received, after midnight, a furtive call from a monk, one of the Bishop's swarm. He handed me a paper bearing no more than a drawing. Two spears crossing an embossed belt. A policeman's belt. It was all I needed to know.

To trumpets and alarums, surrounded by inexperienced lictors, Valentinus would publicly appear, unannounced, to grandly remit a tax, present fish or shrivelled figs to the wounded. In the ancient mummery of leadership, he encouraged the destitute with the words of a Christian agitator, 'Penniless, we own the world', leaving them swindled but satisfied. An ode was composed and sung to him by magnates' children, whose parents nightly prayed for his downfall.

He would scatter largesse to cowed or exultant mobs, though not true coin but wooden tablets painted silver, inscribed with a promise to pay cash 'When Divine Mercy allows'.

In another cumbersome, yet crafty jest, he offered tax rebates to all shrines, on condition that Christians shared equally with their rivals, knowing that they must, in their intolerance, refuse, the Bishop indeed declaring that he could have no commerce with idols and fiends. They lustily applauded a rumour from Bath, of Scots demolishing the Temple of Sulis, killing several children, but were less pleased when Jutes fired Christian altars at Pevensey.

In late July, Valentinus stumbled uninvited into my house, his first visit. He was markedly strained beneath his swagger, wearing his bulk like armour too big for him. He demanded I had all passages cleared – I remembered those at Treves, the hovering eye-emeralds, soundless exchanges, the whispers from motionless lips, the moving shadows. All domestics, even Aurelius annoyed and head-shaking, had to be sent into the garden.

He sprawled, sweating in thick leather jerkin, a big knife on his knee, then, after a long silence which seemed to further embarrass him, astonished me by asking, almost shyly, for information of Roman Britain, a lazy, overgrown student in sudden, unforeseen need of a pass degree.

In my most superior manner, I outlined the old prosperity, feuds, intermittent usurpations, the incipient nationalism, the independent weight of London.

'Caracalla then gave Roman citizenship to all, except slaves of course. Free rights. But if all privileges are free, there is no privilege. No urge to ascend. He devalued Rome, without benefiting Britain and Gaul.'

The porcine, red-veined eyes were as intent as they ever could be. Evidently he was at last groping for more than the immediate, wanting exact reminders of wealthy, pre-Conquest Britain, the metals, sheep, hounds, shellfish, timber, grain, coal, vines. None of them gifts from Rome. The implications were obvious.

'Could the tribes have united, what then?'

'Britain was always a fortress, the strongest in the west. Only the guiding hand was missing amongst the Celts, though the Belgic kings attempted it. Celts hate such guidance. They prefer to die in uproar than to flourish in law and peace. Rome, so to speak, fortified the fortress, provided the guiding hand. Towns, villas, gave muscles to a flabby carcase.'

He nodded, his head ponderous as the slow, strenuous, badly-flavoured breath. 'That body swarms with insects. Hair-lice, crabs. . .'

'Naturally you see the situation perfectly.'

So did I. He had few powers of dissimulation, and I was not surprised when he put in a question about Carausius, then mentioned Constantine, Constantine the Great, knowing him born in Britain but uncertain in which century.

I praised his understanding, his resolution, his appetite for self-sacrifice, hard work, knowledge. Inwardly, I cursed Theodosius' delay. To reject Brunnus had been easy. Valentinus was another matter. Whatever I did, or failed to, I risked my neck. Imperfect timing would be fatal.

He had heard sufficient, was satisfied, offering me my own wine, his broad, smeared grin somewhat conspiratorial. In the lasting weakness of dictators, he believed his own boasts. They boast in order to survive, and end by surviving in order to boast.

Suddenly, against all evidence, with countrysides no less harried, Roman ways almost everywhere blotted out, I was convinced that Britain no longer needed Valentinus.

He shouted for his guards, ready to depart. 'We'll need a sacrifice.' He shook with dull mirth, another smile slithered over him, then he left.

Throughout the last July days, the pace quickened. Saxons and Scots struck east and west, Picts made bloody assaults on London and were repulsed. But Valentinus, after a successful foray against Scots and bacauds, seemed to need further reassurance. Involuntarily fulfilling the taunts of Flavia and Flavian, he ordered, at what he misleadingly called his own expense, public rejoicings in the amphitheatre. This last was significant, for the building, outside the walls, was dangerously vulnerable. Everyone whispered that Valentinus and Brunnus had very private information. I said nothing, unwilling to commit myself anywhere, or to disclose that such information was hidden from me.

Although I did not attend, I was speedily informed of all details of the festival. The crammed populace roared at the salacious satyr-playlets, vulgar sword duels which cost two valuable fighters, obscene acrobats, wrestlers, jugglers. Included was a scurrilous ditty about British Nodens, followed by crude charades of Britain's history, a muster culled from me, unacknowledged puppet-master. Celts, slave and master alike, to raucous pipes, howled crazily for their dead heroes. Useless Bonosus and Albinus, enlarged demigods; Carausius, Magnentius, Allectus whirled swords, overthrew giants and monsters, grabbed the Diadem and redeemed the land, while Trajan, Hadrian . . . names that ring like hammers, were ignored.

Valentinus, sack of self-esteem, feathered, leafed, metalled, parody of Rome at her most insolent, his face caked with red paint, had ridden through tumultous worshippers in a rusty chariot drawn by four lean, white or white-mantled horses, that might have been cows for all they evoked from genuine Romans like Avitus and even Cottanus. He ascended to the Governor's box, and the first to congratulate him was the Armenian, pushing through the indignant notables and assuring him that at this very instant his prowess was being applauded as far away as Thessaly.

'How so?'

'My Lord's tread makes the world tremble.'

Everyone save the Prefect must have known that Thessaly was the last refuge of beldames, viragos and creaking witches. All held breath, Valentinus smiled fatuously, and the Armenian, at once recognized for what he was worth (very little), secured his seat.

Cottanus told me that throughout the ludicrous spectacles, the great Valentinus, destined to overthrow not only Cheru but Theodosius, and beloved of, oh heavens, Nodens, kept glancing about him like an uninvited guest scared of eviction.

In late afternoon, the crowds tramped back to the town they had left undefended, so that they too were, in their way, victorious, lining the streets. 'E-va, E-va, E-va.' The hired bravoes led the ovations. 'Pen Dragon, Pen Dragon.' I too stepped out to witness the travesty, in common cloak and broad-rimmed cap. But disguise was useless, and as the roar at the gates crashed like gigantic waves, an unknown voice from behind whispered to me alone :

'Spain has reached Boulogne.'


This is how history is so often made, as Julius Caesar had cause to know, a whisper from the crowd more stentorian than Stentor. Exceptional men receive prizes from those who watch fortunes, back winners. Eyes had still followed me, prayers assisted me, I was guarded by anonymous weapons.

Valentinus' Triumph left behind suspense, expectation, though nothing unusual was reported, save an immense forest fire in the midlands, lighting the whole sky, dismal laments mounting all night.

More than ever congratulating myself on so wisely turning my back on Brunnus, I also, very gradually, withdrew from Valentinus himself, and, like dogs on the scent, cats in spring, old clients, petitioners and the ambitious young were flocking in greater numbers to my offices, though I very gladly left them to Aurelius.

But Sylviana did not come, as though the gods were warning me off too much pride. Valentinus was still heavily congratulating Metellus on his military flair, his horsemanship, weaponry, air of command, though only Theodosius could rescue him as he stood, woefully parched, feebly drilling a cohort, with his sardonic subordinates gathered as if watching the last antics of the condemned.

I day-dreamed of my own new Britain, purged of the noxious and fanged, no longer choked by precedent. Of pulling Sylviana up beside me, to mingle with statesmen and rulers, sharing secret amusement, and perhaps, more subtle than she had ever realized, causing her a little pain, a tingling perplexity, by approaching her bed without ever quite entering it. I fancied I had got her measure. Skirmishes suited us, battles did not.

Battles, nevertheless, continued. On the last, windless day of July, after the screaming Pictish holocaust near Verulam, Silchester trumpets blared like angry dragons for the crowds to assemble in the Forum : massed faces, rapt, grimacing, already lifting to blurred, sunlit Valentinus, while, encircling them, shambling guards had weapons ready, as if for trouble.

Valentinus stood on the highest step of the Basilica, more guards between him and the lower reaches, where thin Brunnus watched us, alone, as always bent slightly forward.

The Prefect was like a market salesman bawling to conceal the poor quality of his wares by sheer volume of sound.

'What Briton has ever been summoned by Rome to the best places? When has Rome seen Britain as more than a storekeeper's outhouse? Cheap goods, cheap land! Rome takes, Britain gives. We are a forgotten people.'

I could see the Bishop near me amongst the notables, a smile glimmering beneath that youngish, supple skin. He too must have known of events in Boulogne. He could not lose. Victory would swell his tithes, defeat promote his virtue. Behind him, very confident, the Armenian sported an incongruous breast-plate over a spruce blue robe to which he was not entitled.

'Through all eternity . . .' Valentinus raged. How often that last word is followed by the unctuous or foolish, though, that afternoon, it was not. It was a signal. Suddenly, all altered, as though the sky had blinked. The crowd drew breath, the backs of my legs chilled, then Valentinus threw up one arm and with the other pointed down, at Brunnus, isolated, now forlorn. The guards were moving, descending, and , to frenzied yells, were around him, lifting him, unopposed, and, as if from the sleight of a Sicilian conjuror, a bell was round his throat. In abrupt, paralysed silence, it tinkled, the bell worn by criminals and the diseased, cleansing the air, expelling the infernal. A flash, not the bell but a sword, the body gushed, the head was stuck on a spear, already twirling, still stricken with fleeting, surprised affront. Then more spears slanted, jabbed, and the corpse with that dreadful spurting neck was hurled down into the crowd now waving, shouting, maddened as if by song, the bell with its hard clang falling after it.

Valentinus, aflame in false glory, was offering the ignorant and mindless the healing spells of power, himself unaware that power had already passed from him.

# XXIV

Warlocks huddled like grey shrouds on quays cleared by Kentish bands emerging from Wealden trees. They were selling three-knotted cords to ensure a fair breeze from Gaul. Prayers fluttered not to Jeheshua, suffering servant, but to Jupiter Victorious; a flamen was permitted to sacrifice the last knock-kneed ox. In dreams, an enormous raft slid from purple haze over flat water, surmounted by the beaked, ruthless prow of the Roman Empire. On it, gripping the Standards, was the Spanish liberator, born of warm ports and native genius.

Reports spread that Count Theodosius had sailed from Boulogne, perhaps had already landed. Still looking to Valentinus, the cantonal towns, proud of survival, found zeal and courage and chased away Scots, the bacauds trailing dejectedly after them, into the far west. Magnates gathered volunteers to recover villas, hundred of Attacots were drowned in a Severn flood sent by Sulis in revenge for his spoilt temple.

Yet, that first August week, we knew nothing definite from the coast. I was tensed, the future trembled before me, and, almost all work in abeyance, I was glad to welcome even the Armenian.

'You've already heard?'

I jumped up. 'No. What is it?'

The stained face was incredulous, puzzled, suspicious. 'I can't think how you of all people haven't been told.'

'But told what? Let me know at once.'

'I've gone back to Julia.'

Outside, children had reappeared, mysteriously, as if from beneath the earth, once again squatting over dice, playing in drains, pelting old women, chalking mazes for the hops and chases said to derive from Crete and Troy. For them, I was a marginal jotting on an unknown page, though they could see the excitement round my door, the unending arrival of Curials, magnates, contractors and jumped-

185

up officers. Was it not I to whom Britain owed the attention of the Augustus?

Soothsayers were calculating the day most propitious for Count Theodosius' arrival. Day of Hazelnut? Willow?

Valentinus, concealing his dismay as best he could, which was not much, announced that he would greet Theodosius at the coast, with all men available. He requested, with unwonted deference, that I should accompany him.

With Britain still overrun, his cavalry protection was useful for me, but he himself, as usurper, might receive instant arrest. I hoped that this Theodosius was sufficiently intelligent to appreciate civilian help, and was determined to interview him before Valentinus. In my bag was a list of immediate proposals that I must force on him, however bovine he might be. (Soldiers are often close to animals : Junius said that rats and horses could be trained to count, move to order, follow leaders. Admittedly, Valentinus was an unpromising example.)

Pompously, divulging unimpressive evidence, astrologers proclaimed Theodosius a Jovian, Valentinus, inaptly, a Virgo. I myself, more convincingly, was protected by Mars and Venus, amongst scientists and doctors.

Monks informed me, through the Bishop, that a Roman advance force had landed at Richburgh, near the famous oyster-beds. Naval forts were being assaulted, Vandal immigrants revolting against Jute and Angle pirates and promising support for Rome. Saxons were fleeing to hills.

With some fifty riders, great Valentinus set out for the coast. Amongst us was the Armenian, who had apparently used my name to secure a very vague assignment. Despite his boasted travels, he rode badly, his inept plunges at last stopping his talk, though, at a rest-stage, he did utter some nonsense about a humming-bird reminding him of Bactria, where he had gossiped with a Boetian mare.

Metellus was left behind, rather ignominiously in charge of the late Prefect's stupendous and culpable plunder.

Above the Anderidan trees bulged large, smooth hills on which Saxon clusters were being exterminated by peasantry. The river lands were traditionally rebellious but seemed now quiescent, awaiting the outcome. Valentinus avoided all skirmishes, leading us in desperate urgency, fearful of some rival outpacing him.

My destiny waited by the sea. Meanwhile, once again, a succession of burnt hovels, fallen shrines, cowed, suspicious survivors, then a white town like scraps of parchment on a distant slope, a fragment of river, bright muscle along the green.

Summer held. Within two days we saw the walls and camps, the blue slanted waves. Celtic outposts told us, not very amiably, that the Saxons had lost most of their longboats and, fearing or despising horses, had been easily routed. Valentinus was displeased, robbed of his victory.

The harbour was thick with galleys, officers of all nations stalked noisy streets. So many Britons abounded that I wondered why the island had been so wretchedly defended. Too many always want to be kings, too few, like myself, to be ministers. When I dismounted, however, I could see that most of these islanders were more broken-down desperadoes than veterans, herding round begrimed tribal chiefs, jealously eyeing each other or muttering themselves into dubious pacts. Most would have deserted their posts, or so behaved as to have no posts to desert. From them I kept very aloof, and at once left Valentinus, fending for myself with a body of admirers and place-seekers. Aurelius, who could not ride, I had had to leave in Silchester. Perhaps this was as well. A confidant can know too much, and should sometimes be shown it.

The main assault corps had already landed, the Reconquest was fully in motion. We had done injustice to the grim, overworked Augustus. The men crowding the barracks, or sternly off-duty in market or dram-shop, were no fledgling conscripts but professionals from all the world's wars, from Hither Asia to the Saxon Sea. I pointed out burly Victors, yellow-haired Batavians, the hard, bitten faces of Cisalpine Gauls, a picked squad of Julian's Gothic Heruls, Numidian cavalry on superb Cappadocian mounts. Crossbowmen, slingers, cuirassiers, their officers strictly mailed and greaved, their swords vintage Damascus. Still on the beach were siege-towers, vast wheels, heaps of *plumbatae*, the heavily leaded darts.

At sunset, the evening red and strong, the largest galley edged quietly to the pier. It was caparisoned scarlet and silver, a wide, golden flag flapping from the mast, the gangplank with an avenue of Standards burning in sunset splendour, the sea beyond fiery under rows of sails.

Despite glistening cloak woven with wolf-heads and stars, Valentinus, with his fifty, was negligible, made to stand with thousands as shields clashed, arms were reversed, for, preceded by a dwarf bearing a stark white cross, three men were now leaving the admiral's deck as if stepping out of the low sun. Two were tall, bareheaded, with the scarlet cloaks of generals, one of them with the gilded criss-cross leggings and belt of Imperial Companion, a massive gold torque at his throat. The third, somewhat behind them, was another Theodosius, the Count's young son, leading a troop of bristling giants, at whom a gasp went up, for they were black Ethiopians. Then we were all roaring, as Theodosius stood safe on the quay, and, emerging from the crowds, came a file of white-robed priests bearing a high ebony crucifix, before which the two generals briefly knelt, the men from the sun.

That night I spent awaiting a summons that did not come. I now suspected that my gifts would not be needed. I was almost alone, even my most ardent supporters, astounded by evidence of Roman might, losing faith in me. I almost did so myself. Even the wagons following me from Silchester were little in comparison to those from Gaul. The apparition of those giant Ethiopian blacks foreboded a dispensation quite new, in which I might yet claw a foothold but with very few others. Yet such challenges were never totally deplorable. I would not shrink. In my way, markedly unheroic, I had courage. Or perhaps the Empire demanded a new type of hero, and I was he.

The Armenian, always the weather-vane, avoided me that long night.

In the morning, Count Theodosius, the Excellence, permitted some sixty of us to attend him in the damaged fortress. Probably from deliberate policy, tribal ruffians were mixed with officers, all too much like Valentinus, and Curials somewhat like myself. Carefully dressed in senatorial garb, I was yet treated no differently from any of them. In an insult which purpled Valentinus, we had to surrender weapons to slaves whose eyes were contemptuous. (Menials always sense the drift and consequence of those greater than themselves.) We, representatives of Britain, could have been only a herd of wornouts who bolt doors against ghosts, shiver lest birds address them, endlessly count obsolete coins, stare at walls, at flames, hoping to discern smiling, protective faces.

Theodosius retained the scarlet cloak beneath which silver clasps minutely gleamed, hard as his words. His narrow face, steep, rigid, clean-shaven under wheel-cut hair, was colourless beside that of his aides, Maximus and Andragathius, both tall and ruddy. His eyes were of inexpressive light blue, his leanness suggested incessant activity, and I was to hear him declare that he needed work as he did sleep, they fitted like cup and ball.

This man was not only Britain's surgeon, he was the retributive judge.

On his other side, darker, short-bearded like Hadrian, scarlet-cloaked, matching Theodosius in size and indeed presence, legs apart, arms folded, wide-eyed, slightly smiling, perhaps less intractable than his commander, quick and impulsive, stood *that man*, another Spaniard, Magnus Clemens Maximus.

Both were professional soldiers. The days were long gone when Rome entrusted her armies to lawyers and politicians for limited periods.

Theodosius spoke without gestures, as if dictating to a single clerk in his private quarters. He was stiff, disinterested, his voice, though clear, was toneless, using the careful, old-fashioned Latin of the well-read provincial, though behind it glinted a conviction that we were failures, probably treacherous, not immune from prosecution, much sorry truth waiting to be uncovered.

He offered no promotions, but tersely announced his plans. A new Governor would arrive after pacification. London, axle of communications, was the strategic target. A fleet, already victorious over Jutes, was being divided between Thames and Humber. His range of information was surprising. He spoke of the need to exploit a particular rampart defending London's north-eastern approaches. He distinguished between the Foss and Car dykes. Like a chilly schoolmaster he reminded us that the lowest Severn bridge was near Gloucester, among the sheep folk. The Ermine Street was to be cleared, certain pre-Conquest south-western hill forts relieved and re-garrisoned.

He was treating our sufferings like a chilblain. Annoying his own priests, he had permitted the auguries to be taken : understandably, chicken livers and birds' hearts were favourable. With each laconic, immaculate sentence, the red menace of Pictland receded. Here was Rome incarnate, the hands that froze the world. Pictish venom, Attacotic hunger, Germanic and Scanian brutality, were a sottish farce; their animal blood would drown the savages.

I had been right throughout. There had been no Cheru, no Conspiracy : co-ordination, logistics, multiple commissariats, statistics . . . the northern barbarians do not despise them, for they know

189

nothing of them. Only the Goths might be different.

Theodosius ended by evoking the goodwill of Jeheshua, making this too sound like a threat.

I had to establish myself quickly, cancel humiliation by refusing to acknowledge it. Avoiding British unrecognizables, I bravely stepped into groups of officers, one of whom, by fortune, was indebted to my family in Gaul. I learnt that Lympne, so vital at the Conquest, its harbour protected by Thanet, where Claudius had camped, was already taken, helped by Saxon colonists who had cheerfully betrayed their overseas brothers.

The officers soon confided that the forces of Valentinus and his like were regarded as no Army of Britain but merely as untrustworthy federates, over-susceptible to demagogues. Our horses were being sequestered, almighty Valentinus himself must reach London only on his own crooked legs. I smiled, said little. History, politics, become a search for someone to blame, to foot the bill, and no Theodosius would tolerate a Valentinus. Flamboyant gestures, drunken feats of daring, were not for the Excellence, whose immense green crest had the glamour of Rome at its haughtiest.


Count Theodosius, on behalf of Valentinian, Augustus Undisputed, Sun of the West, on his high African mare, silver-saddled, ostrich-plumed, rode from the sea for the taking of London, with hundreds of cavalry and some thousands of foot-soldiers. The progress was designed as much for theatre as for battle. I had bribed myself a horse and was delighted by a glare from the late Prefect, though less pleased to see that the wretched Armenian had also done so, a woodworm seeking the sun.

First to Canterbury, its pale walls and solid towers freed from Germans, its tuns of barley ale, its monks and dazzled civilians. Up the Watling Street dividing the forest, to Faversham, Rochester, London. Years have passed, but I can hear that resounding tread which sounded slower than it really was. Purposeful, implacable, the Imperial Discipline would go on and on until halted by a single will.

From trees and hills emerged ragged fugitives, tribelets with lost names, former rebels, cottagers, gaping at the stir and thud, the fall of late summer light on the Standards, the shimmer of heavy cavalry, the weapons swinging through dust, the trousered Burgundians with bows taller than women, square cloaks fluttering behind them.

Lascivious marching songs would abruptly descend to a growling, regular chant to the Unconquered Sun.

I had observed more : very simple, overwhelmingly significant. Foot-soldiers bore not only sword or bow, but spade and axe. Soldiers of Old Rome had also been farmers : they built, cut, dug; at night-fall, they constructed a camp, a miniature town, impregnable. Now they had returned.

More and more lined the roads waving branches, feathered sticks, sashes, shouting wildly at the two generals, timidly offering apples, cherries, bitter bread, thin milk, briefly silenced by the crested Ethiopians, then by the mountainous trundling siege-engines, the swivelled rams and catapults, the funnels for artificial fire, the carts of hooks, spikes, arrows, of linen, medicine, wine. Like toads after a storm, imperial officials began creeping out with specious excuses, treasuring imaginary wounds and pleas for unearned expenses. Also eager young volunteers, hoary magnates, the timeservers who grub on vast events, Mithraic zealots, Christian deacons unnecessarily beseeching celestial protection on our arms. One unhealthy, shaven group whined that Isis, Star of Sailors, Lady of Alexandria, was pro-tectress of Britain. She had done a bad job. Almost naked captives, necks and hands outstretched, were guarded by toothy, malevolent Britons. These latter would already be exaggerating cowardly am-bushes, hooligan skirmishes, frantic retreats, into epic struggles, nourishing themselves with fantasy.

Each town provided the camp-followers of a victory-bound army, pulling sledges crammed with straw, pots, blankets; bare-breasted whores, pedlars, smiths, farriers, weavers, quacks, ex-convicts with ripped-out nails; dancers and comedians adrift with carpenters, masons, horse-trainers; jobless priests seeking a temple, perhaps a few gods seeking a priest. All greedy for prizes, for vengeance.

Gradually, people were beginning to recognize me, I was becoming acknowledged by Theodosius' own staff, though I had not yet sought audience. Several former agents had rejoined me, informants and retailers. I sent certain messages to Avitus and Aurelius in private code, though to no one else. Rumour might assist my purposes. Repu-tation, like love, feeds on error. I felt better and thought of limping Valentinus, far behind, shrinking to a surly whine, a superannuated village Ajax.

The towns before London had suffered as much from British dis-order as from German battery. Disease and hunger had made many

191

flop. Tax offices had been ransacked. From walls, sliced-off heads of bacauds and mutineers were set in waxen grimace.

Opposition was little more than night raids, overcome with disdainful, efficient ruthlessness. Prisoners were rescued, some to be flogged for insufficient resistance to the barbarians. Nevertheless, Picts still surrounded London, their signs everywhere, in a landscape of death. From a few last huts, pallid survivors were too lacerated, too shocked even to lift an arm. From trees, blackened and leafless, hung bodies of all ages, satiated birds browsing on heads grotesquely jerked. Skeletal corpses, evil details, lay strewn on dry, dirty pastures. Occasional stumps of humanity babbled incoherently amongst verminous ruins, clutching at us through smoke, as soldiers methodically stacked and burned the gristle. One derelict was evidently well-born, though imbecile.

'My own voice . . . used by them. My son's voice, melting, no longer his . . . wooden clothes crinkling. . .'

The Armenian would encounter me with the expression I disliked. Slouching, ingratiating, he seemed less respecting my fortune than calculating my fortunes.

'You, Drusus, my colleague, were never one for daintiness, though you tried to be. When hungry, you drank, when thirsty, you gobbled best bread. You made the rules.'

Amid the dead and the flames, with so much unresolved, I dared not reply as he deserved. He spoke with slimy viciousness of Valentinus, relegated to supervise some trashy camp-followers. 'The Excellence treating us to our deserts, eh! How will he use you?' Without formally addressing Theodosius, I was now careful to be seen near him, as if by right. Once he nodded, without friendliness but with civility. My influence he would have already probed, and indeed I had already conferred with his quartermasters and sent tactful 'replenishments', not, of course, to the General himself, but to his intimate, Andragathius. To Maximus, who seemed everywhere at once, but never remaining, I sent nothing, needing to assess further.

One day, these men with dry voices and unemotional determination would depart, leaving the province to some inexperienced Governor. I was no Metellus, scared of success, no Valentinus, sulking amongst the whores.

He, too, must have been anticipating Theodosius' departure. Once our eyes met, but he only scowled helplessly, seeing me amongst staff-officers. A certain weary pathos covered him. His famous belt and

vaunted sword had been toys too big for him, though, had I been
Theodosius, I would have executed him at once.

Theodosius had authority without charm. He was unimaginable
descending, like Pompey, Caesar, Hadrian, to joke with the men,
praise, demonstrate, or tackle local champions in wrestling, the axe,
the javelin. He was reputed to have fits of moroseness and cruelty.

The forward sky was now lit with Pictish fires, purging the air
before killings. Thin, spasmodic cries, a spy told us, were to restore
the invisible moon.

On the fourth day we saw the high stained walls, turrets, domes of
London, and, as is very well known, superb fortune awaited us. The
main Pictish force was still encamped on our own side of the river,
already trapped between broad water and the Roman army. Before
us now hovered rather than stood a dense, quivering mass very slowly
fracturing into loosely connected armed squads, pelted, daubed with
the usual ferns, serpents, eyes, their shields lifted; skins trailed from
sharp poles, sunlight picked out slings, small axes, mysterious wicker
baskets. Double circles were painted on shields, also on faces which, at
a distance, seemed one-eyed. All were foot-warriors, their cries still
high and eerie.

I was mounted, somewhat apart from the main Roman army, on
a rise amid reserves, messengers, scribes and a small cluster of
cuirassiers who muttered expectantly, hoping for their share of the
blood. Beneath us, in the centre of three cavalry blocks, mantled in
that inescapable scarlet, Theodosius, superbly unperturbed, his son
beside him, was sending runners to both flanks and to the officers
holding regular lines of infantry behind, with small wedges jutting
between the horses. Amongst the scattered Standards were the
feathered, grimly intent Ethiopians.

All was glittering, molten, suspended, about to burst, as the Picts
advanced, very slowly, as if through water. Archers, catapulters,
swordsmen, fire funnellers, the apparatus of punishment. Some
Heruls had slightly wounded themselves, drawing blood to appease
fate.

Theodosius waited; his son's shield glistened, ready to protect him.

The Picts' calls diminished and now, very swift, in long, gliding
motion, they spread out further, the Roman flanks shifting to make
a crescent, Standards shining at both claws, balancing those above
Theodosius. Brazen horse-trumpets suddenly clamoured, then
ceased : expertly controlled, the horses seemed deaf. I felt myself in a

193

theatre, held by actors in a scene that would dissolve with them.

The Romans had only to remain steady, trained on furious packs now within arrow-shot, blurred by dust but flowing blindly into our wide, still crescent, following their blood-call, ravenous for the feast. The rigid figure of Theodosius stifled our fears, and I gladly recalled that Picts had no word for *retreat*, but eight for *panic*. As they neared us, they emitted not war cries but only brief whistles. Their stones and darts, now falling amongst us, had astonishing velocity; one officer was swept from his horse, dismembered before reaching ground. Several men dropped near me but I had no sensations save the urgency to control my horse. Still the cavalry waited, waited, as if carved, and alongside, javelins rose, cross-bows tightened, until, with a single shout, infantry rushed forward, meeting the onslaught in sharp deadly clangs and smashes, war-horns somewhere bayed, like the groans of earth and sky, and, startled, I almost heaved over.

Barbarians rely too much on sheer noise. Their whistles and gulls' shrieks conveyed no orders, no strategy, they merely incited like wine or fantasy. Horse-whinnies now confused them as arrows struck; men reeled and collapsed within feet of Theodosius and the chilling apparition of the glaring Ethiopians; dust swept up in yellow clouds into which catapults discharged rocks that swooped over us in a long, quickly silenced moan and, like giant trees splitting, the dim, flailing Painted Men howled from atrocious wounds.

Maximus, supported by Andragathius on the right, at last moved, riding at half-pace at the next headlong wave, before wheeling as if to flee. Exultant, the Picts followed, leaving their fellows grappling centre and left, meeting the shock of spear and javelin, the slash of sword. Here was the ancient ruse, drastically perfected. Having drawn them in fatally deep, Maximus' riders turned as if on a single axle, masterfully enveloping them, riding them down, jabbing, breaking, crushing. A wild shaft of artificial flame leapt skywards, terrifying the rabble still striving to hack down Theodosius, and scores fell face downwards before him.

Those two Roman generals displayed artistry simple, precise, final, like the runner's winning swerve, the swimmer's dive, the discus lifting, curving through sunlight, falling in unbroken arc : like the tiny clause in a contract, the hinge so deftly inserted, so easily overlooked, which secures a fortune, forecloses on a palace, surrenders a province.

A lord of tactics, Count Theodosius calculated to an instant the several phases of victory. The claws were drawing inwards, the outer

Standards pulling towards each other, trapping the main Pictish impetus which the cavalry now cut into helpless divisions, like butchers slicing joints. To meet others, still swarming from the smashed riverside huts, reserve cavalry sped in further encirclements, driving them towards the carnage while they stumbled and floundered as if slipping on ice.

The last sight of hundreds of dying savages would have been those black African faces under golden insignia and plumes of incredible beasts.

When trumpets sounded recall, the battle lapsed into a pitiless hunt, amply justified, for the destruction of such races is a hygienic precaution. I remembered the Fields of Light.

Picts were driven into the river or rounded up in hundreds, Theodosius' orders obeyed to the letter. British deserters were branded, then had arms or legs torn off. Centurions poured away lives as if emptying jars. Picts had to dig their own ditches, the Britons wailed disgustingly, but the former, clubbed, stabbed, strangled, uttered no sound, no small whimper, their dark cramped faces were locked, their eyes unseeing. What flickering hopes could gods offer them?

To baffle their spirits, if any, Theodosius sited the death pits near the splintered graves of some local deity, then set them ablaze, as all London rushed through the gates to acclaim him.

(The legend of Pictish haunches sold as bacon to hungry London was probably invented to discredit Theodosius in a changed political situation.)

I witnessed power that August, and, amongst the feasting, remembered some immense, steepling pre-Roman temple I had seen or dreamed, its stairway so cunningly proportioned that the humble and penitent saw processions of gods, priests, nobles, apparently ascending into the sky and vanishing.

## XXV

London, always bigger and greyer than I remembered, rejoiced, though the harbour was empty, the Basilica half-burnt, one segment jutting up like a blackened thumb, and, though with much the same faces, the whores had replaced moneylenders on the steps. Theodosius, with an eye cocked overseas, prudently eschewed a Triumph but, on the Day of the Sun, paraded his army, he and Maximus riding together in white robes of peace, while cymbals clashed and iron feet stamped. British troops were excluded. Rome alone must bear the Standards, fasces, silken banners and pennants, the jewelled crosses and weapons, and throw to the ecstatic multitudes newly minted silver, stamped, not very clearly, with the head and divine virtues of the Augustus, Chosen of the Trinity, Supreme Despot.

This silver was sent down all roads, with dispatches about the Pictish rout, the impending Governor, the barbarian shrinkage. This must already be known, blown like thistledown to beleaguered towns, frightened villages, scared, bemused bacauds. Images of blood abounded, but the Standards now radiated magic more toxic than dart or poison.

Theodosius commandeered the Temple of Diana on its muddy hill protected by a thorn hedge and stone blockhouses. Here he received submissions, prostrations, appeals. Leading citizens presented officers with gilded ivy coronets, and festooned the Walbrook Column. More executions followed, to flutes and dances. Some sonorous titles, imperial scarves and emblems were distributed.

Policies were direct. After initial bloodshed, amnesties were offered to all deserters who rejoined the Standards within a month, grain and salt promised to communities that could prove resistance to barbarians. Each area was mapped by staff-officers for the Reconquest. Before the autumn storms, large forces would march west and north, linking with those landing from the ships.

Everyone was expecting Theodosius' promotion to Caesar, though he was careful in all his pronouncements to evoke the Augustus. Around even him would be *agentes*, loitering, flitting between tents, bribing women. Overhearing little, they might have recourse to lying.

Theodosius was no visionary like Emperor Julian. He studied things, not symbols. (He once said he worked not with pens but with bodies.) He had the diligence of his compatriots Trajan and Hadrian. So far, good. But for my ulterior schemes he was too wholly subordinate to Treves : resolute, a restorer, yet dull as metal before firing.

I now took easy place in informal gatherings of powerful officers and citizens; quiet words here, small rankling hints there, imperceptibly made me indispensable. Administration, after all, is the art of procuring one's own corner and using politics in order to retain it. I ensured that all knew that Valentinus had betrayed Fullofaudes, and he was dismissed to insignificant garrison duty in a midland valley.

Theodosius continued to ignore me, but I suspected that this was a precaution against Treves hearing that he was anxious to collect important British loyalties for himself. Andragathius had already taken me aside, unfriendly without being actually hostile.

'The Augustus requires immediate restoration of trade. By the end of the autumn, the Excellence will have completed his commission. The Governor of Britain will be presented with peace, order and, we hope, fullness, plenty. Such as you, will attend to it.'

All Britain was tingling, rising from the Wall to far Dumnonia. Whether I was bankrupt or millionaire was unanswerable, not yet important, but encouraging letters at last arrived from Gaul : from my family, chance acquaintances at Treves; also from British officials, shipwrights, abbots. And bags of samples, first fruits of restored trade-routes. I gathered a large London staff, with some difficulty procured horses. I bribed, cajoled, promised, and was now in position to threaten. As quickly as Theodosius himself, I heard of the last Attacots driven from the western sheep-hills, and magnates sending long-hoarded wine, rope, copper, to secure favour. Himself incorruptible, the Excellence announced the restoration of the wheat tax, *annona*, to pay the troops.

One morning, stepping from a market conference in the pleasant underground Temple of Mithras, I encountered several officers. Two dark brown eyes briefly stared at me, giving me an exceptional tremor, as though Fortuna had taken my wrist. The unruly hair, strong nose, mouth, bearded chin, of Magnus Clemens Maximus. He

197

passed on in silence but something had been exchanged.

I was now attending the Great Council undisputed, carefully detaching myself from freedmen, advocates, surveyors and the like, worthy but inconsiderable. Many old associates began greeting me, recounting adventures always interesting, sometimes uncanny, perhaps not recalled with absolute truth.

Theodosius here was always accompanied by Theodosius the Younger, like his father studious, correct but not affable. During a discussion about whether to supplement the Severn naval strength, Maximus leant towards Theodosius with some suggestion I did not hear; nods and smiles seemed to approve it, but one officer then objected that few boats could be made from air and words. Maximus, followed by Andragathius, joined in the laughter, but, a trained observer, I noticed his fleeting irritation beneath it, and sensed that Theodosius did too. A tiny incident, yet in line with what followed.

The Council over, some of us lingered in the hillside garden above the river. September was blue and sultry, we chattered amongst roses, a pink cloud. Several dignitaries gathered around me. An Illyrian, his keen, ambitious features cut like a hound's, touched my sleeve. 'Is it true, Drusus . . . a great fight in the estuary? We hear of Franks lying dead on the mudflats.'

I replied, but was carefully watching the two generals conversing with their staff, too distant to be overheard. They did not appear unusually serious, were drinking and smiling amongst the flowers, then gazing at a yellow butterfly until it vanished into sunlight. As if unwilling to relinquish the pleasant interval, they began plucking and exchanging roses. Theodosius himself, slowly, even ceremoniously, handed Maximus a red rose, and, Maximus, eyes lighting up, gave him a white. They stood, facing each other, clutching the tiny flowers, distinct from all others, the bright air flat on their faces, and with insight peculiar to me, I was instantly convinced that Britain's fate lay, not with Treves, but with one of these men, both of my own age, both with unblemished and constant success. It did not lie with both.

I must revise my plans. I assessed them like a race-goer betting on champions. Theodosius, the hereditary landowner, reclined at banquets in the old manner, Maximus, a new man, was soon impatient to depart, was always more at ease on camp-stool or tavern bench, joking with inferiors. Both were Christian, but while Theodosius seemed merely to conform to an organization politically useful,

Maximus was a fervid, though erratic believer. Both indeed had sudden, barely controllable angers, Theodosius using anger methodically to crush opposition, while Maximus, more spontaneous, was liable to waste it on mere nuisances : a 'heretic', a lying slave, a talkative woman.

# XXVI

I remained in London checking trade revivals and returns, encouraged when my Dover agents deftly secured a big consignment of wine and pepper. Officers had purchased the few desirable girls, leaving me to content myself with recollections of friendly but long-vanished pudenda: dark elegant scrolls, transparent wisps, florid bushes, downy scatterings, the red, sandy, black, and one mossy patch tinted green and cut into three minute circles, as if to animate Flavia and Flavian. Yet really I desired only Sylviana, less her body than her regard, admiration, submission. Also, her stylish consequence: her way with resplendent nobodies and influential pomposities would have helped me measure Britain's new leaders. Valentinus, Brunnus, Rufinius Sabellinus, even Avitus – all had provoked her scornful indifference, and I myself had not always earned much more.

So as September went golden, I flourished within preparations for Reconquest, with my deals, privy exchanges, information bought at reckless expense. Throughout, my assurance revived, the expectation of something momentous awaiting me alone, and I was right.

A legionary stood before me, respectful, almost devout, with a message delivered in a whisper, at odds with his huge, bearded Lusitanian face. My summons had finally come, not from the Excellence but from Maximus.

That night I sat alone with him in a turret lit only by braziers, a massive boarhound drowsing between them. The moon glimmered through a window beneath which sentries paced, coughed, laughed a little, grumbled. We were far from Theodosius and Andragathius.

The man was restless as ever, striding between walls in a loose, flaunting gown, casting shadows that loomed from the walls like dishevelled wings. While we drank, I examined him minutely as he lurched and halted, gesticulated, went to the window, returned, in and out of the glow, so that, with the headiness of wine and occasion, I seemed to see several of him.

Theodosius' eyes were bone-like : those now accosting me, alternately challenging and hospitable, were younger, quicker, less controlled, more vulnerable. He was not the supernal genius who wins without fighting, but, younger than his years, needing the praise, the warmth he so easily attracted. Closer to Valentinus than he would have cared to admit, he had ability, a certain graceful splendour, was no Constantius inhumanly still above prostrated courtiers. He laughed, waved, scattered gifts without always bothering where they fell, prodded his dog, with identical nods of goodwill, but, I suspected, seeking reassurance from man and beast alike. Womanish in desire to beckon, persuade, bind. Like Sylviana's, his smile did not always reach the eyes, though I could understand his men's limitless fidelity. Theodosius was revered, without love.

As if offering credentials, he was cheerfully revealing his birth-sign, Aries, with Mars rising in the east, denoting the triumphant soldier. Did he realize that it also entailed emotional outbursts and extravagant cravings? Then he asked my own, but did not pause to listen. I was not offended. A more heroic Metellus, he had rich stores of charm, the flattering oil that unlocks defences. I had to warn myself against too facile responses. I was susceptible to these stalwarts from another world. He was agreeing too hastily, before grasping the full seriousness of my remarks. Where Theodosius sat in powerful silence, Magnus Maximus rushed into words, not always intelligibly. He asked fewer questions than his chief. (I judged others by their questions though, in that rapt, buoyant night, I myself asked too few.)

His dark, tangled hair and strong teeth caught the moonlight. 'Men like you are the brothers I've always looked for.' He spoke of his Spanish childhood, the rigours, poverty, the pious, unscrupulous monks, and rekindled my old needs to astonish my family, find an equal, hold the bridge, as I did on that warrior night in Silchester. We were both getting drunk, not on the wine but on high possibilities, irresistible selves. My tongue was loosened, my fears of intimacy gone. Briefly, he seemed the elder, his deep voice slowing, testing his own words, lifting hands as though to impress the very air, with darkness, fire, the sentry's tread, heavy, sleeping London, inextricably involved in his grave matters. Then, at my random exclamation, he quickened, was again stammering in callow anxiety to confide, so that the boarhound raised its great head in a sort of wonder at his moon madness.

'The Excellence is entrusting me with half the army. Sending me

201

north. That's where it all waits, where the chances lie.'

He was boldly tyrannical, enlarged by the obscurities, still unable to relax. Reaching for a stool he forgot to use it, staring at it in perplexity, hemmed in by walls, night, the very island. Then, with the appetites of complete certainty, he changed my life.

'Drusus, I'll need more than a few bales of hay and a couple of mules. I want counsel.'

Behind a quiet inclination I savoured the healthy magnitude of his offer. That it would include dangers did not alarm, though I was not one to declare with Socrates that enemies could destroy but not harm me. If I accompanied Magnus Maximus, they might do both, and they would not be Picts.

Had this Spaniard, now leaning against the wall as if for breath, like a bruiser after winning a duel, heard of Socrates? Probably not, and in his wide ignorance was the widest opportunity of my existence.

Sudden discontent ruffled him, he frowned himself into silence. Imagining he hoarded resentments, social scorns, slights, mishaps in a turbulent career, I vainly tried to recall more of that exchange of roses in the garden, trifling, or perhaps charged with rivalry.

From far above me, his words tumbled out. 'Some places do not exist until I close my eyes. I've seen too much dust, littleness, dryness, like a moneylender's tent. Lairs of nothing. Toothache company. Anyone can grab land, they're all doing it. Better sorts can make a realm.' He grinned wolfishly, then said, indistinctly, with unexpected gentleness, as though to a child : 'Peter and Paul knew that. They built the bright house of the Lord. Everything's probably foretold, but it probably needs a bit of help.'

His strength, his glowing professional path contained a simplicity that would demand my constant vigilance. That Lord, for all his spurious humility, could be as dangerous as Cheru, and more insidious; he might tempt Maximus too lavishly. A religious man is too often spendthrift with violence, wasting and barren, lacking the true imagination.

Fortunately, Maximus had none of Theodosius' asceticism, which institutes horrors more enduring than the lusts of Caligula and Domitian. It may nourish the soul, it certainly impoverishes all else. Never a gross swiller or plunderer, Maximus enjoyed table, bed, the hunt. For both of us, 'worldly' gave beauty without riddles.

We talked through the night. Periodically he slackened, tired, spread out alongside the boarhound, dozed, then shook himself awake, noisily resuming as if he had never ceased, laughing outright at a serious thought.

In return, I felt marvellously free, only intermittently conscious of underwriting the explosive and unpredictable, exchanging guarantees for half-promises. My obsessions rose like fish. Though divided between East and West, the Empire remained too overgrown to govern and defend consistently. The threats were not only from those with fat necks and no minds. Too many citizens demanded rewards for producing as little as possible; such liberties were a charter for feebleness. Yet movement was vital, Europe was not stagnant Asia. Diocletian, Constantine, Julian, greatest of men, nevertheless strove to deny this movement, to freeze the sea, the years, the dance of atoms. Lesser mortals must control it and finally accomplish more. Market laws could be trusted better than eunuchs, bishops and philosophers.

I spoke with more feeling than eloquence. Maximus was capable of eloquence, a risky gift of which I was devoid; I was repetitive, assertive, but I knew facts, invaluable to a receptive pupil.

'Britain could rival Constantinople. The tribes work only when they're hungry. They have too many songs. Their imagination is dry heather in summer. Many generals have feared it. But it can sweep them aloft.'

His cup fell harshly to the stone, he began stroking the hound as if not knowing he did so, and, when he spoke, he seemed to be addressing neither of us, slightly ill-tempered, brooding, heavy. He could keep his feet no longer and, as he squatted by the brazier beside me, I risked touching his arm.

'Here, in Britain, are remains. Extraordinary memories of hideous darkness. Also light. Spirals of light. I believe Britons secretly worship them, though you would not think so from their faces. They live too deep in memories, too little in anything real. But offer them songs, General, wild tales, a bit of malice, then see what comes.'

His face was in darkness, but the curved, huddled body was tense, and for once I forwent caution, was lavish with pledges. I could replenish arsenals, disentangle tin monopolies, readjust conditions so that Britain ceased to be an appendage of Gaul.

He was awake, a young father astonished by parenthood, entranced by my urgency . . . Silchester iron, Chester coal . . . viable links. . . .

Much could be left unsaid. A Maximus could have his garrisons and baths, brothels and monasteries, but the real bases were else-where : roads and smithies, mints, postal stations, mines, even street corners. I had roused him sufficiently, his great hands came together so violently that the dog jerked up, growling with sleepy pleasure or pride.

'Drusus, I march, the crowds hurry to be dazzled. In the north, before they open their mouths we'll have their hearts out of them.'

I could match his phrases, flick out evidence, as no other. 'My General, I have watched my own trees falling, to be sent to lands unknown to the cutters. Woodmen, trees, they are helpless without the overseer. He transforms them to ships, roofs, to fences and palaces, to imperial tables.'

Britain had been stifled almost fatally by the overweight and com-plex, imposed by rulers simultaneously despotic and helpless. If the Diadem contracted to this island capital, it would glitter more fiercely, more assuredly. Before he could exclaim, cry out, I was more coolly repeating Junius' theory of gifted Assyrians, Babylonians, Africans, gradually forgetting their mathematical and engineering talents and most of their language. A vast crumbling.

He was at my feet, head forward on chin, the embers showing his eyes stilled, as if painted. He was the leader, simultaneously eager to be led; a student, yet, like the slumped creature snoring between us, reserving ferocity.

'Emperor Antoninus Pius valued the rescue of one Roman citizen above the slaughter of a thousand enemies.'

Adroitly, I mixed the grandeur, the lost chances, bloody pasts, with occasional fate-tales, which he enjoyed with childish avidity. Maximus, who became a story, loved stories of others. My memories paid full dividend as he listened, absorbed and credulous. I told of a faithless lover danced to death by Faunus; a girl transformed to a river, a forest, a comb; an animal mask enslaving its owner – I re-membered Valentinus; an actor impersonating a hunter, mistaking his hired applauders for birds, and shooting the lot; a girl's dreams becoming a wicked sister, a furred monster, a beautiful youth, an enchanted shoe. Such tales are the hirelings of destiny. The phrase pleased me, pleases me still.

As he lay trapped in my virtuosities, I could see the red rose dangling from his hand, and cold Theodosius receding, convincing me that Maximus had *fortuna* : the magnetism, aura, that evokes song. That night he was firelit son of Jupiter, destined for labours and miracles. The gods' withdrawal had lowered the sky, so that men groped through perpetual glooms. Hercules' club, however irresistible, was insufficient to restore the light. The Genius of Britain demanded more than battle trophies, Asiatic frivolities, the fantasies of omnipotent lunatics. This island, compact and walled, need no longer bleed to death in renting barbarians to defend it from themselves.

I had won. More than any soldier I was dictating policy, distributing offices, replacing stale hierarchies. A man grows by his obsessions, though he must know when to limit them. I had done so.

I was Drusus Antonius Muras, a stiff man, stiff in heart and limbs. I had last shed tears one afternoon years ago, at the sight of something broken. Now I wanted to do so again, in brotherhood with Maximus, and was mortified when no tears came.

## XXVII

Dreams are elusive links with the unseen, parodies of the solid, in which we descend to heights, are devoured by ourselves. In sleep, after the day's successes, I scrutinized a gigantic bill, mysteriously receipted for goods never received and perhaps imaginary. Had Ovid been recalling his dreams when writing that everything changes but nothing absolutely dies? Dismembered gods are eternally revived. Chips of memory survive from the unidentifiable.

After that night with Maximus, most unusually I suffered fever and, as if falling through rotting floors, dreamed continuously.

Halls dissolved into each other, I recognized the imperial palace but with walls and columns so high that ceilings were invisible. I felt, rather than heard, the croak not of frogs but of men pretending to be frogs. Darkness was lit, while remaining dark. I lack ability to explain, but much simultaneously was and was not, like song in the mouth of the dumb. *Transparent, motionless, tinged, floating, blank* – are inadequate. Colours were blurred, as if beneath water. Lamps, crucifixes, statues, were familiar but so angled as to be thinner, taller, sometimes with lines barely discernible. Walls depicted inscrutable figures that would detach themselves and, mere lank skins, drift between layers, layers of dim phosphorescence. Courtiers would bend, as if against the wind, then wither. Fingers without hands, pale eyes adrift in soupy, half-finished heads as if seeking their true place. Others filed by, heads lowered, yet exuding furtive expressions, like monks peeping at women through downcast eyes. Their touch would be furry. On another floor I lay, scarcely breathing, amongst gashed yet bloodless bodies spread as if for sale. Bells swung, dropping not sounds but fish, flickering without water between legs and mouths. Then I wandered through vaguely clad women with averted heads, making way but as if they smelled rather than saw me. Eunuchs, with robes almost touching ground, passed, apparently without feet, some with wings folded behind them. A few addressed me, with vehement gestures and deferential smiles, but too softly to be heard. Nevertheless, I felt myself the only fully live being in the Palace. Big as a stadium, the Throne Room soared from a marsh in which children, neither naked nor clothed, were gradually sinking. Then the Throne shrivelled into a dark hole whose emptiness periodically twitched. A whisper came from a head on a dusty niche. Small fires smouldered. Soon, I too had wings, flying at aching height while statues melted, were reborn with little more than tiny mouths and clawed, elongated left hands. But however high I flew I remained encased in towering walls.

I awoke gasping for breath, drenched, both hot and cold, flinching from the physicians' fiercely white caps and aprons, before fading back into the crowded, abnormal levels of the Palace.

## XXVIII

That dream was soon distant though not quite extinguished, like the glow sometimes seen above crossroads, Mercury's haunt, or strange flames in the sky before momentous events. Some believe that the sky itself is inflammable, the rain preventing universal conflagration.

Less easily than he expected, Maximus won unenthusiastic permission for me to join his ancillary staff. Sombre, dull Andragathius, I felt, was already jealous, but I backed myself to withstand him.

Theodosius, with picked Heruls and Batavians, was to settle the midlands and Silurian west.

Naval forces had already cleared numbers of Scanians, who are always weakened by autumn, which they do not wholly understand, attributing it to uneasiness amongst their gods.

Maximus relied on several hundred mailed cavalry, mostly Spanish, and my own provisioning. As we rode swiftly, he joked, urging us on. He did not need to. The men scented spoils. Despite devastations around them, roads were largely intact. Human squalor was patched with the red-gold crustiness of leaf and sky, what Metellus had called, more than once, the last tattered cloaks of summer. In the dry heat, the roads echoed clearly. I wore not breast armour but thin, cool leather with intricate Samothracian engravings. Very light, it would withstand blade or dart, though necessitating frequent oiling of the body. Everywhere, we met hails of joy, atrocity tales, claims of ingenious or frantic escapes, petitions to join us.

Maximus divided the legion into small, mobile units to pursue fugitives, relieve hill forts, face the wandering Scanians. At first, little resistance, save for a few pelted ruffians who soon scampered into smoky horizons. Despite the gutted post-stations, detailed news preceded us, from secret signals.

I was not tempted to try repeating my Silchester exploits with sword or spear. Death was not my concern. Muddle, indecision, waste, spoilt the live world, the rest could be left to soldiers.

The campaign rapidly became a hunt. Any confederation of Painted Men, Wizards, Vagrants, Scanians, had long palled. Splintered, baffled, nervous, they were seeking home and whatever lurked in bitter mountains, black tarns, eagle-haunted gorges, there to huddle over visions of Maximus, nightmare avenger, winged horseman, breathing out torrents of flame and sowing salt over his enemies' land. Scanians heard plaintive wails from over the rising sea, their gods had not fully accepted the desolate new coastlands presented them, nor drunk gratefully the blood of the defeated. They were twice mauled in open country. First, they fought stubbornly but without 'red root fury', their shield ring defending a giant chief. In the second struggle they soon fled, appalled by a headless raven glimpsed, by them alone, between storm clouds. Our cavalry, obdurate as any northerners, drove them to cliff edge, to deep tidal waters, while Britons slunk from hills after dark to burn their ships and slash the stragglers.

Above the wide, ominous Humber, Maximus permitted some Parii, Jutes with hair dyed blood red, and slit-eyed, short-legged Alans from none knew where, to follow us as scavengers and killers. I wondered about the treachery and torture lately enjoyed by these raw-boned fellows, and Maximus penalized their slightest delinquency with lash or halter. Afterwards, he allowed few prisoners. Picts fought to the last, then often stabbed themselves, soundlessly, as if drugged. Or, superintended by Andragathius, brief killings spurted in remote defiles, under rocks, within small, rough mists. Stinking huts, reddened streams, a line of twitching crosses, a rack of dry heads beneath an ancient tower fixed on a hill like a grim blind face in the sky. I was told that Scots screeched and wailed before being spitted, nailed, stretched over fire, less from cowardice than to release their souls, some lamenting that having left them in safe, far-distant stones or trees, they had lost them forever.

(To detach spirit from body is, I believe, possible but risky, easily exploited by charlatans. We killed, but could not exterminate the Picts. They may dwindle yet never perhaps entirely vanish, like conquered Etruscans lingering darkly on the edges of Rome's bright youth, in children's fears at nightfall, and in sacrifices strictly, though vainly, forbidden.)

British survivors crept from the forest and scarp, and I questioned a number of them. The sullen Brigantes had been decimated, their

209

renown had fared badly. Votads had rushed to defend the Standards; Segoves, with whatever feelings, mostly sent tribute together with excuses to avoid battle.

When at last seeing, across dark blunt hills, sloping heather, the rippling, continuous line of the Wall, towering yet defenceless, I realized in my bones the wicked treason of the Arconi.

Throughout, I was studying my friend and ally. He differed yet again from Theodosius in being no real planner. He relied not on patience, the initial exploration of terrain, tribal dispositions, elementary logistics, but on his own impulse. He made rash mistakes, achieved vivid triumphs, with rare ability to improvise, retrieve a charge almost lost by impetuosity, to feint, swerve, surprise, outflank. In contrast to Andragathius, who, on orders, would have raped Juno or rescued Prometheus, he used self-display like a Standard. He could feign tearful compassion or brilliant indignation, choosing when to pardon, when to agonize. The men cheered his style, his zest for what they could understand. Striding through them, greeting by name some obscure farrier or smith, he handled them like a lover, throwing smiles like largesse (and usually instead of largesse). I considered him appealing, not quite stupid but wilful, though to these crude, war-worn veterans he was a Bacchus, broad-faced, radiant, displaying the irresistible and intoxicating. They thought him fulfilling their decisions, their very thoughts. His belief that all gods were one was that of the whole army, though many soldiers existed only in him. Like all successful commanders, he attracted legends, invented others. He tortured Picts into betraying their smoke-signals, which he then cheerfully counter-employed. He horrified Scanians by, before charging, driving against them some naked lepers, touched by unholy pallor, and the brawny warriors chattered like frightened starlings, fearing not death but the hells of sickness. He spread rumours of a solar eclipse destroying stars but leaving behind an all-seeing, cyclopean eye, which, not existing, still subdued the bacauds beneath Lincoln; others he confused by presenting skins of beer, very fresh, very heavy, which left them stupefied on a frosty moor, so that even Andragathius wearied of spearing them.

Maximus insisted I was nightly welcomed at his ample table, and those hours in the noisy, crowded tent were most profitable, despite Andragathius' sullen, overhanging visage and occasional suspect joviality. Theodosius ate and drank sparingly, as if to embarrass the rest of us, methodically building up his powers. Maximus enjoyed

210

sharing or, perhaps, granting. Also receiving. I procured him an unusual rock-crystal ring which he henceforward wore though, I suspect, quickly forgetting who had given it.

Seating me beside him, he clasped my hands, filled my platter with juiciest hunks, begged advice or supplies with laughing suppliance, and offered to share a supple, demure Brigantine girl. She I refused, then regretted it, not as unsatisfied lust but as lost opportunity to discover hints of her master's private self, if any.

For some nights I saw her regularly, beautiful, dignified, awaiting him while we dispersed. Then one morning, she had changed, was dazed, pale, wandering as if lost, and she disappeared for ever before I could have her questioned.

Meanwhile, Maximus still laughed, gave orders, threw back his dark chestnut hair like Mars dispersing a cloud. 'I'll build a temple to Drusus. Drusus the Provider. He knows so much, he wants so little.' Continuing my instruction, I warned him against high-minded priests and philosophers, in office so often more vicious and incompetent than the Nero who employs them. They disgust me, though, as you have seen, my own stomach is complex. Brutus and Seneca, despite their fine moral style, were greedy moneylenders charging criminal rates. Indeed – Maximus was listening carefully – Seneca almost ruined Britain by his cruel extortions, which helped to produce that dire year-61 revolt of Queen Boudiga, who, fanatical but wronged, wrecked the three largest British cities.

Only once I saw him differently, examining me through eyes smaller, shrewder, thinking himself unobserved.

Onwards, moving west, Andragathius sped off to harry stragglers, and we pushed through heather, boulders, steep gorges. Picts were still fleeing, occasionally daring a night raid, only to recoil, baffled by our stockades. Once I picked up a fur shoe, a woman's foot in it, black and shrivelled. Within sight of the Wall, light was poor despite the round flat sun. Ash hung over fouled wastes. Ravine and hill were wizened, made swarthy by fire. We passed small Germanic settlements of beery, smoky huts guarded by crude, man-sized effigies. Half-starved Britons bemoaned their lost cattle and women, the tainted wells, smashed trees, scalped children. Drunkenly, they cursed Picts, probably erstwhile confederates, offered a dirty osier shield or feeble spear as tokens of fealty. Any German captives Maximus jestingly awarded to a half-witted slave, who now styled himself King of the North. Also, he always hanged two of them and was applauded

211

in strange chant by the survivors. The bodies were refused traditional burning and were buried. Germans hold that burial imprisons the soul, fire releases it to wind and sky. Their women most of us disdained; they seemed bred to be large, fertile and identical. With their curious mingling of servility and pride, the chiefs demanded lands and stipends, which induced Maximus to hang a few more.

From Britons, I more than once heard that famine had entailed a corresponding shrinkage of trees, due to some connection between them and the human eye.

By this time, while cavalry scoured and executioners plied their skills, and Maximus gazed jubilantly at the thick towers and ramparts of the Wall behind which Caledonia shivered and whimpered, I would repair to some stone place, out of the wind, receiving local contractors, seeing to the repair of post-stations, assigning jobs to the wounded.

Reconquest was almost complete. Walled cities, each with tales of courage and tragedy, betrayal, or the ill-starred and inexplicable, swung open their gates. Ovations thundered, petty celebrities knelt in mud. Where the record was bad, Maximus allowed a day's pillage and raping. We were given the usual nonsense of statues leading the attack, fires lit by invisible hands, Pictish bodies crusted with reptilian scales.

Up here, Theodosius was only a rumour, a threat, but scarlet Maximus haughty in the saddle was filling the sky. Survivors, pared almost to the bone, cheered the rebirth of Rome, though, save in dreams, little is ever reborn. History, I discovered, is a jar of coloured essence, periodically shaken. Patterns alter, the essence does not. Like a contract, all is provisional.

Maximus always remanned the Wall garrisons with measured ceremonial. Not only gates were perfected, but also the glaring, menacing statues facing Caledonia. With puzzling celerity, Jews, Libyans, Antiochans . . . took over the shops, whores appeared, songs drifted from barracks, populations began replastering, restocking, settling down. All known Arconi, even suspects, were offered choice of crucifixion, immolation or life service on the Wall. By no means all opted for the last, which I opposed, tactlessly, as I later realized, for they had first to take a most solemn oath, not to the Augustus, not to Theodosius, but to Magnus Clemens Maximus.

I was disquieted, I was gratified. I could already see my own head cut splendidly clear on a restored coinage. My lessons were being

212

absorbed, yet entailing the prospect of civil war, with Theodosius, with Flavius Valentinian Augustus himself, and the redoubtable Jovinus and Severus, perhaps the most crucial confrontation in the island's history. Nothing, however, could halt Maximus. Further south, Wroxeter was recaptured by a dozen men. York, then Chester followed. A patrol discovered that it had captured Carlisle. At York, three old employees awaited me, as if with fingers to their lips. They spoke of the town first beating off assault, then riven by factional riots, a slave rising, dysentery. Yet trade was thriving, even trinkets and hair scents reaching extraordinary prices.

They had more to tell, strictly reserved for me alone. We spoke in a ruined temple, purple thistle growing from walls, a cracked god regarding me with two smiles at once.

Almost everywhere, no finer tribute, such retainers had kept faith. Through famine, fire, battle, they had contrived to pile up hides, cloth, salt, wine, beet, fodder, wax, in most daring hideaways. Accounts were in very fair order. Not one competitor had such assets.

Much would be concealed from Maximus. Where now were the vain magnates, lounging wits? No cymbals clashed for me, no conches blasted, but my empire was emerging from the half-seen, the faintly imagined.

I sat with Maximus listening to glum Curials and indigent traders, until, with a tired smile, a small shrug, I deigned to intervene, with a glib, perfected style not quite natural to me.

'His Munificence, Restorer of Light, must hear that with these gentlemen I can only sympathize, I can almost agree. Their dismay is not to be blamed. Wreckage is almost total, it might seem irredeemable. Yes, granaries, warehouses, cellars . . . earthquake would have damaged less. And yet, take heart. . . .'

I paused, savouring the sharp upturn of heads, the gleam in the brown, round eyes of the Spanish conqueror, then said briskly, 'To serve Maximus invites the goodwill of heaven. Disasters will be attended to, I myself will take them in hand.'

More conversationally, I spoke to Maximus as if we were alone : 'I will report in three days' time. My hands will not be empty.' The astonished, incredulous, aggrieved faces amused me.

Always keeping my word, I was as ever the true artist, moulding, underpinning, embellishing, designing, forever at Maximus' ear, prompting him so that my plans seemed his own, while we clawed back river mouths, estates, farms, restored colour to the land.

213

I was no loveless Armenian. My blood quickened at the general's praise, his embrace, as I envisaged the prosperity we would share. In late October Andragathius joined us at Carlisle, after Maximus had subdued a despairing remnant of Vagrants with a present of gaudy cloth. Later we encountered several thousand Attacots and their families ranged round their sorcerer, an Alder King. The warriors were led by a woman, thickly painted, perhaps blind, who chose to meet us near a circle of tall stones. Andragathius cut them down at will, and we saw those outlandish, bloodstained men and women in defeat, knifing each other before the horses reached them, their faces rapt with calm, distant smiles.

Afterwards, someone reproached Andragathius for spitting the children. He looked somewhat affronted, then growled that as Julius Caesar had cut off hands, why should not he do more? Maximus, sprawling on a bearskin, lazily replied that there were seven reasons, though he disclosed none. He usually treated Andragathius more as an extra limb than as a man worth talking to.

At Carlisle I myself, by mischance, gained a new reputation. A contractor overcharged me for fuller's earth, I mentioned this to Maximus who at once had him publicly flogged, then, as if in afterthought, strangled.

We had halted, to skirmish along the coasts, seeing many frail craft despondently risking the passage to Hibernia. Then, turning south, all Scots finished, a surge of cheering gave us a further prize.

In Fullofaudes' disaster, one of his youngest, most daring officers, Lucius Galerius, was assumed dead, but had actually been captured. Picts hold a debased matrilinear cult of a Great Goddess, who advised against killing him and now, in some last foray, he had been rescued.

Maximus clapped heartily, was several times to praise Galerius' courage, virtue, fortitude, toasting him in very special Gallic wine. Yet Galerius never appeared, nothing further was received, and Maximus ceased to mention him, so that his name was lost, he was never seen and exists in no annals save my own.

Winter ended our campaign, and we settled in a large midland fortress, where several letters arrived from Theodosius. These Maximus kept to himself, though I knew that the Excellence had cleared the south and was encamped at Gwynchester. Wight was retaken, and the fleet had scattered the Scanians and Jutes off the Orkneys. His subalterns held Bath, and loyalists the west highlands. Outposts of Theodosius' and Maximus' forces had now met. I could not forget that exchange of roses. What would happen now?

I collected information from the entire island. It demanded much pondering during short, dark afternoons. The Conspiracy, possibly conceived by 'Cheru', and with some ingenuity, had swiftly degenerated into brigandage, without plan, without future. Savages fall on red, still quivering meat without waiting to cook it, then quarrel. Their negotiations with British tribes had been half-hearted. As a diagram of human behaviour, perhaps human nature, all was pessimistic. Heroism negligible, treachery rampant, loyalist collaboration vitiated by class resentments, wholesale and meaningless wastage. Bacauds destroyed a thousand hides at Chester, Scots burnt huge stores of timber near Gloucester. Corn and barley, amber, gold images, were tossed into rivers : marble columns, ivory vessels, were as often smashed as stolen. Only statues were spared, left lonely, stark, mysterious guardians of smouldering rubble.

More comprehensible was the angry destruction of glass, which had disturbing powers, as if breathing visions from behind the air. Also, the peasants' hatred of documents, those demonic secrets that enslaved their rights.


Fires warmed all floors as the skies contracted and mist shortened the hills. Well sheltered, the troops were in excellent temper.

Now was the chance to induce Maximus to reflect very seriously before the Governor arrived. Theodosius, no doubt, was reflecting to some purpose. So was I. I was bringing Maximus well-chosen gifts, notably a German drinking horn tipped with silver, which he enjoyed fondling, rather lasciviously. Then I insisted on several talks with him alone. A pioneer, I told him, renews and salvages even more than he creates. In an economy that might partially retreat from money to land, he should acquire large villa estates in strategically mapped tribal regions. I would encourage the development of honey, wool, venison. Slavery, now declining, should be confined to criminals and the unteachable. True culture derives not from laws but incentives. Did he know that in China, imperial officials are enrolled from written examinations, each candidate working alone, an armed guard stationed against cheating?

Maximus listened, but with insufficient curiosity, occasionally looking elsewhere. In repose, he could be something of a bore. Also, he had fits of laziness that left him discontented, even querulous. Rather

215

childishly, he still kept Theodosius' dispatches or orders to himself. Nevertheless, much was promising. 'When spring comes. . . .'

Meanwhile, Silchester folk would be looking to me anew, following the victorious campaign, awaiting my return with excited and greedy hopes, they themselves remaining very, very small, once again drifting with fashion, surrendering not to time but to the times, a phrase I reminded myself to repeat to Sylviana. I amused myself by considering some Pictish or Scanian token to be rushed to her by a shining military escort, then refrained. I had tact; I had subtlety. I would flourish better in her speculations, and in Metellus' envy.

'When spring comes. . . .' We had plans, laughter, even Andragathius condescended to tell me a joke, though repeating it too often. All societies, however, even the Jews, cherish a mischief god. Like bad salt, a sick planet, a wayward atom, he upsets balance, corrects torpor, is perhaps a precaution against dispiriting notions of inevitability. Account sheets may disregard him, he does not disregard them. He chuckled his way through Maximus' quarters after a squally day of sleet and chill, provoked, as so often, by religion. Concern for theology, surely, denotes indifference to genuine piety.

In Gaul, an ascetic Spanish bishop, Priscillian, was hawking his Christian beliefs. These included tiresome denunciations of marriage, institutions, the State. He was said to pray naked and insist that others did so too, and preached that the virtuous soul is accidentally imprisoned in evil flesh, to escape only by death, assisted by despair, continence, deprivations. Scarcely a recipe for successful trade. Jeheshua's chief rival, some Persian or Babylonian monster, could himself be eventually redeemed. I myself have no interest in ideas, only in who utters them, and in what tone of voice, and, left to himself, the devout Priscillian would doubtless have benefited society by dying of cold.

Maximus believed himself a Christian, though I doubted whether, in 368, he could have clearly explained Jeheshua's teachings. Priscillian's attack on all government, however, shocked and angered him.

We were all slightly the worse for drink, only Andragathius still upright, like a boulder. The atmosphere was desultory, Maximus stroking his horn, head sinking, several others trying to listen to Marcus, a youth recently promoted for exploits against Scanians. He was, slightly too earnestly, defending Priscillian against obscene, rather obvious jests about his habit of prayer, and the types of female disciple they must attract. Dozing, I was horribly startled when

216

Maximus jumped up, his stool and platters crashing, his eyes enraged, those of a Seneca refused payments legal but monstrous. He grabbed Marcus by the throat, held him like a sack, paused then brutally kneed him in the genitals, dropped him, glared at him moaning, writhing, then at the rest of us, and slammed out.

I never believed people were wholly understandable, and, for me, involuntary exclamations, small but repeated gestures, could reveal sufficient. No one is wholly completed, chance extracts the latent, the unimagined. On that raw, bloody night in Silchester, I had discovered in myself valour hitherto unsuspected. Maximus was showing himself not complex, but elemental, liable to dream of building what he might callously or thoughtlessly destroy.

To remain at his side, strung to his winter moods, might become unwise now that triumph and elation drooped in low November sun and torn clouds, foreboding carrion and hungry stags flitting between tree stumps in monotonous nights thickened by the distant Wall, sharpened by wolf and gale, lit by a moon fast and baleful.

Monotony was brief. Messengers galloped from winter shrouds with news of eruption from a volcano we had rated extinct. Valentinus, mock-Carausius, had been too vividly reliving his glory. He had bribed malcontents, unemployed, the hopeless and disappointed, and was making for London.

Maximus' huge skin cape made him resemble an an overpowering seal. His ill-temper and spite vanished, he was lifting both arms in wrathful gaiety. He looked very hungry.

'I'll deal with him. I alone.'

Unspoken, was a race less against Valentinus than Theodosius, to secure London.

Before hastening out to arouse the troops, he rounded on me, cheerfully, but already looking beyond, into the sky. 'Father Drusus, you're wasted here. We don't need your sword arm.'

This was ambiguous. The we had several meanings; the decision, welcome in itself, would better have made by me. Within the hour, he had gone.

Valentinus had planned the revolt with considerable guile, wheedling into his pack some ageing, exiled officials, mostly Jeheshua-hating Dalmatians, banished servants of Julian, who gave him some air of validity.

Flaunting red boots, an echo of legendary Roman kings, the star-clustered cloak of victory, brandishing like an axe an ivory sceptre

217

topped with a hen-like creature masquerading as an eagle, Valentinus threw an ugly shadow across Britain. He paraded house-slaves in rags, announcing to silent crowds that these were captured legionaries. He managed to storm a mint and issue a few coins of himself in lion-skin, wielding a club, and ringed with 'Unassailable Virtue and Piety.' Voices were paid to hail him 'Britannicus'. Priests of Jupiter Lord of Armies, and Jeheshua Fisher of Men, were forced to pray for his foreordained triumph. A white bull sprinkled with sawdust to simulate gold was inexpertly sacrificed. Britons, still cowed by two years' excesses, tended to flee his recruiting officers, pleading sickness, wounds, even devotion to the Augustus.

With perhaps two thousand infantry and a bare score of cavalry, Unassailable Virtue had to face Maximus, or Theodosius, or both.

# XXIX

Valentinus shouted, gesticulated, proclaimed himself Emperor, hesitated near Verulam, vainly awaited reinforcements and risings, then lunged towards London. Hearing of Theodosius' contemptuous denunciation, then of Maximus' advance, he halted, saw many desertions, and began trailing back to the midlands. Dividing his cavalry, Maximus chased him to Ilchester, surrounded him, forcing him into brief, bloody fight. Easily defeated, disguised as a slave, he fled east, foolishly along Watling Street, into the spears of Maximus' auxiliaries. He was captured, blustering, weeping, imploring, and Maximus, delighting the army, chained him, and in a bear-cage with a naked girl to test his piety, unexpectedly sent him to Theodosius. His fate I never knew. Some maintain he was beheaded, others that he died in exile, in the Scillies. A priest who aided him, for boasting his ability to fly was compelled to leap from a high tower.

369 opened mildly, auspiciously. No tactless woman gave birth to a bull, no comet or winged metalled orb ripped the sky, the sun was undeterred by sacerdotal prattle, and not one god used earthquake to destroy a cattle trough. In the wake of famine, depopulation, squalor, plague had sprinkled its noxious dew, but the cold December had repulsed it. Wild animals slunk back to their lairs, or wandered confusedly in ruined forests.

Politically, the balance wavered. While Maximus spiked Valentinus, Theodosius deftly slipped into London as provisional Governor. All four cantons were now liberated, and he carved out a fifth in the north-west, a cordon against Hibernia, Caledonia, Brigantia, which, honouring the ineffable Augustus, he named Valentia. Tribal dynasties under Paternus and Clemens were established to safeguard the Wall. Attacottic captives were sent for service on the Rhine and Danube. Signal stations and arsenals were restored, forts strengthened or demolished, artillery mounds erected.

Throughout Britain, in an imperial proclamation, the Augustus,

Senate and People of Rome gave thanks to God One and Three, and to the Excellence Count Theodosius, for quelling impious invaders and the vile and absurd Valentinus.

In Silchester, I imagined Maximus' silent fury. Would he turn recklessly? But he remained silent, back in the midlands, corresponding with me only through Andragathius.

Theodosius ordered rites of thanksgiving and expiation. Fires waved on hill, cape, rampart. Cross and Fish were paraded with Standards. London was renamed Augusta, and a Germanic tribe, the Buccinobants, under King Fraomer, imported for the defence. Citizens valiantly denounced all traitors, particularly after the false rumour of the Augustus deciding to show the Diadem in Britain. Valentinian seemed to sit in the sky, watching canals unblocked, customs posts filling, herds, fields, bridges, ships regaining life. A Governor, Civilis, and a Duke of Britain, Dulcitius, were appointed, both friends of Theodosius, and superseding himself and Maximus, who had yet to be officially commended, even mentioned.

That week, Theodosius and his veterans were recalled, sent to the Rhine. All else remained hazy. Maximus should have rejoiced. Yet why was he excluded from citations and rewards? Was he secretly colluding with Treves? He had been joined by his wife, a Briton, and his brother, Marcellinus, a staff-officer. Nominally under Dulcitius, at York, he was evidently confirming his own position, doling out subsidies, enrolling recruits. I advised him to gather some tough Votads.

In return, he sent requests that were barely disguised orders or requisitions, which sometimes left me out of pocket. No great matter, though his elaborate professions of gratitude were too obviously from the stock of Jewish scribes.

My own grandeur was acknowledged from coast to coast, eliciting respect from the Governor himself, though Silchester was giving me less than my due, and no pleasure. People were remote, turning away, vanishing round corners, speaking indistinctly, and I wondered whether adder-eyed Brunnus had wholly departed. Familiar faces were missing, the town very dilapidated, the slave force permanently depleted. The tax-gatherers, rather nervously, had regathered, in the name of Rome Eternal, already demanding substantial levies for the reparations. Guilds, crafts, manufactures, were slowly reviving, but without any enthusiasm to resume municipal office. How often I had urged on Maximus the need to replace compulsory, unpaid public service with well-rewarded careerists. No 367 would recur, if only men had reason to defend their own. Yet I was already being forced to listen to arguments that the late anarchy taught the need for yet more State authority.

Avitus was dead : Venerable Ram, as Metellus had stupidly called him. Fortunately, Marulla had hidden my letters. Some intruders had been ranging the house on pretext of tax surveyance. He bequeathed me less than I expected, and, as executor, the onus of considerable and unprofitable labours.

Metellus, inextricably entangled with Valentinus, had madly attempted to join him, escaped, but in Theodosius' proscriptions was beheaded.

He had always lived in a bubble, in love with appearances, and had committed the blunder of too long remaining himself. Providently, he sent me no incriminating plea. Sylviana, under suspicion, abandoned their home and I found her with some difficulty, living in a wooden slave-hut on the estate of an elderly magnate.

She greeted me with customary lack of warmth, and as though I had never been absent, as though indeed I passed my life idle as Metellus. Otherwise, she was scarcely recognizable. The skin under her high, now gaunt bones, was very dry, her hair grey, only the eyes under the short, tarnished, untidy fringe kept some mischief. When I spoke with some force about the pacification, she interrupted, smiling with intolerable condescension.

'Drusus, you learn nothing.' An absurd remark from one normally intelligent and whom I had taught so much, on whom I had spent so much. She paused rather than hesitated, inspecting me as if I were a second-rate vase or bust. 'My friend, I know you too well. All there is of you. But there should be rather more.'

She astonished me further, not playful but serious. 'Metellus said you were sententious without being resonant.' Her little grin was woefully misplaced. 'You're a professor. You told him in bad prose how to write verse.'

One more reason not to regret Metellus. I left the impudent woman, resolved not to return. She had no more to dangle, but I forbore to be glad of her misfortunes and mental decline. She would regret the loss of a partner in a game known only to herself.

Surrounded by monks and deacons, few of them caring to wash, the Bishop received me like a stranger, speaking only of new religious doctrines, unnecessary and barely sane, and, on my irritated departure, handed me, like a tip, some screed of that mystery-monger Paul, whose Greek made Aurelius shake his head.

I doubted whether Metellus had ever ventured that silly remark about the Professor.

Junius had left Silchester, after reproaching Vesta for our relationship. To enquire more would have been undignified. She herself was tired, bony, less desirable, though I allowed her to continue receiving me. A year later she began refusing me her bed, and could not have been surprised when I ceased to support her. I believe she died soon after.

The young had never appreciated me and scoffed at my sobriety, though Cato would have grasped my hand, Cicero have praised my civic energy. I could quote Propertius and knew some stories which, I was assured, got better and better. But envy followed me, I received few pleasant invitations, and even found myself missing the Armenian, now in London ingratiating himself with the Governor.

I needed to visit Gaul for consultations, but Maximus' affairs and political perplexities still prevented it.

Delayed, I gave some suppers, well-attended, some magnates actually accepting, but they were unsuccessful. I spoke of music, philosophy, even dancers, but guests, eating well, drinking copiously, only wanted advice on tax-evasion, hastened to agree with remarks I did not always make, and, behind my back, attempted to scald me with epigrams. An absurd libel was circulated that, at my parties, prime bores were invited for sundown, lesser bores two hours later, and so on until midnight, the intention being that one group would be leaving as the next arrived, though leavers were invariably swept back by the new lot. I myself, it was said, was always first to arrive.

To repress such nonsense was as impossible as teaching grammar to Picts. I could have told them that wit is the obvious refuge for those with nothing to say.

I abandoned the parties, and instead addressed colleges of merchants and financiers; I was heard gratefully, but was otherwise neglected. Even Aurelius showed disloyalty. I gave him his freedom, which cost nothing, expecting him to request a partnership, for which, indeed, I hoped. But he at once left me, crammed with my techniques and secrets, and, in certain areas, began competing with me. He was, after all, for all his scholarship, a barbarian.

One incident particularly aggravated me. A Belgic timber merchant told me he had married a luscious Syrian, then begged my patronage of a most splendid oriental banquet. 'I seriously advise you, my most esteemed Drusus, to fast three days so as to relish the very best of what she will achieve for you. You especially, of course. She'll do everything with her own hands. Oh, her marvellous side-dishes, Jupiter himself wouldn't refuse her way with swan's breasts. Ginger, you know . . . cinnamon . . Indian pepper creates extraordinary sensations. . . .'

Arriving punctually, I found a barbarian quarrel, the merchant shouting at a furious, slant-eyed slut with hands so soiled that prospects of food were disgusting. She was soon so sulky that no banquet appeared, not even a loaf, and the husband and I were forced to go to the barracks, there, under a new and excessively sardonic bust of Valentinian, to face an ill-cooked lump of boiled lamb, and sour wine, while the fellow at last revealed that he wasn't married, but had merely picked up a very cheap cook.

In contrast, my customers were clamouring in Britain and Gaul. Former contacts with Syria, Africa, Spain resumed with unexpected ease. There's no bad smell about money, rough old Vespasian had said. My father died, but I was preoccupied with acquiring burnt vineyards, ravaged quarries and barley fields, also salting away gold for Maximus, who now hinted an understanding with the Duke, whom he already despised.

His letters arrived, but I never saw him. It occurred to me that he enjoyed company without much liking people. Always somewhere else, he was now a legendary war-lord, glowing, but indistinct and very silent. I heard not his quick excitable voice but the cheers and trumpets, drumming feet, clash of swords on knee-buckles.

I was ready to be placated by some affectionate message, but it did not come, only those requests hardening into the peremptory. Andragathius would be intriguing. Twice Maximus promised to meet me in London, but sent only Marcellinus, who, with Spanish reserve, even hauteur, required my signature, scrutinized my supply lists, was slack about reimbursements, and forgot to invite me to dine.

To Maximus, by special couriers, I sent oblique reminders of the Britain we had sought. The plans, firelight, the hand-clasps, sudden thrills. More openly, I gave advance news of prices, trade exchanges, shortage of rope, currency depreciation, and submitted a new code of weights and measures. For him I charted Britain in terms of woods, sheep, vines, quarries, mines, waters, soil, wastelands, tribes, towns, villas, communications. No land in Europe promised more. The replies remained formal.

By midsummer, a new phenomenon was inescapable. With Theodosius' departure, urban restoration slowed. Baths remained dry, aqueducts broken, streets unweeded. Taxes seemed unspent, but stored for unexplained purposes that none dared question. When I sent protests to the Governor, I was told that the Britons hated towns. I presented a tax-scheme to benefit the farmers . . . perhaps it still lies in some dusty, forgotten alcove.

My health suffered. Flesh rings thickened round my eyes, broken veins showed purple on crimson flesh, recalling Junius' belief that skin reveals faults in the brain. Alarmed, I ceased to hire women. I began to limp, from nagging pains about which I shrank from questioning the physicians, latrine scandal concocting an absurdity about a dismissed slave driving a sharp thorn through my footprint. Working too hard but with loss of spirit, loss of breath, I had spells of inner blackness, my head icy, all thought vanishing, all sense of place and identity lost. Afterwards, I felt release from an evil journey through dim, flitting shapes, soundless and featureless, under dark blocks, phantom, immeasurable. Surfaces had vanished, leaving only their essence.

Aurelius' successor, a Silurian freedman, was badly-trained and untrustworthy, doubling my responsibilities. To escape all this, I determined to visit my brothers in Sens but found continued obstruction disguised as flattery. Maximus, the Governor, even Andragathius asserted that, without me, Britain would collapse. Virtually under arrest, I was left haggling, debating, and having to arrange a triumphant arch to Theodosius, Londoners insisting on it being surmounted by the goddess Britannia holding a cross, raving on a pile of stones.

# EPILOGUE

The rest of my story should be familiar to most of you. I am one of the most famous names in British history, but for the wrong reasons : one of those who, like Nero, is called 'the Great' because of the great opportunities we create, then spoil. I was more responsible than Antony, more intelligent than Pompey and Maximus, more civilized than Augustus with his pretensions and shams. Yet I lost.

Victors, of course, try to destroy the evidence, even the names, of the defeated, so that self-respect compels me to try to restore the balance, efficiently, pointedly. Yet what a pity that my supplanters and betrayers finally proved to be of such mean stature! Armenians to a man.

It amounts to an epilogue, a highly unsatisfactory one, for the Empire, for Britain and, certainly not least, for myself.


Theodosius overcame Alemans, succoured fugitives from Goths, was transferred to settle a rising in Africa, succeeded, then, for reasons still undiscovered, was privately executed.

Flavius Valentinian, Thrice Orthodox, Conqueror of Franks, died as if in one of the Armenian's stories. The Quadi tribe sent envoys demanding lands, privileges, restitutions, the usual insolent rag-bag presented by the defeated. They harangued the Augustus at inordinate length, while he retained that obdurate, back-aching rigidity, trying to stare them down, until, in boredom or fury, he broke a blood-vessel and was dead in an hour.

His sons, Caesars Valentinian II and Gratian, succeeded, the latter predominant, receiving rather surprising help from the younger Theodosius, who, with his father's bloodless talents, expelled barbarians from Illyria and Macedon. Gratian himself campaigned better than anticipated, but his victories then weakened him. While Theodosius defended the frontiers, Gratian complacently retired to

Treves, luxuriantly putting on weight. He over-estimated his own diplomacy, foolishly believing that obsolete coin, empty titles, parcels of wasteland, would placate and divide the fierce but intelligent Goths. He was amiable, literary, with fine taste in courtly inessentials – art, cookery, theology, hunting – inappropriate to the times. As Praetorian Prefect of Gaul, Britain and Spain he appointed his old tutor, the poet Ausonius. Poets cannot administrate, are ashamed of making decisions, they prefer to give and receive pain in curious ways.

Gratian denied himself the prestige steadily being acquired by rivals. He preferred intrigue to workaday judgements. Rather than initiate reform, he argued with priests, accepting sycophancy as sincere. Abolishing his own post of High Priest of Jupiter, he demolished the hallowed Temple of Victory in Rome, ensuring a victory not his own. German mercenaries he entertained rather than employed, while the armies of Britain and the Rhine complained that they were forgotten. An extraordinary neglect, for he had been popular with the legions. He promoted favourites and ignored the Huns as too distant, too legendary, too yellow. He began mixing familiarly with Scythian huntsmen and sentries, stalking the common streets with them, mantled in their furs, brandishing a Scythian bow.

In such folly, he encountered the year of disaster, what that unpleasant Bishop may have considered a Grand Year. The Huns moved west, swiftly enveloping Asia. Goths fled into the Empire and, armed and mounted, were foolishly opposed by Augustus Valens and his eunuchs at Hadrian's City. His behaviour was lamentable, he refused Gratian's offer of help and, in the worst catastrophe since Hannibal, two-thirds of the army perished, and he himself was sliced to bits by Gothic iron.

I was not surprised to learn of thousands of Roman citizens deserting to the invaders, to escape hereditary callings, the tithes, interest rate and debt.

Gratian, inevitably, had to appeal to Theodosius, who accepted, or took, the Eastern Diadem, trounced the Goths, then enlisted them as front-line defence against the Huns.

But what of *that man*? And what of 'Old Drusus'?

By State edict, Britain knew herself at peace. Seasonal fairs reopened, convicts dug and pruned, dunged and dredged. Craftsmen reappeared, as indeed did the shadowy *agentes*. Yet I, and probably I alone, knew that we had tolerable administration but very little government. People waited for others to act, or left to the apathetic Curia duties best done by themselves. They were weasels, clinging to each other's tails. Captious interference and deadweight restrictions were not live authority. Treves had learnt nothing from 367, and was more interested in the codification of Christian books, few of them really necessary. Life was clogged, when it most needed to thrive and bustle. The rabble remained quiescent, but never quite exorcized was that running expectation of some deliverer foretold by a virgin-born madman in woods, while intelligent men shrugged at Gratian, fearing a succession of mayfly pretenders.

A Cirencester magistrate, generally respected, vanished inexplicably. One night, on their couch, his wife found his head in a silver dish, a lemon in his mouth.

The Governor's service was mere demotion ordained by vicious Treves courtiers. Discontented troops accused him of supplying poor rations to avoid taxing his friends the magnates, and were outraged by slights inflicted on Maximus.

Maximus was circumscribed by the spies of the military treasurer. Encamped with some fifteen thousand men, he lacked definite function, while Theodosius' young men won renown in the East.

An under-employed Hercules is a dangerous asset, which Duke and Governor were unable to manipulate. Maximus' demands, sent me from far north, far south, were more exorbitant, more military, and finally the Army of Britain proclaimed him Emperor of the West. He always maintained that refusal would have meant his death. This may have been true.

The Governor fled overseas, the Duke, I believe, killed himself, the officials, grey slugs, wilted before horse and metal; London submitted, and York issued a reminder that there Constantine the Great had set out to conquer the World.

The gamble promised fair returns, though I had no option but to concur. My name had already appeared on proclamations, my seals were flaunted in every city, I was treated by popular opinion as an unofficial but omnipresent minister, though during this period I never once met the Emperor, was merely a provincial quartermaster. Magnus Maximus collected people, but like an illiterate who cherishes books in order to sell them.

All British mints were confiscated, new coins, better fashioned than usual, were used, against my advice, in bribing the tribes, consequently ruining the economy. Maximus was too busy to care.

Drusus must see to it, Drusus must provide. He crossed to the Rhine, collecting every man he could, even from the Wall. Civilians, including many Jews, accompanied him, three times more numerous than the army.

I was excluded. Awarded the grand title Undisputed Lord, I was ordered to co-ordinate affairs from London. I had been snared by a fiery eye, the fluke of charm, a pretence of love, an athlete's magnificence, though had not Propertius castigated Prometheus for straightening men's bodies at the expense of their minds?

My coffers bulged, but I had no leisure to spend and enjoy, now when I most wanted to. Demands arrived incessantly. More grain, metal, timber, artisans. For Strasbourg, Marseilles, Cordoba. . . . Iron, salt, skins, even a wagonload of women for mad Angles. My invoices to the Secretariat received elusive response.

Maximus marched south. He took Paris, Strasbourg surrendered, Treves prepared welcome, his own native Spain raised his standards. His tread resounded through Europe. Gratian, in Gaul, when urgently needed was always hunting, an unwise prerogative. He read fluently, discussed the Divine Nature, fondled his Scythians. City after city acclaimed the Spanish usurper and his motley Britons. Leaderless, the imperial troops dwindled, an entire army under three Scythians deserted to Maximus.

Rousing himself too late, Gratian, so cultured, so irresponsible, fled with a Frankish chief towards Italy and Valentinian II. No town would receive him, Maximus inexorable at his heels. His own Scythians grumbled, then chuckled and departed.

Hunter and hunted were both Christian, their antics scarcely creditable to those seeking true wisdom.

Now desperate, Gratian trailed unsteadily to Lyons, where the Governor sent him promises of fidelity and a safe-conduct in the name of Gratian Augustus, Supreme Victor, the Governor proclaiming himself Protector of the Sacred Person.

Witless from terror and exhaustion, Gratian was received with deference, entertained richly. Monks bawled hymns, the Protector spoke reassuringly of an army's approach. He did not lie. As Gratian reclined at a feast, awarding promotions to all in sight, the tall doors opened and, proudly escorted by the Protector of the Sacred Person, there stalked in Andragathius and several executioners. Within instants, Gratian and his Frank lay headless in a cellar. It is held that the latter had long been negotiating with Maximus, but his favour was unnecessary.

All Gaul, all Spain, fell like unguarded fruit to the new Constantine who, from Treves, sent a respectful embassy to the Sacred Palace, leaving to Theodosius the choice of recognition or war.

That young man had been seriously ill, with the usual whispers of poison by ambitious eunuchs. His discovery reinforced his Christian obsessions, inclining him into the dogmatic and vengeful. Meanwhile he sent Maximus a polite but ambiguous reply, which I mistrusted, though he may still have been genuinely undecided. Gratian had crowned him but had culpably misgoverned. Maximus had been his father's colleague, apparently loyal, and had been ill-treated by Gratian's sire. The legions were weary from the prodigious Gothic War, the aftermath still requiring lengthy, tedious, diplomatic efforts.

Valentinian II, another Christian, though Arian 'heretic', still held Rome, protected by Germans of questionable allegiance. Maximus, as I continually urged him, was consolidating his three great provinces, and let him be, to usefully withstand Goths or Huns, or be overthrown by them. More Germans joined Maximus' Celts, and here I anxiously dissented, in three momentous letters. The State depended too much on these barbarians. Constantius, remember, had even encouraged them to attack the Empire's most superb defender, Caesar Julian.

Maximus rode high, his writ subduing Morocco and all Western Africa. Seeing him like a giant dimmed by a gauze curtain, I envisaged him in that nightmare palace, crouching in prayer before the huge-eyed, implacable god and his eleven judges : or throned miles high, his Diadem throwing sparks over the world. Did he too listen in passages to those with nowhere to go, fear the quiet knife and muttered spell, feel netted by smiling functionaries grubbing on taxes and expense rolls?

My duties altered. I was having to commission Bath sculptors and master masons to fashion his statues, applauded in Ravenna, New Carthage, Alexandria, Constantinople, by mobs with nothing else to do. He was ruling competently, though wasting time executing Priscillian and other deviants in the religion of hate. I believe he actually initiated the policy of making 'heresy' a capital crime. I easily imagined the smile with which he confiscated the ample properties of the Priscillians who so priggishly and irresponsibly despised material goods.

Several years passed, but, Lord of half the West, like a gluttonous child he wanted more. He was bemused by Rome, itself disdained even by Valentinian II, who crept into Milan, seeing Rome for what it was : no Genius, but empty, spectacular palaces and impotent Senate, a scheming Bishop in place of gods outraged or bored, and a mosquito-ridden populace awaiting free doles of Baltic fish and African wheat.

Like any Gratian, Maximus was succumbing to the belief that self-display was achievement. He was an Alexander, discontented with the sufficient, hypnotized by size and space, the mysterious and spurious lure of the East. He saw territory not as desert to be watered, vineyard to be tended, but as a circus yelling for thrills, outsize blandishments, the whip, and some bloody falls. (Cato, you remember, described a king as an animal existing on human flesh.)

He disregarded my admonitions to remain still, occasionally withdraw, reconstruct. The Bishop of Rome disputed his religious supremacy and denounced his persecutions, then expelled him from the Church, but he only laughed. He agreed with my memorandum on rural reform, issued a poll-tax to implement it, then spent it on the army he must lead to Rome. Repeatedly I warned him that real power was not in Italy, not even in Gaul and Spain, but in Britain. He never replied, but denuded us further in wealth and manpower.

Most solemnly - my letters surely survive somewhere, for historians to acknowledge - I besought him at all costs to conciliate Theodosius, and at last he responded, rebuking me in false jocularity for doubting his manliness. I could do no more. Undisputed Lord, I should have been overseeing the West, imperial *tessura* guaranteeing me free residence, women, admission to all councils. Ministers should have been extolling my prescience, the Consistory awaiting my pleasure. I could have guided the Roman Empire into a peace unsurpassed even by Hadrian. No maniacal conqueror, I was the wise and provident farmer.

In his Triumph, the painted, victorious general, in burnished chariot, amid shouts, tramp, blare, had at his back a slave reminding him to look behind him, where fate waited to gut him like a herring. Maximus could only look forward, never pausing. He used all wiles to pull Rome from Valentinian, offering to move troops to Italy, on pretexts of strengthening a projected Danubian campaign. Valentinian yielded, and a British, Gallic, Germanic army crossed the Alps under Andragathius, followed by Maximus himself. With cheerful excuses, he invested Milan, and Valentinian, realizing the truth

230

almost too late, sped east, to Theodosius. In Milan a bishop preached the necessity of accepting fate and avoiding bloodshed.

I held my breath, the world saw my Emperor with thousands of delirious Britons enter Rome itself. As orthodox hero, killer of deviants, he addressed the cringing Senate, his helmet gleaming with massive blue pendants. He denounced Valentinian and the Arians, then proclaimed himself loving protector of Jews. He had won and, without knowing it, had already lost. Rome was a delusion, a mirror expensive but cracked. He was trying to stuff the wind into a wineskin, no longer seeing the world as it actually was. He saw only the distance, and from the distance came retribution.

In the Sacred Palace, Theodosius risked nothing, but had not forgiven Gratian's death. He may have recalled undisclosed tensions between his father and Maximus, he certainly desired undisputed power, in state, in religion. He married a sister of the suppliant Valentinian II, whom he brusquely ordered to renounce Arianism. Jeheshua was more than a god, he was God, no nonsense about it. God and Son were identical. Unobtrusively, he secured a Persian alliance, stilled the Goths, neutralized the Huns with gifts and promises, then collected recruits from both in an army already fierce with Africans and Scythians. Through the winter he was preparing a fleet, then at last arrived in Thessalonica with splendid barbarian cavalry – Goths, Alans, even Huns – spearmen, and Christian insignia. Maximus, his legions immense but undisciplined, trusting him like a god who required nothing else, advanced, then lost a battle on the Save, and a god cannot afford to lose. Desertions followed a night of bewildered dismay. With Marcellinus and a few devotees he retreated to Italy, was trapped in Aquila and, like Gratian, suffered the agonies of betrayal. He had pushed others aside, and by not seeing them, was himself pushed aside. Theodosius, sparing almost everyone else, protecting his family, executed him, the mighty adventure petering out in mud and a flash of swords.

I, the Undisputed Lord, had risked all in Maximus, and lost all. My adherents, parasites and relatives scuttled for safety, ostentatiously turning Christian. Proscribed for treason, I was trundled to Milan in

231

a dirty cart.

Theodosius himself, pretending not to recognize me, examined my case. He was merciful in his way, not magnanimous but contemptuous. I was forbidden to plead, my properties were forfeited to the Treasury, then I was freed, for long, empty days in a dusty suburb.

I am indeed Old Drusus, wrinkled, almost stupid, wandering through lax sunlight where the cold yet poaches my bones, washed up like driftwood. After Valentinian's murder by General Arbogastes, Theodosius the Great reunited East and West, in that unwieldy amalgam that cannot long endure, and may not survive him. He allows me a small pension, and the coarseness that Sylviana so despised has helped me endure vile conditions. Unlike Livy's heroes, I cherish existence, however ignoble. The mouse outlives the lion, according to the fabulists, though to believe it may be rather too convenient.

Had I my youth I would seek opportunities for renewal, 'resurrection'. I wonder if that mountebank Bishop's remark about dying in order to live was as much a joke as he made it sound? He that loseth his life shall save it, the monks chatter, though determined to lose nothing and saving only their energies in begging tax-rebates. The Armenian knew all this, is probably a bishop himself, strolling on waves in an offhand way.

A withered ex-dancer and concubine, so fat that she seems to stand on both sides of me, sweeps my room. I miss not palaces but the liveliness of market and port, my ships unloading, the click and growl of alien tongues mingling with noises of cattle and poultry, masters saluting me, obsequiously presenting receipts. Auctioneers' cries and subtle signs, naked boys swarming up masts to the trembling sails, gulls shredding the sky. The shambling gapers, beggars, touts, thieving urchins, self-important warehouse-keepers and customs men, slaves and sailors hurrying between decks, the corded bales on quaysides, the prows with round, painted eyes and stern figureheads swinging seawards, the sea itself, highway to riches and dreams. I miss them all : tailors offering robes to last forever, stalls of dentists, money-changers, vintners, astrologers, each with its hanging emblem, glistening porters and bearers, the hook-eyed whores ready to pounce. A row of masts, the faded scents, spices, drugs, in old storehouses, the pungency of tar, tallow, cloth, mules, even the stink of dramshop and fried meat, always moved me more than a bucketful of Vergil. After the day's work, I had enjoyed a common tavern, treated just like everyone else, watching the fish sizzle and dirty wine flow, the sun sinking to waves, Jews and Phoenicians wrangling with white-garbed Egyptians, gaudy Arabs, Greeks with sharp eyes, sharp voices, sharp fingers, excitable Ephesians, and names piling up like cargoes . . . Nicodemia, Bythinia, Cappodocia, Tarsus, Tyre.

Compared to a wharf, Milan's pleasure gardens are shabby, the music strident, vendors dishonest.

The hag mumbles, eyebrows twitching :

'Will you have your bread . . . are you awake ?'

'My bread, yes . . . and wine . . . perhaps some wine.'

I overhear rather than listen. Events, not philosophers, show there are no gaps in nature. Everything moves, explodes, dissolves, combines in further designs without losing the germ. The Britons, retrieved by the Empire, are singing epic tales of who else but Maximus, marrying a British goddess of crossroads, Elen, or a Christian holy woman, Helen of Hosts, virgin even after repeated intercourse, which I doubt if Maximus, for all his devotions, would have much praised. His statues are overthrown, but his Genius has escaped into song, which unlocks gates to the unimagined or unimaginable. Now he is Macsen, British emperor and wizard.

The Roman world is too large, too complex, to be understood by any save the exceptional, but it can be condensed, then mastered, by an image. Ironically, Maximus may be such an image. Despite his mad-bull schemes he may yet fulfil my own, so that, if justice survives, I, mistreated, disregarded, swindled, could one day be acclaimed as the true founder of Britain. Before the Conquest, she had heroes but no history : the Emperors valued her exports, but she remained flavourless and without a centre. Today, a Spanish failure is giving her both. He will be the British Eneas, with myself as a sort of Jupiter.

Recently, I was watching birds mate in Vespasian's Gardens. A Briton seated himself beside me. I told him my name; incredibly, it was unknown to him, save that he murmured some rubbish about a new brand of cement. As the birds made their silly patterns, blue against yellow, he recited a lyric attractive enough, then informed me that it was composed by his compatriot, the much-lamented and admired poet, Metellus. Time is indeed mischievous, and unspeakably unjust.

If Britain unites, and finances her own identity, she can flourish.

233

External enemies have neither horses nor intelligence. An incident in Cirencester reveals another, more threatening danger.

A soldier was maimed in the resistance to Scots, the citizens subscribed to his welfare, only to be officially rebuked for insulting the Augustus by usurping the State's responsibility. Compensation should be left to the discretion of the Curia! Modern Rome in a sentence, disheartened, drained of life. Samarthians and Goths are simpler, fresher, more sensible, coveting our lands yet wishing not to destroy but to cleanse our institutions.

Theodosius has inherited his father's banked-down cruelties, and has already precipitated an atrocious massacre, for which the courageous Ambrose, Bishop of Milan, forced him to implore public forgiveness. He has closed the temples and oracles, forbidden the Olympic Games and the Eleusinian Mysteries, and all cults save his own, though I believe the gods have secretly prevailed, and made Jeheshua one of themselves. Religious persecution is commonplace, Theodosius kills Arians as energetically as Maximus did Priscillians, Christian gangsters rip each other apart, and, like tolerant creditors finally annoyed by broken contracts, the lustrous Olympians have abandoned the West, possibly for ever. They demanded too little.

Jeheshua certainly demands too much. Cursing the everyday world, he insists we should reject it totally, though foretelling its approaching dissolution. (In Roman terms, it has probably occurred.) His vanity was unsurpassed, rather pathetic. 'Whoever trusts in me has already passed from death to life.' Even accepting this as mystic metaphor, the precepts of a sensual and charitable merchant are more useful. The land, the realm I offered Maximus, emphatically of this world, would have suited men better.

That Bishop of Silchester, who only very lately, in his old age, actually allowed himself to be baptized, now sits very well in Rome, addressed in a manner of his own devising, 'His Holy Superbitude the Enlightened', and has published an oration, holding that, at root, all gods are only emanations of nature, stages of understanding, spirals of being, enveloped in mystery which nevertheless discloses all.

When I can find listeners, I enjoy discussing 367, and, still sceptical of the Conspiracy, usually blame those deposits left in the blood by primitive, ogreish races, which, however refined by time, cannot be wholly purged. Under a stern Roman hill, Aulus' head, severed centuries ago, still bleeds. The tension between instinct and reason periodically breaks. Plato believed that war was man's natural condition,

Jupiter won heaven through war, Heraclitus held violence the beget-
ter of all societies and institutions. 367 was the ultimate terror,
savagery not for principle but for its own sake. Many feared this,
on a darkened street, or in their own homes, as often as in Fields of
Light.

I am writing not only to assert, to retrieve my position, but to
explore my self-imposed questions. Unlike the fashionable court
rhetoricians, I use words not as decorations but as nails. Like the
Goths, I know what Jeheshua does not, that there are no permanent
solutions, no barriers against movement, we can only reduce the costs.
The Diadem is a device to withstand a Cheru. Huge promises of
deliverance are more fearful than minor injustice. Jeheshua himself
boasted that he brought us a sword, an unnecessary gift, useless
against stupidity, deadly and yellow as Huns, let alone inflation, corruption, unreal notions.

I have seen the State like a lover pursuing identical replicas of
women who have betrayed him and relishing his own pain; he knows
the impossibility of unflawed joy but maintains his quest. The Empire
rotted not through Cheru and mosquito, but through us taxpayers no
longer respecting it. No one seemed actually governing, rulers and
ruled were slaves to torpid routine, riddles were preferred to plain
statements. The most extraordinary monarch can be snuffed out
when the wind changes. (Wait, my readers, for this is to be proved,
again and again, not least in Britain and Italy.) Obvious laws should
produce obvious results. They do not. The obvious seldom occurs.
The favourite charioteer fails at a corner, the inevitable refuses to
happen. On all evidence, Hannibal should have won Italy; the
evidence was wrong or somehow irrelevant. In 367, different tribes,
in similar regions, behaved differently. Over backgammon, a learned
man with a pustulous face assured me that Catiline's plot derived
from class hatreds. It should, therefore it did. Yet had he, like a
banker, patiently examined the conspirators' standing, he would have
found only boredom, feuds, debts – and mischief.

Despite Theodosius, supreme censor, a row of unlucky days
threatens the Roman order. My old story of the priest's women terrified not of fact but of chance, now seems valid enough. I once told it
to Maximus, who roared out a laugh, then looked puzzled and asked
where the joke was. Human behaviour is easy to change, human
nature is not. Junius once told me that, thanks to Prometheus, man's
brain – perhaps not woman's – has enlarged itself threefold, but I see

only perpetual regress and regeneration, endless repetition, behaviour changing but not nature, and fine words emptying of meaning, like the stare of houses for sale or ransacked. Centuries ahead, Britain will be weighted, as if against earthquake, by gigantic columns not to hard Jeheshua or dismal Theodosius, but to God Macsen, once a soldier, who in the scalding time freed the land from monsters. But to what effect?

I had manly qualities, and failed them, like Rome failed her Genius. I am a modest fellow. They may say of me that I brought cloth from Arras, financed aqueducts, made one mistake, but a fatal one.

I would like to have designed the first wheel, chisel, saw, brought fire from heaven. What is there left to invent? Nothing. I desire only to be heard, if only long after my death. If Britain survives, a few towns may be named after me, though, as you see, I deserve more. I hear that London is no longer being called Augusta.

I crawl about Milan, pausing at lithe players in the ball court, at handsome wrestlers. The dirty old woman shoves me apples sprinkled with poppy seed; I would prefer caustic eyes under black fringe that offered less and suggested more. Counting my sesterces, I remember honeyed wine, roast partridges, the carver's delicate motions keeping time to lute and harp. A child sings in the yard, his words not quite audible, but, forgive my tears, sounding like

> 'I am a fish,
> I lie in a dish.'